CRACKER JUSTICE

Janet Post

PINEAPPLE PRESS

Palm Beach, Florida

Pineapple Press
An imprint of The Rowman & Littlefield Publishing Group, Inc.
4501 Forbes Boulevard, Suite 200, Lanham, Maryland 20706
www.rowman.com

Distributed by NATIONAL BOOK NETWORK

British Library Cataloguing in Publication Information Available

Library of Congress Cataloging-in-Publication Data Available

ISBN 978-1-68334-082-9 (paperback)
ISBN 978-1-68334-083-6 (electronic)

♾™ The paper used in this publication meets the minimum requirements of
American National Standard for Information Sciences—Permanence of Paper
for Printed Library Materials, ANSI/NISO Z39.48-1992.

1

Jesse L. Pruitt galloped wide open across the palmetto-strewn Florida prairie. His sure-footed mustang stud, Satan, dodged gopher turtle holes and leaped clumps of broom grass with ease.

Jesse, better known as Prue, swung the twelve-foot-long rawhide whip over his shoulder and sharply forward, snapping it at what he thought was just the right moment and almost cut a chunk out of his shoulder with the popper. His horse shied violently, leaping six feet to the left to escape the whip, nearly dumping Prue as they raced after a squirrelly brown and white cow and her calf.

"Damn you, Satan. I almost had them." Prue slowed the black mustang to a trot and then a walk.

Prue, recently from Texas, was newly come to the Florida frontier to invest his small savings in land. First thing he learned was working cattle in Florida was different. You couldn't do it without dogs and a whip, two things never used by the cowboys out West.

He bought a thousand acres from a young cowboy named Moss Mizelle who told Prue he "didn't want the responsibility of owning no land." The land came fully stocked with two thousand head of Florida yellow hammers, another name for the scraggly Florida cows slowly evolved from the original cattle left by the Spaniards when Ponce de Leon visited the peninsula. Aside from the cattle, the land situated on Horse Creek between Lily and Pine Level was unimproved.

Prue hired a black man named Boarhog Benson, a local cowman, as ranch foreman and all-around help. Benson kept an eye on the ranch and was building a small cabin and cowpens close to the creek. The pens currently housed the one thing besides his horse he had brought from Texas, a two-year-old longhorn bull named Cactus Pete. Prue hand raised the gentle bull and planned to use him to improve his herd.

In Texas, Prue was a cowboy. He rode herd on the Chisholm Trail, cowboyed on several ranches and learned the tough job of a cowhand. But things were different here in Florida. The scrub palmettos and dense hammocks could hide a hundred head of cows and you'd never know they were there. It took a good cow dog to sniff them out and then push them into the open.

The cows he bought from Moss were spread out over the vast Florida prairie. Moss gave him a paper with the Mizelle brand, an M followed by the number two, and the various earmarks carried by his new possessions. But the cows were tough to find. They hid in deep swamps, thick underbrush, thorns and palmetto scrub. And the cattle were small, fast as antelopes, and apt to be rank.

When Prue finally roped one, it often turned out to have someone else's brand. The most frequent brand he saw was a "Q" with a roof over it, called a rafter "Q."

To help in his cow-hunting endeavors, Prue acquired the cow dog named Buzzard and the whip. He made friends with an old trapper and cow hunter named Moccasin Bob Henderson who lived between his place and the McQueen spread. Bob sold him the whip and was trying to teach him how to crack it, while Buzzard was trying to teach him where to look for his cows.

Prue gazed across the open prairie filled with palmettos and clumps of broom grass waving in the slight breeze looking for the cow and her calf. In the distance he saw the rambling tree line marking Horse Creek. Animal trails wound through the palmettos. No doubt there was a gator hole or a cattle wallow beneath those trees.

It might be wintertime on the palmetto prairies, but the weather was still hot and sultry and the wire grass green. Puffy white clouds floated across the clear blue ocean of sky overhead. The air smelled of moist earth and dog fennel with a hint of salt from the sea a mere thirty miles away.

Prue shifted in the saddle as his stomach churned. Cursing his recent foray into the night life of Arcadia, he turned Satan's head toward a hammock covered with oaks and thick undergrowth. Buzzard, following along at Satan's heels, looked up at Prue and made the appropriate course correction.

"I need to find a log," Prue said over his shoulder to the dog.

Buzzard panted and slobbered and kept trotting, which Prue took to mean, "Yeah, me, too."

Buzzard, a big rangy leopard dog of uncertain years with a wide tan forehead, one blue eye and one gray eye, was covered with black, gray, and tan splotches. The dog came to Prue equipped with a vast knowledge of cows and where to find them and a bad temper. Bob presented Prue with the dog shortly after they met. Bob said he never knew anyone that needed the help of a good cow dog more than Prue.

Prue dismounted and dropped Satan's reins. The Texas mustang was well trained . . . usually. This meant the horse would probably still be there when Prue got back from taking care of business. He removed his gun belt and hooked it over the horn of his Texas stock saddle, but pulled out his big Colt horse pistol. There could be snakes. You never know and they were everywhere around here.

Florida cow country had one thing in common with Texas—the country was filled with rough customers, outlaws, rustlers, roustabouts, and layabouts. But here in Florida there were no networks of Texas Rangers, few sheriffs, and no posse. The justice system was in its infancy. It just didn't make any sense to run around unarmed.

"Stay with the horse," Prue ordered the dog and headed into the scrub. Buzzard watched him disappear into the brush and then lay down beside Satan.

Prue found a bush with soft leaves he hoped would not bring on a rash and hung his hindquarters over the first log he came to. Damn all the booze he'd sucked down the night before! His guts rolled. He'd gone into town for supplies and ended up at the Arcadia House, a boardinghouse most of the cattlemen in the area visited frequently.

At the Arcadia House he enjoyed the drinking and talking to other cowmen and the company of a little red-headed gal named Harriett, but he was paying for it this morning.

He stared off into space from his spot in the brush. He could see Satan beginning to wander as he cropped grass. Dang the mustang for a willful, disobedient son of a gun. The sun was already warming the land. Steam rose off that low area to his north where a stand of cypress trees grew. When he looked off to the east and the rising sun he caught a glimpse of something blue and white in the bushes under a palmetto clump. After making use of his handful of leaves, Prue hitched up his drawers, buckled his belt, and set off to see what it was.

Whistling "The Yellow Rose of Texas," Prue sauntered over to the clump of palmettos, bent over, and looked under it. He was shocked to see a pair of huge blue-green eyes staring back at him. He backed up so fast, he sat down. Buzzard spotted him and came over to investigate. When the big dog saw what was in the bushes, he backed away, began to growl, and then he started baying.

"Be quiet, Buzzard," Prue ordered. The dog sat down and panted, which was pretty well his answer to everything.

"Come on out, little girl," Prue said to the child hiding under the palmetto. "I won't hurt you."

The little girl wearing a blue and white checked smock with a torn hem over a white blouse had long blonde braids, a pointed little chin, and sad, sad eyes. Her face was dirty, and one of her high-topped boots was untied. She stared at Prue and the dog and shook with apparent fear. Her mouth was open slightly and her eyes were wide and scared.

Prue stood up, shaded his eyes with one hand and looked around. Where could she have come from? He didn't see any farms or houses, wagons, riders; no place at all where this child could have originated. He took his brown, four-ply beaver off his head and ran stiff fingers through tangled blond hair.

He bent back down and held his hand out to the child. "Come on out darlin', I won't hurt you," he crooned in his soft Texas drawl.

The little girl shrank further into her hiding place beneath the palmetto fronds. Prue would much rather have been on his horse hunting cows than bent over trying to coax this frightened child out of the brush. His head ached and his guts were churning again. But he couldn't ride off and leave her. What would Ma have to say about something like that? Plenty, that's what.

"Come on, darlin'," he said and reached in to grab her. He wrapped one arm around her waist and hauled her out from under the bush. She immediately opened her mouth wide and began to shriek, a high-pitched wail that ate into Prue's eardrums. Drumming her heels on Prue's legs, she doubled over and sank small teeth into Prue's arm, tearing his clean, white, two-dollar shirt.

"Holy Mother of Jesus," Prue swore. But he didn't drop her. He ran out to where his horse was grazing and dumped her on the grass. She leaped to her feet ready to run, but Prue grabbed her around the waist again. "Please, little girl, I ain't gonna hurt you. I just want to take you to your family. Where's your ma and pa?"

The little girl looked into Prue's eyes and dropped to the ground. She wrapped her arms around her body, dropped her head to her knees, and rocked back and forth. Tears streamed out of her huge blue-green eyes, but the wailing stopped. Her crying was quiet. Her shoulders shook with the force of her emotion. Prue never saw so much pain in so young a face. It made tears spring into his own eyes and his heart ache. He felt helpless and completely at a loss. What should he do now?

The girl bent over and buried her face in her lap, rocking back and forth, shaking with those quiet sobs. Prue sat down next to her and put an arm across her shoulders. Buzzard sat on the other side and slowly licked her head and the side of her face with his enormous pink tongue.

Prue stared at the dog. Cow dogs, a wild mix of hound and bulldog, were full of aggression. The work they did was dangerous and the dogs often died doing it. They got gored, snake-bit, cow-stomped, lost, and even shot. They made terrible pets and worse house dogs. But they loved what they did. It was almost impossible to keep them from chasing cows and rooting through the underbrush searching for the animals. Prue marveled at the tender care this rough dog lavished on the child. Buzzard must sense her anguish and helplessness and somehow, instead of acting aggressively, he was comforting her.

The silent sobs finally abated and the little girl lifted her head and looked at Prue. "Where do you live, sugar?" he asked.

She pointed to the north. Prue knew the river was up that way and several homesteads and squatter shacks. She must be from one of them. Prue wiped her face with the torn sleeve of his shirt and picked her up. She didn't scream this time.

She weighed little, hanging onto him like he was her savior. Satan wandered off and tried to play games with Prue when he went to catch him. Prue motioned for Buzzard to get the horse. The dog cheerfully bit the black mustang on the nose to turn him and then nipped at the horse's heels to push him toward Prue. When Prue scooped up the dragging reins, Satan turned his head and tried to bite him.

"I wouldn't a sent the dog after you, if you'd just come when I whistled," Prue told his horse. He set the little girl on the saddle, strapped his gun belt back around his waist, and climbed up behind her.

They rode slowly, Prue asking her every so often if they were headed in the right direction. About two miles from the hammock where he found her, Prue rode into the yard of a small homestead with a cabin, a barn, and several outbuildings. Chickens ran wild in the yard and a milk cow lowed from her pen. When Prue tied up Satan at the hitching rail outside the barn, he saw the cow needed milking.

"Is this your home?"

The little girl nodded.

Prue lifted her down from the saddle and set her on the ground. She looked up at him with more tears in her eyes. When he took her hand and tried to lead her into the house, she balked, digging in her heels and starting the horrible screeching again.

"Okay, okay, please stop," Prue begged. "You can stay out here with Buzzard." He turned to the dog. "Watch her, Buzzard." The big dog wagged his three-quarter length tail and sat down beside the child.

Prue had no idea what he was going to find inside the cabin. He had a pretty fair notion it wasn't going to be good. When he knocked on the rough-cut board door, it swung open. The door wasn't latched. Slowly pushing it, Prue looked into the dimly lit cabin. He immediately shut the door and backed up.

What he saw inside the two-room cabin turned his already wishy-washy stomach to jelly. He'd seen a lot in his thirty years, but nothing to equal the carnage and gore in that small house. He ran to the pump and was sick. Then he vigorously attacked the handle, pumping cold well water over his head.

Prue glanced back at the child. She watched him with staring eyes that seldom blinked. He'd already realized she knew exactly what was in there. She must have witnessed the murder of her parents who now lay sprawled on the floor of the cabin with their blood splattered over everything.

Prue had no idea what he was supposed to do. When his parents moved to Laredo, it was a wild town. But there was a sheriff and some form of law and order. Out here in the wilds of Florida, there was no authority where Prue could report this heinous crime. The closest law was Eli Drawdy, the sheriff of Pine Level, a known drunk who doubled as the town's undertaker.

Prue heard rumors of vigilantes in the area called the Sara Sota Vigilance Committee. The group was highly secretive. There was no way to report the crime to them. If they were interested in securing justice, they'd do it all on their own with no help from the likes of Jesse Pruitt. Everyone knew it was best to steer clear of them anyway, as they were known to use their little group for whatever took their fancy or to further the members' own interests, which from what Prue heard was ridding the community of families just like the one that lived here. They formed for the specific reason of keeping the range land open as grazing land for their cows.

No, the way Prue saw it, the only thing he could do was go back in there, clean up the mess and bury this poor child's parents, if that's who they indeed were. From the girl's reactions, that looked like the case. If only he could get her to talk and tell him what happened. He glanced at her sitting on the ground pulling on Buzzard's big floppy ears. He certainly wasn't going to make her go back in there, not when he didn't even want to himself.

Prue walked into the barn and looked around. It was a simple log structure with two stalls on each side of an open alley. There was a small loft still
filled with hay for the winter. A door led to a room with a corn crib partly
filled with dried corn on the cob, tools hanging on pegs driven into the log
walls. Leather harnesses, bridles, a harness collar, and a saddle all neatly
hung on more wooden pegs. Grabbing a shovel, Prue backed out and shut
the door.

A fat paint pony, two stout mules, one red and one black, and an ancient
gray horse of uncertain ancestry stared at him from a small corral behind
the barn. The gray horse still bore the stains of sweat and dirt from a saddle
pad. Someone recently rode him and didn't brush him off. A saddle lay
upside down against the rail fence with a thick saddle blanket over it to dry.
Parked against the back wall of the barn was a rundown buckboard with its
shafts resting on a sawhorse.

He felt like an interloper snooping into the personal life of these strangers. Well he'd better get used to it because it was going to get much worse
when he went into the cabin.

As he was leaving the barn, the cow caught his attention again. He was
going to have to milk her and take her with him. He couldn't turn her out
on the prairie. She looked like a Guernsey cross, small and brown with big
dark eyes and an enormous bag of milk. She'd come in handy with feeding
the little girl, because from the look of things, he was gonna be stuck with
her, too.

He strode out of the barn with long determined steps and stopped beside
the child. She looked up at him as he laid down the shovel and knelt on one
knee. "Sweetheart, can you tell me your name?"

The girl instantly dropped her head into her hands and refused to look
at him. Buzzard stared at Prue reproachfully. Prue sighed. It would be so
much easier if she could just tell him this was her home and the people
inside the cabin were her folks.

He climbed to his feet and steeled himself to enter the cabin. This was
gonna be awful, just awful.

2

"Stretch him out!" Malachai McQueen snapped his orders. He was used to being instantly obeyed.

Four masked men pinned Jared Webb, a self-confessed rapist, on the ground naked with a rope tied to each leg and both wrists.

The men hesitated and looked up at McQueen as he sat astride the finest piece of horseflesh in Desoto County.

McQueen pulled his personal weapon, a sawed-off double-barreled shotgun, out of the special scabbard on the side of his saddle, pointed it at the closest masked vigilante and twitched it in the direction of the prisoner. "I said, stretch him out. You best remember our motto, Titus. *Death to all traitors.*"

Three of the men moved slowly, reluctantly, to tie the ropes to four trees and pull them taut. The fourth man was McQueen's right-hand man, Sergeant Pelo Berryhill. He moved quickly and efficiently, accustomed to doing whatever McQueen ordered him to do. Webb, stretched tight, screamed his guts out and begged for mercy.

McQueen hated a rapist more than any other form of lowlife. Any man who took a woman against her will deserved no mercy. When he was small, he saw his own mother fight off men. When he grew older, he fought them for her. In her line of work she came into contact with the violent scum of the earth, many who just didn't think paying for her services was necessary.

She was never without the gun he now pointed at Webb. She died when he was fourteen and it was the only thing she left him.

"Now men, this will be just like cutting a stallion or a hog," McQueen said quietly as he lifted his long right leg over the horn of his saddle and stepped off his horse onto the grass. "Unlike a calf, which only has one sack containing both testicles, a man has two, just like a stallion. Therefore, you must make two cuts. Of course, in this case, we will only be making one cut because we are removing just the one organ."

McQueen pulled out his pocket knife and flicked it open.

Webb begged harder. "Please, don't do this to me. She was just a little slut of a nigger gal. Anyone could see she was high yeller. And she was teasing me, flirting all the time with them low-cut dresses showing off her titties and all. Sticking 'em in my face, she practically begged me to take her. So I did. I'm admitting to it. Please, don't cut me!" The last word in this plea was long, drawn out and more like a shriek.

McQueen stood over the struggling man, who twisted and turned in his ropes. "That little nigger gal, as you put it, was only twelve and the daughter of one of the finest men in Arcadia who also happens to be a personal friend of mine. What or who her mama was is no concern of yours. She wasn't flirting with the likes of you. She would never have even met you if you hadn't accosted her on the street. Hold him down, men."

At his command, the four men each grabbed one of Webb's appendages and held it tightly.

"If you don't hold still, Webb, I can't guarantee you won't die. The almanac said signs are in the feet, just right for cutting, and you shouldn't bleed too much as long as you don't struggle."

Webb began a high-pitched screeching as McQueen knelt beside him. With McQueen's first cut, the screaming became a wail of horrible fear and pain. Three of the four men turned their heads. Apparently, they didn't have the stomach to watch. McQueen skillfully slit the sack and yanked out Webb's left testicle, pulling the long cord attached to it out with the organ. He held it in front of Webb's face showing him the cod. The screaming stopped as Webb stared at his lost manhood.

"Open your mouth, Webb," McQueen ordered.

The trussed man shook his head. "No, don't make me eat it, please don't make me eat it. I heard that's what you done to a man over in Zolfo Springs. Please don't make me, please."

"If you don't eat your nut, Webb, I'll remove the other one. I've half a mind to do it anyway." McQueen looked up at the men holding Webb down. "Well, boys, should I cut out Mr. Webb's other cod?"

Webb started screaming again. "No, no, I'll do it. I'll do it, please."

Webb opened his mouth wide and McQueen crammed the testicle in whole. "Stop blubbering and chew. The damn thing is only a mouthful and a small mouthful at that."

Sobbing and gagging, Webb chewed.

"Now swallow."

Webb gagged again, took a deep breath in through his nose, then gulped.

"There," McQueen said as he rose and dusted off his immaculate, fawn-colored, doe-skin riding britches. "Now was that so hard? One less rapist, justice served. You realize Webb, that if you repeat this offense, we will remove the other."

Tears streaming down his red face, Webb nodded and retched.

"Untie him," McQueen ordered.

The men loosened and removed the ropes tied around Webb's extremities. He pulled his legs into his chest, curled into a ball and began vomiting loudly.

"What you want to do with him now, Judge?" asked one of the masked men.

"Nothing," McQueen answered. "He's free to go. He's received just punishment for his actions. The Sara Sota Vigilance Committee has spoken."

One of the masked men retrieved a sorry bundle from behind a tree and tossed it on top of Webb. "Here's yer clothes, Webb. You can go."

Another hooded man walked toward Malachai. Standing close, the SSVC member poked a finger in Malachai's chest. "Judge, I don't like what just happened here. I didn't sign on to castrate rapists. I thought we was gonna get rid of the squatters on my land and push the nesters and farmers off the cattle ranges."

Malachai snarled. "You took an oath Duron. You swore to sustain each member of this band be he in the right or the wrong. And didn't we already run the squatters off your land?"

"Yes, but . . ." Duron Grey, prominent businessman and cattleman from Arcadia, tried to answer.

"But what, Duron? How many farmers' homes have we burned? I think the number is twelve. And didn't you owe the last family a considerable amount of money for horses you purchased but for which you did not pay? And didn't they go back to Quincy and leave without collecting the money you owed?"

Grey's prominent Adam's apple could be seen bobbing beneath the edge of his black hood. "It just don't seem right, Judge, cutting a man like he was a stud colt." Grey's voice trailed off as he turned to mount his horse.

Malachai followed Grey to his horse. "I believe this fine animal was one of those horses you received from the Johnstons."

Grey quickly mounted the horse.

"Didn't you miss the last two meetings?" Malachai grabbed Grey's rein and pulled the moving horse to a stop.

Grey's voice took on the tone of a man who knows he'd better turn this conversation around. Members of the SSVC who missed three meetings were whipped with a stirrup leather. It was in the organization's bylaws. "It'll never happen again, sir."

"No, I imagine it won't."

Malachai let the horse go and Duron joined his three hooded friends. McQueen climbed onto his horse, a rare palomino, and followed by the four members of the Sara Sota Vigilance Committee he headed onto the prairie by the dim light of the setting moon. He lifted one hand as he held the reins of his plunging horse tightly with the other. "Let's ride," he said. Releasing the stallion's head, they galloped away into the dark night leaving Webb still sobbing in the dirt.

The five men rode together until they reached a road leading off to Arcadia. Three of them, all prominent cattlemen and business owners from the area, turned toward town and galloped off with a wave. McQueen and Berryhill, an old army buddy and a lieutenant in the SSVC, turned north toward the Rafter Q.

"What a bunch of gutless, yellowbellied cowards," McQueen said about the three other vigilantes as they rode across the dark prairie. The moon hung low over the western horizon and the sky was dusted with stars.

"They serve their purpose, Judge," Berryhill said.

"They serve their own purposes," McQueen replied. "They'd piss their pants if they knew they were being bossed around by the son of a whore."

Berryhill swiveled his head, glancing around at the dark prairie. "You shouldn't even joke about that, Boss. Someone's gonna hear you one day."

"So what? There's nothing anyone can prove. I'm Malachai McQueen, biggest landowner in Desoto County, a judge and founder at the head of the Sara Sota Vigilance Committee, and I have been Malachai McQueen for nineteen years. Benjamin Jones is dead. He died nobly on the field of battle fighting for the glorious Stars and Bars. Nothing's going to change that. Even the trusted family retainer, my foreman Rooster Barns, believes I'm Malachai."

Malachai, who used to be Ben Jones, stroked his clean-shaven chin, the one that exactly resembled his double, now dead and buried. "The only part of me not like McQueen is this spot I got me on the top of my head."

He removed the hat and gingerly touched the rough scar tissue on the very crown of his head. "When I was eighteen, just before I run off to fight for the Rebs, a half-breed, renegade Apache, drunk as a bandicoot, grabbed me from behind and tried to scalp me. But I told Rooster and old man McQueen when they saw the scar, it happened during the war. And who's to say that's not so?"

"I heard the real Malachai's aunt, Thelma Lou McQueen, is coming to visit. Do you think she'll be able to tell you ain't Malachai?" Berryhill urged his horse into a slow jog to keep up with the longer strides of McQueen's stud.

McQueen frowned and lifted his top hat to run fingers through his sweaty hair. He'd recently received a letter from dear Aunt Thelma announcing her visit. She was bringing her grandson Jeb McQueen to the ranch along her daughter-in-law, a widow, Clara McQueen, for an extended stay.

"She said in her letter, since her son died she's had a hankering to see the old place and the grandson wants to learn about cow hunting from his cousin Malachai.

"She told me working cattle's in Jeb's blood. Working cattle and riding horses is all the boy talks about. She told me in her letter he wants to meet me."

Berryhill hooted. "If he wants to meet Malachai McQueen, he's about twenty years too late."

"Laugh all you want, we got us a real problem, Pelo. I can't very well ask Rooster to fill me in on details I should rightly already know. And you know me as well as anybody, teaching sawed-off runts how to work cows is not and never will be high on my list of shit to do. Besides, I ain't no cowhand. That's what I got men for. Why else do I keep Rooster Barns on my payroll?"

Berryhill turned his head and stared at McQueen. "The little brat is going to stick his nose into everything."

"Not if I have anything to say about it. I heard her and my Uncle Daniel, old man McQueen's youngest son, were living at the ranch when Daniel and the real Malachai went off to war leaving dear Aunt Thelma to care for her son alone," McQueen said. "She lives up Tampa way on a big spread she's been running all by herself. Rooster says she can ride and crack a whip with the best of them."

Berryhill spurred his small horse and cursed when it crow-hopped. "Damn you for a rank piece of crow bait. Your aunt sounds like someone who knows one end of a cow from another."

"Then she needs to teach the boy all about cow hunting herself? I don't like going on roundups. That's why I hire hands. Out there in the palmettos, the bugs eat you alive. There's wolves and mud and gators and snakes. I really hate snakes and I'm not that crazy about them little cracker cows. They're wild and squirrelly. They'll hook you as soon as look at you."

"Boss, you better stay away from this woman. If she knows as much about working cows as you say, she might notice you ain't exactly a hand, and the real Malachai was a legend around here. He could crack a whip and cut you in half. And he could throw a leg over the meanest brute in the stables and ride the shit out of it."

"Don't you worry. I fully intend to stay away from her. I got plenty to do in town with the vigilantes to keep me busy while she's here."

"Do you think she might know something special about Malachai that would tip her off to your impersonatin' of him?" Berryhill asked. "You know, somethin' we don't know nothing about?"

"I have no idea how long she resided at the ranch or what she knows about my early days. And these are questions I really can't ask Rooster since I'm supposed to know. I think you need to snoop around for me, Sergeant. Find out more about dear Aunty Thelma. I'm afraid she may have to have a tragic accident on her way out to the ranch. These are such lawless times you know, anything may well happen. After all this time, so content in my role, I hesitate to leave anything that may threaten it to chance. The day I met Lieutenant Malachai McQueen was the luckiest day of my life. I don't plan to allow anyone, not even Aunt Thelma, to ruin such a comfortable situation."

Ben Jones was born to a lady of the evening in Laredo, Texas. Actually, lady of the evening nowhere near described his mother's circumstances. She was little more than a tent whore, accepting men into a bed located in a one-room hovel in a disgusting back alley of Laredo when Laredo was little more than a quaint village filled with destitute Mexicans, cowboys, ignorant peasants, and other whores. Little Ben slept in the same dirty room unless he was kicked out into the alley by one of his mother's clients while they sported in the shack.

One night, one of those clients, in an expansive mood after a particularly long and apparently enjoyable sojourn in the shack, gave Ben, who was waiting on the steps hoping his mother would feed him soon because he was hungry, a stunning piece of advice. This advice changed Ben's outlook on the world and eventually his future.

The client put one finger under Ben's chin while he straightened his string tie, then he said, "Son, you probably think you're in a pretty hopeless situation. Just remember, you never know when that one moment of opportunity, the one destined to change your life forever, is going to arrive. Always be ready for it. And realize this, every single person you come in contact with holds something of value for you, some way to help you, something you can learn from or take for your own. People are on this earth to be used. You need to be the user not the one used. And don't forget to keep your eyes peeled for your moment."

To make Ben remember him even more, the tall man flipped Ben a gold coin with an eagle on it. To this day, Ben Jones, turned Malachai Mc-Queen, carried that coin. He reached into his pocket as he remembered words spoken to a scared kid so long ago, and found the gold coin. It was his good-luck charm. He rubbed it absently as they rode toward his ranch. What would Aunt Thelma have to offer him? Should he meet her first or just take care never to meet her?

3

The hole Prue dug slowly got deeper and deeper. He wiped sweat off his brow and leaned his elbow on the shovel. Digging anywhere he'd been in Florida was a bitch. Even here on the prairie where there actually was topsoil, the deeper you dug, the more you discovered Florida was just sand. The sides kept collapsing inward.

The little girl sat on the edge of his excavation and solemnly watched it grow. He thought she knew exactly what he was doing and why. When water began seeping into the grave and he could barely see over its edge, he climbed out and laid down the shovel.

"I'm going into the house to get your Ma and Pa. You wait out here."

She looked up at him dry-eyed and nodded. The hysterics seemed to be over. Prue was glad but saddened at her loss of innocence and the pain he knew she suffered. He couldn't imagine what she saw in there or what she felt. He knew the pain of losing a parent, but in one violent action she'd lost everything, both her parents and her life. What was going to happen to her now? He sure didn't know.

He opened the door of the cabin and steeled himself to enter. The inside of the door was splattered with blood and parts of her father. It looked like he was hit at close range by a scattergun. His upper chest and face were a bloody mess. There was no way to tell what he looked like before being shot. The stench of blood and death made Prue gag so he pulled his blue bandana up over his nose.

Holding his breath, Prue grabbed the dead man's feet and dragged him
out of the cabin toward the newly dug grave. When he reached it, he wished
he'd thought to wrap the man up in a blanket so the girl could not see the
destruction caused by the shotgun. Walking fast, he went back into the
cabin, yanked a red and gold quilt off the settle and ran back to cover the
dead man's face.

Breathing a little easier, he returned to the house to get the woman. She
wasn't shot and wasn't bloody. The girl's mother was tiny, barely bigger than
the girl. Her wide-opened blue-green eyes, filming over with death, stared
accusingly up at him from the wood floor. Her throat was bruised and her
neck and head lay at an odd angle. Prue guessed she'd been strangled and
her neck broken. It wouldn't take a giant to do it as fragile as she appeared.

In her hand she held a black velvet jewelry box. It was open and empty.
When Prue rolled her over to wrap her in a blanket off the bed, he saw an
exquisite gold filigree necklace beneath her with a large, blue-green stone
the color of her eyes, hanging from the center.

Prue knelt beside the woman and gently tried to close her eyes. The lids
would not stay down. Like recalcitrant window shades they kept sliding up to
reveal her eyes, eyes the exact color of the little girl's. Prue had to look away.

He could not imagine what happened here. It looked like the woman
was given the necklace as a gift and then strangled. Did the husband find
her with another man and then get shot? The whole scene was crazy and
bizarre. Had the little girl seen what happened or had she been outside,
heard the noise, and found this horror when she returned?

With the woman's staring eyes covered by the blanket, Prue took a good
look at the inside of the cabin. He needed to discover these folks' identities
and the little girl's name. The cabin was neat and clean. A four-hole, wood
cookstove, a counter, and some shelves ran along one wall under a window.
Blue curtains hung from the wooden countertop. When Prue peeked behind the curtains, he saw a big washtub, several crocks, and a slop bucket.

A gray and black speckled metal coffee pot sat on the stove top along with
a huge kettle. A small white enamel washtub lay upside down on the counter next to a plate of biscuits covered with a red and white striped towel.
Dishes were stacked neatly on the shelves. Pots and skillets hung from a
rack over the stove. A pie safe in the corner contained bacon, two loaves of
bread, a can of lard and sacks that probably held flour, corn meal, sugar,
beans, and root vegetables.

The settle was against one wall; a small table sat in the middle of the room
with three chairs. The table was covered with a white cloth embroidered

with riotous flowers of every color on a pale blue background. There was a salt cellar and a china sugar bowl on the table filled with coarse raw sugar.

In the small second room, a large bed covered with a patchwork quilt almost filled the space. When he opened the door of the wardrobe, he saw it contained clothes for a man, woman, and the little girl. He grabbed a green carpet bag out of the bottom of the wardrobe and put two smocks, a handful of hair ribbons and petticoats, and several blouses inside for the little girl. He found her some underclothes in a small chest of drawers and added them to the bag. Bedding was neatly rolled up and tucked under the bed, probably for the little girl. He grabbed that. On an upturned crate next to the bed, he found what he was searching for, the family Bible.

He carried the bag to the tiny table in the kitchen area and sat down on a ladder-back chair to look at the Bible. Inside on the flyleaf was a list of people and their dates of birth and death. The family name was Buttons. The newest entry was Jennifer Elizabeth Buttons born on April 23, 1874, which made the little girl ten. She looked so much younger, probably going to be tiny like her ma. Her ma's name was Elva June Snyder. She and Jenny's pa, Randolph Joseph Buttons Junior, were married in 1872.

Prue carefully closed the Buttons's family Bible and placed it in the bag. He'd spent enough time grubbing around in these folks' life. He felt like a thief stealing their personal secrets. Tossing the necklace into the black velvet box, he shoved it into the bag for Jenny, then lifted her tiny mother in his arms and carried her out to the grave.

Jenny was nowhere in sight and neither was Buzzard. He debated about finding her and bringing her here to watch him inter her folks and quickly trashed the idea. It seemed to him she'd seen enough. He laid her parents in the hole side by side and covered them with the quilt. Somehow, he just couldn't throw dirt on that pretty woman's staring eyes. When they were buried, he erected a hastily crafted cross and went looking for Jenny.

He found her and Buzzard in the barn. Jenny sat on a pile of hay in one of the stalls holding a small fluffy calico cat in her lap. Buzzard squatted on his haunches, panting beside her while watching both of them with extreme interest. A thin trickle of slobber ran out of the corner of his mouth. No doubt, he was plotting some way to get the fluffy cat outside where he could turn it into a tasty snack.

Prue knelt beside Jenny and reached over to stroke the cat. "What am I going to do with you?" he said to her, never expecting an answer.

"I guess you better take me with you," she replied. "I ain't staying here by myself. That's for sure."

Prue was so shocked, he inadvertently pinched the cat which snarled and scratched him. Buzzard, happy to be of service in destroying the vicious creature attacking his master, growled, which made the cat arch her back and hiss.

"Knock it off, Buzzard," Prue ordered the leopard dog. "You can't eat the cat. So," Prue said to Jenny, "You can talk after all?"

"I always could. I just don't much feel like talking."

"I can understand that," Prue said. "I don't think I'd feel much like talking either." He looked her over. She seemed remarkably calm. He wondered if he should ask her now if she'd seen who killed her parents, or maybe give her some more time. Waiting seemed like the best option. "Well, come on then, I best be hitching up that wagon so we can make it to Moccasin Bob's house before dark. I don't want to be spending the night here."

"No, sir," Jenny said, as she got up and placed the cat on the barn floor. "I don't want to stay here neither."

"Which of the mules is the best for pulling the wagon?" Prue asked as they walked toward the corral.

"Pa always uses Buck. He's the big black one."

It took Prue some time to catch old Buck. He liked to get into a corner and turn his rear to you. Prue had a healthy respect for the rear ends of mules. By the time the mule was harnessed and sulking between the shafts, the pigs let out of their pens, the cow milked and hitched behind the wagon along with the gray horse, the pony, his stud and the other mule, the shadows had lengthened. Then when Prue tried to load up the little girl, she balked.

Prue sighed. "What now?"

"I can't leave without Sibby," she explained.

Prue looked at the train attached to the rear of the wagon. "Who in tarnation is Sibby?"

"My kitty," she said.

Prue groaned. "Darling, the cat will never stay in the wagon."

"She will if I hold her." Prue thought Jenny's face was starting to look like Buck's. It also occurred to him the girl had lost enough this day.

"Let's find her," he finally said.

Locating the cat took half an hour, and it turned out dear Sibby had a litter of six half-grown kittens with her. When all seven were tucked in the wagon inside a crate along with Jenny's carpet bag and bedding, they started off.

Prue didn't know what to do with the girl. His place was unfinished, the cabin no more than a lean-to, and besides it was too far away. He couldn't take her into Pine Level or Arcadia. Both towns were more than six hours away at the slow pace he was forced to adopt due to the train of livestock dragging along behind the buckboard. He needed to find a safe refuge where he could think, and someone who could give him some advice. It would have to be Bob.

Moccasin Bob's place on Moccasin Wallow was only about ten miles away. They should be able to get there around dark, even as slow as they were traveling. And maybe Bob would know exactly what he should do . . . maybe.

Prue drove the mule along a small rutted trail across the grass with all the animals ambling behind. There was no rushing the milk cow or the old gray nag. The warm weather of the morning was starting to turn colder as the day waned. A cooling breeze rolled across the prairie from the north, stirring the trees on a nearby hammock and ruffling the mule's fuzzy forelock.

The livestock trailing behind fought and balked at first, especially the red mule, but Buck was strong and eventually all, even the cow, realized they better walk or get dragged.

"Jenny," Prue started. He had no idea how to approach the subject of her parents' murder. He didn't want her to stop talking again, but he needed to find out if she knew what happened. "Were you in the cabin when your folks were killed?"

Jenny looked down at her small hands clenched tightly together in her lap. "How do you know my name's Jenny?"

"I read it in your family Bible."

"Well, what's your name?"

Prue momentarily felt stupid. He'd never introduced himself to the girl. With her not speaking at first and then with the grave digging and all, it slipped his mind. "My name is Jesse Pruitt, but everyone calls me Prue."

Jenny stifled a giggle with her hand. "That's a silly name."

Prue put his arm around her shoulders and squeezed. "Well, it's been my name for thirty or so years, so I guess I'm used to it, silly or not. Now, if it doesn't bother you too much, could you help by telling me if you were in the cabin when your parents were killed?"

Jenny closed her eyes tightly and wrung her small hands. "I don't want to think about it, no, I really don't."

"It's okay, darling, I just need to know so I can help find the man who done it."

Tears leaked out of Jenny's eyes. She wiped them off her face with the back of one hand and sniffed. "I was hiding in the big washtub under the kitchen counter," she finally whispered. "Behind them curtains my ma hung to cover up where we put the slop bucket and all."

The agony of those moments, the ugliness she was reliving to tell him what happened, was so intense, Prue almost stopped her. He hated to see her suffer. But he needed to know. He wanted to know who had killed her folks. If there was a cold-blooded murderer of that magnitude running around in these parts, something should be done to stop him.

"What did you see, sugar? I know it hurts to remember, but whoever hurt your ma and pa needs to be brought to justice before they kill anyone else."

Jenny leaned over on the seat of the buckboard and buried her face in her hands. Prue had to lean closer to catch her muffled words. "There was a man come to visit my ma. I seen him there before. Ma didn't like him, didn't want him to be there, but he kept on coming back. He always came to our house when Pa was off getting supplies or off working."

Prue put his arm around her. "What did he say to your ma?"

Jenny snuggled against him. "He kept asking her to go away with him. He wanted to take me, too."

"What'd your ma say?"

"She told him over and over she loved my pa and didn't want to leave. He'd try to hug on her and he brought her candy and special treats for me. When he was gone, Ma would throw it all in the pig pen. I don't think she wanted Pa to see them."

"Do you know who this man is?"

"All I know is he said I was to call him Uncle Mal."

"Are you sure it was Mal? That's a very strange name."

Jenny shrugged her thin shoulders. "It sounded like Mal to me."

"Well, what did your ma call him?"

"Nothing, Ma wouldn't say his name, ever. And when he left, she'd always ask me not to say anything to Pa. She said it would make him very unhappy."

I bet it would. Prue wondered what Elva was hiding. Must be hiding something or she would have told her husband. Or maybe this Mal guy was her husband's friend. "Did Uncle Mal ever show up when your daddy was at home?"

"Only once. The first time he came over, it was Pa brought him into the house. My daddy told Ma that there was a man to visit that wanted to buy our place. He was only there for a few minutes and he and Pa got into a big fight with lots of yelling. When I looked out the window, I could see a bunch of other men on horses. They all rode off real fast."

"Jenny, what happened when this man killed your folks?" Prue hated to ask her. She'd have to relive it all over again.

But suddenly Jenny wanted to tell him. She sat up tall and brave. "I saw it. Uncle Mal came to the house. Pa was gone for supplies like he did every two weeks. But, for some reason, he came home. I was hiding under the counter because Uncle Mal always tried to hug on me and touch me. When I heard his horse come up to the house, I looked out and I remember telling Ma, 'Oh no, it's Uncle Mal.' She told me to hide, so I did."

Jenny took a deep breath. "Pa came in when Uncle Mal was trying to grab hold of Ma. He was handing her something in a little black box and she didn't want it. Pa was carrying his rifle. He lifted it like he was going to shoot Uncle Mal only Uncle Mal had an ugly, fat gun on his belt. He shot Pa with it and when Ma started screaming and screaming and screaming, he grabbed her neck and she fell down."

The killer must carry a sawed-off shotgun, Prue thought, because Jenny's father was shot at close range by a shotgun and the little girl's description fit. If the killer carried one on his belt, it would make him very distinctive. Few men owned or toted a sawed-off.

"Tell me what Uncle Mal looks like, darling," Prue said softly.

"He's tall, taller than my pa, almost taller than the front door of our house."

"That's good," Prue said. "What else?"

"He has black, oily hair and nasty yeller eyes. His hair always looks like he put lard in it, at least that's what Ma said."

"Are you sure his eyes aren't light brown?"

"No, they're yeller, yeller as Sibby's, and he rides a big ole yeller hoss and wears a tall black hat."

Prue squeezed her shoulders again and Jenny relaxed against him. Pretty soon, she fell into a deep sleep. Poor thing was probably exhausted. All this must have happened yesterday. She'd walked a couple of miles getting away and then spent the night on the prairie. She was holding up like a real trooper.

As Prue drove the wagon down the rutted track toward Moccasin Creek, he wondered what he should do with Jenny and what he was going to do about these murders. Something surely needed to be done. Maybe that vigilante group he'd heard operated in this area would take up Jenny's cause and find the murderer. The vigilantes' form of justice was crude and violent, but as far as he was concerned, in this case that would work just fine.

4

Prue drove the big black mule down a steep incline and into near darkness. The sun was down, with only a red glow shining over the western horizon. Jenny lay slumped against his shoulder snoring softly.

The wagon bumped and lurched as it slowly rolled down hill on the narrow track leading to Bob's place on Moccasin Wallow. The scrub oaks grew taller here and willows crowded the track with their branches hanging low, forcing Prue to duck as he drove into Bob's place. Buzzard pricked up his ears as Bob's pack of dogs began to bark and carry on. All of Bob's dogs except his one house dog were either caged or chained.

When Prue's eyes adjusted to the gloom, he saw Bob standing in the track ahead with his shotgun aimed directly at them.

"Hello the camp," Prue shouted.

Bob squinted and pushed his ancient black floppy hat off his forehead. "Well if it ain't that varmint Jesse Pruitt fresh come from Texas to be a real cow hunter." Bob laughed. "What's a matter, too many bugs, too many snakes, not enough women? Ain't old Buzzard working for ye?"

Prue pulled the wagon in front of Bob's barn, a dilapidated structure created from moss-covered logs, mud, and palmetto fronds. When he moved to get down, he lowered Jenny to the seat where she continued to sleep deeply, one arm dangling off the bench seat. After setting the wagon's brake, he jumped to the ground.

Bob walked over to shake his hand and saw Jenny. His wild eyebrows rose. "What in thunder have you got yourself into, boy?"

Jesse sighed. "You hit the nail on the head, Bob. I got myself into something big and bad. Help me find somewhere to bed down these animals and I'll tell you all about it."

Prue and Bob untied the train of livestock and led them into Bob's barn. Bob looked over the stock. "What? No hogs?"

Prue laughed. "I set them loose."

"Smart move, pigs can fend for themselves. So where did you pick up the little filly and this here herd?"

Prue told him where he found Jenny and about her parents. Bob listened as they tossed some straw in two empty stalls for the mules and the cow. They put the pony and the old riding horse in the corral with Bob's red mare. Prue was forced to disenfranchise a heavily bred cow and a flock of chickens from Bob's last stall for Satan. He put Bob's cow in with Jenny's milk cow. When all the livestock was bedded down for the night, he and Bob went back out to the wagon.

Jenny sat heavy-eyed on the seat looking around at Bob's place in amazement. It was pretty interesting. Bob built his cabin and barn and many small outbuildings close to a swamp and about fifteen feet from Moccasin Wallow. The murky water from the wallow made the atmosphere damp while the thick underbrush and overhanging trees blotted out the sky. High in the trees, a big owl hooted. Prue looked up and saw several of the birds with big round faces staring down at the ground. They probably hoped one of Bob's critters would get loose and provide a meal.

Bob's swamp home was a safe and secretive place. Few people ventured this close to the swamp and those that did would never guess there was a homestead down here. Prue knew Bob had several good reasons for wanting to live in seclusion.

Two hurricane lanterns hung on low-hanging oak limbs. They lighted the glade with an eerie glow, sending long shadows across the well-beaten black earth underfoot. Stinking smudge pots with Bob's own recipe of mosquito repellant filled the air with the smell of pine tar and something that reminded Prue of bear grease and burning chicken feathers. If the smudge pots worked Prue sure couldn't tell. He slapped idly at a buzzing mosquito.

"Jenny, this is Moccasin Bob," Prue introduced the two as he lifted her down from the wagon. The noise from the dogs almost drowned out his voice. He yelled to be heard.

Bob whipped off his floppy hat revealing gray hair pulled tight from his forehead and braided into a queue down his back. His faded blue eyes twinkled at her from nests of wrinkles. Most of Bob's face was covered with a gray beard that flowed over the front of his faded red-plaid, wool shirt. Bob was over six feet tall without a spare ounce of flesh on him. His wiry frame was deceptively strong as Prue discovered the first time he'd met Bob out on the prairie.

Bob had a bull calf by the horns and was having trouble trying to throw it. Prue was riding out from his own place, and for the first time since he'd come to Florida and was hunting for some of his cows. He carried a branding iron for any new calves he found, an underscored "P." The iron was stuck into one of his gun sheaths and attached to his saddle. When Prue saw the old man wrestling with a calf weighing twice what he did, he stopped to watch. He had to admit, Bob impressed him. At one point Prue thought he might get the calf on the ground and hog tie him. When Prue saw the old man running out of strength, he'd jumped off Satan to help.

The two of them quickly accomplished what Bob struggled to do alone, and it didn't make Bob happy at all. The old man put a cussing on Prue when the calf was branded and running back to its mama. Prue still remembered standing with his mouth open while Bob cussed him up one side and down the other for being a sorry interfering so and so. They'd been friends ever since.

"Well, Miss Jenny," Bob said in his Georgia country accent. "Let's get you into the cabin and out of this damp and all these squeeters."

"I thought the smudge pots were supposed to keep the squeeters away," Prue said.

"They do," Bob said. "You should see them dang bugs when the pots ain't burning, clouds of 'em big enough to tote you, me, and the stock right off into the swamp."

Prue laughed as he grabbed Jenny's bedroll and the green carpet bag out of the wagon while Bob, carrying one of the lanterns, took Jenny's hand in his and started to lead her inside.

She looked up and spotted one of the owls, pointing. "Ma told me when you see an owl someone you know's gonna to die."

Bob shook his head. "Oh, no, little lady, if someone I knew died every time I saw an owl, I wouldn't have no friends a-tall. This swamp's infested with owls. They eat my chickens. The stupid chickens roost in the trees and an old owl will land on the same branch next to one, keep scootin' over until he's right up agin him and then blam! Snatch the poor dumb bird's head off. I seen it happen a dozen times."

"That one's purty," Jenny said pointing to a big gray owl with black and white barred feathers across its chest. "He's looking at me."

"That's a hooty owl. He's looking for one of my chickens. Now let's get you out of these skeeters."

Bob's cabin was a one-room log structure, the walls lined with shelves and pegs. Books, cups, plates, food, tools, animal bones, hooves, paws, horns and heads, and bottles filled the shelves. More tools, guns, animal heads, and clothes hung on the pegs. In the places where there were no shelves, bear, coon, otter, and bobcat skins were stretched over the log walls. Bob's bed at the far end of the cabin was heaped with more skins, and there was a huge speckled cowhide covering the wood plank floor near a small table. On the table an oil lamp flickered, casting pale yellow light over the contents of the room.

Prue grabbed Jenny's hand and stopped her just inside the door. He quickly and carefully scanned the floor, table, shelves, and bed before allowing Jenny to step into the room.

Jenny looked around, wrinkled her nose, and stared up at Prue. Prue shook his head and put a finger to his lips. The other most distinct detail about Bob's cabin was the smell. It was an odor that you never forgot and was apt to linger on your clothes long after you left.

The smell was a combination of bacon grease from the skillet always sitting on the small wood heater, which doubled as a cookstove, filthy old man (Bob rarely if ever bathed), the dead animals and skins decorating the walls, and damp and mildew from the nearby wallow, dogs, and snakes.

Moccasin Bob did not get his name from the wallow close to his house. He was named because of his predilection for cottonmouth snakes also commonly known as water moccasins and the fact he always wore tall, lace-up Indian moccasins he made himself.

Bob's collection of snakes lived in the cabin and everywhere on the property. The small outbuildings around the clearing contained wooden boxes and big glass jars filled with poisonous snakes. Bob preferred the cottonmouths, but also collected rattlers and coral snakes. In a wood and wire cage close to his bed, two canebrake rattlers lifted their knobby heads and shook the rattles on their tails in warning.

"There ain't any loose ones are there?" Prue asked before setting Jenny's bedroll on the floor next to the wood heater.

"Nah," Bob said. "I locked them all up yesterday. One of the rattlers bit Sally and I lost her. The stupid gyp stepped on the snake, so's it's hard to blame it, but I loved that old dog."

Prue had never been able to understand how all the dogs and Bob himself didn't end up snake bit and dead. Snakes rarely coexisted with dogs. A known way to keep snakes away from your house was to have lots of dogs or pigs. But Bob somehow managed to keep them all living harmoniously. This was the first accident he'd heard of since meeting Bob and becoming acquainted with his peculiar hobby.

Sally was Buzzard's mama, a big black wolf dog. Prue suddenly realized he missed seeing her come out to meet him. Bob didn't go anywhere without Sally unless she was nursing a litter of pups.

Jenny heard the ominous rattle of the canebrakes and latched onto Prue's leg. "Prue, I don't like snakes," she whispered.

"Me neither," Prue said. "But, if you're gonna be Bob's friend, you have to get used to them. Usually, they're caged up. But if Bob thinks someone's trying to break into the house or if he hears someone sneaking around the property, he sets them loose."

Jenny nodded, but kept her death hold on his chaps.

Bob poked the fire in the heater to life and set the battered tin coffee pot on one of the two holes while Prue laid Jenny's bedroll out close to the fire.

"Where are you going to sleep?" she asked Prue.

"Right here on the floor beside you, darlin'," he said. "Are you hungry?"

Jenny nodded. "Is there anything in this house safe to eat?" she whispered.

"I heard that," Bob said. "And I got just the thing here for you, missy."

Bob pulled a kitchen towel, faded and gray from years of use, off a pan of corn pone. He took two of the fried pieces of cornbread, placed them on a tin plate, and sat it on the table. Jenny sat on one of Bob's benches made of twisted, thick grape vines and raw cypress planks and stared at the crispy pieces of bread. Bob plopped a piece of cold bacon next to them with a flourish, then opened a jar of honey and ladled a spoonful over the corn pone.

"Dinner for my lady," he said.

Jenny looked up at Prue. "It's safe to eat, I swear," Prue told her.

She nibbled at one of the pieces. "It's good," she said around her mouthful. She ate hungrily, even gnawing away at the bacon. Prue figured she probably hadn't had anything to eat since her parents were killed. With her little belly full she snuggled between the blankets of her familiar bedroll and quickly fell asleep.

Prue sat down at the small table that was simply constructed of three rough-cut cypress planks laid over two sawhorses. Bob lifted the cow skin and pulled up a loose floorboard, producing an earthen jug of corn whiskey from the depths beneath the house. He set the jug on the table and poured two tin cups of thick coffee from the pot on the stove. They each added a healthy slug of whiskey to the coffee.

"This a fresh batch?" Prue asked.

"Hell no. This is the good stuff. I been aging it under the cabin. It's maybe two or three weeks old."

Prue closed his eyes. He'd be lucky if he didn't go blind from drinking the stuff. Bob made money on the side distilling corn whiskey deep in the swamp. He grew about fourteen acres of corn every year just for the whiskey. He said it was for his hogs. They were lucky if they even got to taste the stalks.

"What you planning on doing with the gal?"

Prue shook his head. "Don't rightly know what to do. I came here hoping to get some advice from you."

"You going to the law over the murders?"

"I'm gonna have to," Prue said. "The son of a snake that killed her folks needs to be strung up."

Bob slurped his fortified coffee loudly with great satisfaction, sucking the fiery liquid through the whiskers. "Yeah, but what about the little princess?"

Prue's head started to spin. Bob's homebrew was strong enough to burn a hole through his chaps. He couldn't imagine what it was doing to his stomach. "What do you think I should do?"

"Do you know any womenfolk you can place her with? She needs a woman to look after her."

Prue shook his head. He'd shied away from any kind of permanent relationship since his ma had died. It had killed him to see his pa grieve himself to death over her. He never wanted to get close to any woman, because pioneer life was so hard for them. He didn't want to get hurt like Pa. He steered clear of all good women, using the local whores when he felt the need. "Don't you know some old widder woman or an old couple that could take her in?" Prue asked Bob.

"No, I don't," Bob snapped.

"Well, maybe I can leave her here with you for a spell while I ride into Pine Level and report her folks' killing to the law."

Bob shook his head. "I don't think so, Prue. I got me too many mean dogs and too many snakes. And I'm a dirty old man. I don't know nothing about raising no little gal." Bob changed the subject. "So, how's the work coming on your ranch? You got your corrals built, some good stout cowpens for all them cattle you need to be out rounding up this spring?"

"Boarhog is working on the pens. We got some corrals finished and a one-room cabin. I was headed out to start branding me some calves and maybe find some of those cows I own when I ran into the little girl."

"Well, you're gonna need to hire you some experienced hands. Men what knows how to work cows in these parts. You need about one hand for every two or three hundred head. And yer gonna have to get ready for the spring gather. Every March, you and the hands go out on the prairie, round up all the cows you can find, separate out the ones that ain't yers, brand and castrate all the new calves and let them go to fatten up."

"Bob, I know I need some coaching on how things are done around here. And I may not be able to crack a dang whip yet, but I know how to work cattle. It's all I've ever done. I was gonna hire me some help in a few weeks over to Arcadia. Hey, you know what? Somebody in Arcadia told me you once had a family."

Bob went silent for several long moments. He looked up at the log rafters of his ceiling and the palmetto fronds laced between rough-cut slats. Prue could swear he saw a tear at the corner of Bob's faded right eye, but then Bob's gaze cleared and his eyes narrowed into hard slits of steely blue. "I had me a family. Ain't none of your business where they are or what happened to 'em."

Prue got up and poured both of them some more coffee. He hefted the brown jug and dosed Bob's coffee with a healthy amount of liquor and added a drop to his own.

They drank in silence, working through two more cups until the coffee pot was empty. Jenny began moaning in her sleep so Prue got up and softly rubbed her shoulder then drew her quilts higher and tucked them around her.

"She's probably having a bad dream," Prue said. "She saw everything that happened to her parents. I can't imagine how she must feel."

"Well I can," Bob muttered, wiping his mustaches and beard with the cuff of his wool shirt. "I had me a wife and two little girls oncet. But like all the other young fools I knowed, I joined up with the Rebs and went off to fight for the rich planters' right to own black folks. Confederate deserters busted into my house and got 'em while I was away. When I come home after the war, I found the bones of my wife and children a laying all over my kitchen floor scattered there by wild animals. The sons a bitches what done it stole all my old clothes, traded them for their Reb uniforms. That's how I knowed it was deserters. One of them dirty bastards was a sergeant. He left his stripes right there on his Rebel jacket."

Prue took another sip of the laced coffee. "So you know all about taking care of little girls."

Bob scowled. "Just cause I know how, don't mean I'm a gonna do it."

"I just need you to watch her until I get back from Pine Level with the sheriff. He'll know what to do."

Bob glanced down at sleeping Jenny. One of her blonde braids had come undone and was spread out over top of the red and blue quilt. Prue knew Jenny was ten but she was so small and slight she appeared no older than seven. She looked young, fragile, and helpless sleeping next to Bob's wood heater.

"Oh all right," Bob mumbled. "But if you ain't back in two days, I'm hauling her into Pine Level after you."

Satisfied Jenny would be safe in this secret haven with Bob, Prue unrolled his blankets and lay down beside her. Suddenly he sat up. "You sure there ain't no loose snakes in this cabin?"

When Bob had shuffled around the box next to his bed, both canebrakes had hissed and let go with a warning rattle.

"I swear you're a lily-livered sniveling baby, Jesse Pruitt. I boxed up all the snakes after Sally got bit. And I kilt and ate the one what bit her."

"It ain't me I'm worried about," Prue shot back at the old man. "I been around snakes all my life. I'm from Texas, you know. It's Jenny. They scare her."

Prue slept uneasily until daylight. He kept dreaming about the little woman with the incredible eyes. Eyes just like Jenny's. In the morning, Bob woke him up rustling around making coffee. Jenny was sitting up in her bedroll scratching herself like a dog with tears streaming down her face. When she saw Prue, she started to whimper aloud.

Closing his eyes for a moment, Prue took a deep breath. The corn liquor he consumed last night was boiling in his stomach and his head pounded. He really needed to swear off booze. When he opened his eyes again, he saw Jenny's arms and face were covered with enormous red welts.

Bob stalked over to the stove and looked down at the little girl. "Chiggers," he pronounced. "Where did you say you found her?"

"Hiding under a palmetto in the scrub," Prue replied.

"Had she dug herself into the dirt?"

Prue closed his eyes again. It was easier to think that way and seemed to quiet the throbbing in his head. "I can't remember. Jenny, did you dig into the dirt under the bushes?"

Jenny looked up at Prue and nodded. "I'm so itchy," she wailed, digging at her arms and legs.

Prue lurched to his feet. Bob handed him a mug of something that smelled just as awful as it looked. It was an evil reddish orange with brown streaks running through it. Prue could swear it bubbled.

"Swaller some of this and you'll feel more the thing," Bob said.

"What's in it? I've never seen anything that color before."

"Never you mind. It's my secret remedy for what ails you. Close yer eyes and swaller."

Prue, feeling sure the drink could do no more damage than the liquor, held his nose and swallowed. Halfway through the thick evil liquid in the mug, he bolted for the cabin door and was violently ill outside on the dirt. As he walked back into the house, wiping off his mouth on the sleeve of his undershirt, he realized his stomach was settled and he was miraculously hungry. Bob was frying bacon in the filthy skillet. It smelled wonderful. And the throbbing in his head was reduced to a mere twinge.

Jenny sat on one of the benches scratching a large welt on her hand.

"She's covered in chigger bites," Bob told Prue with what Prue could swear was intense satisfaction.

"What do we do?" Prue asked as he sat down beside Jenny, took her hand, and looked at the bite.

"She needs a woman to look after her," Bob said with authority. "You must know some female that can help the poor little mite. She needs to be bathed in oatmeal and then doctored with witch hazel. All I got here is pine tar and horse liniment. Neither one is gonna do her a dang bit of good. Probably eat the hide right off her. Besides, you and me, we got no business bathing a ten-year-old gal anyway."

Prue knew Bob was right, but he couldn't think of any woman within a thousand miles who would take care of Jenny. In fact, the only woman he'd met since he'd come to Florida was Harriett, and she was a whore. He shrugged his shoulders. "You been in these parts a lot longer than me, old man. You're the one that must know of a female we can trust to care for Jenny."

"I ain't been near a woman since I moved down here in sixty-six," Bob said. "At first it was because Donna Jean and the girls was dead. I couldn't bring myself to even go into town and see women laughing and walking around like everything in the world was all right, when I knowed very well it weren't. I hated everybody and everything. I got me some dogs and then I got interested in them snakes. You're the first person I've had here to this place. I take my corn squeezings, my pelts, and snake skins to town, sell them and then git. I don't know no females and I don't want to know none."

They ate breakfast in silence punctuated by Jenny sobbing and digging.

"Jenny gal, you got to stop digging them bites. You'll spread 'em," Bob instructed.

"I can't stop, they itch me so." Tears ran out of her beautiful eyes and down her cheeks as she sobbed.

Prue pushed away from the table and stood up. Jenny had to go to see someone, a doctor or a druggist or somebody.

"You can't just drop this child on anyone, you know," Bob said as though reading Prue's mind. "She's the only one who can identify the man what kilt her folks. From her description and the name she called him, she could be talking about Malachai McQueen, one of the most powerful, if not the most powerful man in Desoto County. If it's him and he finds out she's seen what he done, he'll come after her and he'll kill her sure as I'm sitting here."

Prue threw up his hands. "The only female I know within a thousand miles is a whore named Harriett."

"See, I told you you'd think of something."

5

Harriet Painter sat on the satin-covered bench in front of her dressing table viciously dragging a brush through her long red hair. The hair reached around her back into her lap. She took long, hard strokes, pulling the brush through it from where it parted in the middle to the tips. She sat with her back stiff, her legs tightly pressed together. While brushing, she watched Pelo Berryhill pull his suspenders over his shoulders and stuff his feet into his boots.

She hated the big lout. But this was business. What he did to her was no more than Uncle Buford had done to her when she was eight years old. The big difference was Berryhill paid and now that she was seventeen, it no longer hurt.

When his tall, black boots were on, he walked over to her bench and put a meaty hand on her shoulder. She stopped brushing and stood up. Berryhill's hand was dislodged. He bent to kiss her neck and she ducked away to stand by the bed. Harriet never kissed her clients nor allowed them to kiss her. Her memories of Uncle Buford's thick rubbery lips on hers and on her body were something she would take to her grave.

"Dammit Harriet, don't you care about me at all?"

Wrapping her arms around her body tightly, Harriet turned her back to him. "You owe me five dollars."

Berryhill grabbed one of her hands and peeled it away from her body. He dropped five one-dollar gold pieces into it one at a time, paused, and added a ten-dollar piece. "You know you mean more to me than that. I mean, I ain't just another customer. I come for the loving, sugar. I come here to see you. I love you, little darlin'."

He tried to press his lips to her ear. She quickly avoided this additional unwanted caress and moved to the window. If only he would just go. Each visit he'd become more and more ardent, insisting he was in love with her. Eventually, she was going to have to refuse to see him.

As Harriet closed her hand over the money, someone knocked at the door. Great, another customer, she didn't know whether to be happy or sad. But at least Pelo would now have to leave and she sure needed the money. Danny had grown out of his shoes again and was hankering after a pair of boots. And he wanted a horse so he could become a cowman. Harriet knew horses were expensive to buy and then there was the stabling and feeding.

She'd been fourteen when she ran away from her uncle's house and took her ten-year-old brother with her. She'd had no idea what things cost or how hard it was to make it in this world when you were a woman alone, even with what seemed like a small fortune she'd stolen from Uncle Buford. But the thousand dollars had gone fast and she'd had to keep moving. Everywhere she went, she saw Uncle Buford's face. It haunted her night and day. She felt sure he would be hunting for her all over Georgia.

So, she'd headed for Florida. The farther south she got, the safer she felt. When she'd finally arrived in Arcadia, among the cattlemen and the laughter and gaiety of the wild cow town, she'd felt safe. But the money had quickly run out. Even though she had received a rudimentary education supplied by tutors Uncle Buford hired, being a girl and as young as she was, no one would hire her to do anything that would pay for her and her brother's expenses. It had been so easy to start accepting visitors to her room at the Arcadia House. Men wanted her and they were willing to pay.

The pounding on the door became more insistent. "Ain't you gonna answer it?" Berryhill asked as he grabbed his hat off the bedpost.

Harriet pulled her old green robe tighter, tied the belt around her waist and went to the door. When she opened it, she was shocked to see one of her favorite customers waiting outside on the walkway, holding the hand of a little girl wrapped to her big blue-green eyes in a brown cloak that was obviously not fashioned for a small child.

Jesse Pruitt was a beautiful man. He had long wavy dark blond hair, deep, dreamy brown eyes, and dimples. He was sun-browned and tall with narrow hips and wide shoulders. Any woman would swear he was as handsome as a Greek god. All Harriet saw was trouble.

Berryhill moved to stand stiff-legged beside her at the door. He threw back his shoulders, stuck out his gut, and then stuffed his thumbs into the waistband of his cotton pants. Berryhill and Prue were of the same height and they stared at each other for what seemed like an hour. Finally, Prue whipped off his stiff-brimmed, brown, high-crowned hat and backed away from the door, making room for Berryhill to leave.

Shouldering his way through the door, Berryhill turned to give Prue a dirty look.

"Good-bye, Pelo," Harriet said. Then she turned to Prue, still standing in the doorway. "Who is this child, Prue? Why have you brought her here to me?"

"Her name's Jenny, Harriet, and I have nowhere else to take her."

Harriet saw Prue glance nervously over his shoulder at the gawking Berryhill and sighed. "Bring her inside."

When they were in Harriet's room with the door closed behind them, Prue dropped the cloak from around Jenny's shoulders. Harriet clapped her hands over her mouth to cover a squeak of dismay. The girl's face and hands were covered with huge red welts. "What's wrong with her?" Harriet gasped, immediately concerned the child had some horrible infectious disease.

"Don't worry. It ain't catchy. She got into some chiggers and I had nowhere else to take her to get her some help. You're the only female I know within a thousand miles, Harriet. So I brung her to you."

"Oh my God, she can't stay here. You know what I do for a living." Harriet was beside herself. She couldn't take care of a little girl. She had to work.

"I'll pay you, Harry. I only got a little on me right now, but I'll get more money and I'll pay you. Her parents were murdered right in front of her face. She needs tending and bathing and such, and I need to get to the sheriff to tell the law what happened out at her place."

After only a brief knock on the door that joined Harriet's room to the next, it swung open and a young man dressed in rough wool pants held up by suspenders, wearing big brogans on his feet, entered. When he saw Prue he started to stammer and his face turned red under his carrot-colored hair. "I'm sorry, Harry. I heard Berryhill leave and I thought you was alone." When he saw the little girl, he looked up at Harriet with his eyebrows raised.

"It's all right, Danny. This here is Mr. Pruitt. He's a cowman. Please entertain this young lady for me while I take Mr. Pruitt outside and converse with him."

Harriet grabbed Prue by the lapel of his leather vest and hauled him out on the open walkway that ran the length of the Arcadia House second floor, slamming the door behind her. She looked up and down the walkway. Pelo

Berryhill was gone. "Jesse Pruitt, what can you be a thinking?" She hissed the words into his face from about four inches away.

Jesse tried to back away from her but she hung onto his vest and he was already against the railing. "I need help," he said, pressing his hat over his heart. "Please Miss Harriett. Don't send me away with the poor little thing. She's got nobody and she's covered with bug bites."

Harriet looked up into the late afternoon sky over Arcadia and put the back of her hand to her forehead. She must be losing her mind because she was considering taking the girl in. An idea as bright as the sun had burst into Harriet's head the minute Danny walked into the room. Prue was a cowman. Danny wanted to be one.

"If I take her, and I'm saying if, what do I do if something happens? Where do I go if this murdering skunk you say killed her family shows up here and recognizes her?"

"You'll have to run. Get out of here as fast as you can. Go to my place. I'll draw you a map."

"Run? You're expecting me to take on this terrible responsibility that could endanger me and force me to run. Why should I do such a stupid thing, Prue?"

Prue shook his head and ran stiff fingers through his already disordered hair. "I know it's a terrible thing to ask of you, Harry. But when you were a kid, you were hurt. I can see it in your eyes. I don't know what happened to make you take on the care of your brother, leave your home, and come to Arcadia to take up your profession, but I imagine it was pretty darn bad. This little girl is alone and she's in trouble. Would you abandon her as you were abandoned?"

Harriet felt a hand reach into her chest and squeeze her heart. She remembered being a small girl sitting on her bed, all alone in her room the first time Uncle Buford had accosted her. No one had been there to help her. She nodded. "Okay, I'll do it, but I don't want money."

She took his hand and led him back into her room. Danny had lit the oil lamp and was making shadow animals on the wall for Jenny. She was sitting on the edge of the bed watching him and shyly smiling as Danny galloped a shadow bunny across the wall. Harriet felt a lump form in her throat as she remembered doing the same thing for him when he was little.

"Danny," Harriet started, taking a deep breath. "This young lady has a lot of bug bites and her parents recently died, so Mr. Pruitt brought her to stay with me for a spell. I'm going to help her."

Maybe God was watching out for her after all. Back there at Uncle Buford's when he'd first started on her, she'd stopped believing there was a

God. But after her escape, she'd started praying again. Maybe her time with Uncle Buford had been some kind of test. The Bible said God never asked more of you than you could handle. And now here she was being asked to give back, and help another little girl, alone and lost just as she'd been.

"Prue, this is my younger brother Danny. All he wants is to go cow hunting and learn to be a cattleman. He needs a new pair of boots, a horse, and someone to teach him. You help me with Danny and I'll help you with little Jenny here. She can stay in Danny's room while he's with you learning."

Harriet watched Prue look Danny over. She had to stop herself from defending Danny and building him up so Prue would take on his teaching. She'd looked after her brother for so long, since he was a baby and her ma had dragged them into Savannah to live with her brother, Buford Simpson. Ma had to work in her brother's bakery from before sunup to sunset to feed and clothe them, which left Harriet to care for Danny. She knew he was kind of undersized, scrawny even, and skinny. But he had a big heart and wasn't afraid of nothing.

"Can you rope a cow, son?" Prue asked.

"No, sir," Danny honestly admitted. "But I can crack a whip." Jenny's brother thrust out his chest and strutted. "I can pick a flea off a dog's ear at twenty paces. One of my sister's friends give me a twelve-footer with a hickory handle. He showed me how to use it and I been practicing every day."

Prue smiled. "That's more than I can say fer myself. Maybe you can show me. Can you ride a horse?"

"I can ride anything with four legs, Mr. Pruitt, sir. I surely can. I been riding since I been wearing long pants."

Prue closed his eyes and sighed. "Do you know anything about cattle?"

"Well, I been a working downstairs in the dining room, cleaning up after meals and I been listening to all the cowmen who come in here. They drink and carry on and talk about cattle and such. I know cow work is hard and dangerous, but it's the only thing in this world I want to do. Please take me on, Mr. Pruitt. You won't regret it."

Prue nodded. "I guess it's a deal then, Harry. I got a friend who says Jenny needs to bathe in oatmeal and get doctored up with witch hazel. I don't know. I do know she can't stop scratching."

"Well I too have a friend, a female friend, who will know exactly what needs to be done for this young lady. I thank you Prue for taking on Danny. He's a hard worker and he really does know how to ride and he knows all about horses. He'll do right. I know he will."

"Just take care of that little girl, Harry. And don't forget, she's the only witness to the murders. She said it was a man named Mal who has yellow eyes. My friend Bob said that might be Malachai McQueen, one of the biggest cattle owners in these parts. If it was him what done it, and he finds out she saw him kill her folks, he's gonna come after her or have somebody else do it for him. Be careful where you take her and who you let see her. Don't tell anybody what happened to her folks or what she saw."

Great! Harriet thought. It couldn't be just any man. It had to be Malachai McQueen, Pelo Berryhill's boss. She's heard all about McQueen from Berryhill, and it sounded to her like he was the most evil man on earth.

Prue drew a rough map for her and explained. "Take the north road out of Arcadia. Cross the river and ride to Horse Creek. Head east. When the creek takes a sharp bend to the south, follow it. You'll come to my ranch after riding about three miles. It's right on the creek."

Harriett took the map, folded it and tucked it into the bodice of her corset. Prue gave her a quick peck on the cheek, which for some reason she didn't dodge, sighed and turned to look over her brother one more time. She could see he wasn't real happy to be taking Danny with him. But she would take on the huge responsibility and even the danger of looking after this little girl if it meant Danny was getting what he wanted. He was the most important thing in her life.

"Let's hit the trail, Danny," Prue said. "You can go with me to find the sheriff. I ain't heard much good about him, but he's the only law around unless I ride to Pine Level."

When Prue and her brother were gone and the door closed behind them, Harriet turned to little Jenny who's big eyes shone like jewels out of her tiny face. "Come on, baby girl, let's go find Mae Mae. She can doctor up anything. All the Arcadia House girls go to her."

Harriet quickly dressed, sliding into a dark green, serge skirt with a four-inch waistband that made her tiny waist look even smaller. She shrugged into a crisp white blouse with long sleeves and tightly fitted cuffs and tucked it into the skirt. After putting on her worn out black half-boots, she plaited her hair into one long braid down her back and glanced in the mirror. She looked old and tired. Whoring wasn't much of a life. It was making her old before her time. But what else could she do?

Taking the little girl's hand, she led Jenny down the back stairs to the kitchen. A tiny Chinese woman stood on an upturned milk crate stirring a pot of soup. The soup was simmering in a big iron cauldron blackened from years of use, covering half of the top of the boardinghouse's monstrous cookstove. The soup pot had to hold at least ten gallons of liquid. Mae Mae used a wooden spoon almost as long as little Jenny was tall to stir the bubbling liquid. In a corner of the stove, tucked next to the cauldron of soup sat a shiny copper teakettle steaming with hot water.

At a low wooden table a little black girl was peeling potatoes. She had a mountain of peels in a slop bucket and a kettle filled with potatoes she'd already peeled. Sitting beside the sack of potatoes to peel was another burlap sack filled with peas in the pod waiting for the girl to hull and another sack with apples to peel.

When Mae Mae saw the two come into the warm kitchen, she stepped off the crate and wiped her hands on the crisp white apron tied twice around her tiny waist. She put her hands on her hips and looked little Jenny over.

"What you doing with this little girl child, eh, Missy Harriet?"

"Oh, Mae Mae, one of my customers brought her to me to tend. She's got herself into the chiggers and can't stop itching. Just look at these bites. They're all over her."

Mae Mae had come from China as a child when her parents immigrated to work on the railroads out West. Mae Mae met and fell in love with a giant of a railroad surveyor named Leonard Chapman. Leonard got an offer to come to Florida and work for Henry Plant and the Plant Investment Company surveying sites for the new railroad from Tampa to Punta Rassa. He asked Mae Mae to marry him and they'd been living in the Arcadia House for the last three years.

Well, Mae Mae lived there and did the boardinghouse cooking chores. Leonard, his three mules and his two helpers, traveled and came home to Mae Mae when he could get away.

The little Chinese woman possessed a wealth of knowledge learned from her parents about Chinese herbs and healing methods. She was one of Harriet's few friends at the boardinghouse. Mae Mae had a way of looking you directly in the eyes that made you feel she would never lie to you. The woman's sincerity and warmth had won over Harriet. She'd trusted her before with secrets and personal problems and Mae Mae had never let her down. Now she trusted the Chinese woman to fix Jenny's itching problems.

Mae Mae bent over and lifted Jenny's skirt, staring at the red welts on her knees and the backs of her knees. "Oh my, oh my," she murmured. "You got bites everywhere, little missy."

Harriet turned her head so as not to laugh. When Mae Mae said little it sounded like "rittle." She has a hard time making the "L" sound. When she said her husband's name it came out as Renard instead of Leonard.

Bustling about her kitchen, Mae Mae gathered herbs, oatmeal, and jars of salve into a basket. She turned to the gal peeling taters. "You work hard peeling this here vegetables. I be right back to make sure you work-ing hard."

Harriet took Jenny's hand and followed Mae Mae into the washhouse just outside the back door. In this outbuilding, all the sheets and towels for the boardinghouse were washed. Inside the room was a big stove with giant pots of hot water already almost to the boiling point. Piles of dirty laundry lay in big wicker baskets just inside the door. Two big washerwomen were sorting the sheets from the towels.

Mae Mae elbowed her way past the two women.

"Howdy, Miss Mae Mae," one of the washerwomen said.

"Sara, please you and Clatty May help me fill up a tub for this young lady. She's all covered with the chiggers."

"Lord, have mercy," Sara exclaimed when she saw Jenny's bites. "This chile is plumb eat up."

Harriet stepped forward and helped poor little Jenny undress while the other three women filled up a washtub with hot water. Mae Mae sprinkled tea leaves and some powdered herbs into the water along with some flowers and a big scoop of oatmeal. She stirred it, breathing in the fragrant steam. "Okay little missy, climb in."

Malachai and his foreman, Rooster, were in the hog pen. The weather had turned cooler and Malachai wanted to butcher a hog. He picked out a pig he'd castrated about six months earlier, a two-hundred pounder. "Let's kill this one, Rooster. It's just the right size."

"Okay, Mr. McQueen." Rooster cornered the big pig and held him there while Malachai closed in, shooting the pig in the head with his pistol. Each of them grabbed the dying pig by a hind leg and dragged it out of the pen. All the other pigs were squealing and creating a ruckus.

Rooster slit the tendons on the pig's back legs while Malachai stuck a long sharp knife into the hog's throat. Blood poured onto the ground. Malachai stepped on the pig's stomach, pushing rhythmically to force more blood out and watched as the hog finally expired. Rooster inserted the hooks from a singletree into the slit tendons of the pig's back legs and hoisted it off the ground with a rope tied to the singletree and tossed over the branch of a big oak.

"I like his hide," Malachai said, touching the coarse hair on the hog's flank. The hog was a half-wild pig with a black hide and orange, gingery spots. "His hair is too rough to scrape, you need to skin him. Get the kitchen gal out here to clean off the hide and then tack it to the barn wall. I just might have me some chaps made out of it."

The sound of hoof beats made Malachai turn his head. Sergeant Berryhill was riding back from Arcadia, heading across the open stretch of land surrounding the McQueen homestead. He trotted past the cowpens and into the barnyard on his raw-boned buckskin gelding, leaped to the ground, and tossed the reins over the hitching rail. With quick neat movements, the big man unfastened the girth and belly strap and stripped his McClelland saddle off the sweating gelding. He tossed it over the hitching rail and headed toward Malachai to watch the hog being butchered.

"You look like you had yourself a fine time in town," Mal said to Berryhill.

"It was okay," Berryhill said, looking at his feet and scratching his belly.

Malachai could see Berryhill wasn't happy and by rights he should have been. He just had a fine time with a pretty woman. He should be kicking up his heels. "What's crawled up your backside, Sergeant? You don't look like a man who just had a good time with a gal to me."

"It's Harriet, Boss. I can't seem to make her understand I want her to be my woman. I've been saving my wages and I got me a pretty good size herd. You been giving me one calf every year and I've bought a couple of my own to add to it. I was thinking about striking out on my own and buying some land around here."

"The girl just needs a little schooling, Berryhill," Rooster spoke up from his position next to the hog where he was quickly removing its skin with a very sharp knife. "She don't know what being a real woman is all about. She only knows whoring. She's probably scared."

"I didn't know you were gonna quit me, Pelo," Malachai said. "I never thought you'd go off on yer own."

"I'm a growed man, Boss. I want to start me a family and have my own place. It's not what I ain't grateful for all you done fer me, you understand?"

No, Malachai didn't understand. He depended on Berryhill for a lot and the man was the only person who knew who he really was. If Pelo was to leave him, could he still be trusted? The whole thought unsettled Malachai to no end. He shook his head. It was better not to let Berryhill know how he felt in case he had to take drastic measures.

"You should carry her out to one of the cow camps for a few days of loving," Malachai said. "Have her cook for ye and wash yer clothes and all. Let her know what it's like to be with a man all the time, just one man. How old is she anyway?"

"I don't know," Berryhill said. "I guess she's sixteen or seventeen."

"That's plenty young enough for ye to learn her to be a wife and forget about whoring," Malachai said. "She's a pretty thing, real tiny. I thought about going with her once myself."

Malachai had thought about visiting Harriet Painter, but at the time the only woman he could think about was Elva Buttons. He could hardly believe she was dead. He hadn't meant to kill her. That husband of hers had to go, but Mal had never wanted to hurt Elva. She was just so fragile and delicate and he'd wanted her so badly. She couldn't understand how much he had to give her. And little Jenny was going to grow into such a beauty, just like her ma.

When he'd seen what he'd done to Elva, he'd been horrified. He knew Jenny was on the place somewhere and he'd wanted to spend more time looking for the child. He should have kept looking for her. It was possible she'd seen him ride up and run off to the barn. Malachai hadn't seen her in the house, but she could have been in there hiding somewhere.

He knew Jenny didn't like him. He really should have taken care of the child. She was a loose end and he hated leaving loose ends. They had a habit of coming back and biting you in the ass. But even now, when he knew he should have taken care of the child, killed her too, he wasn't sure he could do it.

The sight of Elva's beautiful eyes staring at him reproachfully, like he'd meant to kill her, which he hadn't, had sickened him and he'd had to leave. He'd run away like a little girl. Mal shook his head to clear the bad visions. It was over. Elva was gone. He needed to stop thinking about what had happened, what he'd done.

"She's got herself a pretty boy, anyway," Berryhill's voice jerked Malachai away from his terrible memories. "She don't need me. He looked to be a cattleman and from his accent probably from Texas. He talked with that Texas twang and he had yeller hair and these pits in his cheeks."

"He's scarred?" Malachai said, not really paying attention to Berryhill. The man was obsessed with that red-headed whore. "I thought you said he was a pretty boy."

"Not scars, pits," Berryhill made two indentions in each of his cheeks with a thick forefinger.

"Oh, you mean he's got dimples," Malachai said, turning his attention back to the dead hog. Berryhill could be an ignorant, dumb ass.

"Okay, yeah, and I guess you could say they're dimples. Well he's pretty enough to be a woman. I doubt if Harriet would even look at me after being with him. He brought a kid with him to see her. Maybe he wants to marry up with her to get himself a mother for his kid. I think he said the kid's name was Jenny. Cute little thing," Berryhill said in a quiet voice. "I wonder why he was bringing her to visit with Harriet."

When Malachai heard the name Jenny, he snapped his head in Berryhill's direction, his heart suddenly hammering in his chest. "You said the little girl's name was Jenny?"

"Yeah, I guess so. I think that's what the Texan called her."

Forgetting all about the hog, and he loved butchering hogs, Malachai grabbed Berryhill's shoulder and led him away from Rooster and the hog dangling from the singletree. When they were well away and behind the barn, he stopped Berryhill. "Sergeant, this is really important. I can't tell you why right now, but I need to know what the child looked like."

Berryhill rolled his eyes toward the late afternoon sky, lifted his chin, and scratched the thicket of black and gray whiskers growing there. "I can't remember much, Boss. See, she was wrapped up in a blanket or a coat of some kind, right up to her eyes." Then Berryhill smiled. "I do remember her eyes, though. They was big and round and bright blue. No, not really blue, more like the color of the ocean out where the water's deep, kind of greenish blue."

6

Malachai guided his horse down a steep incline and into the water of the Peace River. The river was shallow most of the way across. Suddenly, the bottom dropped out from under the horse and Malachai gave the stud his head as he stroked the few feet across open water and found his footing on the other side.

Berryhill crossed behind him, losing his seat in the deeper water and getting a soaking. On the other side of the river, Malachai shook the water off his duster. His high boots had kept the river out, but his breaches were damp. He'd held his sawed-off high, to keep water out of it as well. Malachai urged the stud up the steep bank, and his horse shook from the top of his head to his tail, almost knocking him off. Resettling himself in the saddle, he took off for Brownville at a steady trot.

He regretted setting the vigilance committee meeting for tonight. He wanted to ride into Arcadia and check out Berryhill's story about the girl. What if the whore's Texan had found Jenny at her parent's farm? What if the man had seen the girl's parents dead in that cabin? What if he knew she'd seen them murdered? All these questions could be answered if only he could get away and ride to Arcadia. This was going to be the shortest meeting the committee had ever had.

But once scheduled, the meetings had to be held and everyone, including him, had to attend. Punishment was stiff for missing meetings.

The two men rode into Brownville on the North Brownville Road, then turned right onto St. John's Road. The yard and parsonage barn of the First Methodist Church were filled with horses. Berryhill and Malachai dismounted and added their horses to the rest, tying them to a temporary picket line stretched between two trees. Lights welcomed them into the meeting hall of the church.

Reverend Samuel Whiteleaf was a member of the vigilantes. He had a large cattle ranch south of Brownville that two families of squatters had infested, going so far as to build cabins and fence off land for tilling. He'd joined the committee to find help in ridding himself of the squatters. Malachai and the boys had burned the cabins, torn down the fences, and killed one of the squatters. Whiteleaf had been grateful for about two weeks. Now he was whining about all the violence and threatening to quit.

In Malachai's opinion, the reverend's behavior was typical of all men of the cloth, two-faced and spineless, spouting biblical quotes about love thy neighbor and then hiring someone to kill said neighbors.

When Malachai entered the church, he threw back his shoulders and strutted. He was king here, holding the highest rank, that of judge. His boots echoed off the board floors and his spurs clanked. He pulled his sawed-off out of the holster and placed it on a table filled with weapons. No guns were allowed in the meetings.

He nodded to the reverend and to Sheriff Edmund Daniels from Arcadia. It was handy having a sheriff as a member. Daniels was one of two sheriffs on Malachai's payroll. Pine Level sheriff Eli Drawdy stood by the refreshment table helping himself to coffee. As Malachai watched, Drawdy pulled a metal flask out of his pocket and added a liberal dollop to the coffee from its contents.

Sheriff Daniels as yet owned no land. But he had dreams, dreams of becoming a big shot cattle rancher. Him and his counterpart, Sheriff Drawdy, Malachai could respect. Their motives were plain from the beginning, good old-fashioned greed.

Malachai strode to the front of the meeting room. Most of the nineteen men assembled stood around talking in small groups. When they saw Mal arrive, they moved to sit in rows of chairs arranged by the reverend's lovely wife, Janie Mable Whiteleaf. Mrs. Janie Mable's plump, well-manicured hands also set out the coffee and mugs along with a plate of cakes and cookies. When she saw Malachai, she scuttled into the service area and out of sight. Malachai chuckled. The reverend's hefty wife did not like him at all. Mal grabbed a molasses cookie and munched as he took his place at the podium.

It was Malachai's job to conduct the meeting. He was in a big hurry, so he took roll quickly then asked his lieutenant, Judge Alford Whidden, if there was any old business to discuss. Several members had issues. Malachai noticed Duron Grey was in attendance. Malachai also noticed Duron did not bring up any old business.

Sheriff Drawdy was recognized and stood up. "I just want to mention a certain rapist who was dealt with by the SSVC, recently left the county for parts unknown."

Malachai rapped his gavel and recognized Enoch Pearce.

"I just wanted to thank the group for getting rid of the farmer who bought up some land adjacent to mine and proceeded to till up good rangeland to plant cotton. He and his wife are gone and ain't come back."

After all the old business, Malachai glanced at his watch. It was barely four o'clock. If he wrapped this up quick, he could make it to Arcadia while it was still daylight.

Three hands went up for new business and Malachai sighed. He picked Fines Parker next. Parker worked cattle on one of the biggest ranches in the state.

"I heard of a family of settlers moved in on some of the Babcock grazing land, one man, his wife and little daughter. They already built a cabin and a barn and applied to buy the property at the land office. I think they need to be got rid of."

Malachai pricked up his ears. That sounded like the Buttons family. "You heard a family name, Parker?"

"Nope, not as yet." Parker sat down.

Malachai turned to the group's secretary. "Write that down, we'll look into it."

The next raised hands presented two more similar complaints. It looked like they were fighting a losing battle trying to keep the rangeland open for their cattle. But Malachai enjoyed running the vigilante group. It was there if he needed it.

Cy McClelland was the last man to speak. He stood up, reached over to the end of his row and spit a brown stream of tobacco juice into the spittoon. "I heard me some news t'other day," McClelland said. "I was talking with an Injun from down south at the saloon in Zolfo Springs. He said there's a group of outlaws living in the big swamp down there. They been rustling the Injun cattle and he said they's a planning to come north and start getting ours. He said the outlaws heard we got more cattle up here than God and they be wantin' some of 'em."

All the men started talking at once so Mal banged his gavel. "Here, here," he yelled over the commotion. "Nobody's lost any stock yet. Don't be getting your knickers in a bunch until it starts happening or someone notices a band of strangers that look dangerous riding the range with cows that ain't theirs."

With the majority of the men calmed down, Mal adjourned the meeting. He and Berryhill walked outside. "Sergeant, I have some urgent business in Arcadia. I'll see you later, probably tomorrow."

"Hey, I'll come with you. I'd like to see Harriet again and find out if that Texan is still with her. I can't get his face out of my mind."

"No, sorry, Pelo," Malachai said. "I need you to go home and wait on Aunt Thelma. She should be arriving today or tomorrow. I got a message yesterday that said they left their ranch in Tampa a week ago and were heading this way overland."

Malachai had decided Aunt Thelma couldn't possibly be a threat to his impersonation. She hadn't seen the real Malachai for over twenty years. Time changes a man. She probably wouldn't recognize the real Malachai if she ran into him on the streets of Arcadia, much less be able to tell the difference between Ben Jones and Malachai McQueen, when in looks they were practically identical. He felt solid in his position and if Aunty Thelma started asking the wrong questions, well, she could always disappear.

Berryhill made a face at the news he would be staying on the ranch to meet Malachai's aunt. "Aw, Boss, that ain't no kind of work for me."

Malachai's features drew into a snarling frown. "What did you say, Sergeant?"

Berryhill recoiled, actually backing up two steps and taking his horse with him. "No problem, Boss. I'll go wait for your aunt."

Malachai mounted his horse and galloped toward Arcadia.

It didn't take Prue long to realize the local sheriff was out of town. When he and Danny walked into the sheriff's office, the place was empty. He strode through the vacated office, walked by a desk littered with legal-looking paperwork and opened a door heading into the back of the place. The light was dim in the back but Prue soon realized this was where the prisoners were held. Four jail cells were empty. Cell number-five, right across from the door to the front, held three men playing poker at a table. Outside, two gunshots sounded and none of the deputies even twitched an eyelash in response. Coming here was clearly a waste of time.

A cloud of cigar smoke hung inside the cell, a full bottle of whiskey and two full beer mugs sat on the table and empty bottles of whiskey littered the floor. A keg of beer rested on a stool close to the table. When none of the deputies looked up to acknowledge his presence or got up to ask him his business, he stepped forward. "Are any of you Sheriff Daniels?"

A tall skinny fellow chewing a dead cigar looked up. "The sheriff, he's out a town on business. We're all deputies."

"I have a crime I need to report to someone in authority," Prue pressed on.

"Is it horse stealin' or brand altering or rustlin'?" the cigar-chewer asked.

Prue sighed. "No, it's a murder."

The man took the cigar out of his mouth. "Well then, we can't help you, you got to talk to Sheriff Daniels."

"When will he be back?"

The man smiled and turned his head to look at his two friends. They smiled back, a secretive sort of smile like they knew something special and weren't about to share it with Prue. "I got no idea."

The tall skinny man took a big pull off his beer and began to deal another hand, returning his attention to the game. Prue knew he wasn't getting any help or satisfaction from these louts. He turned and led Danny out onto the board sidewalk.

"Nothing for us here, Danny. I guess we better ride to Pine Level and see if we can find someone to talk to there."

Prue stalked down the boards of the sidewalk swiftly, excusing himself to two older women stepping out of the dry goods store. His boots hammered the boards, spurs rattling musically. Danny had to run to match his rapid pace. The two of them crossed Hickory Street and turned onto Desoto Avenue. Ahead lay a row of saloons, beyond which were several livery stables and then a large set of cowpens. The two swung down a side street to the Arcadia House and picked up Prue's stud horse tied at the rail outside the boardinghouse along with Buzzard, who lay watchfully beside the horse.

The dog had been waiting patiently as instructed. In some ways, Buzzard amazed Prue. He'd never worked with dogs and never owned one as a kid. Buzzard's capacity for loyalty and his intelligence constantly surprised Prue. He couldn't understand why cowmen out West had not taken to dogs. There was no way in hell you could even find your cows in Florida without a dog. And two or three good dogs could stand in for five or six men. With the stud in tow and the dog following behind, they went back to Desoto Avenue and walked down the strip of saloons.

A fight broke out in one and erupted onto the street. Two men brawled in the mud in front of the building. A loose horse catapulted out of the saloon followed by a crowd of onlookers. The horses tied at the rail on the street neighed and snorted, pulling back sharply on reins and ropes tying them to the hitching rail while the loose animal galloped off down Desoto Avenue toward the stable areas. One horse broke his tie and took off running after the loose horse, empty stirrups slapping at its sides. Satan reared behind Prue and pawed the air when gunfire erupted. One of the brawlers fell wounded into the street and Buzzard started barking ferociously at the chaos.

"Quiet, Buzzard," Prue put his hand on the dog's broad forehead, then led Satan and Danny around the fracas. "Come on son, get a move on, it's almost four o'clock. If we hurry, we can be in Pine Level before dark."

Prue found a nervous-looking bay cracker pony, a little thin, but a nice size, not too big and not too small, with good legs and feet he thought might do for Danny. The nag had some age on him. From his teeth he looked about fifteen, but age could mean experience and training, all good things in a horse for a green boy. After several moments of intense haggling with the livery stable owner, he bought it along with a saddle, bridle, and breast collar. As thin as the horse was, the saddle might slip.

"Here you go, boy," Prue said to Danny. "This is going to be your horse. If you take good care of him, he'll do the same for you."

Danny's eyes widened and his mouth fell open. "He's mine? You bought him fer me? I thought you was just looking fer something fer me to ride. You bought him fer me?"

Prue laughed. "He ain't much kid, but he ought to do for a first horse. He looks sound enough and I don't see anything wrong with him. Course he could prove to be a great slug. But I'm hopin' not."

Danny took the reins from Prue and rubbed the horse's muzzle. There were tears in his eyes. He began a careful inspection of his new possession, running experienced hands down the bay's legs, picking up his feet, lifting his tail.

"He could use a little more weight on him, Mr. Prue, but he's a jam-up horse."

Prue laughed. "Then why don't you mount up and try him out. We got to get going."

When the kid mounted, Prue knew the boy was a rider. The horse spooked and sidestepped when Danny had one foot in the stirrup and the boy quickly grabbed the bridle in his left hand and snatched the horse's head close to his left side. With an agile leap, Danny was in the saddle grinning from ear to ear. "Dang, Mr. Prue, ain't he a pistol? That's what I'll call him, Pistol."

Prue waved at Danny, half hearing the kid as he wrestled with Satan. The stud seemed to feel it was a bit much to be asked to continue on this evening without a ration of feed. Prue understood exactly how his horse felt. He was already sick of the responsibility he had taken on. He had his own business, his own responsibilities to handle and riding out to Pine Level looking for a sheriff wasn't on the list. And not only that, somehow he'd acquired a fourteen-year-old boy to add to the ten-year-old girl, the dog, the litter of kittens, milk cow, two mules, and a buckboard. He'd got himself a complete family without even getting married.

When the two of them were mounted, Danny leading the way on Pistol, they trotted across the wooden bridge over the Peace River and then turned toward Pine Level.

The ride to Pine Level was soon interrupted. At the junction where the trail to Pine Level forked off the Arcadia road, a group of six wagons and riders filled the trail. There were women and children as well as three grown men and some older boys. One of the riders signaled to him and galloped down the trail to meet him.

Prue looked past the jumble of wagons, livestock, and people to the glorious open trail beyond, and sighed. A bad feeling about this group of pilgrims was settling into his stomach, and that's when Buzzard commenced to growling.

The man that rode up to Prue and Danny was short and heavyset. He had graying side-whiskers and a scraggly gray and black beard that flew into the air with every stride of the horse. He wore cotton pants, a floppy hat, high black boots, and a butter-colored homespun shirt. A deep frown was etched into his face.

The two men met in the middle of the trail. The heavyset man stuck out his hand. "Howdy, stranger, my name is Willie Starling."

Prue shook hands and introduced himself. The introductions in no way lessened Prue's growing feelings of impending doom.

"Where you folks headed?" Prue asked politely, not in the least wishing to know.

As if he'd been waiting for the question, Starling took a deep breath and started talking. "We just come from Pine Level looking for the sheriff. He ain't there. In fact, the courthouse and jail was slap empty and nobody in town had a clue where to find him."

As if in a dream, Prue found himself asking the one question he knew he shouldn't. "Why were ya'll needin' the sheriff?"

"We bought us a little place north of here close to a ranch owned by a cattle rancher named Duron Grey. We built us some nice cabins, a small barn, and we were preparing the land to plant some cotton and corn. Late one night, a band of men wearing hoods rode down on us, kilt my little brother Joey, burned our cabins and the barn and run off all our livestock. They made it plain we were on land they considered their cattle range, and we better pack up and git."

So, the sheriff of Pine Level was also out of town. He and Danny didn't need to waste any time riding there. But that left Prue dead out of answers to his problems and a place to take his complaint. He had heard the sheriff of Ft. Myers was an upstanding man known for hard work and honesty. But Ft. Myers was a long way away. In the end, he might have to look for a US Marshal in Tampa or go to the sheriff of Desoto County.

He turned to Starling, considering both of their problems. "You said the men wore hoods?"

"Yessir, they done had black hoods over their heads with holes cut in them for the eyes."

"Since you couldn't see their faces, did you notice anything different about any of them, like their horses or what kind of weapons they used?" Prue asked these questions with half his mind paying attention to what Starling said while the other half scrambled to find answers to his own problems.

"One of them seemed to be the leader," the farmer said. "He rode a big yeller stud horse and used a sawed-off scattergun. He's the one what shot Joey."

"Did you notice anything else?" Prue asked.

Starling thought for a moment. "Well, the leader fella was tall and I could see his eyes in the light from the moon. They looked yeller, like a wolf, and the other men called him Judge."

"I think you got hit by the Sara Sota Vigilance Committee, Mr. Starling. They rule this county. Their one aim is to rid the world of all squatters, nesters, farmers, and the like settling the range land. I heard the sheriffs of Arcadia and Pine Level are members." Prue's mind was spinning. Yellow eyes, sawed-off shotgun, McQueen must be the head of the vigilantes, and it must be McQueen who killed Jenny's folks. The more he heard about this man the worse it seemed to get. He was rich and now it appeared he held power over the vigilantes. As Prue was rapidly discovering, he was evil.

"Where you folks heading?" Danny had ridden up beside Prue and now asked Starling the one question Prue had been avoiding because he had a feeling he already knew the answer.

"We got nowhere to go," Starling replied. "We got no money. We spent it all buying the land and supplies to build homes for our families. All we got left is these wagons, the horses, and stock we could round up after the vigilantes drove them off and the little of our belongings we managed to salvage from the fires."

Prue's heart sank. What was wrong with him? Overnight he had become this crusader for the rights of the persecuted against a powerful foe, Malachai McQueen and the Sara Sota Vigilance Committee. Before he could stop himself with reason and logic, he opened his mouth . . . again. "You folks follow me and Danny. You can stay on my place until we get your problems sorted out with the authorities."

Starling's jowled face worked as strong emotion seemed about to overcome him. He reached over to grab Prue's hand, causing Satan to snort and rear and Buzzard to start barking again. Jerking his hand back, Starling waved it. "I thank ye kindly, Mr. Pruitt. It makes my old heart glad to know all the folks what live in these parts ain't dastardly, lazy, and lowdown. I was beginning to think we'd made a terrible mistake coming down here from North Carolina."

Prue looked across his horse at Danny. The boy's eyes were shining as he looked across his horse at Prue. He grinned shyly and tipped his hat to Prue, his carroty hair spiking. Prue took his own hat off and wiped his sweating brow. *Great!* Now the kid thought he was some kind of hero.

The sun set behind them, turning the sky overhead gaudy with bright colors as Prue led the caravan across the shallow ford at Horse Creek and onto a narrow trail winding beside it. Taking a thin cigar out of his vest pocket, Prue struck a match off his boot, lit the cigar, and blew out a cloud of fragrant smoke. What in the world was Moccasin Bob going to say about what he'd gone and done now? He was making a target of himself, putting a sign on his back that said, "Come on, Sara Sota Vigilance Committee. I truly need my ass kicked."

7

Mae Mae led Harriet and Jenny into her rooms and fixed them a cup of tea. She had to leave to finish supper for the boarders, but left Jenny a big plate of sugar cookies, flavored with some rare and expensive cinnamon.

Jenny's bug bites had been treated with the bath and some salve. She seemed so much more comfortable to Harriet. "Is the itching getting better, sugar?" Harriet asked after Mae Mae had gone back to the kitchen.

"Yes, ma'm, it surely is a relief. I thought I was gonna scratch myself to death."

The two of them sat quietly drinking tea and munching on cookies. Harriet was just about to suggest they go back upstairs when someone knocked on the door. Harriet answered. One of the boys that worked for the boardinghouse's owner stood outside.

"Miss Harriet, there's someone out front to see you."

"Thank you, I'll be right out," Harriet said closing the door as her mind worked furiously. With her guts in a knot, she glanced at Jenny. This was probably just some customer. Supper was less than an hour away. Mae Mae would be too busy to keep an eye on Jenny. She'd have to put the girl in Danny's room while she entertained this client. In the back of her mind she fretted that it might be the man Prue had warned her about, but it seemed too soon. How could he have found out she was caring for the child so quickly?

"Come on girl, you can go up to my brother's room and rest while I talk to my visitor."

Jenny's eyes grew round with fear, but she said nothing. She didn't have to. Harriet knew what she was thinking.

Leading Jenny up the back stairs to her pair of rooms, Harriet gave little thought to danger. This was her world. She'd been safe here for over a year. When they reached the top of the steps, she turned the corner onto the walkway in front of all the rooms. There in front of her door was a tall man wearing a filthy duster with a blunt, ugly, sawed-off gun in the holster hanging from his belt.

Jenny took one look at him and began to screech, a high-pitched sound filled with stomach-churning fear. The man wheeled around. Harriet stared into his yellow eyes and froze. Then she gave Jenny a brutal shove, almost pushing her all the way back down the staircase. "Run!"

Jenny stumbled, righted herself and took off down the back stairs like a scared rabbit. But the tall man was quick. He shoved Harriet against the door so hard she hit her head. Stars spun in front of her eyes as she tried to focus. She saw Malachai McQueen, for he could be no other, pluck poor terrified Jenny right off the staircase and stuff her under his arm with the child still shrieking.

He turned and raced past Harriet, who made a futile attempt to slow him down by throwing herself in front of him. He shoved her hard again, this time almost tipping her over the walkway's railing. She could hear him ordering Jenny to stop her screeching.

Harriet recovered her balance in time to look over the railing and see McQueen toss Jenny over his saddle and gallop off on a yellow horse. Uttering a miserable, gut-wrenching sob, Harriet slid to the wooden floor of the walkway where she leaned against the door to Danny's room, tears coursing down her cheeks.

She'd failed. After having Jenny in her care for only a few hours, she'd allowed the poor child to be snatched from her arms. No doubt McQueen would now kill Jenny and the little girl's death would rest on Harriet's soul for the remainder of her years. When she closed her eyes, she could still see Jenny's terrified expression as McQueen tossed her onto the saddle and mounted up behind her.

Dragging herself to her feet, Harriet stumbled into her room. She knew what she had to do. She had to get to Prue. He was the only one who could help. Surely he would do something to save poor Jenny.

Harriet yanked on a pair of her brother's heavy cotton pants and one of his shirts. The only footwear she had was her old half-boots. She laced these tightly, tucked the shirt into the pants, and used the spare pair of her brother's suspenders to keep the sagging britches from falling down. She took her long braid and wound it around her head, then stuffed it under an old pork-pie hat a customer had left in her room some time ago.

She needed a horse. Just about the worst crime you could commit in this county was stealing a horse and here she was about to do it. And she knew right where to go to find one that she hoped no one would miss for some time. Slipping quietly down the back stairs, she left the boardinghouse by the kitchen door. Mae Mae was busy making supper for the residents.

Harriet sped through the hot kitchen, sliding between boys carrying stacks of plates and kitchen maids putting food on platters and pulling fresh-baked bread out of the ovens. She didn't want to have to stop and talk to anyone. She couldn't bear to tell anyone what had just happened to her. She was mortified that she'd allowed that evil man to steal Jenny away. She should have done something. She had no idea what, but she should have stopped him. She should have tried harder. She was always letting men run her over. If she never learned nothing else in her life, it was gonna be to stand up to men and not get hurt and pushed around anymore.

She made her way to Desoto Avenue and turned down saloon row. It was dark, the sun having set while Malachai McQueen was racing out of town with Jenny. The saloons were busy with bright lights glowing from the windows and doorways. Harriet knew it was a common custom for cowmen to ride their horses right into the saloons, sit on them, and drink until they were so inebriated they fell off.

She watched the doors and waited. It wasn't long until a loose horse catapulted out of a saloon, slapping stirrup irons spooking the animal even more, reins loose and dragging.

Harriet, seeing her moment of opportunity had arrived, raced forward and grabbed the loose reins of the crazed horse. Turning the animal in a tight circle, she grabbed the cheek strap on the horse's bridle and vaulted into the saddle, laid low on the horse's neck, wheeled it around and galloped out of town.

She had moved fast and by burying her head in the animal's mane maybe none of the drunks and loafers hanging around in the street had even seen her mount the horse. She hoped the trick worked and all anyone had seen was a crazy horse galloping toward the cowpens. Danny wasn't the only one who knew how to ride.

The horse seemed to be glad to be leaving town. The thin gray was running hard for her. They raced over the bridge across the Peace River toward Horse Creek and Prue.

Prue led the caravan along the narrow track heavily shadowed by willow thickets, tall oaks and cabbage-head palms that followed the winding course of Horse Creek. As it grew darker, so did his mood. They had five more miles to go and the trail would only get rougher the further they got from the Arcadia road. Up ahead were bogs, swamps filled with gators and snakes and deadly patches of quicksand to avoid. He lifted his hand to stop the wagons.

Trotting his horse back to Starling, he found the man drooping in the saddle. *These people are tired*, he thought. They've been through the mill and need rest.

"Make camp here," he told Starling. "The rest of the way to my ranch is across some pretty rough ground. I don't think the wagons will make it in the dark."

Starling's womenfolk climbed out of the wagons and began to make camp. Prue had one foot out of the saddle when he heard a horse galloping at a reckless pace down the trail. Buzzard began to growl and bark.

"Danny, a rider's coming," Prue yelled to the boy as he pulled his big pistol out of the holster hanging from his belt. Danny walked up beside him toting the rifle he'd grabbed out of the scabbard on Prue's saddle. They stood together waiting for the rider to appear.

A gray horse materialized out of the gloom with a small rider clinging to its back. Danny raised the rifle but Prue put his hand on the barrel. "Put it down. It's your sister."

This could not be good. The lump of dread that had been hanging around in Prue's stomach all day was now in his throat. Where was Jenny?

Harriet pulled the gray to a sliding stop in front of Prue and Danny. She fell into Prue's arms sobbing hysterically. "I couldn't stop him, Prue. I tried and he pushed me down. He took her, Prue. He took her."

She must mean Jenny.

"Who, Harriet? Who took Jenny?"

"Him, that Malachai McQueen feller you told me about. He was tall with black hair and yeller eyes. I couldn't do anything."

Tears flooded down Harriet's face and she sobbed as Prue pulled her close and hugged her hard enough to crack her ribs. Why was his heart aching like this? He'd only known Jenny for two days. Yet the thought of her in the clutches of such an evil man made him want to vomit.

"It's all right," he murmured into Harriet's ridiculous hat. He knew everything wasn't all right, but somehow he was going to fix this. He would get Jenny back before McQueen killed her.

"She's such a tiny thing," Harriet sobbed. "What's he gonna do with her?"

"I wish I knew," Prue said.

The folks from the wagons slowly drifted toward Prue and Harriet, crowding around, trying to be polite and not intrude, but obviously filled with curiosity. Prue put his arm around Harry.

"This is Harriet Painter, Danny's sister and a friend of mine. She was caring for a little girl who seen her parents killed. Harriet just told me the same man who drove you off your farm, just stole the child."

Prue watched the reaction of the Starling family. Starling's wife took hold of the old man's arm, her eyes round with shock. The young men were clearly angered and the young women moved into a tighter bunch. They had seen what McQueen could do and they were scared of him.

"That man's got a whupping comin' to him," Starling said. His family murmured their agreement.

"I know, Starling, and I plan to give him one, just as soon as I get Jenny back."

The next morning Prue woke with a familiar black feeling of dread heavy in his stomach. As a beam of light from the newly risen sun broke through the willows, he remembered, McQueen had Jenny. Bouncing out of his bedroll, he pulled on his boots. Starling's womenfolk already had a cook fire burning and were making breakfast. Whatever they had cooking smelled pretty darn good.

Prue buckled his gun belt around his waist, scrubbed his fingers through wild hair, and groomed the tuft of light brown whiskers growing on his chin with a wet finger. Clapping the dust off his hat, he fit it over the freshly smoothed hair and went to see what was cooking.

"Hello, Mr. Pruitt," said a stout matron wearing a faded gingham apron over a dark blue dress. She threw some cold water into a bucket of boiling coffee, dipped a tin cup into it, and handed it to him.

"I'm Emma Starling and I want to thank you for inviting us to stay at yer place. I don't rightly see how it's gonna help our situation, but then I'm just a woman. It could be Mr. Starling knows better than me what to do right now, so I'll keep my jabber box shut. But I'll be thanking you for your kindness. Little enough of that has been shown to us since we arrived in these parts."

Prue smiled into her worn face. "I don't know how it's going to help either, Mrs. Starling. It's always seemed to me that if you keep trying, and don't give in to tyranny or injustice, after a spell, you win. I was just thinking we need to feed the vigilantes some of their own medicine."

The older woman nodded her understanding of Prue's sage remarks. A shy, slender girl with long blonde braids stepped from behind the larger woman and handed Prue a tin plate piled high with grits, bacon, and a huge fluffy biscuit dripping with butter.

"Josey, you get the young man a plate, too," Mrs. Starling said.

Prue turned around and as if by magic, Danny appeared behind him and took a heaping plate from the young woman, smiling broadly. "Thank you ma'am," he said to the young lady then turned to Prue. "Dang me, Mr. Pruitt, if this ain't the best looking plate of grub I seen in a coon's age."

Harriett rolled out from under a wagon and sat up on her bedroll just as Prue was setting his hindquarters on a log to eat. She looked over at him and he felt sorry for her. Her eyes were swollen from crying with deep circles around them. She must not have slept well.

"What are we going to do, Prue? How can we find Jenny?" Harriet asked as she stood up and stretched, rubbing her back. "I'm sure not used to riding anymore. I feel like every muscle in my body is cramping up all at once."

Prue took a big mouthful of grits, wiped his chin, and bit into the biscuit. "I don't know what I'm gonna do yet, Harry," he said after swallowing the tasty morsel. "I been thinking and I still don't have me a good plan. What I do know, is first thing we need to do is get these people to my place. After that, maybe I'll have an idea and we can make a plan."

It didn't take the settlers long to harness their teams and get rolling. By dinnertime they were pulling into Prue's ranch. Boarhog Benson was hard at work on the set of cowpens he was building out of cypress and pine logs next to Prue's small barn. He had a large gathering pen built with several smaller pens, a crevice, and a chute.

The chute was something Prue had used often in Texas. Boarhog had never seen a chute or built one, so the big black man didn't understand what Prue wanted with a chute. It had taken Prue some time to convince Boarhog that it was a good idea. The big man was shaving bark off a rough board for a gate when they rode in. His eyes about bugged out of his dark face when he saw Prue and his caravan.

"Howdy, Mr. Prue, I'm mighty glad to see you. Uh, who these folks you bringing here?"

Boarhog pulled his floppy black hat off his head and mopped at the sweat on his brow with a red handkerchief he removed from the pocket of his roomy black cotton pants. The black man had received his colorful nickname when one of his friends saw him wrestle down a fully grown boar barehanded. Boarhog had taken to stringing boar tusks off animals he killed around his neck. He had quite a collection of long, yellow, curved tusks.

"These folks been run off their property by the vigilantes, Boarhog. I thought we'd let them stay here for a spell."

Boarhog looked over his shoulder up the creek to the north and then whispered. "Why'd you think a fool thing like that? You turn crazy, Mr. Prue? We gonna have dem vigilantes right up our butts afore you can skin a cat."

"I think I'm kind a counting on that Boarhog. If they show up, we'll be ready."

"Now I know you done lost your mind." Boarhog shook his head and stalked off to hang his gate.

Prue put the Starling wagons off to the south of his compound. If he figured right, any vigilantes would ride in from the north. North was where Malachai McQueen's ranch was located. North was where he was headed first thing in the morning to find Jenny. That was the only plan he could come up with. He'd go to the McQueen ranch and look around, see what he could see, then look for Malachai McQueen.

Prue had spent many years on the Texas prairie among Mexicans, Indians and Texans. He'd learned a thing or two about making someone tell you everything they knew and even stuff they didn't. He felt pretty confident of his ability to make McQueen talk. But first, of course, he had to catch him.

That night, the women of Starling's wagons fixed supper for everyone in the camp. Prue and Danny built a bonfire in the center of the well-swept compound. Danny sat next to the blonde girl who had served them breakfast, and Harriet sat next to him. After they'd eaten steaks from a beef the Starlings had to butcher when the vigilantes wounded it, Prue lit a small cigar and sat back to ponder his crazy idea.

"Where do you think McQueen took Jenny?" Harriet asked.

That was exactly what Prue had been asking himself and he'd concluded there was no way to find out except from McQueen himself. There were a thousand places McQueen could have stashed the child.

"Don't know, Harry. I only know where to start and that's at the Rafter Q. I'll be riding out in the morning to find McQueen. I'll make him tell me."

Harriet wrung her hands and looked off into the distance. When she spoke, her voice was soft and filled with sadness. "I can't get poor little Jenny's frightened face out of my mind, Prue. I can still see her looking at me, begging me to save her. And I could do nothing."

Harriet's voice cracked as tears once more began sliding down her face.

Prue put an arm round her slight shoulders and hugged her. He didn't feel like crying. He felt like killing.

Malachai rode slowly. He was in no hurry. The girl had stopped her weeping and wailing an hour ago. She lay like a sack of grain over his saddle.

Smiling, he reached into his pocket, pulled out a chunk of tobacco, and bit off a piece. Saliva flooded his mouth. He leaned over and spit, continuing to munch contentedly. Suddenly he stopped chewing, reached into his mouth, and pulled out a long yellow hair. Wiping off his fingers, he enjoyed his chaw and his thoughts.

Everything was going so much better than he'd thought it would. The girl had been a loose end. Malachai grinned around his chaw. Well that loose end was now draped over his saddle. And for the last three miles, he'd been pondering on what to do with her.

He knew the only smart thing was just kill her and toss her body in a gator hole. But there was only one problem with that idea, he knew he couldn't. No, he had to put her someplace where she would be safe and no one would find her. And who could he ask to look after her? The only person in the world he could trust with something so potentially dangerous to himself was the sergeant. In his heart, Malachai was sure Jenny possessed knowledge that could get him killed.

What he needed was time, time in which to break the girl to his will. It wouldn't be easy. She was so much like her mama. But she was young and eventually, that would work to his advantage.

Elva hadn't given him as much as an inch of wiggle room. She'd remained hard as nails to him, never backing down, never softening her stand. Elva had told him over and over that she loved her husband and would never go anywhere with Malachai. Every time he'd gone to her place and tried to woo her, Elva had ordered him to leave and never come back. It didn't matter how much money he had or what gifts he offered, she wanted none of him.

Jenny squirmed on the saddle and Malachai stopped the stud long enough to pull her into a sitting position. The girl shoved her long hair out of her eyes and held on to the edge of the saddle with both hands.

"You feelin' okay, little missy?" Malachai asked.

The girl ignored him, hunching her shoulders. He reached around her and pulled her closer to his body on the saddle. She was as stiff as a block of wood. The minute he let go of her she scooted away from him.

"Be careful little dove or you'll fall off the horse," Malachai chuckled. "We wouldn't want that would we?"

"Maybe you wouldn't, but I sure would," Jenny's reply was sharp. "I'd love to get down and run. Why don't you let me?"

"You're just like yer ma," Malachai said smiling. "Yer so much like yer ma, I can almost imagine that you're her."

"You killed Ma. I saw you do it."

Malachai froze. She'd seen him murder her folks. He really should just kill her out of hand and get rid of her body. But he knew he wouldn't. She was so much like her mother, just younger and perhaps more pliable. In the long run, this could prove to his advantage. Elva would never have given in and been his wife. This little thing would eventually break.

"Now you forget all about that bad stuff that happened, Elva. Happier times are a coming for you and me, happier times."

"I ain't Elva. My name is Jenny. Don't call me that ever!"

Jenny would be a hard nut to crack, too, but after a month or so alone with just him or the sergeant, she'd change her tune. McQueen smiled as he chewed his tobacco and rode into the night toward his ranch. He reached down and pulled several silky strands of Jenny's hair through his fingers. The girl was already ten. In a few years, she'd be old enough to marry.

8

Late that night after the Starlings were bedded down near Prue's new cow-pens and everyone was sleeping, Harriet crept out of her bedroll. She was bunking with the Starling's single girls. Emma and her husband Will had three daughters and four sons. Two of the sons were grown and had wives and children of their own. The girls were all younger. The oldest was twenty and still unmarried. They were very curious about Harriet and her brother, where they lived and how Harriet was able to take care of them both.

Lying about what she was went against her nature. Harriet was usually not ashamed of being a prostitute. The money she earned kept her and Danny alive. And because of her uncle and what she had to do to get away from him, she tended to be belligerent about her situation. She hadn't asked to be raped and used. And when her mother had ignored the situation in an effort to please her brother, Harriet had known she was on her own. But being around these innocent girls made Harriet even more aware of what her uncle had stolen from her, and it made her wish she could somehow get it back.

So Harriet had followed Prue's lead and said she worked at the Arcadia House as a maid and in the kitchen. When Harriet thought about Prue her face warmed and so did her heart. She knew she was in terrible danger of falling in love with the handsome cowman. He was good-looking. But she'd known some bad men who had looked good on the outside. She knew from her own experiences that looks meant little. But after watching Prue deal with the Starlings, her brother, and little Jenny, she'd started to see Prue in a different light. She'd become aware of qualities in Prue she didn't know any man possessed.

In her experience, men were rough and selfish, taking what they wanted and rarely giving back or even thinking about anyone but themselves. Prue was so different. Danny saw it, too. He already idolized him.

Harriet slipped across the yard and past the dead camp fires toward Prue's partially constructed cabin. The air still smelled faintly of smoke and cooked meat. She quietly ran up the steps to the porch in her bare feet. Entering the half-finished structure, she easily found Prue's pallet. Lifting the patchwork quilt covering his sleeping form, she slipped under it and into bed with Prue. She wanted to touch him and be close to him. Tomorrow she was going to have to go back to Arcadia.

The minute her weight rested on the pallet, Prue bolted into a sitting position with an enormous pistol in his hand. "Who's there?" he growled.

"Shh, be quiet, it's just me Prue, Harry."

Prue ruffled the dark blond hair off his forehead with his palm and set the pistol on the floor. "What in tarnation are you doing here? I almost shot you. You ought to be out there sleepin' with the other women."

"I know," she said, sliding close to him and resting her head on his arm. "I just wanted to be close to you for a spell. I got to go back to Arcadia in the morning."

"Well, it ain't right. What if some of the settlers saw you come in here? I don't want them to think poorly of you."

"I just needed to talk to you for a little while and maybe you could give me a hug." Harriet could feel tears welling in her eyes and her voice quivered. "It hurts so bad that Jenny got stole away from me. You ain't mad at me are you?"

He finally relented. Softening, he put his arm around her and held her close under the quilt. "I ain't mad, Harry. But that Malachai McQueen is a powerful, ruthless man. I'm afraid for Jenny, too, and I can't figure out how to find her and get her back. It's making me crazy. Tomorrow, I'm riding out for the Rafter Q and I don't even know what I'm gonna do when I get there."

"I have to take that horse back to Arcadia tomorrow before I get in trouble for stealing it," she whispered. "Then I guess I'll stay there and work while you go chasing after McQueen."

"I wish you wouldn't . . . you know, do what you do."

Harriet smiled in the dark. He didn't want her to whore no more. "It's the only way I can pay for my room and take care of Danny. Besides, I might hear something, about Jenny. You know."

"I know you need to support yourself, Harry. I just wish you could find some other way. Ain't there something else you can do to earn money? You can read and I know you like books. You got 'em all over your room. You don't need to try to find out where Jenny is. I really appreciate your caring about her and all, but damn, try to think of something else you can do. I mean if you want, you can always come out here and live on my ranch. It ain't much, but it's a sight better than . . . well a sight better than welcoming gentlemen callers into your room."

Jenny's jaw clenched. Prue had just told her she could live here at his ranch and quit whoring. Then she relaxed, sighed, and buried her face in his shoulder. Maybe she would take him up on his offer, later. She wasn't ready to give up her independence. And besides, she wanted and hoped Pelo Berryhill would show up at the Arcadia House and tell her where his boss had hidden Jenny. If she could just find out that one thing for Prue, it would be worth everything else she had to go through.

"Thank you, Prue," she whispered. "Thank you for making me such a generous offer. And thank you for treating me with respect. I truly do appreciate it, but I got to go back to Arcadia fer a spell. I will consider quitting my profession and becoming a good woman, because you asked me to. It's important that you think well of me." Harriet moved away from him on the pallet, suddenly shy of him and the emotional connection she felt growing between them.

Prue touched her on the shoulder, caressing her through the fabric of her shirt. It was a light touch and then he pulled his hand away.

"Tomorrow I'll tell Boarhog to ride into Arcadia with you. He can take one of the mustangs and stable it in town for you. That way when you want to come out here or if you hear something, you can ride out without stealing a horse."

Harriet's smile grew broader and she nestled back into the crook of his arm. Prue sat up and pushed her away. "Oh no, none of that, you had yer hug, now get your butt back to your own damn bedroll."

Before dawn, Prue was out in his small barn preparing for a trip to McQueen's ranch. A trip he had little hope of turning into any kind of success. He had only the most basic of ideas about what he was going to do when he got there. And he had no notion how this trip was going to help him find Jenny. He just knew he had to go. If he didn't do something, he was going to go insane. Shaking out two saddle blankets, he slung both of them over Satan's back. "Stand your ass still," he swore.

Satan was cold-backed. He didn't like the saddle, didn't like the cinch, and was apt to buck for the first five minutes of any given day. After Prue slung on the saddle, he tightened the cinch with a strong tug, kneeing Satan in the guts at the same time, then he buckled the back strap. The horse laid his ears back and tried to reach around and nip Prue on the behind. Prue answered this equine insult with a fist to the stud's cheek as he fastened his duster and bedroll on the back of the saddle along with his saddle pockets. Then he slammed his Winchester in the scabbard and hung his spare pistol, an ancient Colt's Dragoon, off the saddle horn with a piece of leather and added the eighteen-foot whip.

He was getting better with the whip. Last night Danny had given him a lesson. The boy really could pick a fly off a dog's ear with a cow whip. Prue would probably never reach that level of expertise, but he had his lariat rope. He'd been roping since he was old enough to make a loop. Florida cowmen didn't see much use for the lariat, and Prue could see their point. It was hard to rope a steer when you could barely find it hiding in the palmetto scrub. But he doubted whether he'd ever give up using it and there were still plenty of things you could use a lariat to do.

He and the boy were getting to know each other, feeling each other out. He'd taken Danny behind the barn and shown him his pride and joy after they'd eaten supper. Back there covered by a tarp Prue had himself a real Civil War relic, a twelve-pound mountain howitzer.

Prue bought it from a peddler he met on his trip from Texas to Florida. The old peddler had delivered it, given him sixteen rounds of assorted ammo, some black powder and some basic instructions, chief of which was, "don't stand behind it when you're firing, it has a thirty-foot kick."

Prue had yet to try it out. Danny marveled at the gun and asked when he could fire it off. "Fourth of July," Prue had told him. "We'll let off a few rounds come Fourth of July. Since we ain't got no fireworks, this ought to do the trick."

"Do you think you'll ever need to use it?" Danny had said.

"You never know," Prue told him. "I guess it'll be my secret weapon."

Finished saddling Satan, Prue looked around. No Danny. Great, he was worried the kid would try to come along with him.

Buzzard nosed his leg. "Yes, old boy, you can come. I'm gonna need you to help me find a little girl."

Leading Satan out of the lean-to barn, Prue ran smack into the boy. Dang, he'd hoped to avoid the kid.

"Where you going, Mr. Pruitt?" Danny asked, yawning.

"I'm heading off to the Rafter Q before the trail gets too cold."

Danny's heavy eyes popped wide open. "Wait fer me. I'm coming."

Prue put a hand on Danny's arm. "No, son, you need to stay here, watch out for these folks until I get back."

Danny's eyes narrowed. "You can't leave me behind, Mr. Pruitt. I'll follow you. You need me. I can help."

"Help me with what?" Prue yelled into Danny's surprised face. "I don't even know what I'm doing. I'm riding out on a fool's mission. I don't know where McQueen took Jenny. And for all I do know, he's probably already killed her. I'm riding out because I have to do something, even if it makes no sense."

Prue clenched his fists. Buzzard whined and Satan swung around almost stepping on Buzzard's foot. He had to do something or go insane. He'd never been good at waiting around. He liked action, even if it was the wrong action. And without a good plan, he couldn't take this kid into what was surely going to be a dangerous situation.

Danny's head drooped and he dug his hands into his pockets. Prue punched the kid in the arm. "I'm sorry I yelled at you, but I need you here. I'm depending on you to take care of my place and look after these folks for me."

Prue put his left foot in the stirrup and waited. Satan stood still. Prue smiled. Well, well, maybe the stud was learning some manners. But the minute Prue's butt landed in the saddle, Satan's back rounded, his head dropped and he took off bucking. "Whoa, damn you," Prue yelled as he shoved his right foot into the flapping stirrup and pulled the horse's head up. Spurring the stud, he took off at a hard gallop, heading north along Horse Creek.

Malachai McQueen was filled with a sense of contentment and well-being he had not experienced in a long time. The sadness and loss he had suffered when Elva died were gone, lifted away by dear little Jenny. Now that he had her, everything was right with his world.

As he rode into the barnyard of his ranch, he noticed a strange buckboard backed into the wagon barn next to the ranch buckboard and the chow wagon they used for cattle roundups. Who could be here?

Rooster was standing under the eaves of the barn smoking his pipe. He looked up when Malachai rode in.

"Looks like it's gonna rain," Rooster commented as Malachai threw one long leg over the saddle and slid off his horse.

"Who cares?" Malachai answered curtly.

"You should," Rooster replied. "I been hiring for the roundup. Too much rain can cause problems."

"It'll stop. It ain't rainy season, so why worry about it?" Malachai said, thoroughly irritated with Rooster's comments.

"Whose buckboard and wagon?" he asked, pointing at the two conveyances.

"Yer Aunt Thelma's here with her grandson Jeb and the daughter-in-law."

Malachai swung his head around and stared at the ranch house. It looked like every lamp and candle in the place was lit. Damn, why'd they have to come here now? He was going to have to talk to Berryhill and get him to ride out and take Jenny some food and sit with her for a spell.

He'd stashed the girl in an abandoned trapper's cabin deep in a swamp, in a sink hole near a big gator wallow. It was about five miles southwest of the ranch house and impossible to find if you didn't know it was there. He and Berryhill found it one rainy night when they were coming back from a raid. It had been pouring buckets. They got lost in the dark and the horses had found the path leading to the cabin. It had been a relief to get out of the rain. Rats, snakes, and coons had taken up residence, but it wasn't hard to clean it up for the night.

Mal knew it wasn't the greatest place to leave a little girl, but at least no one would find her. She'd been balled up with her knees against her chest refusing to look at him or talk to him when he'd left her. But, no doubt she'd snap out of it.

Malachai tossed the reins of his horse to Rooster. "Here, get one of the boys to take care of the stud for me while I go say hello to my Aunt Thelma."

Rooster grunted and walked into the barn leading the horse.

When he entered the house, Mal stopped and stared. Aunt Thelma must have heard his horse when he rode up because she was standing in the front hallway waiting for him. The old woman was tall and skinny and dressed in men's riding britches, knee-high riding boots and a white long-sleeved shirt. She had a handkerchief knotted around her scrawny neck and a wide-brimmed floppy hat on top of iron-gray hair. She squinted at him when he walked into the house.

"Is that you Malachai?"

"Of course it is, Aunt Thelma." He stepped close to her and tried to give her a hug. The old hag pushed him away.

"Say hello to your cousin, Jeb. He's my son's boy. This here is his mother, Clara."

"Howdy do," Malachai said as he looked over the boy. The kid was dressed just like his grandmother, right down to the handkerchief and the hat. Clara was short and squatty and dressed in what Malachai assumed to be the height of fashion, a pink dress made of some shiny material, tight over her massive belly in the front, and arranged over a bunch of material and bows resting on a mountain of fabric directly above her rear end. Her light-brown and graying hair was curled into ridiculous curly-dos that hung in front of her ears and the rest was tied in the back with a matching bow. The entire get-up on her stubby figure made her look a lopsided three-layer cake.

"I'm sorry I wasn't here to welcome you. Did you find your rooms comfortable?"

Aunt Thelma looked around the ranch house parlor with obvious distaste. "What in tarnation have you done to yer daddy's house, Malachai? It's as gussied up as a two-dollar whore."

When Malachai had first come to the Rafter Q, he'd been shocked to see the McQueens lived like poor folks. They had all kinds of money and apparently never spent any of it on their dwelling. The ranch house was large and solidly built, but primitive. It was a classic Florida ranch house with a breezeway separating the bedrooms from the living quarters. The kitchen was out in the back along with the smokehouse and a springhouse. There was little furniture beyond a basic table made of rough-cut lumber, some chairs similarly constructed, and bedsteads made of logs and saplings. Its best features had been the floor-to-ceiling windows and the wrap-around porches.

Malachai had brought in glass windows, Aubusson carpets, drapes for the windows, modern furniture and installed new doors. He'd made improvements in the plumbing and kitchen. The bedrooms got the same treatment. He'd hired a cook and a maid to keep the house clean along with a kitchen girl to help the cook. Why live like you were poor when you didn't have to? Malachai didn't understand.

The real Malachai's mama had died when he was a boy. His daddy, Mordechai McQueen, had died under mysterious circumstances shortly after Malachai had returned from the war. Cow hunting was dangerous business.

Old Mordechai had made life tough for his newly returned son, demanding he do things Ben Jones either didn't know how to do or didn't want to do, things like working with the dogs, cracking a whip, working from sunup to sunset chasing crazy little cows through bushes and swamps crawling with snakes and bugs. Mordechai had to go. After his timely disappearance on a long ride into a deep swamp, Malachai had settled in, made some deep changes, and life went on.

"When Daddy died, I added a few things and fixed the place up a little," Malachai squirmed under the hag's stare.

"Well I guess you felt what yer daddy liked weren't good enough fer you? And I expect yer wondering why we're here as well?"

Aunt Thelma seemed to have no problem speaking her mind. Malachai figured from the way things were progressing, she was gonna tell him why she was here without any prompting. So he decided to drop any pretense of common civility and reply in kind. "Yes, you could say that. It's been what, twenty years?"

Aunt Thelma bowed up, putting her gnarled hands on straight boyish hips. She had to look up to stare him in the eyes, which she did, piercing him with an icy-blue stare. "You certainly don't mince yer words. Well, I admire plain speaking, so I'll get right to the point. I brought Jeb here to learn about this ranch and take up his inheritance. Half of it does belong to him, you know."

Malachai felt a red-hot rush of anger race through his veins. Who did this little, dried-up, old bat think she was dealing with? Malachai drew himself to his full height and glared right back at her. The two of them seemed to be locked in a battle of who would look away first. Malachai vowed to himself that it would not be him.

"Daddy's will left this place to me and your husband, his brother Daniel. When Daddy died, Daniel had already been in the grave for over four years. There was no mention in the will of dividing the property among Daniel's heirs or giving you any of it. I own the Rafter Q. I have already consulted with a lawyer on this matter. So if that's the only reason you come here, you wasted the trip and you can all three git."

Aunty Thelma didn't back down an inch or blink an eye. It was as though she'd expected as much, but had to give it a shot. In a rapid change of tactics, her voice softened. "I don't understand what's come over you, Malachai. You used to be such a sweet, good-natured boy. I remember how soft-spoken and polite you always were with never a harsh word or an argument out of you. And as a child, you were loving and kind. What happened?"

"The war happened, Aunt Thelma, the war. You'd have changed too."

"I don't know, Malachai. You seem to almost be like some other person. You was always such a well-behaved and generous child, willing to share yer toys, yer puppies, and horses with the help's children. I remember you even gave Rooster's boy one of yer whips. You sure could pop a whip, even when you was little."

Great, she would bring up cow whips. Malachai couldn't crack a cow whip to save his hide. He'd tried it once and almost immediately laid it down after doing his best to take out his own eye.

"Times change, Aunt, people change. If trying to take this ranch from me was your only motive for coming here, I suggest you pack up and head out in the morning."

Aunt Thelma snorted and shrugged narrow, boney shoulders, while Cousin Clara looked extremely uncomfortable. The only one who seemed untouched by the tension in the room was Jeb. He had walked out on the porch.

"Well if that's how yer gonna treat yer relations, I guess we ain't got much to say to each other. But Jeb here is yer kin and the least you can do fer him is teach him how to be a cowman."

Malachai took off his top hat, carefully dusted it and placed it on a shelf by the door, something he should have done five minutes ago, and smoothed his black hair. He moved toward his favorite chair, situated close to the fireplace with an oil lamp on a table next to the chair for reading. "Do you mind if I sit down, madam? I've had a long day."

Clara tittered and Aunt Thelma shot her a dirty look. "Of course, boy, set yerself down."

The two ladies plopped their different-sized rumps next to each other on a settee while the boy came back into the house, knelt by the fire and began poking it into life with a piece of wood. Malachai picked up a small silver bell from the table and rang it. In several minutes a black maid answered the summons. As usual, she wore a frilly white apron over her black dress and sported a sparkling white turban on her head. She stood next to Malachai and waited for his orders.

"Please bring a tea tray for these ladies and some brandy for myself, Gem," Malachai instructed. "And then find Sergeant Berryhill and ask him to come to the house to speak to me directly."

Coffee was no doubt the drink his aunt would have preferred. It was all any of the cowmen drank in these parts. But Mal preferred tea as it seemed to him to be so much more civilized. He'd ordered it for the two of them without considering what they might like because this was his house and the sooner the old biddy learned that, the better.

When the maid had withdrawn, Malachai turned to Aunt Thelma. Things were much more to his liking now. She was on the defensive, needing something from him while he had resumed control, lording it over her from his chair.

"I rarely go on the roundups or the drives. I have more important business here and in town," Malachai told Aunt Thelma. "I'm sure Rooster Barns will be glad to take young Jeb under his wing and teach him how to be a good cowhand."

The old woman gasped, shock plain on her wrinkled face. "What do you mean you don't go on the drives? Yer tellin' me you trust yer help to count the beeves, mark 'em, and take 'em to market? That's plain stupid."

Malachai sat straighter in his chair. It appeared he better watch himself around this old woman. He had changed many things on the Rafter Q to suit himself. Things the real Malachai would probably never have done. But it had been almost twenty years. How would she know what Malachai would or would not do? He relaxed. When Gem brought in the tray and his brandy, he poured himself a large glass and sipped at the silky amber liquid.

Gem set the tea tray in front of Clara who poured for her, Aunt Thelma, and Jeb. "Come sit down and have some tea, Jeb," Clara coaxed the boy. "Look, there are some delicious little cakes and fresh bread with butter."

"I'm not hungry," Jeb said, drifting over to the door and looking out into the dark. There was one lantern lit out by the barn. Malachai thought Rooster or one of the men must be taking care of his stallion. Malachai heard the door open and turned to see the boy disappearing into the dark once again. The kid seemed like a restless, rude little son of a gun.

"I have good employees that take care of the drives for me," Malachai said, responding to his aunt's nosey, interfering statement. "Men I trust."

Aunt Thelma cackled. "Ain't no sech a thing. I bet you a nickel yer being diddled. Yer daddy never missed a day on the range, and when you were young you was just like him, always ready to go on a drive, always rarin' to get out on the prairie with yer horse, yer dogs, and yer whip."

Malachai could feel his face burning. He didn't like dogs and made Rooster keep the ranch cow dogs and catch dogs penned at all times.

"I keep good records. I'd know if I was being cheated," Malachai replied over the top of his glass. He reached into his pocket and brought out the tobacco. The old hag had him needing a drink and a chew.

Clara poured out a cup of tea and handed it to Aunt Thelma. The old bag studied the paper-thin porcelain cup with apparent disgust. Holding it out to Mal she said, "Add me a touch of that medicine of yours to this piss water, will you, Nephew?"

Raising his eyebrows, Mal poured a healthy dollop of his fine French brandy into the tea for his aunt. He lifted his glass. "Cheers," he said taking a sip.

Aunt Thelma polished off her cup in one huge gulp and smacked her lips. "That's mighty fine hooch you got yerself there, Nephew. Now why don't you let me look over them records?"

Mal watched Clara slather a thick layer of butter across several slices of bread and heap two iced cakes on a plate. Picking up a cookie, she added this treat to her projected repast and nestled into the settee to enjoy herself.

"I could tell if the herds are increasing as they should and if the right numbers of calves have been marked and taken to market." Aunt Thelma glanced at Clara munching contentedly. "You look for all the world like a cow, Clara. Why do you eat so much?"

Clara smiled, apparently indifferent to her mama-in-law's insulting comments. "These are very good cakes, Cousin Malachai," she said, then washed her mouthful down with a large slurp of tea. "And I do love a good cup of tea."

Malachai watched with fascination as Clara selected several more cakes and settled back into the cushions. Returning his attention to his aunt, he scoffed. "You can read and cipher?"

There was no way this ignorant old woman was better educated than he was. How could she have learned to read? When she was a girl, and that had to be quite some time ago, women were simply not sent to school and rarely taught to read. He barely could. He'd never gone to school and his mother had been illiterate.

What he'd learned, he'd picked up from some of his mother's "friends" and from an old whore who ran a small café. He'd go in there sometimes when he was waiting for his mother and she'd fix him something to eat and teach him his letters, helping him read from newspapers left over from the morning customers.

His insulting question seemed to startle Aunt Thelma. "Don't you remember, boy? I used to tutor you and Daniel Junior together. He was a lot younger than you and you helped him."

Damnation and hellfire on the old bag! Malachai felt like a pack of cow dogs were running him into a trap, backing him into a tight corner. She was fixing to start dredging up more and more memories about the old days, days he had no recollection of because he hadn't been there, and memories about skills and an education he should possess and didn't.

"That was a long time ago, Aunt Thelma," Malachai said and pushed back his chair to make his escape just as Gem walked in and announced Berryhill.

"Sergeant, have you met my aunt and family?"

"Yes, sir, Mr. Malachai," Berryhill said, doffing his beat up Rebel cap. "I was here when they come. Were you needin' me, sir?"

Relief dried up the flow of acid that had started to eat into his stomach. Malachai rubbed his aching gut. "Madam, you must excuse me. I will bid you goodnight. Sergeant Berryhill and I have important business matters to discuss. Let's go outside," he said to Pelo.

The two men went out on the porch and Malachai drew Pelo away from the door into the dark.

"That dried up old witch is pure trouble," Malachai said as soon as they were out of earshot with the door closed behind them. "I think she suspects I'm not Malachai."

"Come on, Boss. How's she gonna know that? She's just pushin' you to see how far she can go, and what she can get away with, out of pure meanness. What's she wantin'?"

"She wants half the Rafter Q for that whelp. Says he's owed it because it was left to his grandfather."

"You ain't givin' it to her is you?"

"Hell, no. Oh I'd like to give her something all right. I'd like to give her a kick in that shriveled up old ass of hers. Damn the whole mess of them. I'll see all of them dead and tossed into a gator hole first. Shoot, I might just do that anyway before she can start any trouble." Malachai ran a hand over his slicked-back black hair and grinned. "Wouldn't be the first time I got rid of trouble in a gator hole."

Berryhill chuckled. "What was you needin' me fer, Boss?"

Malachai put an arm around Berryhill's shoulder and drew him to the far side of the house in a dark corner of the porch. "I solved myself a little problem and I need you to help me take care of it."

Berryhill's puzzled expression grew strained and tight as Malachai told him about Jenny. "You took a little girl out to that trapper cabin? Boss, that ain't hardly no better'n a lean-to. It's got varmints and snakes living in it and under it. She'll be scared to death."

"I had to, Sergeant. I had no choice. What was I supposed to do, ride in here with her? Good damn thing I didn't with that nosey, shriveled, old crone sitting in my parlor like a spider weaving a web for me to get stuck in. And besides, didn't you hear me? The girl probably saw me kill her ma and pa. She can get me hung."

"Fat chance of that, Boss, with all the law riding fer you on the vigilance committee."

Malachai threw back his shoulders and smiled. Yes, he did have the law in these parts wrapped around his fingers. "I'll leave her there for a couple of days until I figure out something better," Malachai said. "Get some grub from the cook and take it out to the little thing. She's probably hungry. Sit with her fer a spell if you want to and make sure she's gonna be okay."

"I'll go check on her, Boss, but I don't like this one bit. Killin' growed men who done wrong is one thing, stealin' cattle and changin' brands is okay by me, too, and I don't mind runnin' squatters out of town, but hurtin' little girls just ain't right."

Malachai snarled at Berryhill. He'd had more people questioning him and trying to tell him what to do in this one night than in the last twenty years. "You have your orders, Sergeant, now get out of here."

9

Prue slowed Satan to a ground-covering trot as he headed north along Horse Creek. The farther away from his spread he got, the more his mind wandered, turning the problem of finding Jenny over and over in his head. But all the pondering was for naught; he still did not have a plan he felt would work. How was he supposed to get a hardened, powerful man like Malachai McQueen to crack and tell him where to find Jenny? The child could implicate McQueen in a murder.

Prue knew for a fact McQueen had the local law under his control, but what about the US Marshal? And what about the opinions of McQueen's neighbors and friends? If it was discovered he had killed a nice young couple like the Buttons family, leaving Jenny the lone witness to his depravity, people were going to distance themselves from him, if he didn't get lynched, which is what he deserved. Prue had heard the locals were fast to pull out the noose. In these parts, many a man had been hung without a trial or even making it to a jail. A good tree, a heavy rope, and there you had it, cracker justice.

Prue rode on, crossing the creek at one point, his horse splashing the water playfully with one foot and dunking his entire head under to get a drink. Ignoring the antics of the stallion, Prue's head was lost in thought when the sound of an approaching rider snapped him to attention.

Pulling Satan behind a clump of tall palmettos, Prue watched the crossing. Sure enough, Danny galloped into the water at full speed, sending a spray of creek water high enough to douse his bay's head. The horse slowed, shaking off the water as Danny pushed the animal up the bank and stopped to check the mud on the other side for tracks.

Prue closed his eyes. Things couldn't get more complicated or crazy. Why had he inherited this young disciple? He urged Satan out from behind the tree and waited patiently for Danny to discover him.

"Mr. Pruitt, hey I'm sorry. Don't be mad. Harry made me come. She said you'd need my help."

And exactly how was he going to need the help of a green boy?

Well, there was no sense in fighting the inevitable. Apparently, God wanted him to drag a child, any child, with him wherever he went. "It's all right, Danny. I have no idea what I'm going to do when I get to the Rafter Q anyway. You might as well tag along."

Prue thought for a minute as he gathered Satan's reins and started back up the trail along Horse Creek. "Hey, take this lariat rope and start practicing with it while you ride. It might spook yer horse for a minute or two, but I can see handling horses is nothing you have trouble doing."

He handed Danny his spare rope. Danny took it and started to uncoil it. "Should I use my gloves?"

"No, you can feel the rope better if you don't." Prue watched Danny playing with the rope, feeling the weight and trying to make a loop.

"How do I make a loop, Mr. Prue?"

Prue took his own rope and began explaining the parts of a lariat to Danny. He showed him how to twirl it over his head using the wrist to flex as he spun the rope in a circle. Prue tossed it a couple of times, roping a stump, a tree limb, and then roping Danny.

Danny laughed as he struggled to get the circle of strong, stiff rope over his head. "You sure are good at this, Mr. Prue."

"Oh, I ain't that good. If you practice, you'll be better than me in no time."

Danny spent the next hour twirling the rope over his head, getting the feel of the loop in his hand and releasing it to try his horse and see if he could hit anything. The bay cracker gelding didn't mind the rope at all. The horse had had plenty of whips cracked off him. Ropes didn't scare him.

Prue watched Danny while his mind worked at his problem. He was just thinking about going to Moccasin Bob's and asking for help when he noticed the clear water in the creek had turned a muddy brown. He held his hand out to stop Danny and signaled the boy for silence.

Danny's eyebrows rose and Prue pointed to the muddy water. Climbing off Satan, Prue led the horse down a narrow deer trail running through a thick stand of willows close to the creek. At one point, he saw a water moccasin sunning itself in the middle of the deer trail. He held Buzzard back while he prodded the nasty creature with a stick. Moccasins have bad tempers and will attack you if they feel like it. This one woke from its slumber and slowly slithered into the underbrush close to the creek. The sound of whips popping and cowhands yipping drifted to him on the breeze and he knew what was up ahead. Someone was driving a herd of cattle.

Prue didn't know exactly what made him stay hidden and quiet, but he did. When he came to the edge of the willows, a trail opened up leading to an open patch of prairie grass. He could see the cattle with what looked like five hands and a large pack of dogs pushing them across the creek. It was a pretty big herd, maybe five hundred head. Buzzard looked up at him expectantly and Prue motioned for the dog to lay down. Whining, the dog complied, although he clearly wanted to join the dogs racing after the cows.

The cows were bawling and crashing through the undergrowth along the creek as they plunged into the water and waded across. One cow came so close to Prue he could see its brand. The cow had a capital Q with a roof branded on its brown and white spotted hide. Had to be the Rafter Q brand. These must be McQueen's men. But that thought quickly passed as the next two cows to run by him had a capital M followed by the number two. That was his brand or the brand of Moss Mizelle, the cattleman that sold him his spread. Those cows belonged to him.

The cows with the Two M brand on them were followed by several unbranded cattle, then five cows and a calf, all with different brands. Prue saw steers and cows with their ears completely cut off to hide the earmarks. Some of the cows had been branded over so many times there was no making out a readable brand. More Rafter Q cows went by and Prue knew without a doubt these were rustlers.

He backed Satan into the thick underbrush and tied him to an overhanging tree branch. "Get out of that," he muttered to the horse as he slid into the underbrush going from one dense clump of cover to another.

When the hands finally pushed the last of the cows across the creek, Prue could see they were armed to the teeth. Each man had a scabbard on his saddle with a Winchester, and each wore a gun belt. One rode with his rifle laying across his saddle bow, and one had an ammunition belt across his chest. All carried cow whips and knives; none had lariats. They rode on small, thin, muscular mounts that looked like Danny's cracker horse. Two of the rustlers wore shoes like Danny's with strapped-on spurs. These were local men or at least men who had worked cows in these parts for a while. And they were a scruffy, rough-looking bunch. All had beards and mustaches with long unkempt hair. Some wore leather pants and vests, some torn cotton britches. None looked too clean.

The riders had no chow wagon, and they appeared to be moving fast and heading northeast. Prue had heard there were cattle buyers in Orlando that paid good money and didn't ask questions. That could be where they were headed because the more he watched the men, the more positive he became that these were outlaw rustlers.

Backing out of his hiding place, Prue collected Satan, who was still tied to his tree, and slipped quietly back up the creek to Danny. The boy was slicing jerky into chunks with a very sharp knife.

"I spotted a herd of cows being pushed by rustlers," Prue told the boy.

Danny looked up, then slid the knife back into a sheath strapped to his ankle. "We going after 'em?"

"No, I got something else in mind. You always carry that pig sticker strapped to yer leg?" Prue asked as he turned Satan and tightened his cinch.

"If you'd been where we been and seen what me and my sister seen, you'd carry one, too. So what you thinkin'?"

"What I think is, I'm finally getting me a plan," Prue said to the boy after he had climbed back aboard Satan. "Let's ride."

The two of them skirted the herd of cows and the rustlers and kept riding toward the Rafter Q. This time Prue knew what he was going to do. He just hoped McQueen would be at home.

The two rode on into the afternoon with Prue explaining about the rustlers and what he'd seen while they rode. Rustling was big back in Texas. He'd had a lot of experience with cattle thieves.

The cloudy skies of the morning had grown heavier as they rode, and just after the two stopped to eat, rain poured out of the leaden sky. Prue pulled on his canvas duster staring morosely at Danny who had no slicker or poncho. Sighing, Prue opened his bedroll and took one of the wool blankets out of it before rolling it back up. He folded it in half and cut a hole in the middle with his big Bowie knife. Shaking it out, he handed it to Danny.

"Stick your head through the hole. This should keep you dry."

Danny pulled the blanket over his head and around him. It covered all of his upper body and most of his thin horse's rump and shoulders. Prue had seen cowboys out west and here in the palmetto prairie wearing ponchos made out of everything imaginable. Mostly in Texas, the boys had worn serapes from Mexico or used colorful Indian blankets to make their ponchos. He sighed. If it got cold tonight, he was gonna miss that blanket.

It rained buckets for the rest of their ride to McQueen's ranch. Prue wondered if Danny was regretting his impulsive decision to follow him.

The rain fell in sheets and the prairie rapidly turned into a large shallow lake. The horses slogged along in water past their fetlocks. Buzzard trotted along at Satan's heels with his head low and his short tail tucked between his legs.

Everywhere they saw cattle, the animals grazed placidly in the downpour, sticking their heads into the water to find grass or munching leaves off low-hanging oak branches and shrubs.

It took them a while to find the ranch, which was located close to the Myakka River that was not really much of a river, more like a large creek. Once Prue found the river and realized it was the river he was searching for, they headed northeast, backtracking upstream along its path.

They rode into the homestead of the Rafter Q at dusk. Lights blazed in the big log home. Someone was sure here. A single lantern flickered inside the barn. Prue led Danny to the barn and climbed off his mount. Water ran off the duster as he shook the folds. The long raincoat, which also doubled as protection against wind, snow, and dust storms, fell to his ankles. It had a cape-like collar that gave extra protection to his back and slits in the sides so he could grab his gun if needed and ride his horse with ease.

"Stay here with Buzzard," Prue told Danny as he drew off his gloves and tucked them into his pockets. The dog sat down next to Danny's horse. Prue led Satan into the dimly lit barn. The lantern hung on a peg set into one of the support poles in the middle of the barn. An older man with a gray beard wearing a flat-crowned leather hat was brushing a yellow stallion tied to a rope hanging from the rafters. The minute Satan saw the yellow stud, he lifted his head high, laid back his ears, and snorted. Prue yanked hard on the reins in his hand, snatching the stud's head down.

The man must either be deaf or lost in thought because it took a few minutes for him to become aware of Prue and his horse. When he saw them, he jumped and grabbed for the rifle laying across a feed barrel next to one of the stalls. "Hey, there, who the hell are you?" he said, pointing the rifle at Prue.

Prue raised his hands defensively. "I'm just here to speak to Mr. Mc-Queen. Is he around?"

"What you want with the boss?" the man asked, keeping the rifle pointed at Prue.

"I got business with yer boss," Prue snarled. "I ain't here to rob you or murder yer ass, so you think you could drop the weapon?"

The man seemed to appraise Prue one more time, then slowly lowered the barrel of the Winchester. "Who are you?"

The two studs suddenly squealed at each other and the yellow stallion swung around, knocking the old man over with his rump. Satan reared and tried to snatch the reins out of Prue's hands.

"Knock it off, Hammerhead." Prue gathered the reins tight, holding them just under Satan's chin, and backed up the stud three steps.

The old man had been knocked to the ground. He was slow getting up. If it weren't for the two angry stallions, Prue would have gone to his aid. When he finally climbed to his feet, he dusted off his blue britches with his hat and smiled at Prue. "Dang these animals' hides. I don't understand what the boss wants with this nasty-tempered brute anyway. He's up to the house. I'll go tell him you're here. What's yer name?"

"My name is Jesse Pruitt and I've got some important news to relate."

The old man's bushy eyebrows rose but he didn't ask what the business was. He walked with a slight limp as he headed across the well-swept yard to the front of the big house.

Prue led Satan out of the barn and tied him on the hitching rail conveniently located by the barn. The rain had slowed to a mist. Danny huddled miserably close to his horse as if sucking some warmth out of the skinny bay. "The old geezer said McQueen is in the house," Prue told Danny.

"I don't know how I'm gonna keep myself from choking him," Danny mumbled. "He's stole children, killed settlers, and scared my sister."

Prue eyed the skinny kid. He didn't look big enough to choke a wet hen to death. "Please control yourself, son. If you give us away, you'll ruin our chances of finding Jenny."

"I know," Danny mumbled. "It just eats me up that he can get away with all this stuff."

It seemed like an hour before the old man reappeared leading McQueen. After hearing so much about the man, Prue was finally going to meet him. Would he be the devil Prue had come to expect?

Prue's first impression when McQueen got close enough was of a tall well-built man in his forties dressed in tight-fitting tan riding britches and a black coat over a white shirt and black leather vest. He had a black high-crowned beaver hat on his head like a judge might wear.

McQueen strode up, his hands on his hips, and stared at Prue with his thin nose lifted high and a curl to his finely molded lips. Something about his face struck a chord in Prue's memory. He felt like he'd seen the man before.

Buzzard took one look at McQueen and started growling. All the dog's hair was on end and his teeth showed in a hideous snarl. Prue had never seen him react to anyone like this before. "Down, boy," Prue said, placing one hand on the dog's broad head.

McQueen stared at the dog with obvious dislike.

"Well, what you want with me?" McQueen asked in what Prue could have sworn was a voice laced with the smallest hint of a Texas drawl.

Prue put on his most ingratiating smile. "Hey, my name is Jesse Pruitt, nice to meet you."

McQueen did not offer his hand and Prue pulled his own hand back, fished his gloves out of his pockets, and pulled them on.

"Well, what do you want, Pruitt?"

Buzzard made another move on McQueen and the man jumped back, swatting at the dog with his hands.

"You best be tying that nasty beast up," McQueen said. "We pen our dogs here."

Prue turned to Danny. "See if you can put a rope around Buzzard's neck and keep him over by the horses."

He turned back to McQueen who was watching Danny take the dog away. "Mr. McQueen, I saw some rustlers about fifteen or twenty miles back along Horse Creek. They were pushing about five hundred head northeast and plenty of them were wearing the Rafter Q brand."

McQueen's eyes narrowed. "Heading northeast, you say?"

"It looked like maybe they were driving them through to Orlando. You can sell cows easy there I heard."

Glancing at the old man, McQueen's lip curled. "Why'd you come tell me?"

Prue sighed. This man was such an obvious asshole. Dealing with him was already just about more than Prue could handle. "Some of the cattle them rustlers was pushing are mine. I need help to get 'em back. Your ranch was close and kinda on the path the rustlers will take if they're headed for Orlando. They couldn't be more than four or five miles west of here right now, probably bedded down for the night. They can't push them too hard they'll lose too much weight. And then it's been raining like a son of gun for the past six hours. Just now dropped off to a drizzle."

McQueen looked at the old guy again, like he was silently asking for advice. Couldn't the man make his own decisions? He was head of a giant cattle ranch.

The old man stepped forward. "We'll saddle up come sunup and head out. I got me some boys I just hired on. We can get about ten men together plus you and yer sidekick there. Right, Boss?"

"Right, Rooster. You and yer man can bunk with the hands. There's a couple of extra bunks, ain't there Rooster?"

"Sure, Boss, we got at least four empty bunks. I been waitin' to hire any more men till you was ready fer spring roundup."

Prue tried not to grin. This was exactly what he'd hoped would happen. Now he had part of the night to snoop and ten guys to question. At least it was a start. And he was doing something positive to find Jenny. "Come on, Danny. Let's take care of our mounts and haul our gear to the bunkhouse."

"I'll show you where to stable them nags and take you over to the bunk-house and introduce you to my boys. My name's Rooster, Rooster Barns," the old man said. He looked over at Danny and Buzzard standing with the horses. "Put the dog in the stall with yer stud. He'll be all right there. The boss don't like dogs."

The bunkhouse was located some distance from the big house over be-hind the barns. It was crowded and smelled like sweaty cowboys, feet, and cow manure. But as Rooster said, there were four empty bunks. Danny and Prue stowed their gear under two empty beds made from cypress poles and rough-cut boards with stained cotton mattresses filled with God knew what. Prue unrolled his bedroll, minus one blanket, and shoved his saddle and saddle pockets under the bed. Danny hadn't brought a bedroll, so one of the men in the bunkhouse found him one stashed under an empty bunk.

The men hadn't been working long at the Rafter Q, so they didn't have any money. Four started up a poker game playing for matches. Danny lay on his bunk with his hat over his eyes and Prue began oiling his boots. He loved his boots. They were made in Mexico, came up over his knees, and were hand-tooled. The leather was worn, but Prue had kept it oiled when he had the time like now. As he examined the soles and heels he realized next time he was in town, he needed new ones.

"Hey Danny," Prue said. "There's enough light outside. Let's go out and practice throwing the rope some before we turn in."

"Sure, Mr. Prue." Danny couldn't wait to grab up his rope and go prac-tice. They set up a stump and once more, Prue showed him how to make a loop and how to twirl it over his head. First try Danny roped himself a stump.

"Wooee!" Danny crowed. "I done it, Mr. Prue."

"You're a natural, boy. Let me show you how to coil up that rope proper like so it uncoils perfect when you throw it."

Until it got too dark to see, Danny threw his rope and Prue worked with him. The kid was going to be good.

When they got back in the bunkhouse, the poker game was just breaking up. Prue lay down and was closing his eyes to grab a few winks before he tried to get out and snoop some, when Rooster came in to tell the men about the rustlers. He told them to be ready to light out at dawn because the boss was going after his missing beeves.

After Rooster left, all the men crowded around Prue and Danny wanting to know what was going on. They figured Prue must have brought the news of the rustlers. Prue sat up on his bunk and lit his last small cigar. Then he told them about the five hardened outlaws he had seen pushing stolen cattle to the northeast. He told them about the guns. The men decided they better turn in and get some shuteye if they were headed into a gunfight come sunup.

Much later, when the bunkhouse was filled with a cacophony of different kinds of snoring, Prue slipped out of bed and grabbed his boots and duster. Walking softly in his sock-covered feet, Prue made his way past sleeping cowhands to the door. No one stirred as he opened the door and stepped into a chilly night. The rain had stopped and the stars and a quarter moon lighted the sky and the surrounding homestead. Prue could make out the big house in the distance, all lights from the evening extinguished except for one in the back of the house and several in the kitchen shed behind the house. Apparently, the cook of the Rafter Q never slept.

Prue sat on the steps and pulled on his boots as he tried to figure where to look and what he might hope to find. His heart had sunk the minute he left the bunkhouse. Somehow his plan to search the homestead in the night just didn't seem so clear and smart when he was actually getting ready to do it. But the thought of Jenny, lonely and scared, gave him the motivation to look around anyway.

He started at the barn. Grabbing the lantern he'd seen the night before, Prue lit it and kept the flame low. He checked the tack rooms, the feed bins, and all the stalls. He hadn't expected to find anything, but it was a place to start. From there he covered the lantern with a rag he found in the barn and slipped into the barnyard.

The Rafter Q homestead was large. It had the biggest set of cowpens Prue had seen since coming from Texas, outbuildings, barns, and pens for different kinds of livestock. Staying away from the lighted kitchen shed, he went through the spring house, the smoke house, a smaller barn filled with goats, chickens, and sheep.

He made his way to the large pig pen and stared for many minutes into the pen. McQueen must eat a lot of pork. There were over fifty head of pigs in the pens, a lot of them looked like wild hogs. Hogs were a good way to dispose of garbage or anything else you wanted to disappear. They'd even eat a dead human.

Shaking his head, Prue continued to scout the premises. He found two smaller cabins all dark and quiet hidden in woods behind the bunkhouse. He assumed they belonged to that foreman Barns and maybe Berryhill. Though he wanted to, he didn't feel it would be a very good idea to enter the darkened cabins and search.

He was making his way back to the bunkhouse when he heard someone hiss at him.

"Hsst, hey mister," the voice came from the barn.

Prue cautiously crossed the open space between the hog pen and the barn. "Over here."

Prue heard the voice again. It sounded like a kid or maybe a young man like Danny.

He entered the barn, knowing he could be making a huge mistake. Sitting on a hay bale was a boy who looked about fifteen or sixteen wearing boots, a white shirt, and vest and a floppy-brimmed hat like all the local cowhands wore. Who was he?

"You ain't gonna find what yer looking fer here," the kid said.

"What do you know about what I'm looking for?" Prue asked.

"I figure yer looking for that little girl my cousin stole."

Prue couldn't believe his ears. This boy actually knew where Jenny was hidden or at least knew of her.

"My name's Jesse Pruitt, but all my friends call me Prue," he whispered, sitting down next to the boy on a pile of hay. "Are you really McQueen's cousin? I didn't know he had any relatives around here."

"Me and my ma and Granny came in day before yesterday from up Tampa way. Granny and my cousin Malachai got into a big brangle the first night we was here and I left the house. I don't hold with fightin' and squallerin' at all. Don't never fix anything, just makes things worse."

"So what's your name, son?" Prue asked.

"My name is Jeb McQueen and all my life I been told half this ranch was mine. But after all that squablin' night afore last, I don't think Cousin Malachai is in the mood to share. He don't seem to me like the kind to give up anything what's his."

"I think you got that right, Jeb. So what do you know about the missing girl?"

"Well, when they all started hissing and spattin', I went outside. I like it outside. It was cloudin' up, but you could still see the stars and the moon was just a little sliver. Anyway, I was standin' pretty close to the porch and

Cousin Malachai came out and started talking to one of his men, called him Sergeant. They talked about a bunch of bad stuff. I been holdin' on to it not knowing what to do and all."

"You did right, son. Tell me what they said." Prue couldn't believe his luck. This kid just happened to be here and just happened to not like arguing and just happened to end up close enough to hear McQueen talking about Jenny. It was like a sign from God or something that he was doing right.

"First thing he talked about was not being Malachai and being scared Granny would catch on to him. I got no idea what that means. Then he started talkin' about getting rid of me and Granny and Ma if we caused him any trouble. Said he'd throw us all in a gator hole and he done it afore. Then he moved way over into a far corner. I had to scooch myself closer and by the time I done that all I heard was his man saying he'd take her food and watch the little girl but he didn't like it. Oh, and I think I heard something about a swamp."

Prue couldn't hardly grasp the secrets this child had disclosed to him all at once. Apparently, McQueen was some kind of imposter. If that was so and this old lady the boy called Granny knew the real Malachai McQueen as a boy, McQueen could be in real trouble. But not if he took care of the old lady right away. And if Jenny was hidden in some swamp, well at least she was alive. Alive was better than dead even if she was scared and in danger.

Hope along with a rush of new energy filled Prue. He wasn't looking for a corpse. Jenny was alive and if this boy heard right, Berryhill would be heading out to bring her food and watch over her. All Prue needed was a chance to watch for Berryhill leaving the Rafter Q alone so he could follow him and rescue Jenny.

"You done good, boy," Prue said, standing up and brushing off the hay stuck to his pants. "Don't worry none about your ma and granny. Now that we know what he's up to, we can stop him and find the little girl."

Prue turned up the lantern and took a good look into the kid's face. He looked scared but relieved. He must have felt like he was totin' the world around on his shoulders, trying to be a man and deal with all he'd heard on his own. The kid stood up and Prue stepped close to him. He knew better than to give this child-turning-into-a-man a hug. It would humiliate and embarrass. Instead, he reached over and punched the boy in the arm. "You ridin' out with us tomorrow to catch the rustlers?"

The boy's eyes lit. "I ain't heard about no rustlers. Can I really go?"

"Hey, if you turn out dressed and ready to ride in the morning, can't see why your cousin wouldn't let you ride along. You got a horse?"

"I got me a jam-up horse, Mr. Pruitt. I rode him here from Tampa. He's Florida bred and can outrun anything you'll find around here."

"We'll see about that when you put him up against my Texas mustang. Satan can whip anything for half a mile, then he just wears 'em down."

The boy laughed, and for the first time Prue could see what should have been in his face before, youthful exuberance and enthusiasm. With the fresh relief of getting a clue to Jenny's whereabouts deep inside him, Prue could laugh with the boy as they walked out of the barn together.

Rooster met them at the entrance to the barn. Jeb's laugh died abruptly but Prue still smiled. Nothing could kill the joy he felt at discovering Jenny was alive.

"What're you doing in my barn at this hour?" Rooster demanded of Prue.

"I was just checking on my horse, sir," Prue said. "I thought he might be coming on to colic last night when I put him away. He kept biting at his flanks. You know how it is."

Rooster stared into Prue's eyes with a grim expression on his face. "So, is he colicing?"

"Nah, I found a couple of cactus spines stuck in his side, that's all."

"Well you need to get on back to the bunkhouse, then," Rooster said to Prue. "And boy, you need to stop roamin' around all night and get in yer dang bed and stay there," Rooster said to Jeb. "Yer ma and granny will be ready to whup you and me if they find out what you been up to."

"I'll go to bed, Mr. Barns," Jeb said. "And I'll be up and ready to ride out in the morning."

"Oh my Lord," Rooster said as Jeb took off for the house. "The boss must have told the kid he could come. Lord have mercy on us all."

"Don't worry none, Rooster," Prue said. "I'll keep an eye on the boy."

"I thank ye, Pruitt. Yer a good man."

10

After Harriet and Boarhog Benson crossed the bridge over the Peace River, she turned and looked back down the trail. A couple drove up on the bridge in an old covered wagon loaded to the brim, pulled by two hard-working oxen. Something about them called to Harriet.

Boarhog led the gray gelding she stole, and she rode one of Prue's spare horses. She was headed home and back to work. "Please stop, Boarhog," she called to the big man. "I'm going to ride back and talk to those people."

Turning the playful mustang mare Boarhog had given her to ride, Harriet headed back across the bridge toward the wagon.

"Where you going, Missy?" Boarhog turned around in the saddle to stare after her. "Come on back here now, you hear? Don't be messing with no strange folks."

"I just want to talk to the people in this wagon, Boarhog. It won't take me a minute."

Boarhog rolled his eyes showing the whites clearly in his dark face. "I know Mr. Prue would not like this," he muttered.

Harriet urged the mare into a lope, clattering back across the bridge. She waved as she pulled up next to the wagon and looked into the woman's face. The poor lady looked haggard and drawn and her eyes were glassy, reflecting loss and pain. Harriet recognized this look from her own mirror.

"Howdy," Harriet said, shoving the pork-pie hat away from her face. "You folks heading into Arcadia?"

The woman seemed surprised at being addressed by a woman riding astride dressed in men's clothes. Or maybe she was just surprised to be spoken to at all. "I guess so," she said, glancing at the man.

"My name's Harriet Painter. Where're you folks from?"

The man spoke up. "What's it to you?"

Harriet sat back on her horse. Things were either very bad for these folks or they weren't nice people. And though she was young, Harriet was a good judge of human nature. She'd had to learn early to see the good or the bad inside people. Her life and her brother's depended on it. "I don't know," Harriet said. "You two just look like you could use a friend or maybe some help."

The woman leaned down and looked into Harriet's face. "Me and Joseph have had quite a bit of trouble lately. I'm at my wit's end. We just lost our home. It's burnt up, all gone."

The man's face, so stern and hard a moment ago, softened. "I'm sorry I was rude. We've been having a tough go of it lately and I really can't see how you could help us at all. My name is Joseph Fountain and this is my wife, Cora. We bought ourselves a place over on the Buzzard Roost Branch. It cost almost every penny we had and five days ago yesterday we got attacked by a bunch of men in black masks. They set our cabin afire and run off our stock, including my stallion. Now we ain't from nowhere and we got no place to go."

Tears began to flow down the woman's face. Harriet could see she was young and would have been pretty if she only smiled.

"It sounds to me like you were attacked by the Sara Sota Vigilance Committee," Harriet told them. "They've been operating in these parts."

"Why would vigilantes attack us? We ain't got any money. All we owned was our land and that stud colt," Joseph Fountain said.

"It's all about grazing land," Harriet told the two. "The vigilantes have run off lots of people. You ain't the only ones."

"Why don't the law stop them?" Fountain asked.

"I heard the local lawmen are members of the group. But that's just what I heard. Could be true, though," Harriet said.

"It ain't right," Cora said. "It ain't right at all. We sunk all our savings into that place and now we got nowhere to go. We thought about rebuilding our cabin, but those men said if we did, they would come back. Joseph is afraid for us. He's afraid for me."

"He's right to be scared. They killed before." Harriet was making a quick decision. She had no idea how Prue would feel about her doing this, but she had to help these people. She figured the addition of two more victims of the vigilantes to the small group on his ranch wouldn't make much of a difference anyway. And it would give these people some hope and maybe help them get their land back.

"There's a group of folks just like you gathering at a ranch on Horse Creek. They've all been attacked by the vigilantes and run off their land. One of the men lost his brother to the vigilantes." She gestured at Boarhog. "This man here can take you out to the ranch where you can set up camp, stay for a while, and help all of us figure a way to stop them. They're nothing but outlaws masquerading as vigilante justice and hiding behind black masks."

The woman reached her hand out and grabbed Harriet's arm. "Why are you helping us?"

"I really don't know. I just saw your wagon and just knew I had to."

Cora looked at her husband. "Do you think we should do as she suggests, Joseph?"

He slowly nodded his head. "Can't hurt. We got nowhere else to go and if there are other folks like us, we should band together and try to fight for what's ours."

Harriet nodded. "I heard the vigilantes are out to keep the cattle range clear. They don't want no cotton or orange tree planters moving in around here. They don't want fences cutting up the grassland and they've run off quite a few families. My, uh, friend, Jesse Pruitt owns the ranch I'm sending you to and he's trying to fight back. That's why he's inviting folks that been run off to stay on his spread until he can figure out a way to stop the vigilantes."

Mrs. Fountain's tears had dried. She wiped her face off with her shawl and sat straighter, smoothing the faded cotton of her skirt over her knees. Joseph still didn't seem convinced of Harriet's motives or her sincerity.

"This ain't just some cruel joke is it? The people around here have been less than friendly. I don't want to drive these oxen all the way to some ranch to get what's left of our possessions stole or destroyed and maybe get Cora killed. She's increasing, you know." He patted his wife on her shoulder and smiled at her in a comforting way.

"Well congratulations to both of you on the upcoming blessed event," Harriet said. Pointing to Boarhog she waved, gesturing for him to come forward. "This here is real, ain't it, Boarhog? Prue's got a couple of families living out there waiting to get their land back already. I know Prue, if he says he'll work something out and fix the vigilantes for good, he will. Ain't that right, Boarhog?"

Boarhog squirmed in his saddle. "You's right about Mr. Prue, Missy. He will get them vigilantes. He always do what he say he's gonna. I knows him."

Boarhog gazed wistfully over the bridge toward Arcadia. Harriet smiled. Boarhog was wishing he could do as he'd planned, take her and drop her off in Arcadia and get back to the ranch without the addition of a wagonload of settlers.

"It'll be all right, Boarhog. How can helping these folks hurt anything? Prue said he's hoping the vigilantes find out about the ones he's got there already. Adding two more may be what brings them to his ranch."

Boarhog rolled his eyes again. "That's exactly what I's afraid of. I sure hopes you right, Missy. It don't pay to make Mr. Prue mad."

"There are good people in these parts and plenty of them," Harriet said to the Fountains. "I guess you just ain't run into the right folks is all. Something's got to be done to stop the vigilantes and Prue is the right man to do it. Now ya'll back your rig off this bridge and Boarhog will take you out to the ranch."

"I don't know how we can thank you. We were about rolled up fer good," Joseph Fountain said.

"There's no need to try," Harriet said. "Good people have to stick together and fight for what they believe and for the right to live as they choose. Ain't that what our country is all about?"

"God bless you," Cora said as her husband began the laborious task of backing his two massive oxen off the bridge.

"Missy, what you just do?" Boarhog raised his bushy eyebrows and leveled her with a disapproving stare.

Harriet blushed, feeling her cheeks heating. "It was something I had to do, Boarhog. Those folks been driven off their property by the vigilantes just like the Starlings. Maybe if we get enough of them together, Prue will figure out something we can do to get them back on their land."

Boarhog sighed. "I just know Mr. Prue is gonna kill me dead when he finds out I brung more folks out to his ranch."

Harriet smiled and laid her hand on Boarhog's big arm. "Somehow, I think he'll be glad of it. I believe he's got a plan. Now give me the gray gelding's lead rope. I'll take him into Arcadia and stable the mare. You take these folks back to the ranch."

Boarhog held up the lead rope. "You sure you can handle two hosses?"

Harriet laughed as she took the rope. "I know I can. You just get these folks back home."

Boarhog trotted off, looking over his shoulder at her once, a frown wrinkling his broad forehead. The Fountains had their wagon off the bridge and turned back down the Arcadia Road. It would probably take them the entire day at the slow pace oxen traveled to reach Prue's ranch.

Harriet pulled the gray gelding up close to her right knee with the lead rope and began trotting back across the bridge and on to Arcadia.

She had a lot on her mind. The things Prue said to her had made her think and reconsider what being a prostitute was doing to her and her life. When she first arrived in these parts, she had been completely involved in figuring out a way to survive. Now survival did not seem as important. She had some money put by, Danny placed in Prue's care and a completely different future seemed to be within her reach. Even though she told Prue she was going back to work, in her heart, she knew that time of her life was over forever. She would have to find a job that would pay her expenses and not involve selling her body.

After she had placed both horses at the livery stable and told the stable owner she found the gray out on the prairie, Harriet walked slowly to the Arcadia House. As she walked, she took stock of the employment options in the small town. It looked to her as she walked down saloon row, quiet at this time of the late morning, most of the businesses in town catered to wild cowhands and prolific drinking and carousing.

She might find a job in one of these establishments. But would that be any better than what she now did? She'd heard many of the saloon girls took men behind the saloon for some hands-on, tender, loving care.

Next were the shops. There were a few grain stores which hired men because of all the heavy lifting of sacks and bales. There were two general stores and a dress shop with a hat boutique attached. She'd been in there once. The lady that owned the dress shop was from Paris and looked down her nose at Harriet. It could have been the woman, Madame Beauvoir, knew how Harriet was employed or it could have been she looked down on all the female residents of Arcadia. Harriet bought a hat, a lovely little straw confection with a high poke, a short brim, and watered silk ribbons that tied under her chin. Very expensive it had been, too.

But few people in town actually knew what Harriet did for a living. She worked out of her own room and paid the boys working for the boarding-house owner to keep quiet when they brought men to visit. She knew the men tipped those boys generously as well. With some luck she should be able to acquire a position.

She could read and write. Thanks to her mother and the tutor Uncle Buford had hired, she knew how to figure, some world history, and a smattering of French. When she put her mind to it, her English was excellent. It was just sometimes she lapsed into the South Georgia country accent of her parents. It was all she'd heard as a child, and it was the language spoken by most of the people who lived here in Arcadia.

Trekking back up the stairs and down the covered walkway to her room, she was horribly reminded of the night Jenny had been taken from her. A wave of dizziness swept through her, and she shivered when she saw the exact spot where she and Jenny had been standing when McQueen attacked. Shaking the temporary weakness off, she opened the door to her room. It would do her no good to fret about Jenny. Prue said he would save the girl and Harriet had to believe in him.

Her first order of business was doing away with Danny's room. She no longer needed it or the extra expense. Getting rid of his room would allow her to survive on less money, something she had to consider since she was looking for new employment.

After she had changed into her best emerald-green skirt with the high waistband and a starched white shirt, she pulled her flaming locks into a tight bun and tied a black ribbon around her neck with a small cameo dangling from it. Surveying her image in the mirror, she decided she at least looked respectable and that was the image she had hoped to create.

Downstairs she knocked on the manager's door. Mr. Jacob Humphreys was a plump gentleman with a plump wife. Together they ran the Arcadia House. Taking a deep breath, Harriet decided to start here.

Humphreys answered the knock on his office door. As always, he was dressed in a tight-fitting suit of gray cloth striped with thin black lines. He had a mustard-colored waistcoat under his jacket and sported a mustard-colored handkerchief to match in his breast pocket. Under the waistcoat he wore a starched white shirt with a high collar and cravat that seemed to dig into Humphrey's fat neck, making head mobility limited.

Harriet extended her white-gloved hand. He took it and slightly inclined his head, probably as far as it would go considering the collar and cravat. "How may I help you, Miss Painter?"

"Mr. Humphreys, my brother has obtained employment on a ranch outside of town. I won't be needin' the extra room anymore."

Mr. Humphreys scowled. Obviously he was thinking he would now have to find another tenant. "Certainly, Miss Painter, I'll see to that right away."

Harriet cleared her throat and lowered her gaze. "I was also wondering if there were any positions available at the Arcadia House for kitchen help or maybe you might be needing extra help for the dining room."

"Are you asking me for employment?"

Harriet gulped and nodded.

"We are not currently hiring," Humphreys said, lifting his chin to tilt his large head back, and he glared at her out of tiny eyes nested inside rolls of fat.

Harriet took a step backward. From the icy expression in Mr. Humphrey's eyes, it looked as though Humphreys had been listening to the maid's gossip.

With her face red and her hands trembling, she thanked Humphreys with quiet good manners and left the house. She was determined not to let one negative response deter her from her purpose.

Two hours later she returned to the house with her spirits in the outhouse. Either she'd been told there were no available positions, the owners did not feel comfortable hiring such a young lady, single and living on her own, or they recognized her.

Harriet was still determined to find some other way to make a living, but now it looked as though she would have to try the saloons. At least she would receive enough money to live working as a saloon girl. Or at least she hoped she would. She'd heard between pay and tips, they did well enough.

With her heart heavy, Harriet walked through the dining room and into the kitchen. Her deepest desire was to turn herself into a respectable woman, for Prue and for herself. Somehow saloon girl did not fit her image of a respectable woman. Maybe a cup of tea with Mae Mae would help lift her spirits, and maybe Mae Mae would have some ideas. The little Chinese woman was a bundle of energy and enthusiasm for life. Harriet felt like she could sure use a dose of that right now.

Prue wiped soap lather off his face and cleaned the blade of his sharp, straight razor. He'd been up for half an hour and felt ready to get catching the rustlers out of the way. The news that Jenny was alive invigorated him. He could barely contain the urge to confront McQueen and Berryhill and demand they give him the girl, though he knew it was a useless notion. He wished he could tell Harriet that Jenny was alive. He knew she was worried and would appreciate hearing some good news.

The rest of the men were just climbing out of their bunks as Prue pulled his saddle out from under the bed and got ready to head for the barn. Danny rolled over and groaned, "Is it time to get up already?"

"Shake the dust off yer ass, boy. I'm already shaved, dressed, and ready to roll."

Danny slowly crawled out of his bunk and wiped his face with his hands. "Okay, Mr. Prue. Is there anything to eat? I'm starving."

"I heard one of the boys say they got biscuits and bacon up to the big house. You better hurry cause you got plenty to do to get ready for the raid on them rustlers."

When Prue got out to the barn, he found his new friend Jeb saddling a lean, muscular horse, a little on the small side in Prue's estimation. The small horse was a dappled gray and had a Roman nose. To Prue, the horse looked like he would be just as fast as the kid said.

"Hey, boy, I see yer up and ready to ride." Prue opened the door to Satan's stall and let Buzzard out. The dog took off running and shot out of the barn into the early morning. Prue watched the dog race off. Poor animal probably had to take a leak. He grabbed Satan by his halter and pulled him out of the stall. Throwing the lead rope over a rafter, Prue tied the stallion. Jeb walked over, his own horse saddled, and admired Satan.

"Nice horse," the kid said, bending to run his hands over Satan's legs. The stud immediately tried to nip Jeb's rear end, but the kid was too fast, neatly moving aside.

"He's always a pistol early in the morning," Prue said. "He'll do his best to get rid of me for the first few minutes I'm on him, then he settles down. He likes to try a man."

Prue saddled up and led Satan out of the barn. Hands from the bunkhouse were pulling horses out of the corrals and getting ready to take off. So far, Prue hadn't seen McQueen. He did spot Berryhill wandering around helping the hands collect their gear, and when Prue went back into the barn to get his duster and bedroll, he found Rooster saddling McQueen's yellow stud along with a small roan gelding.

He did his best to stay out of Berryhill's way. The man saw him go into Harriet's room with Jenny. Prue held no hopes the man wouldn't recognize him. His one prayer was Berryhill would stay behind to take care of Jenny. He didn't want to have to dodge the man all day and he hated to think of the little girl alone in some trapper's cabin in the swamp.

Satan nickered deep in his chest when Rooster brought the yellow stud out of the barn. Prue was just giving the cinch one last yank before tying it. When Satan neighed, Prue kneed him in the chest. "Knock it off, Satan. We got us a long day ahead. Don't waste any energy on that piece of fancy, yeller hoss flesh."

When all the hands were saddled, and most sitting atop their mounts, McQueen appeared on the porch of the big house and surveyed the assembled. Clapping his black top hat on his head, he strode down the steps and into the midst of the group.

Prue stayed close to Satan, watching for Berryhill and waiting until the last minute to climb aboard the fresh stallion. Rooster held McQueen's stud while he mounted and then swung onto the roan. When everyone, including Danny, was up, Prue put one foot in the saddle. Satan sidled and Prue cursed him. But the horse quickly settled without a fuss as if sensing today would not be a good day to show his ass.

Buzzard appeared out of nowhere, along with six cow dogs following Berryhill. Prue ducked his head down as if playing with the piece of rawhide holding his lariat rope in place. When he glanced out from under his arm, he saw Berryhill turn around and head toward the kitchen behind the big house. Breathing a sigh of relief, he watched Berryhill disappear.

McQueen's fear of dogs must not affect him when he was high in the saddle. The yellow horse danced as McQueen lifted his hand and yelled, "Let's ride."

Prue galloped ahead to take the point. He and Danny were the only ones who knew about where the herd and the rustlers were located. He looked toward the rising sun, turned away from it, and then angled slightly to his left, heading what he figured was southwest. If they didn't run into the herd doing this, he'd lead them to the crossing on Horse Creek and pick up their trail from there.

Setting the pace at a ground-covering trot, Prue led the group of twelve men and two boys across the wet prairie. The air smelled fresh in the coolness of early morning. As the rising sun hit drops of water from yesterday's rain they glistened on the leaves of every tree and bush. Standing water was everywhere. They saw herds of cattle grazing right in the water as if it were nothing. Hailing from a dry part of Texas, Prue rarely saw flooding like this and had never seen cattle grazing in ankle-deep to chest-high water. When he looked around, he realized he was the only one who thought it weird or interesting. Florida certainly was a different place to raise cows.

About dinnertime, Prue figured they were getting close to Horse Creek and still hadn't seen any sign of the rustlers. McQueen rode up next to him. "So, where are all these cows and outlaws, Pruitt?"

"We're almost to the crossing at Horse Creek. Even with the rain, we should be able to pick up the trail there."

Prue had a hard time speaking to the man in a civil tone. It took all his self-control not to reach out and grab McQueen by the throat, snatch him off his horse, and attempt to strangle Jenny's whereabouts out of him. Minutes later they came out of a patch of woods into a clearing. The torn-up earth, flattened grass, and droppings indicating a large herd had probably spent some time there.

"This is where the rustlers brought 'em, ain't it, Mr. Prue?" Danny asked in a breathless voice. He and Jeb had teamed up. The two boys were riding side by side as the group turned northeast to follow the clear trail.

"This has to be them," Prue answered. He signaled to McQueen who rode up. "Looks like they were here overnight, then headed northeast, just like I said."

"How far ahead of us do you think they are?" McQueen asked.

"This is about four miles from where they crossed the creek. From the looks of the flattened grass, I'd say they might have bedded the cattle down here. I'll take a look around and see if I can find where they camped."

Prue loped Satan slowly toward some trees. That's where he would have spent the night. There was plenty of shelter from the rain, and the natural clearing had good enough grass to keep the cows busy and quiet. If it were him, he'd want the cows to move as little as possible in order to save their fat and plenty of good graze would help.

The rustlers must be traveling light. He found evidence of a small camp-fire and spots where two or three bedrolls could have been. They apparently hadn't cooked much, at least not on the dinky fire, and especially with it raining, With that many cows to watch and protect from wolves and other predators like the Florida panthers he'd heard so much about—Moccasin Bob had the head of one stuffed and mounted on his wall—they would have to keep at least two men riding all night. And being rustlers and outlaws they would no doubt be extra nervous.

He galloped Satan back to McQueen. "It's like I thought, they spent the night over yonder in them trees. If they started rolling at dawn like we did, they can't be more than four or five miles ahead. Can't move them beeves too fast, they'll shrivel up to skin and bones if you don't let 'em graze whilst their walking."

"If we ride hard, we should catch up in less than an hour," McQueen said. "Let's ride."

Prue loped back to the two boys. "We should be getting close. The boss over there wants to ride hard and catch them fast. Hey, Jeb, care to let that animal of yours out?"

Jeb yipped and dug in his spurs as an answer. The little gray horse took off like he'd been shot out of a cannon.

Prue gigged Satan in the sides one time with his spurs getting an answering buck out of the stud. Holding Satan's reins tightly, Prue could feel the eagerness and power beneath him. Releasing his grip on the reins, Satan shot off, slamming Prue into the back of the saddle.

Jeb's Florida-bred horse was fast, but so was Satan. The two ran neck and neck for a mile, then the gray started to slow, slacked off his speed, and began losing ground. Satan was in better shape than the gray from being on the trail day after day of his life or Prue felt like the Florida-bred horse could easily have outpaced him. He might look into acquiring some mares out of this stock and starting a herd.

When the boy caught up, the gray was lathered and breathing hard. Satan was lathered up, mostly from nerves, but breathing easily. "You got a fine animal there, Mr. Pruitt," Jeb said, slowing to a walk to give his horse time to cool off.

"I was thinkin' the same thing, son," Prue said smiling. "Satan's got more muscle and I work him every day so he's fit, or I think your gray could have taken him."

They walked together while the rest of the group caught up. McQueen was pushing his yellow stud, sitting high in the saddle like a statue. Riding high like that, Prue thought McQueen would make a great target for attacking Indians or rustlers. Loping along behind the charging group, Prue opened his saddle pockets and took out a bacon and biscuit sandwich. Better eat now or he might not get the chance.

McQueen watched the Texan pitting his stallion against the kid's gray gelding. Anyone knew studs were stronger and faster than geldings. He snorted. Of course the Texan would win. But the kid's little gray was fast, almost pulling ahead before he tired.

There was something he didn't like about Pruitt, but he couldn't put his finger on the exact reason. The man was arrogant and unfriendly, and Malachai didn't feel like the Texan gave him enough respect. He was so far above Jesse Pruitt, the man wasn't fit to rub down his horse. Where did Pruitt get off acting like he knew everything and lording it over the men and telling him, Malachai McQueen, what to do?

After they picked up the rustlers' trail, Malachai began to brood about Aunt Thelma, Cousin Clara, and the kid. He sensed something wrong with that boy. And it was a new feeling. When he'd first met the kid, the boy had seemed okay, slightly disinterested and bored, but normal. Then yesterday, the kid had started treating him like he had a disease, walking away when he tried to talk to him, giving him strange looks, and then avoiding him. After breakfast, he hadn't seen Jeb for most of yesterday. And since Jeb had been on the ride this morning, he'd been staying well away, sticking close to the Texan and that boy he'd brought with him.

Mal didn't understand what was going on in the kid's head, but there was one thing for sure, Jeb thought half the Rafter Q belonged to him. It could be Jeb was pissed off about losing what he assumed to be his birthright and blamed that loss on Malachai. Well, it was plain that as long as the kid lived, he would be Malachai's enemy. It was Aunt Thelma's fault. She'd built up the boy's hopes, making him believe he was a big ranch owner. Now the kid was sour on everything, especially Malachai. Jeb McQueen could cause a lot of trouble in the future.

Malachai snorted and chuckled to himself. He'd see about that. Chasing after rustlers could be a very dangerous business. This morning, when he'd come out and seen the kid saddled up and ready to ride, he'd begun to think his recent run of bad luck and irritating events had started to take a change for the better. If Lady Luck smiled on him at all, if any opportunity should arise, Jeb McQueen would not be riding back to the Rafter Q.

McQueen galloped to the head of his men. In the distance, they could hear the popping of whips and the yipping of rustlers pushing the cows. The occasional dog barking from up ahead had the ranch dogs milling around and whining, wanting to race off, meet the other dogs and get to work. One thing Malachai knew, even though he detested all dogs, working cows in this land would be impossible without them. It was the only reason he kept them around. And he had to admit, the dogs loved the work, racing into a herd of long-horned Florida scrub cows with huge amounts of enthusiasm and aggression.

Holding up his hand for the men to stop, he waited until they were all gathered around him. His chest swelled. He was in charge. Leading men into battle was one of his passions, whether it had been during the war where he made a much better Rebel captain than the real McQueen could ever dream of being, or with the Sara Sota Vigilance Committee, or right now when they were fixing to charge into a band of dangerous outlaws. He loved the gunfire, the action, and the killing.

"Men, the rustlers are up ahead of us. According to the Texan, Pruitt, they're only five to our twelve men and two young'uns. This should be easy, but watch out, Pruitt said these rustlers are heavily armed and they will be desperate. They know if they don't win, they better die, or a rope and a tree will be their destiny. Now take out yer weapons and let's ride!"

As one, his men turned and galloped across the turned-over earth marking the trail. The wet soil was black where the sod had been opened by the passing of many hooves. Rain puddles were brown with mud. Malachai led his men, holding his sawed-off high over his head. In addition to the sawed-off holster hanging from the right side of a heavy gun belt, he also wore a pistol on his left side and carried a Winchester repeating rifle in a saddle scabbard.

They galloped through black mud and puddles, sending sprays of water laced with earth and manure high behind them. Glancing around, he saw the Texan holding the boys in the rear, far enough back to stay clear of the slinging mud. Malachai sneered. It was plain this Texan was a coward.

And it wouldn't matter at all that the kid was hanging back out of the way. Stray bullets would be flying everywhere in minutes. The kid was doomed. Malachai had already made his decision. Jeb McQueen would soon be one less irritation.

Malachai was the first one to see the cattle. It was a large herd as Pruitt described. Three men brought up the rear, pushing the cows, one was on point and one was on the south side, working as a hazer, holding them from running into the woods. As soon as the rustlers saw Rafter Q riders, they fired their weapons. The gunfire alerted their friends and also spooked the herd.

The cows began to run. It was a stampede, but McQueen didn't care. The cattle were running away from his men and right over the outlaws.

The three rustlers pushing cows turned left and headed north, riding hard. The cows bolted straight east and the other two riders took off at a gallop straight south. Malachai signaled for his men to halt, pulling his hyped-up horse to a stop. The animal plunged and fought, but Mal held the reins tightly. The men circled him, horses flinging slobber, foaming sweat, and mud everywhere. The dogs were already racing after the cows. The dogs would try to get in front of them and stop them. It was what they were trained to do.

"Half of you men go with Rooster after the three headed north," Mal yelled over the noise. "The rest of you follow me. Texan, you bring them two boys and come with me."

The two groups split up and Mal opened up the yellow stud again. The big horse flew, closely followed by six men and the two boys. Mal had been in this area before. If he remembered right, up ahead were some thick woods leading down to a slow-moving creek called the Buzzard Roost Branch. He and the vigilantes had rousted a couple making a farm close by. If the rustlers didn't stop in the woods, he and his men should catch them on the branch.

The Texan and Jeb caught up with Mal, each riding fast horses. The three of them rapidly closed in on the outlaws. The rustlers probably rode worn-out nags. Mal saw one of the outlaws glance over his shoulder. He must have heard the pounding hooves closing in because he signaled his partner. The two men dove into the woods, pulled up their horses, leaped off and took cover behind some downed trees and thick underbrush. They were going to shoot it out. Malachai rejoiced.

"Pull up," Mal yelled as the outlaws opened fire with them less than fifty yards from the woods.

The Texan held up his hand. "Follow me," he called to the two boys, heading left in a flanking move. Jeb was close enough to hear and took off with him. The other kid, on a slower horse, had fallen behind. The other boy watched Pruitt and Jeb ride off, but stayed with the rest of Mal's men.

Mal pulled his horse behind a large palmetto, well within rifle range, and dropped his reins as he yanked the Winchester out of the scabbard. His sawed-off was no good at this distance. His men followed, finding cover as best they could. The Texan's boy leaped off his bay horse and crouched behind two small oaks close to Mal's position and pulled a rifle and his whip off the saddle. A hail of bullets flew out of the woods from the outlaws as Mal wondered what the kid was thinking he could do with a whip.

Mal stopped wondering about anything but returning fire on the outlaws. The barrage of bullets from behind the downed trees soon slacked off. Apparently, the rustlers were saving ammo and picking their shots. One of McQueen's men yelped, nicked by a well-aimed bullet. Mal tried to hit the outlaw, rising above his cover to take the shot, but he missed.

The Texan and Jeb had disappeared from sight. Mal searched the woods ahead for some sign of them. The kid had on a white shirt and Mal kept looking for any flash of white against the green and brown of the woods. He thought he saw something white moving behind the outlaws, stood up and risked his life to take a shot at it. The outlaws saw him and fired. Mal heard the bullet hit the palmetto in front of him, tearing up fronds and hitting the trunk. Mal ducked but continued to hunt for Jeb's white shirt.

The boy that had been with the Texan suddenly rose up and fired his rifle. One of the outlaws screamed. At the same time, Mal saw the Texan and Jeb rush the remaining rustler from behind, grab him, and pull the man to his feet.

Mal quickly realized opportunities for killing Jeb were disappearing. This front of the fight was over. He looked around once, then cocked the rifle and took careful aim at Jeb's white shirt. His eyes locked with the Texan's for a second. Pruitt had the remaining rustler by his arm and was about to drag him into the open. Mal briefly wondered if the Texan knew what was going to happen, but didn't care. Shoot, it didn't matter anyway. No one would take a Texan's word against his. His finger tightened on the trigger. Good-bye, pain in my ass.

Just as his finger was pulling the trigger, the popper and tip of an eighteen-foot whip wrapped three times around his wrist. Stinging pain like a branding iron ate into Mal's arm. The rifle flew from numb fingers as the man behind the whip snapped it, yanking McQueen's arm up and snatching it hard.

"I had to stop you, Mr. McQueen," a youthful voice said. "You might have hit Mr. Pruitt. Ain't no need to kill that rustler anyway. Mr. Pruitt and yer cousin got him all right and tight."

Malachai had never been so angry in his life. His wrist and arm burned like they'd been lit on fire. He could barely feel his fingers. He clutched his wrist, his face red and contorted, and turned on this upstart kid that had come with the Texan. "I ain't sure what yer name is kid, but from now on, I better never see yer face."

The kid backed away, shrugged, and coiled his whip. "Don't matter to me, I work fer Mr. Pruitt."

Malachai watched, his guts clenched in a hard knot, as the kid mounted his seedy bay gelding and galloped toward the Texan and his prisoner. Jeb had been within his sights, the kid seconds from death. Malachai could still see it the way it should have gone, a red bloom of blood spraying across Jeb McQueen's white shirt. He'd been robbed by a snot-nosed brat not even old enough to shave.

Holding his injured wrist tight to his chest, McQueen slammed the rifle back in the scabbard and pulled himself aboard the yellow stud. Matters just kept getting worse. For the first time in his life, Malachai felt like his world was spinning out of control. No matter what he did, he was foiled, stopped. The people around him were against him, watching him, wanting to take his land, his cattle, keeping him from accomplishing the things he'd set out to do, things he needed to do. He rubbed his burning wrist. All these people were gonna pay and, somehow, he would regain control of his life.

He stared at the Texan and the two boys standing at the edge of the trees. He wished them all dead. And if that was what had to be done to get his life back and regain control, then that is what would happen.

⑫

Harriet sat on the edge of her bed looking at the sun rise out of the one window in her room. Part of her was filled with despair and part still held onto hope. Yesterday and the day before, she had scoured Arcadia for a legitimate job, any job. No one would hire her. Her reputation either ran before her, she was too young, or she was hampered by being female. Her options had been reduced to two. She could go work in the saloons or take Mae Mae's suggestion and apply at the newspaper.

Mae Mae told her Carlton Jeffers, owner of the *Desoto County News*, needed a copy editor, part-time reporter, and salesperson. The job sounded too far above her abilities. Harriet could write as well as most folks, maybe a little better. She had good grammar skills from her schooling days but doubted her ability to correct mistakes made by a real newspaperman like Jeffers. And on top of that, she was a woman. But Mae Mae said she thought Jeffers held no objections to the hiring of a female and Leonard Chapman, Mae Mae's husband, said he thought well of the man.

Pulling on her half boots and lacing them with her thoughts far away, Harriet decided to go to the Golden Spur first and ask about being a saloon girl. It was a position she figured would be easy for her to obtain. She'd seen the girls that worked on saloon row. She knew she was at least as pretty as they were.

The week was almost over and soon she would have to pay her rent. Her small savings was all she had. She needed to hurry and find some way to earn money. She stashed her money in an old sock inside the mattress but didn't want to dip into the money unless it became absolutely necessary.

Sighing, she pulled a forest-green shawl out of the armoire and wrapped it around her shoulders. The morning was chilly. She walked down the back steps and slipped into the kitchen. Mae Mae stood on her stool next to the woodstove frying an enormous pan of bacon. Her husband sat at the table eating a biscuit loaded with fresh butter. After wiping his whiskers with the sleeve of his plaid wool shirt, Chapman tipped his hat to Harriet.

"Top of the morning to you, Miss Harry," he said, then took another huge bite off the biscuit.

Mae Mae flipped six or seven strips of thick bacon on a plate and set it in front of her husband. "What you doing here, Missy?" Mae Mae asked.

"I thought I'd grab a bite to eat before I went over to the Golden Spur to speak to Mr. Lumpkin about a job."

Mae Mae landed a plate heaped with bacon and biscuits on the table for Harriet at the place across from her husband. "Why you not go see Mr. Jeffers like I tell you? He need help plenty bad."

"I will," Harriet mumbled around a mouthful. "I just feel more like the Spur will hire me. I'm a little nervous about working for a newspaper. What if I can't do the job?"

Mae Mae shook a scolding finger at Harriet. "You don't know nothing until you try, Missy. Why big brave girl like you so scared of something new?"

Harriet shook her head. How could she explain her life to Mae Mae? The little woman couldn't understand how hard it was for her to go out into the public eye when half the residents of Arcadia seemed to know exactly what she did to make a living. "I said I was going to go see Mr. Jeffers, Mae Mae," Harriet mumbled. "I just want to check out the Golden Spur first and see what it would be like to work there. Mr. Jeffers might not hire me, you know. I need to have an alternative plan. I have to go to work soon or I'll be broke."

"Now don't you worry none about Jeffers," Leonard Chapman's voice was deep and seemed to rumble from a canyon inside his nest of whiskers. "I already spoke to him and gave you a Jim Dandy of a recommendation."

Harriet smiled. This big man could make her feel so good. It was no wonder Mae Mae worshiped him. "All right, all right, I'll go."

The good feeling engendered by Mae Mae and her husband rapidly dissipated as she walked through the boardinghouse and out the front door. It was one thing to talk around a breakfast table and quite another to go out into the world on your own and face people you didn't know.

Holding her shawl tightly around her for warmth and comfort, Harriet turned onto saloon row and marched down the street until she came to the

Golden Spur. In the morning light, it looked lonely and dilapidated even though it was the biggest and best saloon in Arcadia. There were no lights coming from inside, no laughter, and no loud music. It was so quiet she was afraid it would be empty. But Harriet knew the saloons never close in Arcadia. Someone would be in there.

She was right. When she walked through the doors, two men were propped against the bar, leaning heavily on it, probably for support. One man sat on his horse drinking a beer in the middle of the saloon. He eyed her as she walked into the establishment. The floor was littered with cypress shavings and horse manure. The place smelled like a crazy mixture of the shavings, spilled beer, manure, and filthy men.

A piano stood against one wall, but no one was playing it at this hour. The tables crowding the floor were empty as well. Walking up to the bartender, a tiny man whose head barely cleared the top of the bar, Harriet inquired after the owner.

"Mr. Lumpkin, he's upstairs in the office," the bartender said, pointing up a narrow flight of steps against the back wall leading to a closed door at the top.

Thanking him, Harriet made her way across the floor with her skirts held high to keep them clean.

She knocked on the closed door, her heart pounding.

"Come in," a rough voice with a thick Georgia country accent called from inside.

The accent reminded Harriet of Uncle Buford. Her insides quaked and she wished she hadn't consumed bacon before coming on this interview. Opening the unfinished plank door, Harriet stepped inside.

She blinked her eyes. Her first look at Bernard Lumpkin was one she would never forget. The poor man had no skin color. He was unnaturally white with pale blue eyes and white hair. His black suit seemed to accent the paleness of his skin and his lips were thick and rubbery, exactly like Uncle Buford's. When he saw her, he licked them with a long, moist, pointed tongue.

"Close the door behind you." Lumpkin did not ask, he commanded, as though used to telling people, especially women, what to do.

The office was so small. The thought of closing herself in with this strange man was frightening, but she did it. When the door was closed, Lumpkin rose to his feet. Harriet was not a small girl but she had to look up to see his face. A ridiculous thought passed through her mind. She could just picture this giant standing next to the miniscule bartender.

That thought kept her from opening the door and bolting for freedom. With the door closed, Harriet could smell Lumpkin. Apparently bathing was not something he did frequently.

"What you want, girl?" Lumpkin asked, and then tapped his left temple with a long skinny forefinger. "Hey, ain't you one of them whores that works out of the Arcadia House?"

Harriet resisted the impulse to close her eyes. He knew. "My name is Harriet Painter, and I came here to inquire whether you were hiring girls to work downstairs."

A nasty leer started at the man's thick mouth and narrowed his eyes. "So, you want to work for Bernie Lumpkin?"

No, Harriet did not want to work for this man at all. When he came out from behind the desk, she backed against the door. "I think I've made a mistake, Mr. Lumpkin. This is not the right kind of employment for me after all."

Lumpkin put one big hand on the door behind her and towered over her. Harriet pressed herself as close to the door as possible. To get out, she realized, she'd have to pull the door inward. Lumpkin knew that when he told her to shut it. Why on earth had she done so?

"Maybe I could make you change your mind," he whispered, dropping his head close to hers.

Harriet felt the bacon and biscuits coming up and couldn't stop the impulse. Gasping, she put her hands on Lumpkin and pushed, then bent over, and vomited all over his shiny black boots.

The string of profanity, cursing, and invective that issued from Lumpkin's mouth would have been funny if Harriet wasn't so frightened. When Lumpkin stepped back to shake her breakfast off his shoes, Harriet snatched the door open and bolted down the steps and out of the saloon into the fresh morning air.

Breathing deeply of the cool air, she walked rapidly down saloon row, finally stopping at the corner of Hickory Street and Desoto Avenue. If she turned right, she could go back and hide in her room. If she turned left, she could continue her job search by talking to Mr. Jeffers at the newspaper.

Taking her handkerchief out of her crocheted handbag, Harriet wiped her mouth. When she put the handkerchief back, she searched through the depths of the bag for a peppermint stick she knew was in there and wrapped in a twist of paper. When she found it, she broke off a small piece, stuck it in her mouth, and sighed with relief. If her breath smelled as bad as it tasted, she would probably offend Mr. Jeffers and he would never hire her.

Straightening her shoulders, she marched resolutely down the street toward the tiny office of the *Desoto County News*. It was a half mile walk. When she got closer, she saw a wagon pulled up outside the office loaded to the brim with furniture. A team of four mules dozed in their tracks in the warm morning sun, eyes half-closed and one hind foot cocked. Three small children and a woman dressed in faded calico sat on the high, bench seat of the wagon.

Harriet stopped and waved to the children. They smiled and waved back. As she turned to walk into the office, a distracted man dressed in a faded flannel shirt and brown pants ran right into her.

"Excuse me, Miss," the man said as he removed his floppy black hat and executed a small bow. "I didn't see you there. Did I hurt you?"

"It's quite all right, please don't mind me. I am perfectly fine."

Harriet hesitated at the threshold of the door to the newspaper. She turned and watched the man step up to the wagon and speak urgently to the woman. She could not help but overhear him tell his wife the newspaper could do nothing to help them.

Looking the wagon over again, the haphazard manner in which the furniture and belongings had been thrown on and tied down, along with the harassed expressions of the couple, it all seemed to say Sara Sota Vigilance Committee to Harriet.

"I'm sorry, sir," Harriet began. Walking over to the wagon, she stared up at the family and then looked at the man. "Have ya'll been displaced by vigilantes?"

He turned to her, his eyes wide with surprise. "How did you know?"

Harriet took a deep breath. Boarhog was going to be so angry. "It's happened to quite a few families. I have met several of them recently and I know of a place you can go where you may be able to receive some help."

Behind her a voice spoke. "I'd be interested to know of this place as well, young lady."

Harriet turned around to find a gentleman of medium height in a plaid suit with gold wire-framed spectacles perched on his upturned nose. Standing between the two men, Harriet felt her face flush. What had she done?

"Are you Mr. Jeffers?" she asked.

"I am indeed," He answered smiling. He had a small neatly trimmed mustache over his smiling lips. His brown eyes were kind behind the spectacles.

Harriet felt relieved. He was so ordinary looking. After the Lumpkin debacle, ordinary seemed so comforting.

"Please tell me about this place," the man from the wagon said. "My name is Horace Temples, and this is my wife, Margaret, and my children.

The vigilantes attacked us and drove us off our farm two weeks ago. We've been trying to find a sheriff or a lawman of any kind to give us some help. None of the men we talked to had any interest in helping us. One, a Sheriff Daniels of this very town, said he'd have us arrested if we caused any trouble. Mr. Jeffers here said he will write and place our story in his newspaper, but doubts whether it will help us at all."

"I've run other stories like yours to no avail, Mr. Temples," Jeffers said. "However, I have received several threats, some written, saying if I run any more my business will be burned down. So far, this has not happened. And as any newspaperman will tell you, we hate to be dictated to about what we can and cannot publish. I will write your story and run it, but I hold no hopes that it will cause any more than a small ripple in the daily life of those here in Arcadia."

Harriet took a deep breath. "There is a ranch not too far from here on Horse Creek owned by a man who has allowed several families displaced by the vigilantes to camp. I believe he hopes to lure the vigilantes into attacking his place where the united forces of all the displaced families will be able to defeat these outlaws who are masquerading as representatives of justice."

She took a step back to observe the effects of her words. Hope bloomed on Mr. Temples's face and incredulity on Jeffers's face.

"Are you serious, Miss?" Temples said.

"Of course," Harriet answered. "I'll give you directions to the ranch. It's still early. You should be able to make it by nightfall with that team of mules pulling."

"And they'll let us stay there?"

"Just tell the foreman I sent you. His name is Boarhog Benson. He'll probably bluster and swear, but he's kind at heart and will show you where to camp."

Temples grabbed both her hands. "I can't thank you enough, Miss. We done lost hope. We don't want to go back to Tennessee, we can't afford to, and there ain't nothing back there for us anyway. We've been camping out on the prairie and going from Pine Level to here trying to get the law on our side and we're just about give out."

Jeffers had been watching this exchange quietly, one finger moving the spectacles up and down the bridge of his small nose. "This is quite interesting," he said. "I wish I could go out to this ranch with you and speak to these other displaced people. It would make an interesting story, perhaps even a series of stories about each family and their travails. But I am currently short personnel and can't leave the office. It's a pity, such a wonderful story. I'd really like to speak to that rancher."

"Uh, Mr. Jeffers," Harriet had made her decision. She might as well jump in with both feet. "I came here to apply for that open position here at your newspaper. I heard you needed help."

Jeffers turned his entire attention on Harriet. "Indeed? Can you read and write?"

"I have received an education of sorts," Harriet said. "I had a tutor as a girl. Mrs. Barfus taught me reading and writing and said I had a talent for expressing myself on paper. I do love to read, but I don't think I qualify to make corrections of anything you may write. However, I would like to learn, Mr. Jeffers. I would try very hard and put my heart into working for you."

"Are you the girl Leonard Chapman told me about? I think he said her name was Harriet Painter. Is that you?"

Harriet nodded.

"I will give you a chance, Miss Painter, under one condition. You ride out with these folks and get me the stories of all the families staying on this ranch. What did you say the owner's name was?"

"I don't think I did. His name is Jesse Pruitt. He's from Texas."

"Do you know Mr. Pruitt well enough to get some of this story from him as well?"

Harriet nodded. "Oh yes, Mr. Jeffers. I can get Prue to talk all about what he's done." Harriet couldn't believe it. He was going to hire her and send her back to Prue. This was like a dream come true.

"Then why don't you go change your garments, pack some things, and take these folks out to Mr. Pruitt's ranch."

Temples had climbed back onto the seat of his wagon and was listening to Jeffers. He nodded when Jeffers offered Harriet the job. "That sure would be dandy, Miss Painter. We'd be beholding to you if you could guide us out to that ranch."

Trying her best to be practical, but feeling like she was walking through a dream, Harriet stood up straight and took a deep breath. "I will be glad to work for you, Mr. Jeffers. You'll need to show me what to do and tell me everything I need to get for you to write the story. And if it's not too much trouble, could you tell me how much money I will make?"

She had to know. If it wasn't enough to pay her room and board, she didn't know if she could stand it. She wanted this position so badly, she could taste it. It meant so much, freedom from whoring, a position of respect in the community, and perhaps a way to make a living she would even enjoy.

"I imagine I could pay ten dollars a week and some of your expenses, depending, of course, on the quality of your work, how fast you learn, and how much you are able to help me."

Ten dollars. It wasn't nearly as much as she made off the men, but at the moment it seemed like a fortune. It would pay for her one room and leave her with a few dollars to spare. She stuck out her hand. Mr. Jeffers shook it. "I'll get you some pencils and a book of blank paper into which you may inscribe your notes."

"Thank you for giving me a chance," Harriet said. "I won't let you down."

13

Prue had seen McQueen line his cousin up in the sights of his Winchester. But Prue had just grabbed the outlaw by the shirt. If he dropped the rustler, the man might take off running. It all went so fast, his mind churning trying to decide what to do. He'd just made up his mind to let go of the rustler and shove Jeb out of the way when he'd seen Danny snatch the Winchester out of McQueen's hands with his cow whip. The rifle flew into the air before McQueen could fire and Jeb was safe.

Prue figured Jeb hadn't seen McQueen take aim at him. He'd been involved with catching the outlaw. The boy was pulling a pigging string, a thin strip of rawhide used to tie the legs of calves together for branding and castrating, out of his pocket, his attention focused on that. When he pulled it out, the danger was gone, and Jeb wrapped the string tightly around the rustler's wrists.

The outlaw began squalling the minute he was tied. "Please let me go, mister," the man begged. "That's Malachai McQueen over there. He and them infernal vigilantes of his already cut me like a stud colt. He'll kill me now. I know it."

"Stop yer belly achin' and hold still," Prue said, cuffing the resisting rustler on the side of his head. "I don't have no idea what yer talkin' about, but if you don't stop fightin' me, I do know you won't have to wait for Mc-Queen, I'll take care of you myself."

The rustler ceased squirming and fighting his bonds. Falling to the ground, he sat hunched over with his head in his bound hands.

McQueen and the other men walked up leading their horses. McQueen immediately recognized the captured rustler. "Damn if it ain't Jared Webb the one-cod wonder."

The sight of the bound man seemed to cheer McQueen, whose face had been mighty long, a big frown cutting across it, and eyes narrowed in hollow sockets.

"Stand up, boy," McQueen ordered Webb. "You gonna hang now. No more living life as half a man. We caught you dead to rights. Get me a rope boys, we're gonna have us a hangin'!"

Webb began blubbering, crying into his hands with his back shaking from the sobs. Prue stepped forward. He wasn't going to stand for a lynching if he could stop it. "Hey, McQueen, don't bother with the rope. I'll take Webb into Zolfo Springs. The sheriff there can hold onto him until the circuit court gets there to try him."

McQueen turned on Prue and snarled, showing long, yellow teeth. They looked like wolf fangs to Prue, and with the man's yellow eyes shooting bullets of hate at him, McQueen was a scary sight. "This man is my prisoner. These are men from my ranch. I hired them and they'll do as I say. Who the hell do you think you are anyway, Texan? You done yer duty and led us here. Now part yer cows out of that herd and git. We don't need yer opinions or yer ideas on how we Crackers take care of justice in our country." McQueen turned to the five riders behind him. "Men, string up that rustler. We done caught him red-handed. He's guilty of cow stealin'. All those who agree with me say aye."

The cowhands behind McQueen kicked the dirt and hemmed and hawed. They looked at the dead rustler laying in the dirt with half his head blown off. Ants were already starting to crawl across his face. Then they looked back at McQueen. As one they replied, "Aye, sir, let's hang him."

McQueen was in his element. He looked happy to Prue. "Let's go boys," Prue said to Danny and Jeb. "There's no way we can go against all these men. If they want to hang Webb, I guess that's what they're gonna do. We got us about twenty head of cattle to find and roundup."

"Hey, boy!" McQueen yelled to Jeb. "Where you going? I thought you were a McQueen. Where're yer balls, son? What's a matter? Got no huevos?"

Jeb turned back and stared at Malachai McQueen. He straightened his back and thrust out his chest. "We McQueens don't lynch men or presume to dispense justice without benefit of the law. This country has a system set up to deal out justice. When you choose to step above it, you become a criminal yourself. You know, Cousin Malachai, if I didn't know better, I'd say you weren't even a McQueen at all."

The sound of thundering hooves alerted the group to incoming riders. The remainder of McQueen's hands rode in ponying two horses. One had a dead outlaw strapped to the saddle, head flopping loosely against the flapping stirrup. The other carried a live outlaw with his bound hands resting on the pommel of the saddle. Half of the dog pack, including Buzzard, raced in behind the men.

The riders and dogs roared into the camp kicking up mud and dirt as the horses slid to a stop and milled restlessly. The dogs were tired, tongues dragging the ground as they panted. The ranch's three went over and collapsed under some bushes while Buzzard trotted over to Prue and began acting like a puppy wanting some attention.

"Get down," Prue ordered the big dog. Buzzard jumped up, planting his paws on Prue's chest. "Yes, I'm glad to see you." Prue ran his hand over the dog's broad forehead and rubbed his neck and chest.

McQueen strode over to Rooster, who was in charge of this second group, tilted his head back and demanded, "Where're the other one?"

"He done jack-rabbited on us, Boss," Rooster said. "We shot one and the other dummy fell off his horse. Bass there caught him when he tried to run."

Buzzard, sitting on Prue's boots, took an instant dislike to McQueen, curling his lip and growling from deep in his chest. Prue didn't think anything of it and was unprepared when the big leopard dog suddenly leaped at McQueen, grabbing his arm and tearing a huge hole in his slicker.

Quick as greased lightning, McQueen had the sawed-off out and aimed at Buzzard. Prue stepped between them, hauling on Buzzard's old leather collar. "I got him, McQueen. He's a good cow dog. Ain't no need to shoot him."

McQueen bared teeth seemed remarkably similar to Buzzard's. "If he jumps on me again, I won't hesitate."

"Fair enough," Prue replied, pulling Buzzard a short distance off. Prue ordered the dog to lay down and turned his head to hear what McQueen said to Rooster.

"Leave that piece of cow manure on his horse," McQueen ordered. "We got one of them varmints ourselves and we was just fixin' to have us a hangin'. Now we got us two to string up."

McQueen walked over to the men holding Jared Webb. "Toss another rope over that branch, boys. We'll have us a double hangin' party."

Prue didn't want to stay and watch. He knew the men would be hanged no matter if it was here or in town. Hanging was the punishment for cow stealing, especially in this part of the country where rustling had become a raging epidemic. Just the same, he'd rather not be a party to a lynching. It was wrong for one thing and when you did things like that it always seemed to come back and bite you in the ass.

"Let's go, boys," he said to Jeb and Danny.

"I can't believe yer letting McQueen hang them two," Danny said, his eyes betraying a sudden loss of faith in Prue.

"The three of us got no chance to stop him," Prue said. "I would make a stab at it if I thought we had a prayer of succeeding. I can't condone putting you two in harm's way to save a couple of rustlers who will be hanged sure as I'm standin' here whether it's done by the law or Malachai McQueen. They were caught with the goods. Now we need to get going. It's more important to me to save Jenny than to waste my time fighting McQueen for the lives of two outlaws."

Danny's eyes slowly lost their rebellious expression. "We do need to get back to the Rafter Q and save Jenny. You're right about that, Mr. Prue. I done almost forgot about her, poor little mite. But I wish we could stop McQueen from hangin' 'em. Somehow, it just don't seem right."

"I know it ain't right, son, but you got to make choices in life. Sometimes those choices are hard. It's never easy to pick who should live and who should die. And I'm choosing to save Jenny. I hate to think of that poor little girl spending another night in captivity. She's alone and probably scared to death. Now let's get going. We got cows to round up before they end up twenty miles from here in some snake and gator infested swamp."

The three of them headed for the horses. Satan had wandered off, dragging his reins through mud and manure. Prue cursed the capricious beast and wiped the muck of his reins. When they mounted their horses and were out of McQueen's earshot, Prue turned to Danny. "I saw what you did with that whip. You saved Jeb's life."

"What?" Jeb said, clearly startled.

"Danny saved your life. McQueen had you in his rifle sights and Danny snatched the gun out of his hands with that cow whip he's always popping."

Danny was the one looking surprised now. "I thought he was gonna shoot the rustler, and I was afraid he'd hit you, Mr. Prue. I couldn't see who he was aiming at."

"I could. He had that Winchester aimed right at Jeb's chest. I guess he figured it was an opportune moment to rid himself of a relative with some claim against his ranch. And he was seconds from doing it."

"It's got to be because of the ranch," Jeb said. "It's like I already told you, Mr. Prue, I was supposed to inherit half of it when my granddaddy died. My cousin must figure I'm still a threat. I just don't understand why. He said his lawyer already checked into it and I ain't got no claim."

"You never know what's going on in Malachai McQueen's head. I think he just likes killin'. Now let's get going and round up my cows. I got a lot to do and then I got to find Jenny. This day's getting over too fast. I hate to think about her alone out there for another night."

The cows turned out to be in a bunch with several of the Rafter Q cow dogs watching. Every time one of the cows would try to break out, a dog would bring it back. Buzzard raced off joyfully when he spotted his new friends. It took the three of them along with Buzzard about an hour to part out the ten cows with calves and a bull bearing the Two M brand. When they had finally been convinced to leave the safety and comfort of the herd, Danny cracking his whip along with Jeb, Prue began the task of driving them back to Prue's ranch. This bunch would make a good start to catching up his herd.

They slowly drove the cows south, following Buzzard Roost Branch. When it intersected with bigger Horse Creek, Prue stopped them. "You boys look pretty confident. Think you can take them to my ranch yourself?"

Danny's eyes narrowed. "Why?"

"I got to ride for the Rafter Q. This will be the best opportunity I'm gonna get to find Jenny. McQueen will be tied up getting that bunch of cattle back to his ranch. It should take at least two days. Even if he leaves his men to handle it, I should be able to cut out after Berryhill the next time he goes to visit Jenny. I have to go, boys. I hate to leave driving these cows up to you, but I think you'll be fine. That's if you want to work for me, Jeb."

"We can handle it, Mr. Prue," Jeb said. "And I'd rather work for you than be anywhere else on earth right now. This is what I was born and bred to. Could you tell my Ma where I'm at?"

"I'd be proud to," Prue said. "Now, you two follow the creek until you get to the ranch. Can't be more than eight or nine more miles. Lay up for the night if you have to. Light yerself a big fire to keep off the wolves and other varmints. One of you watch cows and the other one can catch some sleep. Take old Buzzard with you. He seems to know more than all of us how to manage these critters. I wish I'd had him out in Texas."

"Be careful, Prue," Danny said. "I sure wish I could go with you."

"Stay at the ranch. I should be there tomorrow or the next day depending on if I find Jenny." Prue tipped his hat to the boys, turned the horse, and galloped off. Buzzard didn't even try to follow. He knew his place was with the cows.

Prue rode hard, pushing Satan who was tired and cranky. His being tired was really a blessing because he was too worn out to take his irritation out on Prue. A fresh, cranky Satan was something indeed.

It was after dark before Prue reached the Rafter Q. The place was quiet. Prue tied Satan to a tree branch three feet over the horse's head. "Get out of that," he muttered as he headed for the barn, bent low to conceal himself in the shadows.

The barn was dark. The yellow stud and Rooster's roan were still gone. There were several stalled horses and only two empty stalls. Prue hoped that meant Berryhill was here.

He left the barn and made his way toward the two houses he knew housed Rooster and Berryhill. One was lit. He slid around behind it keeping close to the building. It was a two-room cabin of cypress logs set high. It had a front porch and an outhouse. There were two windows in front and two in the back.

Prue pressed himself against the logs next to a window and risked a look inside. Berryhill was sitting at a rough-hewn table on a bench with an earthenware jug in front of him and a gray tin mug. He took a swig out of the mug and slammed it on the table.

Prue ducked out of sight. It looked like Berryhill was drinking. Good, he hoped the man got good and drunk. Hurrying back to his horse, Prue quickly made a plan. Berryhill was either drinking himself into a coma so he could sleep or fortifying his nerve with drink so he could go out to the cabin in the dark and take care of Jenny.

Searching in his saddle pockets, Prue found a set of hobbles, clapped them on Satan and took off the horse's bridle. He hung it on a tree branch and let the horse go so he could graze. Part of Satan's grumpiness had to do with being hungry.

With the horse taken care of, Prue took his one remaining blanket out of his bedroll and headed back to watch Berryhill's cabin. The light was still lit, and when he checked, he saw Berryhill sleeping with his head on his hands at the table. Prue took the blanket, wrapped himself in it, and put his back to a tree. From his position, he could watch for Berryhill to come out of the cabin. When the man put in an appearance, Prue would follow him to Jenny.

14

Harriet rode the mustang mare Prue gave her, enjoying the day and her newfound freedom. She felt as though she didn't have a care in the world. She still worried about Jenny, but Prue would find her. Prue possessed an ability to get things accomplished. He had energy and integrity.

Harriet had complete faith in the Texan. He seemed so solid to her, a comforting presence in her life that had never been there before. He was someone she could rely on. Danny had been her only comfort for years, but he was also a huge responsibility. She had an image of Prue in her mind. When she was feeling scared or uneasy, she would look at that image and feel the warmth and solidity he projected. His presence inside her gave her courage to reach beyond her usual comfort level and try new things.

Her new friends, the Temples, drove their mules pulling the loaded wagon behind her. They crossed the bridge out of Arcadia three hours ago and followed the course of the creek. The going was rough. It started to rain again and the trail, really little more than a deer trail, was mired in mud. It was a good thing the Temples had four mules pulling their heavily loaded wagon. The large, tan-colored beasts were ornery, but strong, and Mr. Temples was a good man with mules.

When Harriet looked behind her to make sure the wagon was close, she saw Mr. Temples drive it into what looked to be only a puddle but proved to be a deep pocket of mud. The mules strained in their harnesses. Temples cracked his whip and called to the mules. "Hey mules, get up there mules."

The mules moved the wagon a foot, but that foot actually put them deeper in the mud. Harriet climbed off her horse to help. Temples ran to the mules' heads while his wife picked up the reins. Temples grabbed the lead mule's headstall and pulled, trying to turn the mules to the left and onto some drier land. The big animals strained. The wagon rocked but went no further.

"Get them out of their harnesses," Harriet said. "Are they broke to ride?"

Temples wiped clumps of thick black mud off his face with a red handkerchief, clearing it out of his eyes. His clothes were covered. "Yeah, they ride fine. But I don't want to leave the wagon. It's got everything we own on it."

Harriet studied the landmarks she remembered and figured they were only two miles from Prue's ranch. The sun was setting, the clouds in the western sky deep purple. Streaks of sunshine broke through in places creating an eerie twilight.

"It's going to be dark soon. I can ride hard to the ranch and be there in half an hour, before dark, but it would take me some time to get a crew together to come pull this wagon out of the muck. You're gonna need more horses or maybe a couple of oxen. There's man out there with a team of them. I don't think we can pull this wagon free of the mud in the dark, and we need to get your wife and children somewhere safe for the night."

Temples rubbed his face with his left hand and looked up at his wife sitting on the wagon seat. She nodded. "I'll send Mrs. Temples and the children with you and I'll stay here with the wagon."

Harriet nodded. That seemed like a good idea to her. Temples quickly dropped the trace chains and pulled all four mules out from between the shafts. Stripping off their harnesses, he left bridles and blinkers on two of the mules. His wife climbed down, and he threw her up on one of the mules. Then he placed his little daughter in front of her. Harriet figured his oldest boy was at least ten. When Temples put the boy on the mule's back, the kid gathered his reins as though he knew what he was doing. Temples tossed the youngest boy, a strapping child of what Harriet thought might be about eight, up behind his older son John.

"John, I'm putting you in charge of Ann, your little brother, and your ma," Temples said. "Buck here will get you wherever you need to go and Molly Mule will follow him."

"I know, Pa," the boy said, as he straightened his back. "You can trust me to take care of them. I'll be back in the morning to help get that wagon out of the mud."

Harriet smiled. John sat tall, but his dangling legs didn't even reach past the sides of the draft mule. He had taken on the role of a man and she could see the pride in Temples's face.

"Let's get going. It's almost dark," she said, urging her mare forward. "I'll be back at first light for you, Mr. Temples," she called over her shoulder.

Horace Temples stood beside his wagon holding the lines of his two remaining mules. The man didn't wave or smile. He just watched them ride into the gathering dusk.

Mrs. Temples was quiet during the ride. Other than to tell Harriet to call her Maggie, she said nothing. The mules walked along willingly behind her mare, but they tended to be slower than her mare who stepped out at the walk. It was about dark when they rode into the barnyard of Prue's ranch.

Harriet spotted Boarhog feeding the longhorn bull. He was tossing some grass hay into the bull's pen as they rode up to the barn.

When he saw her, his eyebrows rose to his hairline. "Lord have mercy on my poor pitiful soul," he moaned when he saw her and the mules. "What you done dragged to Mr. Prue's ranch now?"

Harriet jumped off her mare and walked to the pen leading the horse behind her by its reins. "I found some more settlers displaced by the vigilantes, Boarhog. This is Mrs. Temples and her children. Her husband stayed behind with their wagon. It's stuck in the mud up the trail a ways."

"Don't tell me, it's stuck because it's loaded to the top and all they had to pull it was two mules."

"No, they had four mules," Harriet replied smartly.

"Why you bringin' more of these folks out here, Missy Harry? Ain't we got enough already?"

"Prue said he thought more displaced settlers would help draw the attention of the vigilantes, Boarhog. So I brought more. Besides these folks have nowhere else to go. They've been living out of their wagon for two weeks. And there are children involved. I had to help."

"Course you did," he mumbled. "Well I cain't go out there and haul their wagon out the mud till mornin'. Take the lady and the childrens up to the house and bed them down there."

Harriet smiled. He was grumpy, but beneath his rough exterior was a vast wealth of kindness and a big heart. "I knew we couldn't get the wagon until morning. It's pretty stuck."

"Over the axels?"

"Oh, yes, I'm afraid so."

Harriet just managed to get Maggie Temples and her children comfortable when she heard the crack of whips and the yipping of cowhands pushing cattle. Rushing out of the house, she was just in time to see a harassed Boarhog opening the gate to the cowpens and a small herd of cattle running into them pushed by her brother and a boy she'd never seen before. She saw Buzzard and she saw Danny but no Prue. Where was he?

Glancing back into Prue's cabin, she saw Maggie covering little Ann up and the two boys rolling out bedding for their own beds. "I'll be right back," she said to Maggie. "My brother just rode in and I hope Mr. Pruitt is with them."

Maggie nodded, but didn't seem to care about anything beyond her children. Harriet could understand that. They were all probably exhausted as well. It had been a long day and a long time since the woman had a place to rest.

Grabbing a jacket and shrugging it on over her boys' shirt and pants, she rushed out to the cowpens. It seemed to her wearing boys' clothing had become the norm instead of the strange. When she got to the pens, Danny dropped out of the saddle. As soon as his feet hit the ground, Harriet grabbed him and hugged him hard.

"Stop it, Harry, everyone will see," he said, pushing her off and holding her at arm's length.

"I'm so sorry," Harriet said smiling. "I guess you've become too great and important to hug your sister."

"It ain't that, Harry. It's just my friend might see."

So Danny was becoming a man and embarrassed by emotion, afraid he might seem weak in the eyes of his new friend. "Where is Prue, Danny, and who is this boy you've brought here?"

"He's a friend of mine and Mr. Prue's. I ain't got time to talk to you now, Harry. I got things to do."

"I see," Harriet said. "But I have so many questions. I'll go up to the house and leave you be, but you tell me where Prue is first."

"He's gone to find Jenny. I hope he done found her already. We left him earlier today. It took us all this time to drive these ornery critters ten mile. Thank the Lord we had that dog. He knows more than the pair of us put together about pushing cows."

Harriet had to smile at that comment. All she'd heard for months was how badly Danny wanted to be a cowman. Now he had a job working cattle and just listen to him talk.

"I hope Prue finds Jenny as well. You must have a lot to tell me about your adventures. Come up to the house as soon as you unsaddle that horse and talk to me. Don't make me come find you."

"I will, Harry. Now leave me be and let me do my job."

Prue waited in the dark for Berryhill to come out of the cabin and do something, anything. But all Berryhill did for five hours was snore away on the top of his table. Prue dozed in his position, waking up to check on Berryhill occasionally and then going off in another doze.

The first rays of the sun were beginning to light the eastern sky when Pelo Berryhill shook his head and stood up. Stiff and sore from hours with his head on the table, Berryhill stretched and rubbed his back. Prue folded his blanket and went to check on his horse. Hobbled, Satan hadn't gone far. He'd found a good patch of grass a short distance from where Prue left him and was grazing.

Prue retied his blanket on the back of his saddle inside his bedroll and took off his hat. He rubbed his hands through his matted hair and shot a short prayer off to God that soon he would find Jenny.

He took the hobbles off Satan and tied him to an overhead branch. When he got back to his position outside Berryhill's cabin, he saw Berryhill putting his hat on and getting ready to leave. As quietly as possible, Prue slipped back and untied Satan. He figured Berryhill would have to go up to the kitchen and get food for the girl, then saddle up. At the thought of food, Prue's stomach rumbled. That bacon sandwich he'd eaten on the drive yesterday seemed a long time ago.

Prue moved Satan behind the tree and hunkered down to wait. It didn't take Berryhill long. From his position, Prue could just make out the barn. When he saw Berryhill come out, mount up and head into the woods, he climbed aboard Satan. For once, the ornery animal behaved. He must be tired, Prue thought, or this uncharacteristic show of good nature would never have happened. But sometimes animals sensed the importance of a situation. Maybe Satan knew he needed to behave because it was important. Naah, he was just tired.

Berryhill took off toward the south and the river at a trot. When Berryhill turned even more to the south, Prue began recognizing landmarks. A stand of thick cypress, willows, and water oaks marked the beginning of a swamp. Berryhill turned, looked once behind him, and disappeared down a narrow deer trail into the woods. Luckily, Prue saw the man stop. He quickly moved Satan into some thick brush and thanked the Lord for making Satan black and not a paint horse or a white horse. He could never understand the Indians' love of painted and white animals. They made you into a sitting duck.

Prue held back and waited until Berryhill was out of sight, then he dismounted and led Satan onto the trail. There was something very familiar about this area, but Prue couldn't remember ever being here. He felt like he should know where he was.

The trail led deep into the swamp. Pools of black water crossed the trail. The ground was spongy under Prue's boots, water seeping into his tracks.

The smell of rotting vegetation and damp earth competed with the scents of flowers and green plants and leaves. Several times Prue had to follow Berryhill's fresh tracks as they meandered around muddy spots or avoided the deeper pools of water.

Sunlight streaming through the trees announced a clearing up ahead. Just as Prue was thinking he better look for some cover, a loud crash followed by a string of curses stopped him in his tracks. Feeling very exposed on the trail, Prue moved into the cypress, wading into water, pulling a very reluctant horse behind.

Doing his best to be silent, Prue led stomping, splashing Satan through the shallow water and muck, deep into the swamp. He was looking for a place to leave the horse, somewhere the animal wouldn't get snake bit or eaten by a dang gator. As it was, the pair of them were providing a feast for a bunch of hungry skeeters. He kept making note of landmarks, weird trees, big rocks, or an extra-large cypress knee. It would be so easy to get lost in this mess. It was gloomy as a dungeon with the trees completely covering the sky.

Luck saved him from running slap into Berryhill. He tripped over a tree root under the water and fell. When he looked up, Berryhill was storming around the outside of a cypress shack, little more than a lean-to, heading straight in Prue's direction. The shake roof of the shack was covered with moss and leaves and collapsed on one side. The door looked newly repaired. It hung open and Prue couldn't see inside, it was too dark.

Berryhill was frantic. Prue could hear him calling. "Jenny, Jenny girl where are you? Come back. Uncle Pelo has some grub for you. Cook sent you some cakes. Jenny!"

Prue stopped dead in his tracks. His breath caught in his chest and his heart beat rapidly. He was afraid Berryhill would see him and horrified to learn Jenny was missing. He rapidly backtracked into the depths of the swamp. Once he felt safely hidden, he stopped and looked around to take note of his surroundings again. His boots were wet, but his feet were thankfully dry. His pants were soaked and his leather chaps were wet to his knees. It was a good thing he had on these fancy Mexican boots. They came up over his knees, and might save his life if he stepped on a snake.

A small hammock off to his left offered some dry land. He sloshed over to it and towed his horse up the small rise. At the top, he found a tree and tied Satan. Then he headed back to the cabin. If Jenny had escaped, she could be anywhere, but most likely she was dead. He would just have to accept he was too late. This swamp was filled with snakes, gators, panthers, bogs, and quicksand. There was no way a little girl could make her way out of here alone.

Berryhill's frantic voice echoed through the thick woods and off the water. He kept calling for Jenny over and over. Prue took the opportunity to slip unnoticed up to the cabin and inside. His lip curled when he saw the awful conditions inside the shack. There was a small bed tucked next to the back wall. The floor had been swept clean of debris, leaves, and filth, but the pile of sweepings still remained in a corner. Uneaten food had collected a pile of interesting bugs. Enormous palmetto bugs climbed across a chunk of cornbread along with ants and smaller roaches and beetles. Prue shivered. With the door closed, it would be dark as night in here.

When Prue lifted the girl's blanket, a small white and black feather dropped out of the blankets. Prue picked it up and turned it over and over in his fingers. Why was an owl feather important and what was it doing here? He took off his hat and tucked the feather into his hatband, then slid back out into the clearing.

Far off in the distance, Prue could still hear Berryhill crashing around and calling for Jenny. Prue walked all the way around the cabin looking for footprints. He found Berryhill's big clodhoppers all over the clearing but found one print he couldn't identify. If he hadn't known better he would have thought it was an Indian moccasin. He stopped. There was one person he knew that wore moccasins.

Prue stood up and took another look at his surroundings. Could it be? Was this the back way into Moccasin Bob's swamp home? Walking carefully, bent low, Prue circled the clearing and the cabin. It took doing it twice, but he found what he was looking for. Behind the cabin was another moccasin print leading directly into a clump of palmettos and willow saplings. Prue pushed them aside and found a game trail leading south, deeper into the swamp.

A tiny flicker of hope grew in Prue's chest. Bob's moonshining operation had to be around here somewhere. Moccasin Wallow must form out of all this water moving south. Maybe Bob had found Jenny. Maybe she was safe.

⑮

Malachai McQueen was angry and upset. Even hanging Jared Webb didn't improve his mood. Watching the outlaw take his last breath should have put him in a jolly frame of mind as it usually did. Instead, he felt like he was falling deeper and deeper into a dark hole from which he could not escape.

It all had to do with Aunt Thelma and that kid, Jeb, and the Texan, too. Jeb rode off with the Texan, choosing a stranger over his own kin. It wasn't right. Ever since he'd accidentally killed Elva, his world had spiraled down and down and down. Malachai just wanted to regain control. There had to be a way.

Riding well out in front of the cattle, Malachai headed for home. Rooster and the men would bring his cows and the others, the cows with different brands and earmarks, home. There, the men could sort out the ones belonging to cowmen he knew and return them. The others would get their brands changed to the Rafter Q and maybe get their ears whacked off. Finders' keepers, that's what he always said.

Thinking about the one hundred or so head he'd just been gifted, Malachai smiled for the first time. Maybe things weren't so bad after all. Aunt Thelma and her relatives could be dealt with, harshly if necessary.

Maybe a raid by the vigilance committee would cheer him up. They hadn't rousted any sodbusters for over a week. When he got home he'd send out a message calling for a meeting.

Putting these positive thoughts into his head and thinking about all his blessings cheered him up. And after all, he had Jenny. Sweet little Jenny was out of the hands of people who could harm him and safely tucked away. He'd keep her hidden in that swamp for a month or so, until the old battle-ax was out of his house and back in Tampa where she belonged, taking her baggage with her. After she was gone, he might bring Jenny to the house. Why not? He could tell the men she was the daughter of one of his friends who had died. That would work. Then he would have Jenny with him all the time.

Thinking about bringing Jenny to his home buoyed his spirits so much, he started whistling. Things weren't so bad after all.

When he rode into the Rafter Q, he was feeling very chipper. He put his horse up on his own since Rooster and the men were some hours behind. Then he went looking for Berryhill. He wanted the man to ride out and call a meeting of the vigilantes. Might as well do that right away. Maybe there was some news about some squatters or a new family of settlers, and he wanted to share his news of the rustlers he hanged.

He looked for Berryhill in his cabin, in the kitchen, and in the bunkhouse. Berryhill was not on the property. He checked the barn and found Berryhill's old buckskin gelding missing. Grinding his teeth, Malachai cursed the sergeant. The man should have finished taking food to Jenny by dinnertime. He better not have ridden into Arcadia to see that whore.

Stomping up to the house, he threw himself into his chair. Staring out from under brooding brows, he saw Clara sitting on the settee stitching something. The woman was always sewing. She must have piles of samplers and cross-stitch projects piled up somewhere.

He rang the bell for the maid and got the cook. "Where's Gem?" Malachai snarled.

"Gem took sick. She tole me if you was to ring, I should answer it."

The cook was a fat black woman, probably bigger than one of his steers. But she cooked like a dream, food Malachai liked. The cook's name was Ruby and she was Gem's sister. Getting good help out here in the sticks was not easy. Reconsidering his harsh tone, Mal spoke nicely to her. "I'm sorry if I was rude. I'm tired and hungry. Can you fix me a plate of something good? You know how much I like yer fried chicken."

Ruby had her hands on her massive hips with a frown creasing her face. When he told her he liked her food, a slow smile started. "I got some cold chicken in the kitchen right now left over from supper, Mr. Malachai. You want some greens and some taters with it?"

Malachai closed his eyes. "Yes, thank you. And do you have some fresh bread?"

"Course I do. Who you think runnin' dat kitchen? I always got fresh bread."

She turned around quickly for a woman of her bulk, creating a breeze that ruffled Mal's hair as she swished out of the room.

Mal went into the dining room to eat. In minutes Ruby set a plate overflowing with food in front of him. She slipped between the table and the sideboard and poured him a glass of white wine. Even his servants knew white wine went with chicken.

The sun was setting. Bright light entered the house from the western windows. Motes of dust danced in the light. Mal thought he needed to get on Gem about dusting when she was well enough.

The fried chicken was golden brown with a thick crunchy crust. Mal bit into a thigh, his favorite piece, and groaned. Polishing off the rest of the thigh with gusto, Mal followed the chicken with heaping forkfuls of greens and mashed potatoes and big bites of fresh bread.

"You never used to eat chicken when you was a boy," Aunt Thelma said from the doorway to the sitting room.

Hearing her voice behind him almost caused Mal to choke. He swallowed quickly and swigged half his glass of wine. "People change," he mumbled.

"You'd always tell everyone who would listen that chickens were busy little birds that laid eggs and never did no harm to nobody. That's what you used to say. When you were real little, you'd chase them all over the yard, catch one, you was a fast little dickens, and bury yer face in its feathers. We ate chicken here at least two times the week, and you never touched a bite of it."

Mal's mean mood was getting worse. He tossed down the rest of his glass of wine. "I must have been a boring little sissy boy. As you can see, I've changed. I love to eat chicken. Fried chicken has to be my favorite food."

To illustrate his point, he tore a huge mouthful off the thigh and smiled around it at Aunt Thelma, chewing with his mouth wide open.

She snorted and whirled around, stomping back into the parlor where no doubt Clara was still cross stitching.

Mal was just starting on his third thigh when he was startled by hoof beats pounding right up to his front porch.

Pushing back his chair so forcefully it fell over backwards, anger swelled Malachai's chest. Nobody, and he meant nobody, rode up to his front porch. They stopped at the barn. His front yard was raked to perfection every day. There were plants and shrubs out there he cherished.

Mal strode to the front door and yanked it open. Berryhill stood on the porch, his eyes wide with horror or fright or both, his Rebel cap in his hands. The man's face was ashen under his tan. Mal forgot to be angry about Berryhill's transgressions against the raked yard. He'd never seen the sergeant look like this.

"What's wrong Sergeant? Why'd you ride across my yard?"

"It's the little girl, Boss. Jenny's gone. I looked all day and didn't find a thing. She must have drowned in a pond or got ate by a gator."

Mal backed up rapidly, his hand on his chest. He felt like his heart was going to explode. Jenny couldn't be gone. She was all he had left of Elva. In his mind, Jenny had already taken Elva's place. He lunged forward, grabbing Berryhill by the throat, choking the big man and screaming. "No, she's not gone. She's still out there. She has to be. You left her, didn't you?" He shook Berryhill hard. "Didn't you?"

"No, Boss, I swear, I been lookin' fer her all damn day. She just up and disappeared."

Pain went shooting through Mal's head. He closed his eyes and released Berryhill's throat. "She can't be gone," he said, his voice a whisper. "She's too little to run into the swamp. She'd be too scared."

"I know, Boss, I know. That's what I thought. I looked and looked fer her. I been all over that swamp. All I found after wading through water and muck and dodging snakes and gators all damn day was a still where someone's cookin' up corn squeezins."

Hope blossomed in Mal's breast.

"You found a still? Is someone using it?"

"It looked in pretty good shape. It ain't been used in a couple a months, though, probably cause corn-growin' season is over."

"Why didn't you check it out better? There has to be a path leadin' somewhere. Whoever tends the still don't just fall out of the friggin' sky."

"It was gettin' dark. There was no way I could follow any trail in that swamp at night. There ain't hardly no light gettin' through the trees during the day. At night, it's like the bottom of a deep hole. I figured you and me would go back there in the morning time and look for a trail."

Mal sat down on a bench placed in the hallway for visitors. He put his hands on his face, fingers digging into his flesh, and closed his eyes again. All he could see when his eyes were closed were Elva's beautiful eyes. They were filled with reproach and stared at him accusingly. "I'm so sorry, Elva. I'll find her, I swear."

"Who you talkin' to, Boss?"

"Myself, who the frig do you think I'm talkin' to? Ain't none of yer damn business anyway. We'll head out at first light and we'll find Jenny." He stood up and glared at Berryhill. "You better hope we find her."

Berryhill backed down the steps. "I do, Boss, you know I do."

Harriet sat at the kitchen table in Prue's small unfinished cabin and sucked the tip of her pencil. The lead had just broken. She needed a knife to sharpen it.

She had one story about the Starlings finished and another about Joseph and Cora Fountain almost done. When she read over the Fountains' story it made her tear up. The couple loved each other. They were devoted to having a life together and raising their unborn child. The vigilantes had destroyed all their dreams, taken all they owned, and pounded it into dust.

The door slammed. Harriet looked up as Danny walked over to her chair. "Me and Jeb are heading out in the morning. We got to find Mr. Prue and help him. Can't leave him out there alone, not with that McQueen son of a buck after him. I got to help him find Jenny."

"You sure have taken a liking to Prue," Harriet said.

"He's a real cowhand, Harry," Danny said, pulling out another chair and sitting down. "You should a seen him catch that outlaw. He fought to save McQueen from lynching him, too, but he had to leave them two rustlers to their fate. He explained it to me. It was either save the rustlers, and they would a been hanged later anyway, or find Jenny."

"I'm glad you like him," Harry said. "Hey, you still got your knife? I need it."

Danny pulled the knife out of the sheath strapped to his right calf and handed it to Harriet. "Be careful. It's sharp."

"I know," she said. "You always did keep it that way. Having it saved my life when that man got the jump on us outside of Jacksonville. I was sorry you had to use it and all, but glad you did."

"He would have stole all our money and killed us dead fer sure," Danny said. "That was the last time we both fell asleep at the same time."

"Live and learn, huh, little brother? Do you like this Jeb boy?"

"I like him fine, Harry. When we was fightin' the outlaws, McQueen tried to shoot him. I stopped him with my whip. Snatched his Winchester right out of his gun hand before he could shoot. I thought he was after Mr. Prue. I saw my duty and I done it."

"I'm glad you saved him. I think he will be a good friend to you. Maybe for life."

Harriet handed the knife back to Danny. He returned it to its sheath, stood up, and pushed the chair back under the table.

"Well, Harry, I'm gonna turn in. I got my bedroll spread over by the Starling's fire. Jeb's over there with me."

"They sure have a couple of pretty daughters," Harriet teased.

"Shucks," Danny's face flamed as red as his hair. "It ain't the girls. Mrs. Starling cooks the best grub I ever ate."

Harriet put her pencil down and stood up. "Are you too big a man to give your sister a hug before you go?"

Danny stepped over and hugged her hard. "I'm proud of you, Harry. I'm proud you got yourself another job and quit . . . you know, quit."

Harriet smoothed his wild hair. "I understand, Danny. I never meant to hurt you. It seemed like the thing to do and back then I really didn't care. It didn't seem all that bad, not after what Uncle Buford done to me. Now, it's like I'm a different person. I can't feel sorry for what I did. It fed us for over a year. But Prue made me see it ain't no way for me to carry on my life."

Danny hugged her again. "I love you, Harry. One day I'm gonna go back and get Uncle Buford for what he done."

"It ain't necessary," Harriet told him. "What's passed is gone and can't never change. If we go back, it will be to see Mama. I know she wasn't the best mother to either of us, but after Pa died and she had to take care of us on her own, it was probably real hard. I know. She was scared of her brother. He was a lot older than her and held all our lives in his hands. She had to look the other way, I guess. Though, to be sure, she was always so tired working eighteen hours a day in the bakery, maybe she didn't know what he was doing to me. I'd like to think that was it. Now you be careful out there, you hear? And bring Prue and Jenny home with you."

At first light, Danny and Jeb saddled up and headed back to the Rafter Q. The two of them rode through the early morning following Horse Creek as it meandered north then curved toward the east.

Thick fog hung over the land. Danny ran right up on a spooky old cow and calf and never saw them until he was two feet away. Steam rose off the creek adding to the moisture and fog. Neither one of them said anything. Last night, they had had a fine old time with Starling's daughters, eating good grub and singing songs around the campfire.

Danny started thinking about Prue as he rode. He liked the man and was kind of hoping Prue and Harry would marry up. Not that either of them gave any sign of being in love or of having more than a liking for one another. It was just a feeling Danny got when he saw the two of them together, kind of started him thinking about them as a couple. Danny thought it would be a good thing. He'd love to say Jesse Pruitt was his brother.

Harry had a tough time back in Savannah, living with Uncle Buford. Danny had been too young to understand any of it. And when they first got to Arcadia, he was still a kid. At first he didn't know or comprehend

what Harry did to pay for their room and board. It never occurred to him
to ask or wonder about it. The room was paid for and every morning Harry
gave him lessons in reading and writing and doing sums. He didn't like the
learning part, but reasoned it was better for a man to know as much as he
could. It wasn't a good thing to have people around that knew more than
you, especially when you were a man.

When Harry's visitors would come around, she would give him some
money and tell him to go to the store and buy himself some stick candy. He
sure loved peppermint sticks, and so did Harry.

And for a long time, he hadn't understood why Harry hated Uncle Buford so much. He remembered the first time he'd become aware of what
Harry did to earn money. At the same time, he'd figured out why Uncle
Buford made her cry. When they lived in his uncle's house, she would come
to him in the mornings and cry in his arms. When he would ask her what
was wrong, she would dry her eyes on her nightgown and say it was nothing,
just a girl thing.

It hadn't been that long ago, just about when he turned fourteen, he
figured out what she was doing. He'd overheard a man staying in the boardinghouse tell another man that Harriet Painter was a fine looking whore
and he just might get himself some of that later on in the evening. Danny
knew what the word whore meant and he'd been shocked. But it all made
sense. Suddenly he understood why he couldn't go to her room when she
had guests and why she had so many strange men calling on her.

Learning about it like that had made him mad at first. How could she
do such a thing? He'd stormed around the town, stealing a horse and riding hard across the Arcadia Bridge and out into the prairie. The hard ride
cleared his head. He realized she'd done it for him, to take care of him.
For a few terrible moments, he'd wanted to ride that horse right off the
bridge into the water. Then Harry would be free of the responsibility he
presented. He was a burden, forcing her to have sex with strangers. But he
knew how much his dying would hurt her and she'd suffered enough.

He'd ridden back to town, returned the horse, and rushed home to try to
talk Harry into quitting. He'd cried with his head in her lap and begged her
to stop. Harry told him a little about what Uncle Buford had done to her.
How it didn't matter if she took men to bed with her, she was ruined as a
woman anyway. She'd said after Uncle Buford, she could never give herself
as a virgin wife to any man, so what difference did it make if she earned
money in this way?

Danny was stricken to his soul by what she told him. How could he have
missed it? How could he have lived there with his uncle and not known that

she was suffering? Tormented, he promised her he would get revenge for the wrongs against her childhood by Uncle Buford. Harry held him as they both cried and then dried their tears and swore she would quit whoring as soon as she could find another way to pay their bills. Danny felt sick over it, trying to put on a happy face for her because he knew there was no stopping Harry when she was set on a course.

That was when he'd decided to become a cow hunter. He figured if he earned enough, he could take care of Harry the way she cared for him all those years. And that was when he decided one day, no matter what Harry said, he was gonna have to take a trip to Savannah and give Uncle Buford exactly what he deserved for hurting Harry. A man could only live with so much on his conscience.

Danny and Jeb rode out together like old friends. The day was clear and crisp after the recent rain. The fog slowly cleared as the sun warmed everything. It was like riding through a magical world and Danny enjoyed every minute. He put his dark thoughts behind him. This was the life he'd always wanted.

"Ain't this great?" Danny said to Jeb.

"It sure is," Jeb said. "Being a cow hunter is all I ever wanted to do in my whole life. Between my ma and granny, I been kept in the house and forced to go to school. They only let me out after I done all my lessons. I never wanted book learnin'. I just want to ride the open prairie under the blue sky, push cows, and work beside other cowhands."

"How'd you get them to bring you to the Rafter Q?"

"I'm finally old enough to make them two listen to me. Granny said this was supposed to be half mine, so I told her I wanted to come here and take it up. Now Granny's got herself a tidy little ranch up near Tampa. But she wouldn't let me work it until I turned fourteen and then I had Jasper Collins watchin' everything I did. The man stuck closer to me than a tick on a hound. He taught me some, how to ride, how to crack a whip and how to push cows, where to be to keep them together, where not to be. But he always made me stay behind, out of the way. I never had no fun at all. And he never let any of the other hands talk to me. Granny said they was all ignorant sons a bitches and I was the boss's grandson."

"Got any ideas about how we can find Mr. Prue?" Danny said. "The only thing I can think of is we better start lookin' at the Rafter Q. Otherwise I have no idea of where to start lookin' fer him. He's out there following Sergeant Berryhill to find Jenny and there's no way we can figure out where he went unless we wait until the sergeant heads out and follow him, too."

"Then that's what we'll do. We'll watch Berryhill and wait until he rides out with supplies for the girl, and head out behind him. That sounds like just about the only plan we got."

"You got any idea what we should do when we get back to the ranch? Prue said yer cousin tried to shoot you and it is his place. If we're gonna follow Berryhill, we need to hole up somewhere until morning and we might want to consider stayin' someplace besides the Rafter Q."

"I know Cousin Malachai doesn't like me but Granny and I have every right to be at the Rafter Q whether he likes me or not. I can't imagine him trying to kill me with Granny and Ma around. He ain't that dumb. And I'm gonna need to tell Granny about him trying to shoot me out there on the prairie."

"You really think it's a good idea to tell yer grandmother yer cousin tried to murder you? What can she do? Won't it just get her all upset and cryin'? I hate it when a woman cries. Rips me up inside."

"Granny is a knowin' one, she is. She won't get upset and she'll know what we should do. Ma ain't good at much besides sewing and cookin'. She likes cookin' but Granny never lets her. Granny says it's beneath Ma to cook for herself. When Granny ain't lookin', Ma sneaks down to the kitchen and bakes pies and cakes. I love her, but she's as useless as tits on a boar when you got any kind of problems. Granny will know what we should do. We'll tell her about the little girl, too."

Danny shook his head and admired the beauty of the morning. The birds were singing and in the distance he could hear a bull gator grunting. Pretty soon, from what he'd heard, the male gators would be roaming the countryside looking for mates.

No, he wasn't putting too much hope in an old lady helping them find Jenny. But maybe she could keep McQueen from killin' Jeb. The best thing she could probably do for his friend was haul him straight back to Tampa because Malachai McQueen was a very bad man. Danny had no doubts about that at all.

16

After seeing the path leading into the brush and the moccasin track, Prue decided to ride. It could take him hours following the trail and the tracks through the swamp. And Prue had no doubt it would be a bitch to follow. Moccasin Bob was a devious character and his still was out here somewhere. Protecting it would be a priority, which meant it would be hidden and the paths to it from Bob's homestead virtually invisible.

Backtracking across the front of the cabin, he listened and heard Berryhill screaming his guts out for Jenny deep in the swamp. That was definitely not the way to go. Wading back to the hammock where he'd left Satan, he found the horse eating Spanish moss off the tree. A long streamer of the gray stuff was tangled in his bit.

"All you think about is yer stomach," Prue said, snatching the rope off the tree. The horse nodded his head, shaking the moss out of his forelock.

Prue mounted Satan and rode out of the swamp. When he reached dry land, he took off at a gallop, heading southwest. Riding Satan as hard as he dared, he skirted the swamp, hoping he was headed in the right direction. His stomach rumbled and growled and he began to envy Satan his moss.

Familiar landmarks cheered Prue and gave him some hope. Moccasin Wallow appeared close to the track Prue followed. It flowed through a cut filled with scrub oaks, thick willows, briars, and no doubt, snakes. Bob lived in there where the wallow came to an end. Maybe the old man found Jenny. It was his only hope, and he'd staked everything on that hope.

When he reached the cart path leading down to Bob's place, his stomach began knotting. What if he was wrong? What would he do then? And where else could Jenny be? Dead in that swamp was the only other possibility. And he didn't want to think about that.

Satan sensed Bob's place and the other horses and livestock before Prue knew they were getting close. He didn't have to urge the stallion into a trot. The horse picked up his pace as food and equine companionship beckoned. Prue could just make out the barn when Bob stepped in front of him with a double-barreled shotgun. Both hammers back, it rested across his folded arms.

Bob grabbed Satan's reins and pulled him up. "I thought you'd never get here. I swear to God I thought I was gonna have to load the little filly up and come get you myself. Where you been, boy? What in the hell is going on?"

Relief flooded Prue. His legs wobbled as he tumbled off Satan and hugged the old man, hanging on with his arms around Bob's neck. "You have her here? Oh my God, I was never so glad to see a moccasin print in my life as when I saw yours at the edge of the clearing. I almost dropped to my knees and cried then and there. And the owl feather, did you leave that for me?"

"Get off me, boy. What in tarnation's the matter with you? I ain't no woman. Quit yer huggin' on me. This old gun could go off at any moment."

Bob pushed Prue off and carefully dropped the hammers on the shotgun. "Almost got yer stupid self blowed to smithereens. Of course, I left the feather. Did you think it blowed in the winder?"

Prue started laughing. He laughed so hard he couldn't stop. He had to bend over and grab his side, it hurt so bad.

Bob took Satan's reins and began leading the horse to the barn. "Now I knowed you done lost yer mind. Go say hello to the princess. She's had a pretty rough time."

The relief Prue felt when he realized Jenny was safe was so intense, he could barely walk. He tottered to Bob's cabin and opened the door. The stench was familiar and comforting. Jenny was sitting on Bob's bed playing with her fluffy cat, Sibby. When she saw him, she squealed, threw it off her lap, and ran toward him. "Mr. Prue, Mr. Prue, Moccasin Bob saved me. He sneaked me away from that dreadful cabin and brought me here. And now you're here, too. Ain't it wonderful? I'm so glad to see you."

Tears rolled down her emaciated face. Prue grabbed her up and hugged her close, right to his heart. She was so thin and he was so glad to see her. He buried his face in her loose hair and cried like a child. "Jenny, baby, I was so worried. Harriet is worried. I thought I'd never see you again."

He held her out so he could look at her. "Didn't they feed you?"

She squirmed out of his embrace, landed on the floor, and smoothed the wrinkles in her dress. "They tried to. I wouldn't have none of it. That evil man sent some big fat guy he called Sergeant out to bring me food. I was glad it was him and not Uncle Mal." She shivered. "I don't ever want to see Uncle Mal again."

"Were you scared, darlin'?" Prue led her back to Bob's bed and sat down beside her. The insulted cat stopped licking her fur and returned to Jenny's lap.

"I was at first. When he threw me over his saddle and galloped out of town, I was purely terrified. Bouncing along on the front of a saddle ain't exactly comfortable and I didn't know what he was gonna do to me. He knows I saw him kill my folks. He kept kissing on me, kissing my hair, and talking strange about Ma. I think he either planned to kill me or keep me locked up forever. Sometimes I think he thought I was my mother."

"He might be crazy, Jenny. From what I've seen of him, he don't always seem to be in his right mind."

"Yer right, Mr. Prue. Sometimes he'd talk like a normal person and then he'd go off and start callin' me Elva and talking to me like I was my ma. And I didn't like that cabin he put me in at all. At night, I had to sit with my back against the wall and I couldn't sleep because things would crawl all over me if I did. I got me a stick and whacked anything that moved. It was so dark in there and out in that swamp. You couldn't see no moon and no stars at night. And then it rained. But I got to likin' the dark, because the fat man only came in the daytime."

Bob slammed into the cabin, banging the door behind him. Beneath the bed, an ominous rattling announced the presence of one of Bob's pets. Prue's feet rested on the floor. When he heard the snake, he snatched them off the boards. "Are they caged?" Prue whispered.

"They're under there in a box. Stop worrying. You're acting like a little girl. No, not a little girl, all the little girls of my acquaintance are very brave." Bob tossed his wooly animal-skin vest on a hook and began to stoke the fire in the woodstove. "Is anybody hungry?"

"Bob, I'm about gut foundered," Prue said. "I can't remember when I last ate, but I do know it was a long time ago and weren't very much."

Bob opened the pie safe and took out a sack filled with a slab of bacon and started whacking off slices. He tossed them into the fry pan. A Dutch oven with a lid sat on top of the stove. Bob lifted the lid and stirred the contents. Then he lifted one of the hole covers off and stuck the pot over the hole. There was no telling what was in the pot, and Prue didn't care as long as it was warm.

Taking Jenny's hand, Prue patted it softly. "Did McQueen hurt you?" he asked through clenched teeth. The man had better not laid a hand on her.

"No, he just left me there in that place. It smelled and I was cold all the time."

"It's a good thing it was cold," Bob said. "Snakes stay hidden when it's cold. I suspect in the summer, that cabin is infested with moccasins. I think I caught a few in there for my collection. I may have got me a coral snake in that dump, too. Can't remember. And if it was warmer, the skeeters would have toted you off come nightfall."

"The skeeters were pretty bad anyway," Jenny said. "But skeeter bites don't even come close to what chiggers do to a body. I'd rather be eaten alive by skeeters than have one chigger bite."

Prue hugged her. "You sure have had a rough couple of weeks, sugar. But that's all over now. I'm gonna take you back to my place in the morning. I'll get Harriet to come out there."

Bob grinned. "So who's this Harriet? You planning on inviting her to live with you? What you do, boy?"

Prue felt his face heating. "It ain't like that, Bob. She comes out to visit. Her brother works for me, she don't live there."

Maybe Bob had it right and it was like that, Prue thought. Having Harriet out there all the time wouldn't be so bad. He could use her help with Jenny and maybe she could cook. It was one of those things he didn't know about her. Fact was, there were a lot of things he didn't know about Harriet Painter, but what he did know, he liked.

Bob winked at him. "Sure, Prue, whatever you say. I did hear some interestin' news when I was getting supplies at the general store in Gardner. Someone said there's a ranch on Horse Creek where folks that have been run off their land by the vigilantes can go and camp out. By some chance, would that happen to be your place?"

Prue sighed. What the hell? "Yeah, I got me a family or two of sodbusters camped out past the barn. What of it?"

"Could be ya'll be getting a visit from the vigilantes. I also heard they know about what yer doing and they ain't happy."

"It's none of their dang business what I do on my own land. But I figured they would pay me a visit sooner or later. That was kind of the plan."

"Using yerself as bait?"

"Sometimes you got to use a live calf to catch a panther," Prue said.

"I'm right there with you on that," Bob replied. "Got me a heck of an idea how to take out this bad guy of Jenny's."

"What you thinkin', old man?" Prue asked with a grin. "Can it be Malachai McQueen is about to have a very bad day?"

Harriet rode into Arcadia and straight up to the office of the *Desoto County News*. She was feeling a little nervous about presenting Mr. Jeffers with her work, but in her stomach was a small thrill of excitement as well. She felt good about what she had done and wanted him to see it.

She tied up her mare at the hitching rail in front of the offices. It was early; the streets of Arcadia were just beginning to come alive. She left the ranch before dawn in an effort to get the stories she wrote to the newspaper and get back to the ranch before dark. Last night two more families showed up at Prue's ranch. They said they heard settlers displaced by the vigilance committee were being allowed to stay at a ranch north of Arcadia on Horse Creek.

Harriet was shocked. It was amazing how news could spread in a place that was so wide open and as sparsely populated as the Desoto County area. The two families, the Crockers and the Kicklighters, had pulled their wagons behind the cowpens and set up camp. The two new families made the total living on Prue's ranch five. Harriet didn't count the numbers of folks, but it must be running close to forty souls displaced by the vigilantes and living at Prue's ranch.

She pulled the saddle pockets off her saddle and carried them right into the building. Jeffers was busy placing small raised metal letters called sorts into a composing stick by hand. Two helpers were doing the same thing. When all the lines of text had been tightly placed together on a form, the page would be inked and mounted in a press.

Harriet watched as Jeffers finished his lines of type. The man adjusted his glasses and came over to talk to Harriet.

"Hey there, Miss Harriet, did you bring me some news?"

Harriet beamed. Suddenly all her nervousness vanished, replaced by the excitement of her new profession. "Oh Mr. Jeffers, look, I have two whole stories written for you and more news I have yet to write. Two more families arrived at the ranch last night and set up camp. We have five families and over forty people out there."

Jeffers took the book with her stories carefully inscribed in her best handwriting and opened it. He adjusted his glasses again and sat perched on a high stool with one foot tucked behind a leg of the stool. Harriet could barely stand still while he read. When he was through with her first story, the one about the Temples family, he shut the book and looked at her. Harriet felt her stomach lurch quickly followed by a wave of nausea. What would she do if he didn't like her work? She loved writing about these people she was meeting. She loved talking to them and listening as they poured out their hearts along with their stories.

She found she actually held her breath as she waited for him to say something, anything. Finally, he smiled.

"This is quite interesting, Miss Harriet. You've managed to create a compelling look into the lives of this family and what it meant for them to be driven from their homes by a band of outlaws masquerading as the law. Good job."

Harriet felt blood rushing into her face at his praise. This was the first thing she had ever done in her life that had meaning and he liked it. "Thank you, Mr. Jeffers. I put my heart into it."

"And it will be on the front page of the news with your name under it. There's just one thing. Do you mind if I use the name Harry Painter? That way more folks will read the story because they'll think a man wrote it. I hate to do that to you, Harriet, but it would be a good thing for both of us."

Harriet sighed. All this work and the credit would go to some man that didn't even exist. Why couldn't she have been born a man? But she was realistic and her friends did call her Harry, so what did it really matter? It was her material, she wrote it, and people would read it because it was going to be on the front page. "I don't mind, Mr. Jeffers. I know you went out on a limb to hire me. I'm just glad I can do the job and you think what I wrote was good. Harry Painter it is."

"I have one question," Jeffers said. "Have you spoken to Mr. Pruitt yet? We need to get his story into print as soon as possible."

"He hasn't come back to the ranch. I expect him to return shortly. As soon as he arrives, I shall talk to him and write down his story. My brother is out looking for him as we speak."

17

Danny and Jeb reached the outlying pastures of the Rafter Q before the sun rose above the trees to the east. They rode hard, hoping to catch Berryhill before he headed out to bring Jenny food. They were within a mile of the homestead when McQueen and Berryhill came out of the trees, riding together. When Danny saw them, he put his hand out to stop Jeb and held a finger across his lips to keep him silent.

The two of them quickly withdrew into some heavy underbrush and watched the two men pick up a trot and head toward the south and the river. When Danny saw the direction the men were taking, he dropped quietly off his horse and led the animal deeper into the woods. Jeb did the same and the two watched as McQueen and Berryhill rode by close enough for them to hear some of what the men were saying.

None of what Danny could hear made sense. McQueen was talking about a trail and a still. Were they going to feed Jenny or what?

When the two men had ridden past and Danny felt safe, he turned to Jeb. "Did you hear what they were saying?"

"Sounds like they're going out to hunt for a still. I didn't hear them say nothing about the little girl."

Danny climbed back on his bay cracker horse. "I think we need to follow them anyway. If all they're doing is hunting a still, then we'll come back and talk to yer Granny."

Jeb nodded and the two boys set off to follow McQueen and Berryhill. The men hadn't gone far, maybe six miles, when they turned onto a deer trail running deep into a swamp. Danny could see cypress trees tall enough to block out the sun running for miles. A flock of white curlews took off as the riders approached the cypress. The swamp looked to be huge.

He held back and waited for McQueen and Berryhill to pull ahead. "We might as well stay here for a while. We get on that trail into the swamp and McQueen will be able to hear us. If he looks behind, he might be able to see us. Ain't no place to go, the trail's pretty narrow and we can't get off to the side and into cover if we're close on 'em. Out here in the open we could hang back like and stay in the trees. In there, ain't no way, we'll be like sitting ducks."

"Do you think they're looking for a still or going to take care of the little girl?"

"I don't rightly know, Jeb. I didn't think McQueen was going out to see her only Berryhill was bringing her grub and all. That's what you said."

"I heard my cousin tell Berryhill to take her grub. I never said McQueen didn't go see her. Maybe he's got the time and wants to see if she's all right."

"I guess so. All of a sudden I ain't feeling very good about any of this. I wish Mr. Prue was here so he could tell us what to do. I sure hope we find him in that swamp, but I can't see how it's all gonna work out now that we're here and all. Watching McQueen and Berryhill together made me scared. Those two men are very bad. You know, Jeb, it's possible Mr. Prue's already been there and rescued Jenny."

"Yeah, that's a good possibility except McQueen didn't look all that worried and if Jenny was out of his control, I think we would be able to tell. He'd look scared and mad and all and we'd notice. He didn't look worried to me, he looked fine. You want to quit lookin' fer Mr. Prue and go back to the ranch?"

That was exactly what Danny wanted to do. He didn't like the looks of the swamp and didn't want to go down that trail leading into the dimly lit forest. The woods were thick on both sides of the trail. From experience and from listening to stories told by cow hunters, Danny knew all kinds of predators lived in swamps. Creatures that could kill like panthers, bears, wolves, gators and snakes to mention a few. And that was just the wild critters. The most dangerous creatures of all, Berryhill and McQueen, were in there as well, perhaps lying in wait. What if they heard him and Jeb? What if they knew they were being followed?

Because he was afraid and didn't want to admit it in front of Jeb, Danny went against his better judgment. Squaring his shoulders, Danny mounted up, pulled his horse's head toward the trail leading into the swamp and urged him forward. "Of course I want to keep lookin' fer Mr. Prue. He's in there and we're gonna find him and Jenny, too."

The two rode slowly into the woods. The deer trail they followed meandered across hammocks and down into deep ponds of water. It was easy to see the tracks from McQueen's stud. He had shoes on all the way around that left a clear imprint in the damp earth.

They followed along watching the tracks and keeping well back for an hour. The sun was right overhead as they rode into a clearing with a cabin falling into rubble in the center. Danny looked right, then left. He couldn't see McQueen or Berryhill. He began to get that horrible feeling you get when you've done something very stupid.

"Stop right there," McQueen said from behind them.

Startled, Danny spun around in his saddle. McQueen stood behind his horse with the sawed-off pointing right at his chest.

"You too, Cousin."

"Hey Cousin Malachai," Jeb said in a calm natural voice. "What a surprise to find you here."

Berryhill snarled. "No it ain't. You were following us. You must a thought we was greenhorns. Ain't no sech thing as you can tell. Now, what'd you think you'd find in this swamp? Me and yer cousin here, we was just going to do us a little hunting. Ain't no call fer you two to follow us. Now get down off that horse before I unload this pistol in yer belly."

The two boys looked at each other. Danny could see Jeb's frightened face, white with two huge, staring blue eyes. Danny nodded and both of them climbed off their horses.

McQueen clapped Danny's gelding on the rump and sent it trotting toward the cabin. Jeb's gray followed.

Danny's mind spun with options and ideas, none of which seemed to be worth a damn as he watched his horse trot away. When the reins fell off the saddle and dangled loose in front of the gelding's face, Danny's horse stopped and looked back. The bay's one good quality, he'd stay ground tied. But it didn't matter none now. McQueen had them for sure.

Jeb knew what to do. He started in on his cousin. "Me and Danny were just coming down here to hunt, too," he said. "I heard there's a lot of deer in this swamp. I been wanting to get me a big buck while it's still cold enough to hang him. You don't need to be pointing that sawed-off at us, Cousin Malachai. We're cousins you know. We're kin."

Malachai sneered. "Yes, we are cousins. But I'm afraid I'm going to have to cut that relationship a little short. Tie their hands, Sergeant."

Berryhill took two pigging strings out of one of his saddle pockets. He quickly tied both Jeb's and Danny's hands tightly behind their backs. Danny flexed his wrists and fingers but couldn't move at all. The rough rawhide cut into his flesh. Jeb seemed to be just as tightly bound.

"Why are you doing this to us, Cousin Mal?" Jeb asked. "We ain't done nothing to you. We're kin, you and I. We got the same grandfather."

"Think I don't know that kid? Now shut up and save yer breath. Screamin' and talkin' ain't gonna get you untied or any help. This swamp is in the middle of nowhere and big as Texas. Now walk!"

McQueen shoved Danny forward with the barrel of the sawed-off shotgun. Jeb got the same treatment from Berryhill and his pistol. They stumbled along, tripping over roots and shrubs and uneven ground, awkward with their hands behind them. McQueen pushed Danny into a thick bunch of scrub willows and vines and suddenly a huge hole opened up in front of his shoes. Rocks had been placed in a row around the hole's edge and a tripod stood over the opening with a rope hanging down into its depths.

"Jump," McQueen ordered Danny, giving him a shove with the sawed-off. Danny dug in his feet. "Please, Mr. McQueen, don't push me in there."

Danny had never been this scared in his life, not when he and his sister were attacked while alone on the road, not during the firefight with the rustlers, not ever.

"Get yer sorry ass in the hole." McQueen growled and pushed him harder with the gun, gouging a hole in his spine. Danny leaned back, hitting at McQueen and the shotgun with his bound hands, digging the heels of his shoes deep into the wet soil.

"Don't do this, McQueen. You're making a big mistake." Danny tried to keep the fear out of his voice and talk like a man. He had no idea how deep the well was. It could go down a long way. However deep it was and however long the fall, Danny knew McQueen planned for Jeb and him to disappear into this well and remain there forever.

"I ain't making no mistake. I'm getting rid of two troublemakers," McQueen snarled. "Now git down there!" McQueen placed his boot on Danny's rump and kicked him into the hole. Danny jumped then fell about ten feet, landing hard on rocks and the broken bucket. He grunted and rolled onto his rear. He had to lift his head high. There was more than a foot of water in the well.

Danny heard a noise like a hammer hitting a ripe watermelon, looked up and saw Jeb drop into the well.

"Jeb, you okay, buddy? Jeb answer me."

Danny crawled toward the spot where he thought Jeb had landed. It was slow going on his knees, trying to keep his chin above water. He only had to cover a short distance, but crawling with your hands tied behind your back was a lot harder than you'd think and Danny couldn't see a thing. The only light in the well was from the entrance to the hole ten feet above his head. Trees and thick brush shaded the well, blocking what little light from the sun managed to penetrate the swamp.

Above him he could hear Berryhill demanding Mal pull up the bucket rope. "You ain't leaving them that rope are you?"

"What difference does it make? It's old and rotten and their hands are tied. You think they're coming out of the well by pulling themselves up the rope with their teeth?"

Danny heard a crash and pieces of wood dropped around him. When he looked up, he saw McQueen's boot stomping the tripod to pieces. Only a thin stick ran across the mouth of the well holding the old rope. "There! Happy?" McQueen asked Berryhill. "Now let's roll, we gotta find Jenny."

When Danny was sure Berryhill and McQueen were gone and weren't going to throw the rope into the well along with any hope of ever getting free of this trap, he turned back to reviving Jeb. His friend still hadn't moved.

"Jeb, talk to me. You all right?" Danny couldn't see the dark lump of Jeb's body but he knew it was there. The well was about five feet wide and the darkness so thick, Danny couldn't see his friend even though he knew about where he was. Jeb lay still as death. Frantic and afraid Jeb's face was under water, Danny head-butted him.

"Wake up, Jeb, wake up. You'll drown, buddy, wake up."

Either the head-butting worked or the cold water did the trick, but Jeb started to come around. He groaned and gagged on the water in the bottom of the well. Choking and spitting, Jeb rolled onto his back, holding his head up high enough to get his nose out of the water. "My leg," he moaned. "I can't sit up."

Jeb's head splashed back into the water. Danny was terrified his friend would drown and there was nothing he could do to save him. Then he got an idea. Sitting down, he shoved his feet under Jeb's head, lifting Jeb's head and upper body on his legs. His friend's head was above water and Danny sighed with relief. At least Jeb wouldn't drown in front of his face.

"He means for us to die down here," Danny said.

"If that's his intention, he's doing a good job. I think my leg's broke and I'm half drowned." Jeb's voice was weak and he wheezed, pulling air noisily in through his nose.

They were in a terrible situation, hands tied behind their backs and dropped to die in the bottom of a well. Something heavy slithered across one of Danny's arms. "Don't move, Jeb. There's snakes down here."

Prue slept in his bedroll beside Jenny. The pair of them stretched out on the floor next to Moccasin Bob's wood heater. Light tried to stream in the filthy window of Bob's tiny kitchen. Prue rolled out of the bed quietly so as not to wake Jenny and yawned. Jenny was safe. He looked down at her sleeping deeply and a bubble of happiness lodged in his abdomen. He'd almost given up hope of recovering her.

He poured himself a cup of the sludge Bob called coffee and sat down at the table. Bob came into the cabin quietly, carrying a copy of the *Desoto County News* under his arm. "You two better get up and get ready. We need to get out of here as soon as possible. Them two varmints that stole our Jenny could be arriving here looking for her at any minute."

"What have you got in mind for them?" Prue asked as he gnawed on a flapjack from the night before, dunking it in some cane syrup to soften it up.

"Never you mind," Bob said. "It's nothing fer you to worry about. Pack up Jenny and skedaddle. You can sleep well tonight knowing my critters will be a earnin' their keep."

Prue took that to mean Bob was going to set a trap for McQueen and Berryhill that employed his snakes. He almost felt sorry for them.

When Jenny finally woke up she seemed like her normal self. She smiled and sang to her cat and insisted Prue bring Sibby with them. The kittens had taken up residence in Bob's barn eating the fine crop of mice and rats Bob had been allowing to accumulate due to the snakes all being in boxes instead of on rat patrol.

Prue saddled the pony for her and soon discovered Mr. Britches was a mean, nasty son of a buck with every vice a horse could possess. He bit, kicked, and tried to lay down while Prue was tightening the cinch. But when he tossed Jenny into the saddle, the little rascal settled down and behaved, which was a good thing because Satan had taken the pony in dislike. And if Mr. Britches had done one rank thing to Jenny, Prue planned to turn the stallion loose on him. But that had not proven necessary.

The two of them trotted out right before dinnertime. Bob whistled around his homestead rounding up crates and jars and hauling them all into the house. He looked up from dragging a big wooden box into the cabin and waved as they rode out. "You take care of our Jenny," he called after them.

"I will, Bob. And thanks for everything. I'll be back as soon as I can."

"I love Mr. Bob," Jenny said as they made their way down the grassy track that led out of Moccasin Wallow swamp. "He found me in the cabin. It was almost dark and I was crying. He said he heard me and thought I was a hurt animal. He was just coming to see what the noise was and he found me. I was never so happy in my life when I saw him. At first I thought I was dreamin', but it wasn't no dream, he was real. And then he carried me back here on his shoulder right through the swamp. I would a been scared but after staying in that cabin, the swamp was a nice place, and Mr. Bob was with me and I knew I never had to see Uncle Mal again because Mr. Bob promised me he'd take care of him."

Jenny talked all the way to the ranch. Prue listened to some of it and answered any questions she asked, but his mind kept drifting miles away. If Bob knew about the settlers camped at his ranch, then the vigilantes did as well. When he got home, he planned to set all the settlers to work getting ready to be attacked, because there was no way the Sara Sota Vigilance Committee was going to take what he'd gone and done lying down. They were going be insulted that their work had been tampered with and they were going to retaliate. Well, let them.

The sun was setting when a very tired Mr. Britches toting a very tired Jenny trotted into the barnyard of Prue's ranch. Boarhog Benson had just thrown some grass hay into the cowpens and dumped a bucket of corn into a trough. The cattle Prue recovered from the rustlers milled around in the pens and began eating the hay and the corn. Boarhog was backing out of the gate when he spotted Prue climbing off Satan. He dropped the bucket and ran arms waving wildly. "Mr. Prue, Mr. Prue, Lord have mercy, we thought we was never gonna see you agin."

Boarhog grabbed Prue and gave him a hug that almost busted his spine, then the big black man spotted Jenny. He backed off Prue. "Oh my, oh my, wait until Miss Harry see you done found the chile. She's here too, ya know? She done moved in."

"Harry's here? What happened?" Prue was glad she was here but couldn't understand why.

"She gonna have to tell you all about that herself. I don't understand it, but she's writin' stories about all these folks living here."

What Boarhog told him didn't make a whole lot of sense to Prue. He'd just have to get the story out of Harry when he saw her. "Boarhog, I'd like to introduce you to Miss Jenny Buttons. Jenny, this is Boarhog Benson, my foreman."

Jenny dropped a tiny curtsey. "Pleased to meet you, Mr. Benson," she said. "If you take care of Mr. Britches, watch out for him, he kicks. Oh, and he bites, too."

Boarhog's eyebrows rose. "He do what?"

Prue laughed. "Oh yes, little Mr. Britches will catch your ass if yer not careful."

Boarhog grumbled as he took the pony's reins and led him to the barn with Satan. "He better not try none of that stuff on me. I knows how to handle ornery little varmint ponies. Oh yes indeed I does."

Harriet walked out on the porch of the house. Prue saw her and smiled. She looked different somehow, more mature, and self-confident. She was wearing a white blouse and an old brown skirt and carrying a bucket of what looked like slop for the hogs. Her hair was pinned up at the nape of her neck. Prue thought she looked beautiful.

When Harriet spotted them, she dropped the bucket, spilling slop all over herself and the porch as she leaped down the steps and ran across the yard. "Prue! Jenny!"

She swept Jenny into her arms and hugged the girl close. "I've never been so glad to see anyone in my life," she said into Jenny's hair. Holding the girl at arm's length, she knelt in the dirt and looked her over. "Did that man hurt you?" she asked, her face pinched, her voice cold.

"No, Harry," Jenny said. "He just left me in the swamp by myself. Moccasin Bob saved me. Moccasin Bob is going to make Uncle Mal sorry he was ever born."

Harriet stood up and looked up into Prue's face. At first, she smiled shyly, then she grabbed Prue by the shirt collar and kissed him on the cheek. "I'm so glad you're back. I've got so much to tell you. I got a job, Prue, a real job. I'm working for the newspaper. I write stories and they're gonna be published. Ain't that something?"

Prue pushed his hat to the back of his head and rubbed his forehead. "I'm glad to hear that. I'm right proud of you. Where's Danny?"

18

Malachai McQueen was mad. The first thing he'd seen when Berryhill showed him the path leading from the clearing around the cabin into the brush was a footprint.

"I can't believe you didn't see this footprint," he said to the sergeant. "You searched all over this area, found this trail and never saw this print." Mal stood up. "Damn, here's another one and this one's different. We got a boot print here and what I think is some kind of moccasin print over here. Both of them are fairly fresh, maybe only a day old. You should a seen 'em, Sergeant!"

Berryhill took off his cap and mopped his brow. "I was so worried about the little girl being all alone and lost in the swamp."

"Obviously, she wasn't alone at all," Mal snarled as he yanked the bridle over his horse's head and threw the saddle against the front wall of the cabin. He buckled a set of hobbles on his stud and set him loose while Berryhill did the same.

"Boss, why can't we ride?"

"If what you told me about the trail to the still is right, the horses will just slow us down. They'll get in the way and we'll have to tie them up. I don't want to have to worry about them."

"What should we do with them two boys' horses?"

"Unsaddle them and throw their gear into the cabin. Then slap them on the ass."

Berryhill quickly pulled the saddles and bridles off the boys' mounts. Lifting his hands high, he clapped his hands. Both horses wheeled around and took off into the swamp without looking back. Grunting, Berryhill hefted both saddles, toted them into the cabin, and tossed them in a dirty corner.

Mal led the way as they pushed through thick palmettos to find the tiny trail Berryhill said led to the hidden still. Berryhill found a partial print from the moccasin on a small patch of wet dirt, but no more boot prints. The trail led through thick brush, palmettos, willow scrub, vines, scrub oaks, and a lot of plants Mal didn't know and didn't want to know. This place was a jungle. Half of everything growing in here was probably poisonous and the other half had thorns. Overhead, tall virgin oaks, pines, and cypress shaded the swamp, casting it into everlasting dusk and gloom.

After only ten minutes of plowing through the underbrush, they popped out into a clearing. The sun broke through and the bright light almost blinded Mal.

Under the trees, close to a deep spring, Berryhill showed Mal where the moonshiner manufactured his corn whiskey. Whoever ran the still built several lean-tos to cover his equipment and keep it protected from the elements. Empty earthen jugs stoppered with fresh corks rested on a wooden pallet ready to fill with brew. Three oak barrels sat under one lean-to. When Mal lifted the lid on one, he could smell the sour mash that had once been in the barrels, the raw material used to cook up corn liquor.

A large tarp covered something in the center of the clearing surrounded by a mountain of split firewood. Mal pulled back the tarp. Under it was a huge, covered copper kettle with copper tubing worming its way out of the lid. The tubing ended over an old wooden table where three empty jugs sat waiting to get filled with corn whiskey.

"Nice setup," Mal said.

Berryhill found another pallet under the lean-to with more jugs. "Look, boss, these are full."

Berryhill lifted one and plucked out the stopper. He sniffed, then rested the jug on his shoulder, tilted it, and took a sip. He gagged, gasped, and smacked his lips. "Dang me, that's good stuff."

"Put down the jug. We got more important things to do. We can come back and confiscate all this liquor after we find Jenny."

Reluctantly, Berryhill set the jug on the pallet, put his hands on his hips, and looked around. "This sure is a sweet setup. He gets the water from the spring, fresh and pure as a virgin, and cooks up his whiskey without nary a chance of getting caught."

"Well, he did get caught. We found it," snapped Malachai. "Now where is the trail that leads out of here?"

Glancing back at the pallet of jugs one more time, Berryhill led Malachai to a trail leading south out of the clearing. This path was clearly marked and easier to follow, the dirt packed from heavy traffic. Whoever manufactured corn whiskey in this clearing had been doing it for a while.

Mal bent down to look for tracks, and was rewarded. Another one of those moccasin tracks was planted smack in the middle of an ant pile. Checking further, Mal crowed with excitement. "Sergeant, I found Jenny's footprint."

Berryhill was taking a leak off the trail. He adjusted his britches and bent over beside Malachai to stare at the small print. It was a perfect little boot print with a pointy toe.

"It looks like her shoes, Boss. This must be the right path."

"We found her, Pelo. We found Jenny. This trail is going to take us right to her. The poor dumb son of a bitch that took her from me is gonna pay. I'm gonna stretch him out like a hog and cut him."

The trail led across a creek with an easy ford and into a plowed field. By the time they walked around the edge of the ten-acre field, Mal's feet were starting to hurt. Riding boots weren't made for hiking all over the state. They finally located the exit from the field. This time the trail headed south and west into thick swamp. Mal stopped to look for tracks and was rewarded with another of Jenny's footprints.

The going got tougher. A larger body of water appeared next to the trail. The pond or wallow was shallow, wide, murky, and still. Apparently the swamp drained into this pond. The trail skirted the wallow for at least a mile. They had to cross many small creeks that drained the swamp, running into the larger pond. They spotted deer and turkey tracks. And in the water, Mal could see the eyes and snouts of a lot of gators. There were gators on the banks sleeping in spots where the sun broke through. Not a good place to take a dip. Water birds waded in the shallows catching frogs and small fish. A flock of small white egrets covered a tree hanging out over the wallow.

Suddenly Berryhill, who had taken the lead because Mal's feet were killing him, held up his hand for Mal to stop. Up ahead, a mother bear was drinking out of a small creek draining into the wallow. She looked up, swinging her big black head around. Upstream of her, two cubs splashed in the water. Mal and the sergeant hunkered down waiting for the bear to leave. It was too risky to shoot the animal. They had no idea how close they were getting to the home of whoever had taken Jenny. A gunshot might alarm him into running with the girl.

Mal crouched down behind a bush, his knees aching and his left heel throbbing where, no doubt, a large blister had formed. High overhead he heard the flapping of wings. When he looked up, a gray and white owl as big as a Rhode Island Red rooster stared down at him. The owl seemed to look right into his eyes, then lifted its great wings and swooped at them. Mal ducked as the enormous bird flew by inches over his head. When Mal looked up, the bird was over the wallow and the bears were gone.

They walked down the trail for another hour. Twice Mal spotted Jenny's little boot prints. His heart soared. He would get her back and make this kidnapper pay. The feeling he'd had for days, of his life spinning out of control, would stop. This had been a good day. Already he'd taken care of the kid. Jeb wouldn't be bothering him anymore. And when he got back to the ranch, he would take care of Clara and that interfering old bat Aunt Thelma.

Filled with an overwhelming sense of relief, self-confidence and inner peace settled inside his head and heart, feelings he hadn't had in days. The blister on his left foot and the one forming on his right big toe were his only annoyances.

The two of them stopped when they reached the end of the wallow. The swamp fell away to open grassy areas and clumps of trees. Up ahead, Mal could see corrals, a barn and a cabin situated under tall oaks and soaring cabbage palms.

After only a few seconds of searching, both of them found many moccasin prints and one of Jenny's delicate little boot prints. The man wearing the moccasins brought little Jenny here.

"She must be in the cabin," Mal whispered. They crouched behind a thick stand of palmettos with giant cabbage palms sprouting out of the clump and towering overhead. "Do you see anyone?"

Berryhill strained his eyes, shading them with a big hand. "Nope. I don't see no people. I can see some horses and a milk cow. Looks like a couple of mules in the corral next to the barn."

Mal stepped behind one of the palm trees and stared at the barn. He could see the mules, too. One, a big black son of a gun, looked familiar. When he scanned the compound for any other signs of life, he saw nothing. "Maybe there's nobody home. Let's move closer."

The two of them moved from one tree to the next, keeping hidden from the cabin. Slowly, they worked their way around to where they could see the cabin's front door. Standing at the edge of the wallow, Mal could see a clothesline behind the cabin. Hanging from the line was a little girl's white smock and two blue-green hair ribbons. They belonged to Jenny. He'd given her mother those ribbons. Elva must have given them to Jenny.

"She's here," he whispered to Berryhill and pointed at the clothesline.

Berryhill nodded and they moved behind a tree closer to the cabins. Empty wooden boxes were piled neatly under the tree. The lids sat on the ground next to the boxes. Each one had holes drilled into them. What could the moonshiner be doing with these boxes? On the other side of the tree were hutches filled with rabbits. A long row of elevated rabbit cages held at least a hundred head of rabbits of all sizes and colors. Maybe the moonshiner sold rabbits and carried them to town in the crates.

Mal shrugged his shoulders. Who cared about a rabbit-growing moonshiner? He was about to die a slow and very painful death.

They slipped closer to the cabin and Mal still hadn't spotted any people. Across the raked yard of the compound, dogs began barking. Berryhill dropped to his knees as the dogs howled and barked loud enough to wake the dead. They waited, holding their breaths while the dogs barked. When no dogs showed up to chew them to pieces, Mal looked at Berryhill. "Must be penned up," he whispered.

They waited several more minutes, holding their breaths, eyes strafing the compound for any signs of movement. When no one showed, Mal made a run for the cabin, pressing himself hard against it. He saw one window and crouched under it. Taking a deep breath, he stood high enough to peek in the window. It was dark inside. The small amount of light that filtered into the cabin through the dirty window barely lit the interior. It looked like no one was home.

Feeling braver and more confident, Mal moved to the front of the cabin. The door was made of rough-hewn timbers. It wasn't barred from the outside and Mal could see no lock. He still hadn't heard anyone or seen any movement either inside or outside. He was starting to think whoever had taken Jenny had packed her up and carried her into town to look for her folks. But why would he leave her clothes hanging on the line? She must be inside the cabin. Perhaps she was sleeping and her benefactor was out getting supplies or selling corn liquor.

"Let's go in," he hissed in a hoarse whisper to Berryhill.

Berryhill's face was tight, eyes busy scanning the compound, watching the barns and woods. He drew his pistol. "Okay, Boss."

Mal pulled his sawed-off out of the holster and held it in front of him. Berryhill moved to the other side of the door as Mal reached his foot forward and booted it open. The hinges creaked as the door swung inward.

The two of them stood in the doorway with their guns drawn and pointed into the dark cabin. On the bed opposite the door lay a small bundle covered with a blanket. Mal scanned the cabin. The only light filtering inside was from the filthy window in the kitchen area. It looked empty except for the bundle on the bed. That had to be Jenny sleeping soundly, exhausted from her ordeal in the swamp.

Mal motioned toward the bed with his gun. Berryhill nodded and stepped into the cabin, making his way with extreme caution toward the bed. Mal followed behind him, sweeping the room with his sawed-off.

Mal passed a woodstove with a fry pan half filled with grease sitting toward the back near the pipe. He sniffed. The place reeked. Stuffed animal heads hung on all the walls along with hides and sets of paws dangling on hooks, cow horns, and antlers. Under the dirty human and rancid bacon-fat odor hung a different smell Mal couldn't place. It smelled kind of like cooking cabbage.

Berryhill never made it to check the bed. He was just reaching out to pull back the blanket, only a foot away, when he suddenly froze and exhaled all his breath in a loud whoosh.

Mal froze, too. "What's wrong?" For some reason he was still whispering though clearly the cabin was vacant save for the bundle on the bed. Was that Jenny? Was she alive?

Berryhill turned white under his tan. He slowly motioned to the floor with his pistol barrel, holding as still as death.

That's when Mal heard the first rattle. It was muffled but quickly became clearer. The sound caused ice to slowly encase his spine and spread into his veins. Gooseflesh flowed up his arms. Both he and Berryhill stood staring like statues as the mother of all canebrake rattlesnakes slithered from under a rag rug on the floor beside the bed.

They'd all been killed by snakes, was Mal's first thought. No one was alive in this place. They were all dead from snakebite, including Jenny. Another rattle answered the first one. Mal slowly turned his head and an even bigger rattler slid out from under the woodstove. That snake lay between them and the door.

But the rattlers were the least of their worries. When Mal looked back at the open door, the light from outside illuminated the interior of the cabin and it was crawling with snakes. How had they missed them? Snakes were everywhere, under the table, on the table, coming out from beneath the kitchen cupboard, hanging from the rafters overhead, and when he looked closely at the head of a dead boar on the wall, he saw a coral snake hanging out of the boar's mouth.

Berryhill was going to panic. Mal could see the sergeant's eyes widening, showing the whites. He looked like he'd seen death. His gun hand was shaking badly. His mouth was working but no sounds were coming out. The canebrake was inches from Berryhill's boots. Even though Berryhill had frozen in place, it sensed his presence and coiled up, mouth open, fangs gleaming. Mal had never seen a rattler that big. It had to be eight inches in diameter and ten feet long. The snake's head was as big as a cat.

Completely lost as hysteria claimed him, Berryhill fired the pistol wildly. Forty-five caliber bullets smacked into everything but the snake.

"Stop shooting, you stupid motherless sod. Yer gonna shoot me," Mal screamed at the sergeant. As the sound of his voice echoed throughout the cabin, a hundred snakes coiled up, hissing, mouths gaping, and over it all he could hear the dry rasping sound of dozens of rattles.

Mal started backing slowly out of the cabin. Plain and simple, it was get out now or die. This was a trap. Someone had deliberately lured them here with Jenny's footprints and the clothes on the line and sent them into this den of death.

A loud rattle behind him froze his retreat in its tracks. He looked over his shoulder and gave an involuntary shriek. In addition to the canebrake slithering out from under the woodstove, another huge rattler lay coiled behind him. This one looked like a diamondback, and it had to have twelve or more rattles at the end of its tail.

Berryhill suddenly lost all control, leaping high and backward. His gun, still waving wildly, flew out of his shaking hands. Berryhill had moved fast, but the canebrake was faster. As Berryhill leaped, the rattler struck, hitting Berryhill's boot and glancing off. The sergeant's jump took him crashing into Mal, knocking the sawed-off out of his hands. Berryhill almost landed both of them on top of the diamondback. A cottonmouth water moccasin dropped off the rafters and flopped heavily on Mal's shoulder.

Unable to contain the scream that burst out of his mouth, he grabbed the snake by the tail and threw it on Berryhill. The moccasin instantly tagged Berryhill on the cheek.

Furious and terrified, the sergeant threw the snake to the floor. He lunged at Mal, firing off a string of profanity with his hands outstretched, grasping fingers turned to claws. Before Mal could stop him, Berryhill snatched Mal's spare pistol out of its holster, spun around keeping his back pressed tightly to Mal, and began firing wildly. Mal dropped his shoulder and slammed it into Berryhill's back, shoving him toward the open door. Berryhill teetered for a moment on the balls of his feet then plummeted face forward still screaming curse words and still firing the pistol. The diamondback struck him in the thigh as he fell to the floor.

Mal's heart hammered inside his chest as he gasped for air. He was never so glad to see anything in his life as Berryhill laying flat on his face stretched from where Mal stood to within inches of the door. The huge diamondback was pinned under Berryhill. Another moccasin struck Berryhill in the neck as he lay on the floor moaning and twitching. A pigmy rattler struck one of Berryhill's flailing hands, latching onto a finger.

Wasting no time, Mal jumped on Berryhill's back and danced down the sergeant, planted one last boot on top of the sergeant's Rebel cap as he leaped through the cabin door and out into daylight.

⓳

Harriet was so glad to see Prue return to the ranch. It seemed like years since she'd seen him, though it had only been a few days. She sat on a bale of hay next to Jenny watching him getting ready to speak to the group of settlers gathered to listen.

Bales of hay had been set in a semi-circle around a wagon bed. There were now seven families living at Prue's ranch, all displaced by the Sara Sota Vigilance Committee. For the first time in her life, Harriet felt like she was part of something important. She felt like she was someone and with Prue's help, she was making a difference in the lives of those around her.

Prue climbed onto the wagon bed and surveyed the gathered settlers. With his hands on his hips, his stiff, wide-brimmed hat pushed back off his forehead to reveal his ruffled blonde hair, Harriet thought he looked very handsome and strong. To her, he seemed filled with self-confidence and power, characteristics she knew she often lacked. Men and women sat on the bales around her, holding their children and gazing at Prue with hope in their eyes. He had promised to help them and they believed he would. Harriet believed he would. He was above all a man of his word. If he said he was going to do something, he did.

Earlier, Harriet had told him about her job at the newspaper and he had given her an interview. At first she'd felt weird asking him questions and talking to him as though he were a stranger. But she'd soon forgotten the strangeness as she pulled details, emotions, and plans out of Prue with her questions.

She found she was getting good at helping people reveal their stories. She'd already spoken to all the families and filled her notebook with them.

Prue would be the last and most important story. She'd sat up late last night writing it out so she could take it to Jeffers today. She wanted everyone to know how brave and caring Prue was. She hoped her writing did his story the justice it deserved.

As she watched him start to speak to these people, folks whose lives had been destroyed by the machinations of one evil man, her heart welled with love. Somehow over the past week watching Prue, seeing how he cared for folks, how he took care of Danny and how hard he worked to save Jenny, she'd fallen in love with him. It had been so easy. He was truly a hero.

"Folks," Prue began. "I know you all are getting tired of sitting on your hands waiting for something to happen. I know you're tired of worrying about your families and wondering if you're ever going to get back on your land. I hope that's going to happen soon, but I'm gonna be honest, I can't promise you anything. What I can tell you is very soon the vigilantes are going to come here and attack us on my ranch. I heard while I was gone that just as you new folks heard about this place being a haven for those displaced by the vigilantes, so they have heard. And they will be coming."

Prue stopped his speech as the gathered families began talking excitedly among themselves. He held up one hand and they instantly quieted. "I don't want any of you to be afraid or worried anew by this fact. When I invited you all to stay here, I knew they would come. Only through our strength, the strength we get from presenting a united front against them, can we defeat the Sara Sota Vigilance Committee and achieve our goals."

The noise in the crowd once again rose to a loud chorus of questions and voices talking among themselves. Prue held up his hand again and the voices died. "I have a plan. It will take all of us working together, but I know we can defeat these outlaws and villains who would try to take away our land and our right to pursue our lives as we wish to. How many of you have plows and animals that can pull them?"

Every family raised their hands.

"In the morning I'll show you what I want done with the plows. Then I want everyone who can sit a horse out rounding up cattle. Right now I don't care what brands are on the cows, just bring every cow, calf, and bull in. For every ten head of cows a family brings into the ranch, I'll give that family one calf. Boarhog, I want temporary cowpens all over this property, enough space to hold whatever these folks can round up."

The noise and talking rose to new levels as the families all wanted to talk at once about these plans Prue was making. "One more thing, any man that has a good rifle and a good eye come talk to me right now. Then I want to meet with the heads of all seven families to plan our defense against the attack that I know is coming."

Prue jumped off the wagon bed and Harriet, moved by his speech to tears of joy and love, rushed forward. She grabbed him by the arms and pressed herself against him. Her heart was pounding with pride in him and love. She prayed he could return her affection.

Looking down tenderly into her eyes, he brushed a callused hand across her shoulder. She could feel the strength in his touch through her blouse. "I'm proud of what you've done, Harry," he said, with his warm brown eyes shining. "You've done good getting this reporter job and writing these stories about the settlers. You've helped a lot of folks."

He hugged her then and kissed the top of her head. She reached up and touched his cheek. "I have to ride into Arcadia and take what I wrote to Mr. Jeffers. I'll probably have to stay in Arcadia for a few days to work and all. But I won't be having gentlemen callers up to my room ever again."

He grabbed her around the waist and swung her in a circle, lifting her feet off the ground. "That's great news, Harry. I knew you could do it."

Harry blushed as his praise raised her hopes of making him love her. If he knew her thoughts, what would he say? Shaking off his hands, she smoothed her hair and touched her hot cheeks. "I'm worried about Danny, Prue. He still ain't come home and I can't think where he is."

Prue stared off in the distance. "I'm worried, too. Maybe after he and Jeb couldn't find me, they just went to the Rafter Q to see Jeb's ma and his granny. I tell you what, if he don't come back today, I'll go looking for him in the morning. Whatever, don't you be worrying none. I'll make sure he gets back here safe and sound. After all, I need him. When all this mess is over, he's supposed to help me gather up my cows."

"What about the settlers? Aren't you going to stay here and help them fight off the vigilantes?"

"I plan to get them ready, ready to fight off anything whether I'm here or not. There's plenty of men here that can stand up to them outlaws as long as they do as I say and stick together. If they stand together as a group, there ain't no band of vigilantes that can back them down. After all, the vigilantes ain't trained fighters. They're just a bunch of ranchers and storekeepers trying to keep newcomers off the cattle range. They need to learn what cattlemen out West had to learn a long time ago. Settlers are going to come, progress is going to happen and there's nothing they can do to stop it. Ask the Indians, they know."

Harriet ducked her head, shyness suddenly overcoming her. She had something she wanted to say to him but didn't know if she had the nerve or the ability to put what she was feeling into words.

Prue saw her looking at the hem of her skirt and lifted her chin with one finger. "You got something stuck in your craw, girl? Spit it out."

She laughed. "What you done for these settlers is really amazing, Prue. I'm so proud to know you and I'm . . . uh, well I just wanted you to know I like you. I like you a lot."

Her heart was hammering so loudly in her chest, Harriet knew Prue must be able to hear it. Her face felt like it had turned bright red.

"Look at you blushing like a girl sitting by herself with a man for the first time."

When Harry looked up at him, she saw he was smiling at her with kindness and warmth in his eyes. She balled up her fist and punched him in the chest. "Stop teasing me, Jesse Pruitt. You must know what I'm trying to say."

He hugged her with one arm and started walking back to the cabin. "I know, Harry, I know what yer thinking. But we still got a lot to do and a lot to learn about each other before we jump into anything. You know I ain't on the hunt fer a wife. The life of a cattleman's wife is a hard one. I wouldn't want anything bad to happen to you, Harry. I don't want you to die young. I seen it too many times. Look at all the women here on the ranch with these families of settlers. They're old before their time. They're gonna die in childbirth or from disease cause there ain't no doctors out here or they're gonna get worked to death caring fer kids and houses and farms while their old man is out hunting cattle. I ain't ready to wish that on any woman. It happened to my ma and I don't want it to happen to you."

Harriet's heart plummeted into her feet. He didn't want her. Well, he'd never know how he had just crushed her. Standing tall and straight, she shrugged his arm off her shoulders. "I got to go saddle up my mare. Promise me you'll find Danny and take care of him. And tell me what you got planned for Jenny? Are you gonna keep her with you or give her to one of these families to take care of?"

Prue looked thoughtful. Shoving his hat off his forehead, he rubbed his eyes. "I ain't give it much thought. Come to think, you better take her with you to Arcadia. Things here are gonna get rough in the next week or so. I expect McQueen to bring the vigilantes down on our heads. I hope we can hold our own, but I don't want to take the chance of losing Jenny to him again."

Harriet gasped. She figured Prue was expecting McQueen to attack the ranch. That's why he was preparing the settlers. But it had never occurred to her Jenny would be in danger of getting captured by Malachai McQueen again. Such a thing must never happen. "I'd be glad to take Jenny with me. She needs new clothes and a new pair of shoes. She's about grown out of her little boots and they are worn slap out."

"That sounds like a fine idea," Prue said. "Let me get you some money so you can buy yourself something nice, too."

"Jesse Pruitt, I don't need your money. I got plenty of my own." How could he offer her money when he didn't want her to live with him or be his wife? Of all the nerve.

"Okay, Harry, you don't need to be biting my head off. I still want you to take a little extra money in case Jenny needs anything or wants anything. She deserves to be babied after all she's been through."

"I'm sure," Harriet said. "Just don't you go forgetting about Danny. I have a bad feeling something awful has happened to him."

"I know, Harry. I'll head out in the morning to find him. Don't you be mad at me fer telling you how I feel. I swear, it's nothing against you personally. I just don't want to see you drug down like all the rest of these pioneer women. You deserve a better life. One filled with fancy clothes and perfume, wine and candlelight. You'll find yerself a nice city man and he'll treat you like a queen. I ain't never gonna be able to do that, Harry. Life out here is always gonna be hard and dirty."

A small glimmer of hope flickered inside Harriet's breast like a match flame in the wind. It truly wasn't her. He had nothing against her. It was just that he wanted her to be pampered and knew he could never do it. How could she tell him all she wanted was for someone to love her and give her a home and a family, someone she could always depend on? And she'd seen Prue was that kind of man. If he took on a wife, she'd be kept safe and he would work like a dog to see that woman and his family were well cared for.

Smiling, she took his hand and squeezed it. "I know, Prue. But you best remember if you ever decide you want a wife and a family, I'll be waiting for you. Always."

Laughing, he threw a careless arm over her shoulders and walked with her to the cabin. "Get your stuff and Jenny and skedaddle. Do you need Boarhog to ride with you?"

"He always comes whether I need him or not. Just to the Arcadia Bridge."

"I'll tell him to saddle up yer mare and Jenny's Mr. Britches and a horse for himself, too. I want you and Jenny to be safe, Harry. And I'll always look out fer you and Danny. You know that."

Yes, she knew that. It wasn't in his nature to allow anyone he cared for to be hurt if he could help it. That was one of the reasons she loved him and would always love him.

Danny was cold. The water in the well was spring water and it was icy. The sun couldn't reach any warming rays into the depths and the mud and rock walls were damp and cold as well. Jeb's head was heavy where it rested on his legs, legs that had lost all feeling. He needed to do something fast or it was gonna be lights out for both of them just as McQueen had planned.

"Jeb, wake up, buddy. You have got to sit up or we're never gonna get out of this well."

"We ain't gonna get out of here anyway. My leg hurts so bad I'm afraid to move at all. I can't stand the pain." Jeb's voice was weak. Danny had begun to fear his friend was going to die on him and soon.

"Listen to me. I can get us out of here but you got to sit up and get off my legs. I got a plan."

Jeb snorted. It was a pathetic sound. Danny wiggled his legs trying to regain some feeling in them. He hadn't felt anything moving in the water for a while. It was probably too cold for snakes. It must have been a rat or some other creature that had crawled over him earlier. He knew snakes did not like cold. When he shook his legs and moved them up and down, Jeb's head flopped.

"Stop moving, Danny. Yer making my leg hurt."

"I don't care, buddy. Please try to sit up. I'm telling you I got a plan."

"What? To drown me so you can get out yerself?"

Jeb lifted his knees up, dumping Jeb off his legs. "I'm telling you, sit yer ass up. My hands are tied too, you know. I can't help you."

Jeb groaned, but began pushing himself into a sitting position with his good leg. Every time his broken leg moved he cried out. Danny could hear his harsh rasping breaths and his friend's teeth grinding. He hated to make him hurt like this but if Jeb couldn't sit up on his own with his head out of the water, they were both going to die down here.

As soon as he was sure Jeb was propped against the stone and earth wall, Danny sat up and began wriggling. Being thin and small had always been a source of extreme disappointment for him but right now he was glad to be small and agile. It was a piece of cake for him to bring his bound hands from behind him, under his butt and feet and into the front. As soon as his hands were in front of him and he was sitting solidly on the bottom of the well, he felt around his ankle for the knife he knew was there. The trick would be to pull it out of the sheath and not drop it. If he dropped it into the water, he might never be able to find it again. It was too dark and the bottom of this well was muddy in spots, rocky in others, and filled with holes and crevasses.

His hands were so cold and they were about numb from his wrists being tied so tight. His fingers were hard to move and they felt strange like they belonged to someone else. He inched his pant legs up until they were over his knee just to be sure he wouldn't have to fiddle with them once he got the knife out of the sheath. When his fingers touched the sheath in the dark and he felt the handle of the knife, he breathed a sigh of relief. The knife was there.

In his head, Danny had known the knife was there. It was always there. Every morning he put it on and some nights he never took it off, sleeping with it still strapped to his leg. But even that knowledge hadn't been enough. The fear he felt at being down in this well was so extreme, he had actually worried that the knife, along with any hope they had of getting out of this hole, was gone.

He grabbed the blade carefully with his thumb and forefinger, sliding it up and out of the sheath. When he had it out of the leather, he grasped it tightly in his hand. Now for the tricky part. Carefully, he turned the knife upside down. Holding it with the blade pointed up, he began sawing at the rawhide.

It was slow going. His range of movement was limited. He could only move the blade a tiny bit at a time.

"What are you doing?" Jeb asked. "My leg's gone numb. I can't feel it anymore. Do you think that's bad?"

Danny looked up, still sawing away at his bonds. One piece of rawhide had already come apart and he had more movement in his hands. "I'm getting us out of here, that's what I'm doing," he said just as another piece of the pigging string popped and he wrestled his hands free.

Reaching out in the dark, he felt around and found Jeb. "Lean forward," he told his friend.

"You're free," Jeb said. "How'd you do it?"

Danny quickly cut through the rawhide holding Jeb's wrists. "Just used something I've been keeping by me for a couple of years. You never know when you might need a hidden blade. This one's just saved my bacon for the second time."

Jeb rubbed his wrists then began feeling his legs. "I think my leg's gone numb from the cold water."

Danny stood up, feeling shaky on his feet. Even the short amount of time they'd spent sitting in the water had him as weak as a cat. It wouldn't have taken much more time for them both to succumb to the cold. "That's probably a good thing for now cause it's gonna hurt like a bitch when I pull you out of here."

Danny found the bucket and the rope. Yanking on it, he tested it for strength. It wasn't that thick of a rope and was probably half rotten to boot. When he pulled on it, the tripod holding it up collapsed and the rope dropped another foot. If the whole affair held together long enough for him to climb out it would be a miracle.

Once again Danny found himself thanking his lucky stars he was a runt. "I'm gonna climb out of here. I'll be back in a minute," he told Jeb.

"Please don't leave me down here long," Jeb pleaded. "I'll go crazy."

Danny could hear Jeb's teeth chattering. His friend was in a bad way. He tried to make light of it. There was no use panicking. It wouldn't do no good. "I'll be right back," he said to reassure Jeb, but in reality, he had no idea whether he could get out and if he did he didn't know where his horse and his lariat rope were. And he needed that lariat and a horse to get Jeb out of this hole.

McQueen could have ridden off with both their mounts. Or he could still be up there. Danny didn't know what he was going to find when he climbed out of the well. And if he couldn't find his horse and his saddle with the rope on it, he'd have to think of some other way to rescue Jeb. He'd have to try to use the rope from the well and pull Jeb out himself and he wasn't sure it would hold his bigger friend or if he was strong enough to haul him up. He wasn't even sure the rope would hold him.

Grabbing the bucket rope, Danny put his feet against the side of the well and began hitching himself up, climbing the wall of the well with his feet while he pulled himself up a foot at a time with the rope. It only took him a couple of minutes to scale the wall in that fashion. When he reached the top, he threw himself over the edge. Landing on one of the rocks bordering the well, he lay there breathing hard like a landed fish. He'd made it.

Rolling over on his back he stared at the trees and the sky overhead, glad to be alive, thankful to be out of the well. Now he had to rescue Jeb. Sitting up, he got on his hands and knees and crawled through the thick brush surrounding the site of the well and peaked out.

Moving a palmetto frond aside, he stared at the clearing surrounding the cabin. The first thing he saw was McQueen's big yellow stud cropping grass. The horse was hobbled. On the other side of the cabin, he spotted Berryhill's buckskin. What had they done with his and Jeb's horses?

He stayed where he was and watched the clearing for a few minutes. All he saw was the horses quietly hunting for grass. Moving inches at a time each with their two front feet tied closely together, they had to balance on their hind legs and kind of hop forward. Danny noticed the horses seemed calm. Everything was quiet. He could hear birds, bugs, frogs, and a gator grunting from the swamp. He climbed out from under his concealing palmetto slowly and stood up. Man, he was glad to be out of that well.

With the clearing empty except for the horses and no apparent signs of McQueen or Berryhill, Danny ran to the cabin. Where were their horses?

20

McQueen turned around and looked into the cabin. The diamondback was out from under Berryhill and coiled up across the man's legs. Berryhill twitched a couple of times and lay still. The snake hissed and opened his mouth wide every time Berryhill moved. There was nothing Mal could do for the man. If he wasn't dead already he would be shortly.

Turning his back on the cabin and the horror inside, Mal strode resolutely toward the barn. The feeling he'd had inside that his life was spinning out of control had evaporated. All that was left was a cold emptiness.

In the barn he found a tired old gelding that looked familiar napping in a corral with two mules. He knew these animals. They belonged to Jenny's family. Whoever had taken her brought the livestock here to this place of death in the swamp. When he looked in one of the stalls, he found the Buttons's milk cow placidly munching on a pile of fresh hay. All these animals had been fed. The cow had been milked. Whoever planted the trap that killed Berryhill hadn't been gone long. Maybe they were here . . . watching.

With his shoulders hunched against the feeling eyes that followed his every move, Mal caught up the old gelding. He searched the barn and couldn't find the first piece of tack. After the trap with the snakes in the cabin, there was no way Mal was searching through any of this man's belongings for a saddle, and he certainly wasn't going back into the cabin. He found an old lead rope hanging from one of the barn rafters, made a noose out of it, and slipped it over the gelding's nose to make a halter and a set of reins. Then he jumped on the animal's back and guided it out of the barn. As old as the nag was, it should be easy to ride.

The horse was ancient and had a backbone that rose an inch off its back all the way from its withers to its tailbone. Mal could feel it digging a crease in his backside. Every step the old horse took rammed his family jewels into the gelding's withers. Anything but a plodding walk was out of the question. It might permanently cripple him if it didn't turn him into a woman. This was going to be a very long ride.

It took him eight hours to cover the twenty miles to the Rafter Q. Several times the old horse had just stopped and began to crop grass. No amount of kicking, cursing, or swearing could make the beast move. Mal jumped off and led him. Swearing a blue streak, Mal finally abandoned the animal on the prairie, vowing he would return to shoot it dead as soon as he had a weapon. He walked the rest of the way to the Rafter Q.

The moon was up and so was Mal's temper as he climbed the steps to his home. The place was lit up like there was a party going on. When he slammed open the door, he left it that way. First thing he did was go straight to the gun cabinet in his office and remove his spare sawed-off shotgun and ratchet a full load of shells into the chamber. He set that aside and pulled out a Winchester repeating rifle and loaded it. Opening the drawer at the bottom, he pulled out the old Navy Colt, a pistol he'd owned for years and loaded it.

While he loaded his weapons, Rooster came out of the parlor. "I thought I heard you, Boss. Where's Berryhill?"

Mal looked up and snarled. "What are you doing in my house?"

"I was just in here talking to both Mrs. McQueens. Clara's son is missing. She ain't seen him since he left with the men to roust the rustlers two days ago."

"He's a meddling, interfering little son of bitch," Mal said in a cold flat voice. "If something bad's happened to him, he deserved it."

"You ain't seen him?" Rooster asked.

Mal stood up. Colt in the holster on his left side, Winchester under his arm, he crammed the sawed-off in the empty holster on his right side. Armed, he felt like a man once more. Looking up, he saw Jeb's ma, Clara, and Aunt Thelma come out of the parlor cross the hall and stand beside Rooster in the doorway of his office.

"Jeb ain't come back from the raid on the rustlers," Aunt Thelma snapped out like a drill sergeant. "What's happened to him?"

"I got no idea," Malachai said. "He went off with the Texan and his boy and I ain't seen him since. I didn't know I was supposed to watch him."

"You had no right to let my boy go off with strangers like that," Clara said softly. "Something terrible has happened to him. I just know it." Clara began sobbing so Aunt Thelma wrapped an arm around her waist and patted her on the back.

"I thought he was a man and could decide for himself where he wanted to go," Malachai sneered. "I didn't know he needed a keeper, or had to ask his ma's permission to go play with the other boys."

"He's only sixteen. He ain't even old enough to shave. I trusted you to take care of him," Aunt Thelma said in a voice laden with acid.

Malachai had had enough of just about everybody and everything. His day couldn't have gone more wrong and he had no intention of letting this bunch of meddling fools ruin his life with their whining and interfering. He shoved Aunt Thelma aside and headed for the door. There was business to take care of, settlers to run off, and a Texan to kill.

When he rammed into Aunt Thelma, she grabbed his arm. "Don't you run off before I've had my say."

But it was Clara, dear, sweet, fat Clara, who attacked him. "Where is my boy?" She screamed the last word, pushed Thelma's arm aside, and latched onto Mal's right wrist. Her mouth worked but no noises came out, her eyes wide and dilated, hysteria plainly only seconds away. "You don't care about him at all do you?" she wailed. "He's my boy and he's gone. I know you had something to do with it. You hate all of us. You don't care about any of your family. And we all know why. Oh yes, we figured out your dirty little secret. You ain't even one of us. You ain't a McQueen. You never been one and you never will be."

That got his attention. He stopped in his tracks just outside his office, peeled her chubby little fingers off his arm and looked into her narrowed blue eyes. "And what is it you figured out, Clara?"

She circled him then backed up into the hallway working her way toward the front door. "We know you're not really a McQueen. You couldn't be. Mother says you don't know about any of your relatives. Folks you met and should know, like her. She says she used to take care of you when you was little and when you was in your teens, she sat down at the supper table with Malachai McQueen every day for dinner. She says you ain't interested in things you loved as a child. Mother says you look like Malachai might have looked as a growed man, but there's something wrong with you inside that ain't nothing like Malachai. She says nobody changes that much. Not even a war should have changed the way you feel about animals, dogs, and work you used to love. You hate the dogs and you can't even crack a whip. Rooster and Mother both told me Malachai could handle a cow whip better than any man on the ranch when he was just a boy. You ain't Malachai and you done something with my Jeb. You're afraid he's gonna take this ranch away from you, ain't you? Where is my boy, you sorry excuse for a man? What have you done with him?"

Malachai laughed and looked at Rooster hovering protectively over Aunt Thelma. "You don't think I'm Malachai McQueen? That's pure craziness. Come on. Tell them who I am Rooster. We been together for twenty years. You know me."

"Yeah, I know you all right. I know you ain't the Malachai I knew as a boy. I've knowed since you killed Mr. Mordechai you can't be Malachai McQueen. The Malachai I knew could never a hurt a fly much less done away with his father. When you and that criminal Berryhill came back off the ride without him and all you had was a lame story about Mr. Mordechai disappearing into a swamp, I knowed you kilt him. But I love this ranch. I stayed here and did what needed to be done to keep the Rafter Q going. You sure ain't interested in cattle ranching. Where the hell do you think all yer money comes from? Cows, that's what. No, you ain't Malachai. Miss Thelma is right. You must have killed Malachai in the war and come home with that son of a gun Pelo Berryhill to take over Malachai's inheritance just cause you look so much like him. Well you might look like him, but he was quality and you ain't."

Aunt Thelma spoke up for the first time. Her wrinkled face, thin to the point of emaciation, was pulled into an evil leer. "We know who you ain't but we don't know who you are. We're gonna find out and you're gonna hang for killing my brother and his son, the real Malachai."

Malachai finally reached the breaking point. Who did these interfering busy bodies think they were? He was Malachai McQueen and he was the one with the guns. He pulled his sawed-off out of the holster in one smooth move and fired it directly into fat, dumpy little Clara, thoroughly enjoying the look of shock on her face. The force of the blast, a direct hit to her chest, smashed her through the open front door. She backed up two more steps, fell over, and tumbled end over end down the stairs.

Mal turned the gun on Rooster next. "You should have told me what you were thinkin', Rooster. We could have worked out a deal. I need you on the ranch. But it's too late fer that now."

Mal's next shot hit Rooster as he bolted through the door. The shotgun blast hit him in the back and knocked him down the steps after Clara. He took a dive, shooting off the porch head first landing with a sickening thud on the ground with one leg over Clara's waist.

"You're next Aunty Thelma." Mal swiveled his gun around looking for Thelma. She bolted, running down the center hall into the back of the house screaming for Gem. Mal could hear her boots pounding the wood floors as he chased after her. He threw the Winchester back on the floor of the hallway and carried the sawed-off shotgun in both hands. Where could the old bitch have gone?

He looked for an hour and couldn't find hide nor hair of her. He was headed back to the house when he spotted her running toward the back of the cook house. Cocking the shotgun, he fired off a shot. The spray of pellets peppered her. He saw blood stains blossom on the back of her white shirt, but she was so far away he couldn't be sure of a kill.

Walking slowly, keeping the shotgun low and aimed in front of him, Malachai headed for where he'd last seen Aunt Thelma. She could have armed herself. She could be waiting to get him on the other side of the cook shed. Then he heard screaming and wailing, which he recognized as coming from Ruby, the cook.

When he got to the corner, he peered around and instantly relaxed. Thelma was down, face down in a bed of turnip greens with his cook Ruby bent over her sobbing her heart out.

The greens were the only thing growing this time of year in the kitchen garden; the rest of the garden was tilled and awaiting the spring planting. Mal made his way down a row of mustards to where Thelma lay.

"Back away, Ruby, I don't want to have to shoot you, too."

The black woman was in her nightgown, a voluminous affair made from yards and yards of white cotton, but her head was still neatly covered in the familiar white turban.

"Lord have mercy, you done kilt her dead, Mr. Malachai," Ruby wailed, tears making shiny streaks down her fat brown cheeks. "Why'd you hurt Missy Thelma? She ain't done you no wrong."

Blood seeped out of multiple wounds on Aunt Thelma's back. Mal poked her with the toe of his boot, shoving her over. She flopped onto her back, one arm slung over her head, mouth open, eyes shut. She looked plenty dead to him.

"It's none of yer business, Ruby, and if I were you, I take myself back to bed and stay out of matters that are clearly no concern of yours."

The large woman climbed slowly to her feet. Mal thought for a moment of getting rid of her as well, but it seemed so wasteful. She really was a great cook. And who would believe her word over his? She was only a darkie, fresh out of Georgia where she'd been a slave most of her life.

"Yes, sir, Mr. Malachai," Ruby said as she lifted her nightgown above her ankles to walk back to the house servant's quarters. She glanced over her shoulder once, then disappeared into the house.

Mal took one more long look at Aunt Thelma laying in the turnips. Good riddance to the whole mess of them. They should never have come here poking their noses into his business.

Mal holstered the shotgun and stalked back to the house. He went into his room and threw some clothes and toilet articles into a leather bag. Grabbing the bag, he headed to the barn. When he realized he was going to have to catch and saddle his own horse, he cursed Rooster for getting involved with Aunt Thelma and her God-cursed family.

It took him half an hour to catch Rooster's roan gelding. The horse was the only one in the barn. It was cantankerous and always booger hunted. Two characteristics Malachai would never have tolerated in any of his own mounts. When he finally got the animal saddled, he was hot and sweaty and in a foul mood. When he tried to strap the leather bag to the saddle, the roan spooked and reared.

Malachai had had enough bull for one day. He grabbed a buggy whip out of the tack room, made a noose out of a rope, tightened it around the roan's neck and tied the other end to a ring bolted into the wall of the barn. Then he beat the horse with the whip while it plunged and choked until his arm got tired. When he took the rope off the horse's neck, it stood quietly, dripping with sweat, head drooping. Satisfied the animal wasn't going to give him any more crap, Mal mounted up and headed for Brownville.

He'd stay with Reverend Whiteleaf and his lovely wife while Whiteleaf sent out messengers to round up the committee members. Tomorrow night, they would ride on the Texan's ranch and kill all the damn settlers camping there. Malachai McQueen wasn't playing any more.

Malachai had finally figured out there was something very fishy about the Texan. He was connected to too many events involving Malachai or the vigilantes. First Berryhill told him it was a Texan that brought Jenny to Arcadia to stay with the whore. Berryhill's description of his Texan exactly matched Jesse Pruitt.

Then Pruitt showed up at his ranch to tell him about the rustlers and brought that boy with him. And then that boy and Jeb left with the Texan and showed up later at the cabin where they were holding Jenny, Jenny's gone, and Berryhill is dead. Now the same Texan had a bunch of settlers living on his ranch. Settlers Mal and his vigilantes evicted from their land with prejudice during the last month or two. Somehow that Texan was in the middle of everything bad that happened to Malachai during the past couple of weeks—everything. And Mal planned to see he was punished for it—with prejudice.

21

Danny was beside himself. Their horses had run off or been driven off and he could find none of their tack, no saddles, bridles, or any of the other gear they carried with them. He looked all over the clearing, taking a good amount of time. His concern for Jeb grew bigger by the second. He was sure if he didn't get the injured boy out of that well soon, Jeb would die. He stuck his head in the cabin but saw nothing. It was dark in there, one side was in a sorry state of collapse, and he didn't see the saddles.

After a fruitless search behind the cabin, in two rundown sheds and the outhouse, he stopped at the well. "You okay, Jeb?" he called down.

When his friend didn't answer, he grew more worried and dropped some dirt into the well. "Jeb, are you down there. Come on buddy, answer me."

"I'm here."

Danny could barely hear the faint reply. "Hang on, man, I'm looking for my lariat rope. The horses and our gear are gone."

"Hurry," drifted up from the well, Jeb's voice weak and raspy.

"Damn!" Danny cursed. He figured Berryhill and McQueen must have driven off the horses while they were still saddled. Thinking there might be some rope in the cabin hidden in a dark corner or a cabinet, or maybe something, sheets or anything he could use to make a rope long enough to pull Danny up, he went back to look inside one more time. When he opened up the door, went inside and began looking around, there the two saddles were, tossed in a dark corner.

What a fool he was. Cursing himself and praying he was in time, he grabbed his saddle, bridle, and the lariat and dashed over to McQueen's big yellow stud. He tossed the saddle blanket and saddle on the horse together all at once, tightened the cinch, slid the bridle over the big horse's head and took off its hobbles. For a stud, the animal had great ground manners. Danny couldn't have been more happy to discover this; he didn't have time to fight with a bronc.

Prue added a saddle horn to Danny's McClelland saddle, constructing it of wood and leather, while he explained no saddle should be without one. Jeb secured one end of the lariat to his makeshift horn, and led the stud through the brush to the well.

"Jeb, brother, are you awake?" he called into the well.

Making a loop with the end of his lariat, he dropped it into the well. "Jeb, can you hear me?"

"I'm here, Danny," Jeb finally replied.

"Slip the loop over your head and shoulders and tighten it under your arms, I'm gonna pull you up."

Danny felt the rope moving as Jeb grabbed it. Hanging into the well as far as he could, Danny saw Jeb in the dim light propped against the wall trying to fix the rope under his arms. It looked like he was too weak to accomplish even this simple task.

Snatching the end of the lariat off his saddle horn, Danny tied it to a nearby tree and pulled his gloves out of his saddle pockets. It was no trouble to slide down the rope into the well with the leather gloves on. When he got into the well, it took a few minutes for his eyes to adjust. It seemed as though Jeb had gone off in a faint when he tried to put the rope around his body. The boy lay with his head slumped in his lap, the lariat rope hooked over one arm.

In a matter of minutes Danny had the rope around Jeb, pulled tight under his arms. Praying his friend remained unconscious, he climbed out of the well. With the lariat back on the saddle horn, Danny urged the stud to move forward, pulling Jeb out of the well. Danny knew when Jeb woke up because that's when the screaming started.

The first stop Prue made was Moccasin Bob's as he rode out to search for Danny and McQueen's cousin Jeb. Bob was busy gathering up snakes. Pelo Berryhill's body lay in front of the cabin face down. One look was enough for Prue. Berryhill was swelled up like a toad.

"Looks like Berryhill got tagged a couple of times," Prue said as Bob came out of the cabin with an eight-foot rattler. He had hold of the big snake behind the rattler's huge head. The snake's mouth gaped revealing a nasty set of fangs. The snake was strong, twisting, and struggling, but Bob's sure grip was like iron. Old Bob had held many a snake and knew exactly how to do the job. Bob coiled it in a box he had ready and quickly dropped the lid on top.

"I think McQueen sacrificed his companion here. There were boot prints down his back."

"What, he walked over him?"

"It sure looked that way to me. Check out his cap."

Prue didn't really want to look at Berryhill again but at Bob's suggestion moved closer. Sure enough, Berryhill's Rebel cap was indented by what looked like a boot. On the dead man's back was another boot print. "I guess McQueen will turn on anyone to save himself."

"I think you could say that," Bob said.

"Hey, I got to go back to where they kept Jenny. Danny and McQueen's cousin are missing. Harriet said they went looking for me. I'm afraid they followed Berryhill or McQueen to the swamp and got in trouble. Would you mind taking a break from the snake roundup to come with me?"

Bob was just about to go back in the house. He carried a long stick with a loop of thin rope at the end and a burlap sack. "Sure, let me shut the door here. Don't want these critters getting out. You got no idea how hard it is to catch them once they get loose."

Prue didn't want to know how hard it was. He wanted nothing to do with snakes. One look at poor Pelo Berryhill made him wish to stay as far away from Bob's pets as possible, not that he'd ever had much of a liking for critters that slithered.

While Bob saddled his horse, a gentle red mare, Prue looked around. "What happened to the old gelding I brought here from the Buttons's place?"

"McQueen rode out on it . . . bareback." Bob broke into loud guffaws. "I wish you could a seen it. That old nag has to be thirty if he's a day and his backbone's like a knife, sticks up two inches. When McQueen climbed up on him, I almost fell out the loft I was laughing so hard. I swear it probably took ten hours fer him to get back to his ranch on that old shuffler. Would a been faster for him to ride the milk cow or just walk. All that ancient piece of hossflesh has got for gaits is a walk and a plod. And he'll stop on you and there ain't no gettin' him to move again."

Prue smiled but he was getting more and more worried about Danny. He'd kind of hoped to find him at Bob's. Even though the kid had never been here or met him, Prue hoped Bob found the boys or they followed the trail through the swamp and ended up here.

He and Bob urged their mounts into a lope as they headed around the swamp. Prue pushed old Satan to move forward. The black stud couldn't seem to get his mind off Bob's red mare. Several times the stud tried to circle around and get behind her. But Prue was way ahead of him.

Bob turned into the swamp before they reached McQueen's trail. He said he knew a shortcut. They heard screams while they were still deep in the swamp, way before they reached the cabin.

When Prue heard the screams, he knew they were from someone in a lot of pain. He wished they could travel faster, but the trail was narrow and threaded its way through bogs, quicksand, thick underbrush, and around larger bodies of water crawling with gators.

The first thing he saw when they popped out of the woods into the clearing was Danny bending over Jeb McQueen. The McQueen boy was the one screaming, and Prue breathed a sigh of relief. Not that he was glad to see Jeb laying on the ground, he just didn't want to have to tell Harriet Danny had been hurt.

22

Bob was on the ground first, bending over the kid and talking to Danny. Prue had to wrestle with Satan. The animal was becoming more and more of a pain in the ass about the red mare. She must be coming into season. "Bob, why'd you have to ride that hussy anyway?"

That was when McQueen's yellow stallion got a whiff of her and all hell broke loose. The two studs weren't that good of friends anyway, and with the mare in breeding season prancing around right between them, the fight was on. Prue was mad. He wasn't going to lose his cow pony over a mare.

The stallions were on each other tearing with their teeth and striking out with their forefeet. A stud's forefeet are his greatest weapon. A stallion can stand on his hind legs and lash out like a prizefighter. Prue pulled his pistol and fired a shot into the air. The gunfire slowed the yellow stallion but Satan took advantage, ignoring the shots and latching onto a chunk of the yellow stud's neck.

"Get yer frigging mare," Prue yelled at Bob.

The mare was dancing around as though enjoying all the commotion on her behalf. Her tail was cocked sideways and she was pissing everywhere. The smell of her urine drove both stallions insane. The yellow one tried to mount her while Satan was still hanging on to his chunk of neck.

"I'm going to shoot that yellow bastard," Prue yelled to Bob.

"No, don't do that," Bob answered. "I'll get old Sally."

Bob grabbed Sally's dangling reins and dragged the mare into the cabin, slamming the door on her. Prue could hear her inside, crashing into the walls. But she soon quieted down. It was dark in there and horses are always quieter when you take away their sight. Prue was grateful the walls of the cabin held up to her and did not fall down.

The two stallions still circled each other, squealing and striking out, but without the mare in the middle of them, Prue was able to get Satan's reins and tow him to a tree where he tied him to a branch over his head. No amount of pulling back and rearing would free him from that.

With Satan out of the way, Prue grabbed McQueen's stud and tied him the same way in a clump of scrub oak and willow on the opposite side of the clearing. Horse fight out of the way, he was able to greet Danny and discover what was wrong with Jeb. One look was enough. The boy's left leg was badly broken, bone ends sticking through his pant leg.

Danny grabbed Prue and hugged him. "I ain't never been so glad to see anyone in my life," he gasped in a breathless voice. "I done just finished pulling him out of the well where Berryhill and McQueen throwed us. He's been screamin' and I don't know how to help him."

Prue saw tears in Danny's eyes and knew the boy was at his wit's end. Some experiences will put age on a man. This one was forcing Danny to grow up fast. "Danny, this here is Moccasin Bob," Prue said, introducing the two of them. "I brought him with me for just such an emergency as this. I never knowed him at a loss in any situation."

"I'm right happy to meet you, Mr. Moccasin. I'm happy to see both of you here. I was about to lose my mind."

"Just call me Bob. I knowed Prue about six months now and he can get into more trouble than any man I've ever met. It hunts him down, I swear."

It turned out Prue was right and Bob did know what to do. He'd been doctoring animals his whole life. "People ain't much different from animals," Bob said as he began cutting Jeb's britches off with his Bowie knife. "Now that especially goes for broken bones. A broke leg is a broke leg whether it's on a dog a horse or a boy. Broke leg horse you shoot, a broke leg dog can be fixed up. Now this broke leg is gonna require some special treatments. We got bones sticking out."

Bob sent Danny off in search of Spanish moss while he went to his saddle and pulled a small vial of cloudy liquid out of one of the pockets. He held it up. "This stuff is pure gold."

"Is that what I think it is?" Prue asked.

"Pure rattlesnake venom. It'll keep the wound clear of dead flesh and it's a powerful good medicine for fighting infection. Just happen to carry a little with me all the time."

Prue shook his head. "You ain't putting that crap on the kid's wounds. It'll kill him."

Bob hung his head, then perked up and uncorked the vial. He took a tiny sip and made an awful face. "I drink some every day," he gasped when he could speak. "Keeps me safe when one of the ornery ones bites me. But I got another idea. I got a pallet of corn squeezins aging over by the still. I'll go get me a jug. Now that's good medicine."

The alcohol couldn't hurt so Prue let Bob fetch a jug and liberally splash it over the torn flesh of Jeb's leg. Neither one paid any attention to the kid's screams. They'd both heard worse and seen worse in their time.

After splashing on the liquor, Bob made Jeb drink some. It wasn't long till the boy passed out from weariness, pain, and being drunk. With Jeb unconscious, Bob quickly splinted the leg, wrapped it in Spanish moss soaked in corn liquor and bound it up with strips torn from old blankets Danny found in the cabin.

"How we gonna move him?" Danny wanted to know. "Anytime he moves at all he starts to hollering."

"Me and Prue will make us a travois. The Indians use them to haul everything. I seen it down here and I know Prue probably seen plenty of Indians using a travois in Texas."

Prue did know what Bob was talking about. He cut willow saplings while Danny and Bob tore up more of Jenny's sheets. It didn't take long to set up a drag for the boy behind Berryhill's buckskin gelding. When they had him loaded, Prue climbed aboard Satan and took the buckskin's lead rope. Danny climbed on the yellow stud since he was by far the best rider among them. The stud was quiet when Danny was in the saddle. Only Satan showed his butt when Bob led the mare out of the cabin.

"You should see the mess she made in there," Bob said.

"It doesn't matter. I doubt if anyone will ever live there again," Prue said.

Because of Jeb's condition, Bob stayed with the little group, riding on to the Rafter Q. When they got there they discovered the place in the process of completely coming apart.

Prue rode in first, walking his horse past empty cowpens that were filled with cattle only days before. They stopped at the barn, which was as empty as the cowpens. There wasn't a horse in any of the stalls or even in the corrals attached to the barn. Prue tied up his horse and pulled Bob aside.

"Something bad has happened here, Bob. I ain't never seen the pens empty or the barn. Keep the boys in the barn until I come get you."

Bob climbed stiffly off his red mare, rubbing both knees then his back. "I ain't cut out for this riding business anymore. I forgot how bad it makes my reumatiz kick up."

Prue touched Bob on the arm and whispered. "If I come back a runnin', haul your tired aching butt back on that mare because we got to skedaddle."

Bob nodded. "I got you."

As Prue walked out of the barn, he saw Bob bending over to tend to Jeb on the travois. First place he went was the bunkhouse. There should be ten hands living here. When he opened the door, all he saw was empty bunks, rolled up mattresses, trash and empty tin plates sitting on the table, no hands in there.

Turning up the hill, he headed for the big house. It was late afternoon and one oil lamp shone through the front window. He walked around back to the cook house. A pot bubbled full of something on the big stove and Prue could smell fresh bread baking. Someone was here.

He went into the house through the back. From the porch he opened a screened door and went into the kitchen. A large black woman sat on a stool churning butter, the butter churn held between her legs. When Prue walked in she jumped, knocking the churn over and spilling buttermilk everywhere.

"Lord have mercy, you bout scared me to death. I thought Mr. Malachai done come back to finish us all off."

"My name is Jesse Pruitt. I'm looking for the two older ladies that were staying here. I brought Jeb McQueen home with me. The poor kid went and broke his leg."

Tears began coursing down the woman's shiny brown cheeks. "Poor Miss Clara done got herself shot and kilt yesterday. Mrs. McQueen is laying in her bed about dead. Mr. Rooster got his self shot dead and all the hands done run off to get jobs somewhere else. Only me and my sister Gem and the pot boy is left to take care of everything. We done let all the cows go loose because it's too much for us to draw water for them and feed them. Ezra let the horses out too and the pigs. I can't let them starve or die of thirst cause we can't do all them chores by ourselves."

"What are you talkin' about?" Prue demanded. "Who got shot and who did the shooting?"

"Mr. Malachai done shooted up the whole place. He come home and got in a big tussle with Miss Clara. They was shouting at each other and then he shooted her. He shoot Mr. Rooster in the back and then he chased poor old Mrs. McQueen all around the house and the yard and shooted her out back by the cookhouse. I seed him shoot her. I thought fo sho he was gonna shoot me too. He looked like the Devil hisself."

That must have been what happened after McQueen left Berryhill in the cabin to die. He came right here and started killing folks. He must have gone out of his mind. It sure sounded like the work of a crazy person.

"You said Mrs. McQueen is still with us?" Prue hated to have to tell Jeb his ma was dead. The kid was in bad shape himself. Maybe the old lady would live so he would have some family to hold on to.

"That ole biddy sho is a tough one. We put her to bed, me and Gem, and we been nursing her best we can."

"Where did Mr. Malachai go after he, uh, shot up the place?"

"He saddled him a horse and high-tailed it out of here like the hounds of hell was chasin' him is what he did. I knowed we ought to go tell the law, but who's gonna believe the word of us niggrahs against Mr. Malachai? Me and my sister decided to just hold on best we could, take care of the old missy, and wait for help. You's our help, mister."

"I wish I could do more for you, but I'm sorry to have to tell you I brought you another patient. Miss Clara's son has a badly broke leg. He's out on a litter in the barn. If you don't mind too much, I'm gonna bring him up here and put him in his bed."

"Mind? How we posed to mind anything? We just niggrahs. All we do is what we been tole to do and with all the white folks dead or hurt bad, we got no idea what that is."

The large cook bustled around, picked up the churn, mopped up the spilled liquid and then stood up, wiping her hands on her starched white apron. "I'll go get Gem to pull down the covers on the chile's bed and get his room ready. If the boy's hungry, I got chicken soup and some fresh bread gonna come out the oven in just a minute."

"I don't know how hungry he is but I'm starved and I have two other fellows with me. Can you feed us, too?"

"Sho nuff can. Now that be something I knows how to do. Ya'll just come on into the kitchen after you settle Mr. Jeb in his bed and I'll fix the three of you mens a plate." Ruby fussed around the kitchen some more while she filled Prue in on the remaining details of what had been going on around the Rafter Q. It was a sad tale with too many deaths.

"I'll go get Jeb," Prue told her. "And if it ain't too much trouble for you, we'll take you up on that offer of food directly."

Ruby shook her apron at him, shooing him out of the kitchen. "Den go get the chile, he needs to be in his bed."

Prue went back to the barn with his head reeling. It sounded like Mc-Queen had flipped his lid. How was he supposed to tell Jeb about his ma? Best to wait until they knew how bad his granny was hurt.

When he got back to the barn, Danny was sitting on the barn floor beside Jeb so Prue pulled Bob into the tack room and shut the door. With the smell of leather and neatsfoot oil hanging in the air, he told Bob what had happened at the ranch. "Things here have gone from bad to crazy," he said to Bob.

The old man's eyebrows flew up. "What now?"

"I think McQueen's coming apart at the seams. He came here after losing Berryhill at your place and shot everyone except the servants and the hands, then he high-tailed it out of here. The servants, two older black women and a little boy, are taking care of Jeb's granny, she's the only one of his family that survived the shootings."

"Weren't there a bunch of hired cowhands here getting ready for the spring gather? Where'd they go?" Bob asked, trying to keep his voice quiet so Jeb wouldn't hear.

"The hired hands pulled out. When they heard all the shooting, they came up to the big house to discover the cause of the ruckus and found the foreman dead. There was one other maid, a mulatto girl, she run off with one of the hands. The house servants that stayed let out all the stock cause it was too much for them to take care of."

Bob nodded. "Sounds like the old lady is lucky some of the servants are still here to take care of her."

Prue nodded. "She is, but from the way the cook was talking, they don't have no place else to go."

"She's probably right. This is their home as much as it is McQueen's. You know, McQueen didn't appear too tightly wrapped last time I saw him neither. Happen the man ain't playing with a full deck no more, if he ever was. Smart thing for the help to do, letting out all the stock." Bob paused, took his old hat off and scratched his gray hair. "So the boy's granny ain't dead? What kind of shape is she in?"

"The cook says his granny is still hanging on. But she's wounded pretty bad. McQueen killed Jeb's ma and I sure don't think it would be a good thing to tell him that now."

"You could be right there. Let's get the boy on up to the house and into bed."

When they came out of the feed room, Danny left Jeb laying on the litter and came over to stand beside Prue and Moccasin Bob. "What's going on?"

"Tell you later," Prue said. "Help me tote Jeb up to the house."

When Jeb was tucked into bed with Gem's help, the cook produced a bottle of laudanum and dosed the boy. Drowsy and in pain, Jeb closed his eyes, unaware his mother was dead and his grandmother seriously wounded.

"Let me have a look see at the old lady," Bob said to Gem as they left Jeb's room, closing the door behind them.

Gem rolled her eyes. "Ain't right," she said. "It ain't decent. It ain't right for gentlemuns to go into a lady's room. It done matter if she's sick or been shot to hell, it ain't right." In spite of her objections, Gem opened the door to old Mrs. McQueen's bedroom. Mumbling under her breath that no good would come of this and she didn't know what the world had come to when mens were allowed into a woman's bedroom, she ushered them in, taking a stand beside the bed with her arms crossed and a deep, disapproving frown on her face.

Granny was awake, her gray head resting flat on a pillow, her gnarled hands clutching the edge of her blankets. When she saw Prue and Bob, she pulled them up under her chin. Prue thought she looked in bad shape. Her face was gray and the hands clutching the blanket shook.

"Who are you?" she whispered and then broke into a fit of coughing.

Gem's face softened and she laid a big hand on the old lady's shoulder. "Now Missy McQueen, you hush and lay still. These mens just brought home yer grandbaby. He's gone and got his self a broke leg. We put him to bed and he's gonna be jest fine so's don't you fret yerself none."

Jeb's grandmother looked pretty sick to Prue. He glanced at Bob. Bob was eyeing the old lady.

"Sounds like she's got water in her lungs," Bob said to Gem. "We need to get her higher on them pillers, so's it will drain and she can breathe better, understand? One of her lungs probably deflated. If the good one can't drain out the blood and fluid collecting inside, she'll get the pneumonia and die on you."

Gem nodded and Prue and Bob gently lifted Jeb's granny while Gem added two pillows to the one behind her head. When Mrs. McQueen was settled, she smiled at Bob and Prue could swear there was a twinkle in her eyes.

"Thank ye both. That's much better," she said, then broke into another fit of coughing, which produced some phlegm. Gem tenderly whipped the old lady's lips. Reaching out a thin hand, Mrs. McQueen grabbed Bob's arm. "You get that imposter and you kill him," she said to Bob and Prue. "He's not a McQueen you know. Been passing himself off as one for years. My fault. I should have come here a long time ago. I thought, well I thought things were fine. Who'd think such a thing could happen?"

㉓

Harriet and Jenny rode side by side. It was raining steadily and they both wore ponchos made by Boarhog. Harriet's hat kept the rain out of her face and Mrs. Starling had given Jenny a hat to keep her head dry. Neither one of them was comfortable, but Harriet was reasonably dry under the make-shift raincoat, and she knew Jenny had to be at least as dry as she was.

After all that had happened to her, Jenny seemed happy enough. But Harriet knew from experience that all the troubles she'd suffered in the past weeks would eventually catch up to her. The little girl put on a brave face and Harriet loved her for it. They'd stayed an extra day at the ranch because Jenny was just too tired to ride and Harriet kept hoping the rain would stop. Now Harriet worried she was late with her stories.

Boarhog Benson rode behind, his rifle over the pommel of his saddle, water dripping off the wide brim of his straw hat. He had a sour look on his face Harriet associated with the breakfast they'd consumed before leaving and the weather.

In spite of the steady rain, every man on the place that could ride was on the prairie bringing in cattle. Boarhog built temporary holding pens for the cows all of yesterday and hadn't appreciated leaving the work to squire her and Jenny. But Prue insisted.

While most of the men and several of the women took off to hunt cows, four older men hitched their teams to plows and began plowing a five-foot-wide swath completely around the barn, cabin, cowpens, and outbuildings of Prue's ranch, starting at the creek on one side and finishing at the creek after circling the place. When they started plowing at the creek, they dug the plows in deep, tearing a gully into the bank around the creek and plowing right into the water. At the other end of the circle, they did the same thing. Water began moving into the plowed rows slowly. Add the steady rain and an instant swamp formed in the torn earth.

Harriet knew Prue had a plan, but he'd been quiet about what it was, simply assigning the tasks he felt necessary to carry it out and leaving to find Danny.

Harriet hoped Prue would come home with her brother before she had to leave, but there was still no sign of him and it was past time for her to get back to Arcadia. Come sunup, Boarhog appeared on the front porch and told her and Jenny the horses were waiting. They'd gulped down eggs, bacon, and biscuits cooked up by Mrs. Starling, donned the rain gear and mounted up for the ride. Harriet carefully wrapped her notebooks in oil cloth and stashed them in her saddle pockets to keep them dry.

Aside from the rain, the ride to town went fast. Up ahead, Harriet could see the bridge. She knew Boarhog wanted to get back so she cut him loose. "There's the bridge, Boarhog. We'll be fine now. Make sure you take this dog with you. Ain't no place for an animal with this much energy in Arcadia."

Getting rid of Buzzard turned out to be no easy task. The animal had taken a liking to Jenny and wouldn't leave her.

"Tie a rope to Buzzard's collar and drag him off," Harriet snapped.

Boarhog gave it a try. "Look, Miss Harry, this ole dog done laid down. I think he might bite me."

Buzzard pinned his ears to his head and tucked his short tail between his legs. Every time Boarhog tried to get near him with the rope, Buzzard showed his teeth and growled.

Boarhog backed slowly away from the dog, white showing around both eyes. "I don't think he likes me, Missy, and I know I don't likes him. You want this string on him, you better come off that hoss and do it yerself."

"Oh just forget it, Boarhog," Harriet said, fed up with the rain and the dog. "I guess he's made up his mind to belong to Jenny."

Jenny laughed. "He's the best dog ever," she said. "He's my friend."

Well that did it for Harriet. If Jenny wanted the dog, she'd have him, even if, as she figured, Buzzard would probably prove to be a giant pain in the behind. Harry stopped Boarhog from riding away. "Hand me that rope, Boarhog, just in case I need to tie him up."

Boarhog handed her the braided length of hemp and briefly touched her hand. "You be careful, Miss Harry, and take good care of our little Jenny."

Harriet watched for a moment as Boarhog galloped his horse back down the trail. Then she turned her mare toward Arcadia. "Let's go, Jenny. I've got to bring these late stories to Mr. Jeffers."

They dropped Mr. Britches and her mare off at the livery stable. Shaking water off her hat and poncho, Harriet helped Jenny do the same. When she looked outside, the rain stopped, so she folded the rain gear and put it with the saddles.

As she was leaving the livery stable, she tried to palm Buzzard off on Mr. Peterson, the man who ran it. He said he would look after the dog so they put him inside a stall. They were only ten steps out of the barn when Buzzard rejoined them. Mr. Peterson came running out of the barn waving his arms.

"That dang animal dug a hole under the stall wall. It's three foot deep," Peterson fumed. "I'm gonna have to fill it. If a horse was to fall in the thing, he'll break a leg fer sure."

"I'm so sorry, Mr. Peterson," Harriet's face burned bright red. The dog hadn't even been here five minutes and he'd already proved himself a nuisance.

Peterson grabbed a shovel that was leaning against the outside wall of the stable and stalked back into the dark barn. Harry watched him go and took Jenny's hand. In her other hand she carried her saddle pockets filled with stories and Jenny's small carpet bag with a few items of clothing in it.

"I have to go to my job first, darling. We can go to the room later."

Jenny nodded and the two of them trotted down saloon row with Buzzard stalking majestically along beside Jenny swinging his big head back and forth, watching everyone and everything. As they walked rapidly by the Golden Spur, Harriet turned her head away, praying she wouldn't see horrible Mr. Lumpkin now or ever again.

But when she came abreast of the saloon, she couldn't resist one look. And there he was standing outside the saloon at the top stairs by the swinging front door. He was talking to a man who for some reason seemed familiar to Harriet. The man's back was turned to her so she couldn't see his face. But the way he stood and moved his hands made Harriet think she knew him. He was overweight, short of stature, and wearing a bowler hat just like Uncle Buford used to wear. She shivered, wishing she'd worn a warmer jacket. The rain made her clothes damp under the poncho.

Brushing aside a feeling of uneasiness engendered by the sight of Mr. Lumpkin, she and Jenny arrived at the newspaper office. She took the rope Boarhog gave her and tied Buzzard to a lamp post. He sat down and with a long face watched the two of them go into the office.

Once inside, Jenny became fascinated by the machinery and wandered off to examine everything and ask Mr. Jeffers's printing assistant, Jacob Bembry, a thousand questions.

Jeffers took her notebook and all its stories and led her to his desk. Harriet goggled, unable to stifle a giggle when she saw the piles of paper, notes, file folders, and copies of the *News* along with copies of other newspapers stacked on the top. They warred for open space with tin cans filled with pencils and pencil shavings, ink bottles, quills, and two dirty plates containing remnants of what could have been Mr. Jeffers's dinner.

A strange man stood behind the desk idly reading the most recent issue of the *News*. The man presented a very imposing figure. He was tall, well over six feet, his heavy muscles evident under a brown coat and a black leather vest over a white shirt. A very large black mustache was waxed to perfection under a strong nose with a decided hook. His gray eyes were sharply penetrating when they looked up from the newspaper to stare at Harriet.

Harriet felt herself coloring. Who was this man? Jeffers noticed her discomfort and introduced them. "Harriet, this is U.S. Deputy Marshal, Bill Short. He's come here from Tampa because someone showed him your articles in the *News*. He's going to investigate Malachai McQueen and the vigilantes."

Harriet couldn't believe what she was hearing. He'd read her stories?

Jeffers turned to the Marshal. "Marshal Short, this is the young lady that wrote those compelling stories. I know the byline reads Harry Painter, but Harry is short for Harriet. Harriet, meet Marshal Short."

Harriet stuck out her hand and the marshal shook it just as though she'd been a man. "I'm very happy to make your acquaintance," she said. "It's wonderful that you came all this way for these people. They deserve someone to stand up for them."

Marshal Short found a chair for Harriet and himself. He took her hand. "Now, little lady, I want you to tell me everything you know."

Prue and Danny left the Rafter Q early the next morning. Prue felt like a new man. A good dinner and a huge breakfast along with the first decent night's sleep he'd had in a while had him feeling like a million dollars. If it wasn't raining a regular gully washer, he would have whistled. He and Danny wrapped themselves in rain gear from head to toe and trotted their horses out of the Rafter Q toward his ranch.

The situation at the Rafter Q was distressing. Bob went home to feed his livestock last night and to finish catching the snakes, but promised to come back to the Rafter Q as soon as he had his own affairs in shape. He swore he would check in on Jeb and Jeb's granny.

First thing Prue did this morning, even before he ate the fine breakfast cooked up by Ruby, was to tell Jeb his mother had passed. The boy was stunned. He took the news quietly, saying little. But from Prue's experience with young men, he could tell Jeb was hurting. When he and Danny told him good-bye, all he'd said was how grateful he was to Danny for saving his life. He could tell those two would be friends for life.

Prue felt better about leaving the servants with Jeb and Mrs. McQueen after Bob said he would come back and help out, just as long as Bob didn't feed Mrs. McQueen any rattlesnake venom. He'd made the old man promise he wouldn't, even though Prue put very little stock in Bob's word where snakes were concerned. The old man seemed to think snake poison would cure about anything. Bob also promised to keep an eye on Jeb and do his best to cheer up the boy.

Prue would have stayed on at the Rafter Q to help out if he hadn't felt such an urgent need to get back to his ranch.

"I think McQueen rode off to gather his vigilantes," he said to Danny.

"Will he attack yer ranch?"

"The way I figure it, he should be attacking the ranch tonight or maybe early tomorrow morning."

"How you know that?"

"Timing, boy. I know it's on his mind. I stuck my big ass in his face by putting all them settlers he run off on my land. He's got to be fighting mad anyway. His life's gone into the outhouse ever since I showed up. I know he's coming for me. I can feel it."

The rain was a blessing. It figured right into Prue's plans. He hoped for a flood. Boarhog Benson could predict weather better than any human being Prue had ever known. He assured Prue it was going to rain cats and dogs, and even though it didn't do so immediately, the rain showed up just as Benson predicted.

When Danny and Prue arrived at the ranch, they had to cross a deeply plowed stretch of ground five-feet wide. Satan and Danny's bay both floundered in the deep mud. Danny was forced to get off his horse and lead it across the mud while Satan leaped and plunged and pulled clear of the mire. Prue couldn't wipe the smile off his face. He turned to Danny. "I love it when a plan comes together."

"What?" Danny said. The boy was coated with black mud from his face to his boots. Clumps of black goop hung from the boy's hat. He'd lost one of his shoes and it took ten minutes of digging to find it.

"Nothing," Prue told him. "I was just talking to myself."

When they rode into the ranch homestead, Prue stopped and stared. Every open inch of the place was covered in cowpens bulging with moving cattle. The pens looked to be hastily constructed. They were made of saplings stacked five feet high between two pieces of Boarhog's home-milled lumber. The lumber posts were set eight feet apart, two together with space between the two posts to stack the saplings. It was a simple but strong way to construct a fence, and it looked to be holding the cows. The saplings still had leaves on them and the cattle were busy stripping off the leaves and eating them. Prue hoped the vigilantes would show up before the leaf supply ran out.

The rain picked up. When Prue looked into the sky, all he saw was a uniform leaden gray. He and Danny rode their horses right into the barn glad to get out of the weather. Boarhog was in the alley between the stalls cutting more of his fence posts. When he saw them ride in, he dropped the saw and walked over to Prue.

"Do you see all them cows, Mr. Prue? There's hundreds of them. What we gonna do with all them cows? As soon as they finish off the leaves, they gonna bust out. I just knows it."

Laughing, Prue climbed off Satan and shook out his slicker. "I hope they hold on long enough to provide us with a little support against the vigilantes, Boarhog. Are any of them ours?"

"You wouldn't believe it Mr. Prue, but there's a hundred head of cows in that bunch what are ours. Most of 'em got calves with them, too. We's rich, Mr. Prue."

Prue put his arm around Boarhog's shoulders. "I hate to tell you this, but we're gonna have to let them out."

"What! You jokin' with ole Boarhog, ain't you? I been building pens from sunup to sundown for three days. The farmers keep on bringing 'em in and now we ain't got no more room and you gonna let them out?"

"Not just yet, Boarhog, but that is the plan."

Boarhog tilted his head to the side as a smile of understanding slowly grew on his face. He wagged a finger at Prue. "I get it now. I sees what you got planned. It's devilish, that's what it is, Mr. Prue, pure devilment."

"I hope so, Boarhog. Did Miss Harriet go back to town?"

"I took her and the little missy into town myself yesterday morning. That dang dog of your'n stayed with them. He tried to bite me. He's bad, Mr. Prue, pure bad."

"I hope he takes care of Jenny," Prue said.

Danny unsaddled the horses while Prue, putting the wet slicker back on, made his way out into the rain to check on the cattle and the settlers. From the look of things, the place was as ready as it could get for an attack by Malachai McQueen and the Sara Sota Vigilance Committee. Whatever the vigilantes expected, Prue was sure it wasn't going to be what they got. He had a secret weapon.

He found Willy Starling hunkered inside his covered wagon drinking coffee. He had erected a tarp and his wife built a small cook fire under it with a bucket of boiling coffee hanging over the fire on a tripod.

Prue stuck his head in the opening of the wagon. "How are things coming, Willy?" he asked.

Mrs. Starling was sitting on a three-legged stool beside her husband darning socks. When she saw Prue, she got up and climbed out of the wagon to let Prue in. Prue tipped his hat to her, which caused rivulets of water to run into his face.

"Howdy ma'm," he said as she climbed out.

"Come on in here where it's dry, boy. Emma, fetch the lad a cup of that coffee and have Hank and Dale come over to the wagon so we can all talk."

Hank and Dale were Starling's two grown sons. Space inside the wagon became severely limited with the two big Starling boys sitting on a steamer trunk, Willy in his chair, and Prue on the stool vacated by Mrs. Starling.

"I heard from servants at the Rafter Q that McQueen has become dangerously unbalanced," Prue said. "He shot up his own relatives and rode out. I think he's gonna gather up vigilante members and ride on us here. Word that the settlers he's displaced are gathering here is all over the county."

"I ain't quite sure what you got planned, Mr. Prue," Willy said. "But we rounded up a mess of cattle. And old man Carter and my pa plowed a heck of a swamp around this place."

"I saw that when I come in," Prue said. "All this rain sure helped."

"What else do we need to be doing?" Dale Starling asked. "My family is getting right nervous waiting."

"Load every rifle, pistol, and shotgun you have and sit tight," Prue said. "They will come. I got me a secret weapon up at the house, a little something left over from the war I bought on my way here from Texas, a howitzer."

Will and his sons' mouths flopped open. "You just happen to have yerself a cannon?" Will stumbled over the words. "I can't believe it. Boys, this man has a cannon."

Dale and Hank giggled like little kids. "He's got a cannon," Dale said to his brother and poked him in the ribs. "How on earth did you get something like that and where you been keepin' it?"

"I bought it from a peddler. He had a wagonload of military artillery, ammo, and guns he collected after the war. He was pulling this cannon behind the wagon, a neat little mountain howitzer. I had to have it. He delivered it to me about a month ago on his way to sell some guns to the Seminoles. I bought it because I like cannons and I guess I thought it might make a good lawn ornament one day. I never in my wildest dreams thought I would have to use it. Now I'm glad I made him show me how to load and fire the thing and include some ammo in the sale. He had a pile of canister shot all packed and ready to go and he threw in a couple of friction primers and showed me how to make quill fuses when they ran out."

"I can't believe we got us a cannon." Will's eyes were round as marbles.

"It's just a small one, a twelve-pound howitzer. It was originally designed to be disassembled and packed on a horse into the mountains. This one's on wheels. I ain't fired it yet, so we need to pray it doesn't blow up in our faces." Prue couldn't stop smiling. He was proud of the cannon. It had been his secret weapon all along and part of his plan to defeat the vigilantes. He was thrilled to share the knowledge of it with someone and discover they were just as excited and happy about possessing the weapon as he was.

"What's it fire, ball?" Hank asked.

"I have six twelve-pound balls and ten rounds of canister shot," Prue told them. The canister shot is deadly. It's like a tin can with one hundred forty-eight mini-balls packed inside with sawdust. When you fire a round, the can comes apart like a shotgun shell and sprays the mini-balls in a three-hundred yard area. The old man told me it was lethal to two-hundred fifty feet."

"Holy Mother of God," Dale said quietly. "Now that's what I call a secret weapon. Can we go look at it?"

"It's under a tarp behind the barn. When it stops raining we can wheel it out and figure out where best to place it. Then I'll teach you both how to load and fire it."

"I saw that tarp covering up something with wheels back there," Dale said. "I thought it was just an old buckboard you were storing under the tarp. Damn, I can't believe we got us a cannon. I can't wait to load it up and shoot it."

Prue laughed. Will's boys were just like him. The thought of loading and firing the cannon had them as excited as two kids in a candy store.

"Who you going to get to mind the cattle?" Willy asked.

"I need two men on horseback come dark time," Prue said. "I don't think the vigilantes will attack us until around dawn. Anyone around them cows from now on needs to be mounted. Keep all your children away from them. Can't underestimate the danger of a crowd of cows like that. A clap of thunder, a rifle shot, or even a bunch of kids making too much noise or a dog could cause them to stampede. God knows what they'll do when we fire off the cannon. I been in a stampede before and it's about the scariest thing I know."

"What else do you want us to do, Mr. Prue?" Dale asked. "We're right grateful for ye taking us in and we want to do everything we can to help out, you hear?"

Prue smiled. "I'm gonna need you boys to help me with the cannon. Sleep with yer boots and yer britches on this night."

The flap of the wagon opened and Emma Starling stuck her head in. She handed her sons tin mugs of coffee. "I just heard there's a rider approaching the ranch," she said.

Prue shook his hat. "Thanks, ma'am. I'll be going out to see who it is."

The rain was slacking off as Prue climbed out of the wagon. The sun was nothing but a fuzzy shiny spot on the western horizon as it prepared to set. Prue looked out over the cattle and saw a tall man walking in leading a big black horse. Clapping his hat on his head, Prue strode toward him taking in details of the man and his dress. From his clothes, he seemed to be an important man. He wore a black suit, the coat with long tails. His shirt was white and he had on gray britches, a black leather vest, and tall black boots with silver eagle spurs. When Prue got close enough, he saw the badge of a US Marshal on the lapel of the man's jacket.

Prue stuck out his hand. "Howdy, sir, my name's Jesse Pruitt. What can I do fer ya?"

"Marshal Bill Short. I'm here to see what you got going on. Someone brought a bunch of stories about you and your ranch to my attention. They were in the *Desoto County News*. I read them when I was up in Tampa. I heard you got a lot of settlers here that were run off by a group of vigilantes. I was wondering if you knew where I might find those vigilantes."

Prue listened in astonishment to what Marshal Short had to say. He couldn't believe Harry's stories had gone all the way to Tampa. He felt pride in her accomplishments almost as though they had somehow been his own. Harry had come a long way in a very short time. "Yes sir, we do have a bunch of settlers got run off their land camped out over yonder."

"So the stories are true and the girl had it right?" Short sounded surprised.

"Did you ride all this way from Tampa expectin' the whole mess to be a made up fairy tale?"

"You have no idea how many wild goose chases I go on every year," Short said. "And then, half the time when I get somewhere to investigate a crime or a situation, it's already been resolved. I just got to check out everything and make sure I got my facts straight before I do anything. I represent the United States Marshal Service. This ain't no fly-by-night operation you understand."

"Yes sir, I think I do understand. Now you let me help you put up that horse and we can go talk to the settlers. You can hear their stories for yourself." Prue was still feeling slightly confounded by the arrival of a real US Marshal. Short's appearance on the scene filled him with hope. The vigilantes were a serious problem. They had killed helpless citizens and frightened families of honest folk into abandoning their land. Still, Prue never expected help from the government and he couldn't believe something as simple as a story in the newspaper led to the arrival of Marshal Short.

Shaking his head he led Short to the barn, which at this point was about slap full of horses and mules, not to mention the team of oxen. But they'd find somewhere they could stable the Marshal's big horse even if it meant them dang oxen would be out in the weather. Big old things should be fine in one of the cowpens with the rest of the cattle, but Prue knew better. The oxen were trained draft animals and worth a lot of money. Still, they could spend the night in the corral adjacent to the barn. A little rain wouldn't hurt them.

"So, do you think you can put me in the way of finding these vigilantes?" Short asked after they sandwiched his gelding into a makeshift stall in what used to be Prue's loafing shed.

"Well sir, you could be in luck. I got a feeling tonight is the night we're gonna get us a visit from the Sara Sota Vigilance Committee. Stick around. I think we're in for a fight."

24

Harriet was walking on a cloud. She had Jenny's hand in hers as they made their way toward the Arcadia House, but she floated so high she could barely feel the boards of the sidewalk beneath her boots. Her stories had made it all the way to Tampa and they had possibly helped affect the downfall of the Sara Sota Vigilance Committee. Marshal Short said he was here to put an end to their activities. If he was successful, it would be due to Harriet's stories, because if he hadn't read them, he wouldn't even be here.

When they got to Arcadia House, Harriet led Jenny around back. "We're gonna have to go up the back steps," she told Jenny. "That dang dog of yours will stir up too big of a commotion if we go in the front door. He might even get us kicked out."

Jenny's eyes rounded. "I'm sorry, Miss Harry. But I do love Buzzard and he loves me."

"First chance we get, we're riding back to Prue and dumping that animal with him. He needs to be out working cattle, not taking up residence in our bedroom."

Jenny hung her head, but she laid a hand on Buzzard's back as she walked and the big dog never left her side. When they went by the kitchen, Mae Mae came out of the back door. She stood for a moment on the porch mopping her forehead with her apron. When she saw Harriet and Jenny she clapped her hands together. "Missy Harry, you got little girly back. Oh, I so happy."

Mae Mae gave Jenny a hug. "You big girl. I so glad to see you. How your chigger bites?"

Jenny giggled. "I still have a couple behind my knees that won't go away, Mae Mae. But mostly your bath fixed me up pretty good."

"I got some more ointment we put on those bad bites," Mae Mae said. "Well, Missy Harry, how you do with that job? I been reading the paper and I saw all those articles you wrote. You damn fine writer."

"I'm doing good," Harriet said. "I just dropped some more stories off at the newspaper and Mr. Jeffers wants me to go back to Prue's ranch in a couple of days and follow up on what's happening out there. Tomorrow he wants me to dress up and try to sell some ads. I'm not too sure about talking to shopkeepers and such. I hope I don't mess it up."

"That's very good," Mae Mae said. "We proud of you, me and Leonard and all of us here at Arcadia House. So why you sneaking up to your room the back way?"

Harry pointed to Buzzard. "It's the dog, Mae Mae, he's taken a fancy to Jenny and she to him and you know I hate to upset her. She's been through so much. As big and dirty as he is, I don't think the management would appreciate him in the dining room or the lobby and probably not in my room either."

Mae Mae put her small hands on her hips. "He look like hungry dog to me. Let me see what I find for him to eat."

She left for a few moments, and reappeared toting a huge bone with chunks of red meat still attached. She handed it to Harriet who gingerly held it in front of her with two fingers. "Thank you, Mae Mae, for everything you done for me."

The Chinese woman hushed her. "No never you mind. All of us women got to stick together you know. Now I go get back to my cooking."

Harriet lugged the enormous bone up to her room. When they were inside, she presented it to Buzzard. It was too big for the dog to hold up. He dragged it under the bed and disappeared under there with it. They could hear him grinding and chewing.

Jenny sat on the bed. Her eyes were huge and Harry could see she was close to exhaustion. The stress of the past weeks had the little girl worn out.

"Lay down, sugar. Here let me take off your boots. Tomorrow, we'll go out and buy you some new clothes, a new pair of boots, and a new collar for that dang dog. You rest and I think I'll rest for a while with you."

Harry consulted the little watch she wore pinned to her shirt. It was almost four. "We can rest until supper time. Then we'll go down and eat, come up here, and start going through all this stuff I got piled around. I might have some of my older clothes that could fit you."

Jenny smiled and closed her eyes. Harry took off her own boots and lay down next to her. It would be good to get out of these pants and put on a dress. She was planning her next article, one about Prue and how he vanquished the vigilantes single-handedly, when she fell asleep.

"Wake up, Miss Harry. I'm getting kind of hungry." Jenny shook Harriet's arm. Harriet's eyes flew open. Where was she? For a minute she couldn't remember. She must have slept for a while; it was dark outside. When she looked at her watch, she leapt to her feet. Holy cow, it was after six. If they didn't hurry, they would miss the last sitting for supper.

Harry poured water into the wash basin and found clean washcloths and a towel. She had Jenny wash her face and hands while she pulled on a skirt and blouse. Lacing up her boots, she looked at Jenny. "You get that dirty smock off. There's a clean one in the bag."

Harriet splashed water on her face and helped Jenny tidy up and lace up her boots. She quickly rebraided Jenny's blonde hair and pulled her red mane into a knot at the back of her neck, securing it with several long pins she found on her dressing table. It was good to be home where all the stuff she needed was close at hand.

The two of them, all clean and dressed, headed for the door. Buzzard appeared from under the bed and whined to be let out with them.

"You stay here," Harriet ordered the dog and thought for the hundredth time he needed to be back on Prue's ranch.

The big dog sat on his haunches and watched them leave. "That animal will probably eat all my shoes and destroy the room before we get back," Harriet said to Jenny as they headed down the open walkway outside all the rooms to the stairs leading to the main house.

"No he won't," Jenny assured her. "He's really very well behaved, for a dog."

"Jenny, he's a cow dog with no house manners. He's used to the open range and sleeping under the stars at night. He's going to hate it here with us and cause all kinds of trouble, I just know it. As soon as I can, I'm taking him back to Prue's ranch."

Harriet opened the door to the dining room for Jenny. The two walked in just in time to be served. Harriet found two seats next to each other at the long table seating ten in the middle of the room. She held Jenny's chair for her to sit and then sat down herself. She showed Jenny how to put her napkin in her lap and then looked up to see who was seated around her. She knew most of the residents but there were always a few new faces.

The waiter filled her bowl with hearty vegetable soup as she took stock of the other guests. When her gaze reached the head of the table, only two seats from theirs, her heart stopped beating and she froze. All the blood in her body rushed into her head. It was him! She jumped to her feet knocking over her chair.

"You followed us," she hissed, unaware of the spectacle she was creating, poor Jenny staring up at her or of anything else in the world but Buford Simpson sitting at the head of the table looking for all the world as though he owned the place.

Grabbing Jenny's hand, she turned and bolted from the dining room. Her only thought was to get away, as far away from her terrible uncle as possible. Uncle Buford was fat, but quick. He ran out of the room right behind them, pounding up the stairs in their wake.

Harriet, fumbling in a panic with her key in the lock, got it opened just as Uncle Buford reached them. She and Jenny fell into the room with Buford on their heels. Buzzard was waiting just on the other side of the door. He'd heard them on the walkway and heard Harriet put her key in the lock. When Buford appeared in the doorway behind them, Buzzard launched himself at the fat man, growling horribly. Buzzard knocked Uncle Buford flat on his back and grabbed him by the throat. He shook Buford Simpson like a rag doll, all the time snarling and making an ugly noise deep in his chest.

Uncle Buford screamed as flecks of saliva few from his mouth. He pushed on Buzzard's chest, shrieking. "Harriet, save me please save me. Don't let him kill me, please."

Harriet stood in the doorway gasping for breath, working furiously to compose herself. Seeing her uncle had been a terrible shock. But she was no longer a child under his control. She was a grown woman with a job and a good life. He had no power over her. In fact, because of Buzzard, she now had the power, the power of life or death over this man who terrorized her childhood.

"Come here, Buzzard," she called to the dog. Buzzard let go of Buford's throat and turned to look at her, but remained crouched over Uncle Buford with his paws on either side of the man's shoulders. Blood flowed from several deep wounds in Buford's neck. Blood stained his white shirt and white satin tie. Harriet saw the dog look at Jenny and realized Buzzard was not protecting her but was protecting the little girl. Somehow Buzzard had instantly perceived what Harriet had not. Buford was no longer a threat to her. He was a threat to Jenny.

"Jenny, call off the dog," she said quietly.

Jenny, who hid behind Harriet's skirts, stepped into the doorway. "Come here, Buzzard," she said softly.

The dog looked at Jenny, looked once more at Buford slobbering and blubbering beneath the dog's chest, hands now clutching the bleeding wounds on his neck. Buzzard growled once more, like a final warning, and leaped into the room, falling to the ground and rolling like a happy puppy at Jenny's feet.

"Stay away from us, Uncle Buford. I don't know why you came here, but you can pack up your bags and go right back to Savannah where you belong. There ain't nothing here for you." Harriet slammed the door and leaned against it. Sliding slowly to the floor, sobs shook her entire body as she sat on the worn carpet of her room.

"Who is that man, Miss Harry? Why did you run away from him?"

"He's my uncle," Harriet said when she could speak. "He hurt me when I was little like you. He hurt me bad."

"What's he want now? Does he still want to hurt you? Buzzard won't let him, you know. He don't like that man. He don't like him at all."

"I don't know what my uncle wants, baby girl," Harriet said as tears started running down her cheeks again. "I took some money from him when I ran away. He could be here to get it back. Whatever the reason, he came here looking for me and now he's seen you and I'm afraid he might want to hurt you, too."

"What are we gonna do, Miss Harry?"

"I don't know," Harriet said. "I guess we'll have to think of something."

Prue kicked a dried clump of mud with his boot and uttered a curse under his breath. He'd been so sure the vigilantes would come last night. For two nights, the entire camp had waited, torches lit, guns loaded. But no vigilantes came riding across the prairie into his ranch.

Not only did he have seven families of settlers waiting, seven families of settlers he had to feed, but now he had a US Marshal under foot. All of them trusted Prue knew what he was doing and until this very moment Prue thought he did know.

Maybe McQueen was smart enough to figure Prue planned this as a trap. Maybe McQueen had no intention of falling into it no matter how well Prue baited it. Maybe this whole thing was going to be a bust.

With no rain, the mud in his plowed swathe dried. The cattle in the pens were hungry. Fifteen head of heifers and one bull knocked down Boarhog's temporary enclosure behind the barn and wandered his homestead all night. The heifers got into everything, while the bull destroyed one wagon. The big animal terrorized the Dale Starling family, knocking their wagon over and goring a hog.

Prue shaded his eyes and looked into the distance. The only good thing he saw were clouds. It looked like it was going to rain again. That would at least help keep the man-made swamp around his place wet. They needed that swamp to slow down McQueen's men. Prue had no idea how many he might bring with him. He hoped McQueen brought every last member of the Sara Sota Vigilance Committee. Prue wanted to knock them all out in this one action.

Marshal Short hailed Prue as he walked back toward the house. *Great! Short is the last man I need to talk to.*

"Howdy Marshal. Looks like rain, don't it?"

"Listen, Pruitt, we've been waiting up all night long for two nights. I can't stay here forever. I thought you said the vigilantes would attack night before last. What's going on?"

Prue sighed. "I don't know why they ain't showed up yet, Marshal. Believe me, I don't want these families kicking their heels here much longer either. And if you think I'm happy about having two hundred head of restless, hungry cows penned up by sticks and string only a few feet away from my home, you're crazy."

"Well, what's your plan now, Pruitt? We supposed to just sit here for another night?" Marshal Short sucked on a dead cigar. Prue could smell it and see flecks of tobacco stuck in the Marshal's pearly white teeth. The man was so close Prue thought he detected the aroma of the man's hair oil.

"Listen, Marshal, if you want to go back to Arcadia, go on. We can handle the vigilantes ourselves. That was my plan in the first place. These people got no place else to go until the vigilantes have been dealt with. We'll be just fine until they come here. And I assure you, Malachai McQueen will come. I know the man. Even if he thinks this is a trap, he'll come. He won't be able to stop himself. That's just the kind of man he is."

Short backed down and stuffed his hands in the pockets of his black coat. A coat now rumpled from two nights' worth of sitting up with a rifle across his lap. Every man in the camp was in a mean mood from waiting. The women weren't too happy either.

"I'm really gonna have to leave tomorrow if they don't show tonight," Short said. "I got business to attend to back in Tampa. I was hoping to get this thing worked out a little faster. I hadn't really planned to stay in these parts at all. I was just comin' down here to check out the situation and see what needed to be done. I already stayed more than I should have."

"Hey, Marshal. You do whatever you need to. Tonight, we'll set up just like we done last night and the night before. McQueen will come. I don't know what's keepin' him."

Prue decided to visit Will Starling. There was something solid and comforting about Will and his wife. He found Will eating breakfast. "You folks doing all right?" Prue asked.

"We're fine, just a little wore out," Starling said.

"I know the feeling. You all rest a while then I'm gonna need your boys to help me get some feed together for these cows. If we don't find something for them to eat, they're all gonna bust out fer sure."

Will nodded. "I'll gather the men up after dinner. What is it you want us to do?"

"I think if we go into the woods and cut some branches down and haul them into the pens, it'll keep them quiet until tomorrow. I'm really hopin' the vigilantes show up tonight. I can't think what's keepin' them."

"That Marshal feller is getting a little antsy. If he ain't happy, he needs to get his self out a here," Willy said with his mouth full of fried potatoes.

Prue accepted a cup of coffee from Emma and sat down at the Starling table, a small fold-up affair with room for two. "I wish he would go. At the moment, he sure ain't helping things. I'm about sorry this is draggin' on so long. I thought McQueen would a been here two nights ago."

"It ain't yer fault, Prue. You're doin' all you can. Things would be fine and you wouldn't even be worried if Short weren't hanging over yer shoulder a pushin' you."

"I know," Prue said. "One good thing though, it looks like it might rain."

㉕

Pacing the floor did little to alleviate Malachai McQueen's irritation or impatience. It took two days to bring together all the members of the Sara Sota Vigilance Committee. It was almost nine o'clock, but finally all were assembled in the meeting hall of First Methodist.

Rain hammered the tin roof as he stood outside a closet in the meeting hall's back room. Inside the closet, Reverend Whiteleaf moved furniture and boxes. The reverend's hands trembled as he passed a burlap bag holding fifty-seven black masks, one for each member of the committee, to Malachai. The masks were kept in a closet in the meeting hall under boxes of old hymnals, vases, faded altar cloths, and a broken podium.

"You're not going to require me to go along, are you?" Whiteleaf's voice trembled just like his hands. "I don't have any rain gear and it's pouring buckets out there."

Malachai smiled. "Everyone's going on this raid, Reverend. You wouldn't want to miss the most important run we've ever made, would you?"

"No, of course not. But it's my horse, you see. He's lame. The wife let him get into the grain bin and I think he's coming on to a founder. And then the rain, I take cold so easily and with improper rain protection, I'll get a soaking. I've never had the money to purchase a good slicker."

Malachai laid an arm over Whiteleaf's narrow shoulders. "I'm sure we can find you a mount, Reverend, and a poncho to keep off the rain. Now take these masks and pass them out. Make sure you keep one for yourself."

The two men entered the meeting room through a side door. Talking ceased and a hush fell over the men inside. Malachai felt their attention on him. He felt his own importance filling him. It was like the finest wine. It made his head spin. He climbed onto a table and spread his hands wide to welcome the members of the committee and to embrace them all and inhale their energy. He took a deep breath.

"Fellow members of the Sara Sota Vigilance Committee, it's so good to see all of you together on this momentous occasion. I'm sure you all have heard of the Texan, Jesse Pruitt, and how he's been taking displaced settlers onto his land, succoring them, feeding them hope, and keeping their dreams of making a home on our range land alive."

All eyes focused on Malachai. His chest swelled. "This Pruitt has pulled down his pants and stuck his naked hind end in all of our faces. He's made fools of every one of us. He's made the Sara Sota Vigilance Committee, an organization whose very name used to strike terror in the hearts of every squatter and sod buster, look like a bunch of stupid incompetents. He's single-handedly undone a large amount of what we worked hard to achieve. We can't let that go unpunished. We can't let him get away with what he has done. It's up to us to finish what we started. The squatters must go!"

Malachai shouted the last words and the members of the committee cheered and hollered out their agreement. Rebel yells and whistles filled the room as Whiteleaf passed out the masks. When he was done McQueen took the sack from him. Three masks remained inside. McQueen took one and handed it to Whiteleaf. Then he pulled one out for himself. One mask remained in the bag, and he held it up for all the members to see.

"This mask belonged to Sergeant Pelo Berryhill. That low-down Texan killed him. Shot him dead in the back. I saw it with my own eyes and I buried the sergeant beside my mother and father. Tonight we will avenge Sergeant Berryhill and we will right the wrongs perpetrated by this Texan. Tonight we will string him up and hang him for his crimes."

McQueen climbed off the table to more cheers. Sheriff Daniels of Arcadia moved between the tables and chairs to stand beside Malachai. "Judge, I need to have a private word with you about some disturbing information I've recently received."

Malachai pulled Daniels off into a corner by the refreshment table. Bless old Janey Mable Whiteleaf. She put out quite a spread. "What's going on, Daniels?"

Daniels shuffled his feet back and forth nervously and Malachai's stomach churned. What had the man heard to make him so nervous?

"I had a report of some serious doings out at your ranch," Daniels said. "One of your ranch hands came into my office and told me you shot up yer own kin folk. He said you killed yer cousin and yer foreman, shot 'em dead, and you left old lady McQueen shot up but still alive. This sounds like something I'm going to have to follow up on. Word of this gets around and I didn't act on it, well my ass will be in a sling fer sure. What happened out there, Judge?"

Malachai's throat tightened like he'd never be able to swallow again. He wasn't that worried about Daniels. Daniels was easily taken care of. What upset him was the news that Aunt Thelma might still be alive. If the old lady survived, she could be marshalling forces against him right now.

Aunt Thelma had money and power. And her name gave her power in Desoto County. The McQueen name was so well known in these parts, mostly because of him, that anyone bearing that name would instantly draw attention. Her word would carry authority and people would listen to what she said.

"Nothing that need bother you, Sheriff," Malachai said. "Surely you don't think I had anything to do with shooting my own kinfolk?"

"I'm just telling you what I heard, Judge. And the high yeller gal that come into town with the cowhand, said the old lady is telling anyone that will listen you ain't a McQueen."

What terrible luck. Why couldn't fat Clara have been the one to survive? But no, it had to be that nosey, interfering old hag.

Malachai threw an arm around Daniels's shoulder. "Listen, I got a great idea. This Texan I'm talking about, Jesse Pruitt, he has some fine land on Horse Creek and a sizable herd of cattle. Now after we hang him for killing my sergeant, I believe you should be the one to inherit his land and those cows. That land is just what you've been looking for. It's a half-day's ride to Arcadia and as pretty a piece of land as you could ask for right on the creek. Getting the paperwork pushed through should be a cinch."

As if by magic, Daniels forgot all about trouble at the Rafter Q. His mind grabbed hold of the idea of possessing the land on Horse Creek, currently owned by Jesse Pruitt. McQueen could see the dollar signs shining from Daniels's beady blue eyes.

"That land surely does sound exactly like what I was looking for, Judge. You think we'll be able to roust the Texan and all them squatters?"

"Sheriff Daniels, this is the Sara Sota Vigilance Committee you're a talk-in' about. There is no doubt in my mind that before this night is over, the Texan will be hanging from a tree limb and all them squatters and sod bust-ers killed or vanquished to the ends of the earth."

Daniels smiled and Malachai could see him thinking about the land and the instantaneous realization of all his dreams.

"One more thing, Judge," Daniels said, then stopped and looked around as though checking for anyone listening. "I heard there's a US Marshal come to town two days ago. He didn't stay long and I can't find anyone who knows why he was here or where he went. He did stop in at the *Daily News*, and Jeffers has always been an enemy of the committee. There's been a couple of stories in his paper about the Texan and them squatters. Now I didn't read none of them, but a couple of folks have mentioned the articles to me."

Malachai frowned. What would a US Marshal want in Arcadia? And why would he speak to the newspaper editor? Mal put looking into the marshal in the number-one position on his mental to-do list. Best not to dally on finding out why that marshal was here.

The two of them strolled out of the church meeting hall into the stormy night. Trees whipped back and forth in the wind as sheets of rain poured out of the sky.

"We sure picked us a bitch of a night to go riding," Daniels said, as he pulled on his rain slicker and buttoned it all the way up under his throat.

Malachai smiled. "This is the best weather for a raid. During the war, my most successful sorties were under cover of a rainstorm. The enemy can't see you coming and the sound of the rain covers the noise of galloping horses. The enemy is usually just as concerned about taking cover from the inclement weather as you are, my friend. We couldn't have asked for better weather."

With that final word, Malachai tugged the brim of his top hat low over his forehead and found his horse on the picket line. Rooster's roan stood with his butt to the wind, tail clamped to his backside. All the picketed horses stood that way, head low, ears back as they tried to stay dry in the driving rain. One of the roan's ears swiveled back and forth at the sound of McQueen's voice. Malachai noticed with satisfaction that the horse tucked his tail even tighter. Old Roanie had finally learned who was boss.

Malachai untied the reins and tightened his cinch, giving it a final yank to make sure it wouldn't slip. He missed the yellow stud. He'd loved riding that horse. Not only was it dead broke, but it fit Malachai's image of himself, tall, flashy, and a stallion. The roan was smaller and a gelding. The animal had no flash and no dash. Well, after all this was over, he would get himself a new stallion. He kind of fancied the Texan's mustang. Black would definitely suit him.

When the men mounted their horses, including the Reverend White-leaf, Malachai galloped to the head of the fifty-five men. "Form up in two columns," he yelled over thunder rolling in the distance. McQueen had his sword with him for this special occasion, the real Malachai's army sword. He pulled the old blade out of the saddle scabbard and raised it high. "Forward, ho," he called as he spurred the roan into a fast trot.

They headed out of Brownville toward the river. McQueen charged the roan into the water and was soon across. He climbed the high bank on the other side and looked back. Reverend Whiteleaf sat his horse, his own horse miraculously cured of laminitis, high on the other bank.

Malachai pulled Daniels aside as the rest of the men climbed the bank and reformed into columns. "I think the Reverend needs to be taught a lesson when we get back from this raid," Malachai said. "Maybe he'll feel differently about what he owes us when his cattle are all missing and his ranch house burned to the ground."

Daniels pulled his short-crowned black beaver hat with the wide stiff brim and silver concho hatband lower on his forehead. "I reckon the good reverend has had himself a change of heart. Turned coward on us. He'll have to pay. He swore the same oath all of us did."

"Oh yes, he will pay," McQueen said. "Let's ride."

It took them two hours in the driving rain to cover the eight miles to Horse Creek. It was as dark as the inside of a coffin. Heavy clouds covered the moon and stars. The horses constantly stumbled and tripped as the riders pushed them to trot across ground they could barely see filled with puddles of standing water and mud holes. Every man was miserable. It added to their tempers. Each man was pretty edgy by the time they turned the bend in the creek and grew closer to Jesse Pruitt's ranch, a spot most of the county seem to know where to find.

McQueen, in the lead, held up his hand to stop them when he felt they were close. He called two of his best men forward. Bud Dawkins and Dusty Rhodes were two of the younger members of his group. Most of the men were older, cattlemen, shopkeepers, lawyers, and doctors. These two were the younger sons of two of the cattlemen. Their fathers owned good-sized spreads on the big prairie close to Lake Okeechobee. They'd been suffering from an influx of cattle rustlers and settlers and were some of the vigilantes' biggest supporters. Not to mention Dawkins and Rhodes were rough and rowdy cowhands and enjoyed the raids more than most.

"You two scout around and find the ranch and these settlers. I'm gonna light us a fire up under those trees so you can find us when you get a good look at where we need to be going. I know we got to be close and there's no sense in all of us blundering around in the dark."

The two men, really not much more than boys, smiled showing their teeth. "We got it covered, Judge," Dawkins said.

Malachai watched them ride off and consulted his watch. It was only ten minutes after midnight. The two boys should be back in an hour. They couldn't be that far from Pruitt's ranch, and that would leave then four or five good hours of dark to wrap up this ugly business.

He had Daniels build a large fire with the help of Duron Grey and Fines Parker. They'd just got the blaze roaring good when the rain let up. But with the passing of the rain, a cold wind began blowing. Cy McClelland pulled a felled tree limb close to the fire and began feeding dead limbs into the blaze.

Malachai stepped away from the fire and pulled Judge Whidden aside. "I'm sure glad the rain's stopped."

Whidden nodded. He was an older man, toughened from years of working cattle. His face turned to leather years ago and his body didn't carry an ounce of fat. He'd served as a judge before the current Desoto County was formed, sitting on the bench in Manatee County and then in Desoto County. He'd been known as the hanging judge then and he was the hardest man Malachai ever met.

"Judge, as my lieutenant, I want you in charge of capturing Pruitt. I'm planning to conduct a hanging here tonight."

Whidden spit an enormous gob of tobacco and saliva onto the ground between them. "Suits me fine," he said. "Sooner he gets strung up for what he done, the better. You know me, I don't believe in diddlywackin' around."

"You take the boys, Bud and Dusty, with you. They should be a big help."

As the wind grew sharper, the men huddled closer to the fire. About one-thirty the two scouts returned.

"We could see yer fire for a mile," Rhodes said as he warmed his hands on the blaze.

The flames leapt high illuminating the dripping canopy of oak leaves overhead. Malachai looked up and saw the moon coming from behind a cloud. That was a good omen. But he'd already known this raid would be successful. He was always successful. The only thing nagging at him was Aunt Thelma. How had the old bag survived? She could cause him a lot of trouble. He'd have to ride back and take care of her. There was no way he would allow the McQueens to drive him out of his own home, a home he had fashioned into his idea of the finest and most comfortable place in the county.

Rhodes and Dawkins stood close to the fire and spoke to McQueen and the assembled vigilantes, telling what they saw on their scouting run.

"There's some kind of plowed strip surrounding the place," Rhodes said. "We left the horses behind and crossed it on foot. It's kind of muddy in places. The place is lit up like daytime. Fires are burning everywhere and there's a lot of torches and lanterns. This should be a piece of cake. And there's spoils for all of us. Pruitt's got a lot of cows penned up, maybe two hundred. We should all end up with a few head."

"Did you see the settlers?" Malachai demanded.

"Oh hell yes we saw them," Dawkins said. "Looks like a regular circus going on with tents and wagons and such. But we didn't see many folks walking around and we didn't see the first guard. There were a couple of women working at one fire making food. We saw one old man taking a leak. An old lady was up walking a baby. She walked that kid all over the place. But everyone else seemed to be in bed asleep."

"You done good, boys," Malachai said. He couldn't believe his luck. No guards, all were probably fast asleep. They wouldn't know what hit them. "How far away is it?"

"About a mile up the creek from here," Rhodes said. "We just followed the creek and we found the ranch right where you said it was."

"Warm yourself for a few minutes and then get ready to ride," Malachai told them. "This should be over way before dawn. It'll be like killing pigs in a pen, easy."

Malachai pulled the roan off the picket line and began loading shells into his rifle. He slid it back into its scabbard and pulled the sawed-off out of his hip holster. The shotgun was full of shells. He checked the gun's action, cocking it then releasing the hammer. When he was sure that gun was in good working order, he checked the old pistol.

He sure missed Pelo. The sergeant had been with him since the war. He felt like his right arm had been cut off. Somehow, Mal knew it was all because of the Texan. Jesse Pruitt was at the bottom of all the pain and suffering Malachai was forced to endure over the past weeks. And it was payback time.

The rest of the men pulled their mounts off the line and checked their weapons. The flickering light of the fire illuminated them as they tied their rain gear to their saddles and tightened cinches and girths. Malachai mounted up and looked at his men. They were a pretty tough group, and most were experienced raiders. This should be easy.

The men gathered around him. He motioned to the two boys. "Bud and Dusty come back and said there's no sentries and the settlers are sure enough there. I want you men in quick. Bud there said there's plenty of torches burning. They must like light. Well we'll give 'em plenty. Take the torches and set the place afire. The boys said there's over a hundred head of cattle penned in the area around the barns. Be careful. We don't need them stampeding until after we're out of there. Try to limit yer fire to a sure kill. The Judge and Bud and Dusty are gonna go after Pruitt. The rest of you concentrate on taking out the squatters. Does everybody understand?"

The men nodded and murmured agreement. Malachai lifted his hand. "Let's ride."

26

Harriet climbed off her mare and walked back to help Jenny. Mr. Britches had balked at the bridge, refusing to set even one of his small hooves on the wooden planks. When Jenny smacked him with her crop, the little son of a gun laid down. Jenny had to climb out of the saddle quickly or get her leg pinned under the fat, lazy, contrary animal.

Grabbing the reins, Harriet pulled on Mr. Britches. "Come on you sorry little slug," Harry cursed. "Get behind him and push, Jenny."

Jenny looked up at Harriet with her eyebrows raised. "You got to be kidding, Miss Harry. He'll kick my head slap off."

Harriet and Jenny had packed their bags and raced to the livery stable where the two animals were kept the minute Buford Simpson cleared off the walkway outside their room. The only place Harry would feel safe with that man around was with Prue. She couldn't get to his ranch fast enough. And now this ridiculous pony would not cross the bridge and it was getting dark. What were Jenny's poor dead parents thinking when they bought this pony for her? Everyone knew ponies had the worst temperaments of any animal alive except maybe a mule, and Mr. Britches was no exception.

Buzzard started to bark. That scared Harry but didn't even get an ear twitch out of Mr. Britches, who sat on his haunches like a dog. Harriet glanced toward Arcadia. Scanning the road, she prayed it wasn't her uncle coming after her. Far across the bridge three cows grazed in the roadway. Harry sighed with relief. "Cows," she said, pointing for Jenny's sake.

Unable to resist the temptation of a hot chase, Buzzard shot across the bridge toward the cows.

"Come back, Buzzard," Jenny yelled. The big dog ignored her, intent on catching cows and having a whole lot of dog fun.

"Leave him be, Jenny. He'll follow us when we get across the bridge. We have to ride right by those cows anyway."

Harriet returned her attention to the reluctant pony. In all her days she'd never had to deal with a creature this ornery. Ponies were all mean little animals, but it seemed Mr. Britches was the king. Grabbing the lead rope tied around her mare's neck, Harriet walked behind the pony. "Hold his reins, Jenny, I'm going to drive him over this bridge if it's the last thing I ever do."

Harriet lashed the pony's rump with the rope. "Get up, you sorry critter," Harry snarled as she whacked him again with the lead rope.

The fat pony lurched to his feet and without hesitating charged Jenny with his ears laid back and his teeth bared. The girl screamed and let go of the reins. Mr. Britches tore by Jenny, almost knocking her off the bridge into the river, raced across the wooden span and disappeared into the woods beside the river with Jenny's carpet bag slapping and the empty stirrups swinging.

Tears of fear and frustration filled Harriet's eyes. "Damnation! Why do I always cry when I'm not sad, I'm furious."

Jenny took her hand. "It's all right, Miss Harriet. I'll walk. Let's get going."

"You can't walk all the way to Prue's ranch. It's too far. We'll have to ride double on the mare. I hope she doesn't give us any trouble. I've had enough dealing with cantankerous animals for one day."

They trudged across the bridge leading the mare. When they got to the other side, Harry tossed Jenny into the saddle and climbed up behind her. The mare laid her ears back and hopped a couple of times, then settled down to a fast walk. Harry sighed with relief. Riding double wasn't that comfortable, but they were back on the trail to Horse Creek.

The sun darkened as the sun set and evil black clouds rolled in from the west. Harry didn't care. She'd ridden to Prue's plenty of times and could find it in the dark and in the rain. Getting away from her uncle was all that mattered, and saving Jenny from him was everything that was important. That would not change if they got wet or had to ride all night.

They had just about reached the ford for the creek when Harry heard horses coming up behind them. It sounded like more than two, which was frightening. Who could be riding out this way so close to dark and at such a pace? The horses sounded like they were galloping.

Holding tightly to Jenny, Harry looked down the road. Up ahead was the creek. Harry could see the willows and oaks that grew on its banks. When she turned in the saddle to look back down the trail, it was empty. She was just about to turn away when a carriage pulled by four horses trotting out at a fast pace came around the corner and began closing the gap between them.

Harry shivered as though a cold wind had blown across her shoulders. She spurred the little mare into a lope and headed for the ford.

"What's wrong, Miss Harry?" Jenny's voice was thin and reedy with fear.

"I don't know who's in that carriage, Jenny, but I'm afraid, terribly afraid."

Harriet huddled over Jenny determined to protect her no matter what. She slowed the mare and guided her over the bank and into the ford at a trot. That's when the first shots zinged by over their heads.

"Stop, or I'll shoot you, Harriet," a familiar voice shouted from inside the carriage. "I don't want to accidentally hit the little girl."

Closing her eyes, Harry pulled the mare to a halt.

"Don't stop, Miss Harry, please. He won't shoot us, he won't." Jenny turned in the saddle and clutched Harry's riding jacket lapels. "Keep riding. We can make a run for it."

"No, Jenny. I know Uncle Buford. If he says he'll shoot me he will. He cares for nobody but himself and has no conscience. I can't let him shoot me, the bullet might hit you." Tears flowed down Harriet's face. What a terrible day this had been.

Harriet could see a black man driving the carriage. He looked familiar. Harriet recognized the driver as Tiberius, one of Uncle Buford's personal servants. No doubt Henry was inside. That was Uncle Buford's valet, a huge black man utterly devoted to Uncle Buford. Henry did everything for her uncle but wipe his rear and Harry thought he may have done even that on more than one occasion.

The driver put the four-horse team slowly over the edge of the bank and drove them into the ford. Harry waited patiently, having ridden the little mare to the top of the other side. She gazed longingly at the trail leading off into the woods that went to Prue's. It was so close. If only she could make a run for it.

"Get off the mare." The carriage stopped close to her at the top of the bank on this side of the ford. Her uncle stepped out with a double-barreled shotgun pointed at her midsection.

Harriet climbed off the mare slowly. This all felt so unreal, like a bad dream. Soon she should wake up and everything would be better.

But it wasn't a dream. Uncle Buford stood in front of her in a cream-colored suit with a matching waistcoat of cream satin. His shirt was white, the cuffs large. She saw his familiar gold and diamond tie pin in the cream satin tie and his tiger-eye cufflinks. She knew his gold watch, the size of a turnip, was nestled in his watch pocket. She could see the chain.

"Get over here, girl. I ain't going tell you twice. How about I just shoot you instead and the little one can go with me."

"Come with me, Jenny," Harriet said taking her hand and leading her toward Uncle Buford's carriage.

"I'm not going," Jenny said and took off running down the hill to the creek, across the shallow water of the ford and into the woods.

"Go get her, Henry," Buford said. The big servant raced by Harriet, cleared the creek, and tore into the woods after Jenny.

"When he brings her back you tell her to behave," Buford said in a low voice. "If she doesn't, I'll make her and I know you don't want that, do you, Harriet?"

Harriet shook her head. She couldn't escape the feeling that this was all a dream. She could barely feel her feet on the ground and her spinning head was making her nauseous. Just the sound of her uncle's voice brought back memories, the feel of his hands on her, the dread she experienced each night as the sun set, wondering if he would come to her room as she slept. And now all of that was going to happen to Jenny. Poor Jenny saved from McQueen only to fall victim to a monster from Harriet's past.

In minutes, Henry appeared at the top of the bank with Jenny tucked under one meaty arm. The girl kicked and squirmed and Harry could hear Jenny putting a cussing on him. Harriet felt close to swooning. She'd been hanging on to the hope Jenny would elude her uncle's servant.

"Take the carriage onto the trail, Tiberius," Uncle Buford ordered the driver.

Buford put his hand on Harriet's arm. The flesh burned under her jacket. His grip tightened, then he let go and stroked her hair. He bent his head and nuzzled her ear. "You still look as young as ever, Harry. Be nice to me and I'll leave your little friend alone."

"Let her go, Uncle Buford," Harriet said in her sweetest voice. "She'll only cause you trouble. I'll be nice to you if you just let her go."

Uncle Buford shook his head and put a finger to his lips. "Tut, tut, my girl. Why would I let such a tasty little angel go? And as long as I have her, you'll do exactly as I wish. Such a comfort to me, I assure you."

Harriet turned on her uncle, scratching at his face, her fingers turned to claws. "You're a beast and you will not hurt Jenny. If you do, I'll kill you."

"You always were full of spirit," Uncle Buford chuckled, grabbing her fists and easily bringing her under control. "And such dreams. But I have you back now and I have the girl. I'll get what I want from both of you and you'll have nothing to say about anything."

Henry set kicking and screaming Jenny on the ground beside Harriet. Uncle Buford slapped the girl hard across the face. "Be still!" He ordered Jenny.

Tears glistened on Jenny's cheeks and Harriet felt like dying. How could she have brought this on Jenny?

Buford put his hand on Harriet's neck and pushed. Harriet was forced to bend at the waist. "On your knees, girl," Buford ordered her, pushing harder on her neck.

Harriet had no choice but to drop to her knees.

"See your friend Harriet?" Buford said to Jenny in his meanest, oiliest voice. The sound reminded Harriet of the hissing of a huge snake.

Jenny nodded, her eyes huge, Henry stood behind her, dwarfing the girl.

"If you don't stop screaming and start doing as you're told, Harry here will suffer for everything you do." Buford pushed Harriet even further down until her forehead was pressed to the muddy earth. "You understand me, girl?"

"Give me my cane, Henry," Buford ordered.

Henry climbed into the carriage and returned quickly with an ebony cane. The cane was made of a black wood and had a carved ivory handle. The carving in the handle was of slaves being whipped.

Harriet's back was rounded, her knees under her and her cheek pressed to the moist sandy soil. Her red hair had come out of its bun and lay spread across her shoulders on the mud and sand. Uncle Buford's meaty hand still pressed her neck, pushing her closer and closer to the earth. Harriet wished it would open up under her and swallow her forever.

"I have no idea what you are doing running all over the countryside dressed in boys' clothes, Harriet Painter," Uncle Buford said in his coldest voice. "I brought some of your old clothes with me in hopes we'd be reunited. Right after I administer your punishment, you will change your clothes. I find the sight of you dressed in pants offensive to my eyes."

The first blow of the cane to her back was a terrible shock. When she opened her mouth to scream, sand filled it. Choking and gasping for air, she pushed hard against Buford's hand. But it was huge Henry that held her down now and Buford's cane came down on her back over and over again, until from lack of air and pain everything went black.

When Harry woke up, her head was resting in Jenny's lap, and she lay across the cushions of her uncle's carriage. The windows were open and a damp, cold breeze blew in, ruffling the curtains.

Her back ached unbearably. She groaned and tried to sit up.

"No, Harry, please lie still," Jenny whispered. "He beat you so badly. I thought you would die."

Harriet groaned and looked around the interior of the traveling coach. Uncle Buford slept with his head lolling on the velvet head rest of his seat.

"Where's Henry?" She said softly. It would be better not to wake her uncle.

"He's sitting up top with the driver."

"Help me up."

Jenny lifted her to a sitting position. Every bone in her body ached but she'd been caned by her uncle before. He was an expert, nothing would be broken, but she'd have bruises for a week. "Where are we going?"

"He said we're going to visit your mother. Where's that?"

Harriet closed her eyes. Every bounce the carriage took made her bruises scream. "He's taking us back to Savannah."

27

Danny climbed out of the tree he was using as a sentry post and motioned for Prue to join him at its base. He said nothing, just pointed, and Prue spotted McQueen's two scouts entering his compound.

Prue was parading around his ranch wearing a dress and holding a bundle that looked like a baby. He'd covered his hair with an old shawl. Under the voluminous skirt, he wore his pistol, and inside the baby bundle was his Winchester.

"I seen them two scouts slog through the mud barrier," Danny whispered. "They pussyfooted over one of the drier spots, looked around for a few minutes and left."

"I sure hope they go back and tell their boss we're asleep on the job and the place is open to an attack."

"Come on," Prue said. "Let's go wake up Marshal Short."

The marshal was sleeping under one of the wagons. Prue tapped him on the shoulder.

"They're coming," Prue said, tearing off the skirt and tossing the fake baby into the back of the wagon.

"Glory be," Short said as he pulled on his knee-high boots and scrambled out from under the wagon.

"We're in for a hell of a night," Prue said. "He sent in two scouts. I got no idea how many men he brung with him, but the way I figure, it's got to be at least fifty."

Danny picked his teeth with a sliver of wood while he waited for Prue to give him an order. The boy appeared excited about the prospect of a battle. He danced from one foot to the other and kept pulling his hat on and off his head and raking his hair with his fingers.

"Danny, go to each wagon and wake all the men. Tell Dale and Hank Starling to come to the barn and get the secret weapon up on the hill. Get the rest of the men into position in the trees around the perimeter. Make sure they know not to shoot at any of the raiders until we're shot on ourselves. We got a US Marshal here. I don't want anyone being charged with murder. And remember to tell them to light all the torches we placed in the trees and the lanterns, then not to come out of them trees for nothing and I mean nothing. And get the women folk and the children up to the house, all of them."

"Are Dale and Hank gonna fire the secret weapon?" Danny asked.

"What secret weapon?" Short said.

"Come with me, Marshal. I'll show you."

Hank and Dale showed up as Prue was pulling the tarp off his twelve-pound mountain howitzer. The brass barrel sparkled in the light from Hank's lantern.

"Well, I'll be dogged," Short said. "That's a cannon."

"Sure 'nough is," Hank said. "We got us about sixteen rounds for it too. If this don't send them vigilantes running, nothing will."

"You fired it before?" Short asked.

"No," Prue said. "We're just gonna have to pray it doesn't blow up. The peddler who sold it to me said it's got a thirty-foot recoil. I already told them two boys about it and where to put it. There should be plenty of room. Hitch a mule to it, boys, and haul it up the hill to the house. I always did mean for it to sit up there, I just never knew I'd have to defend my property with it."

"I been around when one of those guns was fired," Short said. "I was just a kid. The recoil is deadly. I surely would like to watch you shoot it once you get it loaded. Where you gonna want me to be during this gunfight? You know I want the leader, that McQueen character."

"I'd like you to stay with me. I'll be where a lot of the danger is but you'll have the best chance of spotting McQueen and taking him down. And I will make it up to the house to help with firing the cannon."

Short nodded and they headed for the barn.

"Get mounted," Prue said to Short. "You'll need to be on a horse. I'm gonna go wake up Boarhog. He's in charge of the cows."

Boarhog's loud snores issued from the hayloft of the barn. When Prue climbed up to wake him, he saw Boarhog slept with his rifle across his belly and in his boots. Prue shook him and stood back. He'd done this before and was ready when Boarhog bolted into a sitting position, slamming a cartridge into the rifle's chamber at the same time.

"Who's there?" Boarhog demanded, blinking the sleep out of his eyes.

"It's just me, Boarhog. We got visitors. Time to put a whupping on those vigilantes."

Boarhog grinned showing lots of white teeth. "Sho nuff, Boss. We gonna put one on 'em."

Prue clapped Boarhog on the shoulder. "You bet. You know your position?"

Boarhog shuddered. "Why I got to man the cowpen gates, Boss? Them cows is hungry and tired of being in them pens. Some of them old cows done tried to hook me yesterday and I was giving them food. And that crazy bull you brung from Texas is on a rampage. When he ain't fighting with the other two bulls in the pens, he's breeding every cow he can mount."

"I'm counting on the cows wantin' to get out and I guess it's about time to let old Cactus Pete go with them. Get on your horse and wait for my signal."

"You really gonna fire off that old piece of brass?" Boarhog asked as he climbed out of the loft and went to fetch his horse.

"It's my secret weapon," Prue said. "If it works, the vigilantes are finished."

"If it works," Boarhog mumbled.

Short and Prue saddled up. By the time Prue was in the saddle the first shots were ringing through the woods. Prue looked into the trees. He could see some of the men in the light of the torches crouched on the platforms they built high in the branches. The second shot came from one of those men. Prue wished there was a way for him to see what they were seeing and be on his horse at the same time.

Another shot rang out. Danny called down to him from a tree. "Mr. Prue, they're in the mud on the west side."

"Let's go," Prue shouted to Short. Drawing his pistol, Prue galloped Satan toward the western edge of the homestead, a place he'd concentrated the plowing. It was the best access for riders coming in from Brownville or Arcadia, there was good cover right up to the mud and the creek bank was low. A lot of water had run into the furrows from the creek on the west side. It was a slop hole.

When they got to the plowed swath, Prue saw his plan had been effective. Ten horses were mired in the mud up over their girth straps. The men had come off. One was dead, shot in the chest. Two men were still stuck in the mud with the horses and the rest had fled into the trees. A shot zinged passed him. He wheeled Satan around and took off along the perimeter with Short right behind him. Following the plowed swath, he headed for the wagons and the tents belonging to the settlers.

Prue and Short galloped along the plowed strip. When they got to the wagons, they ducked into a sheltered place between two wagons and spotted a group of raiders headed for the mud. It looked like more than twenty riding straight for Prue's man-made swamp.

Prue turned Satan and stopped the marshal. "Got to get back to Boarhog. This is the tricky part of the plan. I'm gonna need your help."

Short nodded and looked at the approaching raiders. "Are any of them McQueen?"

"No," Prue said gathering his reins and sitting deep as Satan danced and tossed his head. "Can't tell from this distance in the dark. He used to ride a yeller hoss, you could pick him out anywhere. Now, I got no idea what he's riding. The yeller stud is at his ranch. He usually wears a top hat. Look for that. Now let's ride. I got to get to Boarhog."

They took off galloping toward the barns and the cowpens. Boarhog sat on his horse, resting his head on one fist propped on his knee. He looked ready to drop into a doze.

"Open them gates, Boarhog. We're gonna have to get the cows out and headed toward the back of the property where the settlers are camped." Prue pointed toward the north edge of the ranch homestead.

"Oh Lordy, Lordy, they's gonna tromp everything them settlers own into the ground," Boarhog moaned.

"Stop moaning and groaning, Boarhog," Prue said as he reined in Satan and spun the horse in a circle. The stud could feel the excitement and the close proximity of cows. The stallion loved working cattle. "I got no idea if they'll run over the tents and wagons. They may and they may not. I've seen a stampede flow around wagons and tents and even people and horses like a river around rocks. You never know what cows are gonna do. Now get them gates open."

Boarhog opened the gates one at a time, leaning down and doing it from horseback. Prue urged Satan into the pens, right into the middle of the herd. The stallion snapped at the cows and pushed them with his chest. Cows didn't bother Satan. The mustang had been working cattle like this since he was two and just broke to ride. The horse had some close calls and had been hooked a couple of times, but mostly the cattle respected him, his size and his teeth, and got out of his way.

Prue began pushing cows out of the gap and into his ranch yard as Boarhog and Short positioned themselves so the cows would move away from them and toward the back of ranch compound where the settlers were camped. When all of the gates were open and all the cows released and milling around looking for food and mooing, Prue took out his pistol.

"Get ready," he called to the two men.

Prue, Short, and Boarhog blocked the cows' escape to the south where the creek, house, and barns were. Boarhog took out his whip and cracked it. The cows' heads came up. Then Prue fired the pistol.

The cows began moving slowly away from the shots. Prue wished he had Buzzard, the dog would get them moving. It looked like the cows were so desensitized from being in the pens and around people nothing would get them moving. And then they got some help from an unexpected quarter.

A huge boom echoed through the trees to the west. Dale and Hank had fired the howitzer. The cows jumped, several bolted leading a charge away from the loud noise. After Prue fired his pistol a couple more times, the rest of the cows followed the lead cows heading toward the north and suddenly they were in full stampede. All two hundred headed off at a dead run for the settlers' camp with Prue, Short and Boarhog galloping on their tails.

In part, Prue had been right. The stampeding herd flowed around the wagons. They did mash some tents and trampled some of the settler's gear, but missed a lot of stuff and steered clear of the wagons. When the cows made it beyond the campground, they pounded their way toward the mud moat moving like one giant organism. Boarhog, Prue, and Short were hard on the cattle's heels, yipping and cracking their whips. Prue was doing his best with the whip; Boarhog was an expert.

The minute the riders were clear of the wagons and tents, Prue saw the raiders. Three torches burned in trees close to the plowed-up mud hole. Prue could see at least eight head of horses stuck. But the mud had dried considerably this far away from the creek. The rain added some moisture, but ten of McQueen's men crossed the mire and were regrouping when the stampeding cows came through the campground.

The cattle led by Prue's Texas bull rushed the mud hole. The cows hit the mud moving fast. Several stumbled; none got stuck. Florida cows are light, not even six hundred pounds, and they were used to gator holes, swamps, and quicksand. The mud barely caused them to slow their pace. The herd flowed across the mud stomping six head of horses to their death, the other two managed to scramble out of the way just in time. It was a brutal and bloody sight.

The raiders stopped and stared, stunned by the stampede. Usually you can hear a stampede coming for miles, but the cows had only been running for about a hundred yards when they hit the campground. There was no advance warning for the vigilantes. They were caught off guard and many were on foot. The ten on horseback regrouping on the ranch side of the mud were swept back across the moat with the cows. Some made it; some did not. The men on foot on the other side disappeared. Prue couldn't see what happened to them. It was too dark. He heard yelling and screams over the sound of pounding hooves, mooing, and frightened horses.

"This is finished, let's ride for the house," Prue called to Short over the commotion.

Short peered into the dark at the rear of the stampeding cattle to see if he could spot any raiders. Prue figured he was looking for McQueen.

"He ain't here," Prue shouted as he wheeled Satan and galloped for the house.

The cannon fired one more time. Prue pushed Satan into his fastest pace, leaving the lawman and Boarhog behind. He raced up the hill to the house and leaped off Satan before the horse had stopped. Hank and Dale were loading the cannon again. A cloud of smoke surrounded the weapon so thick Prue could barely see the two men at work. The smoke quickly spread. Prue couldn't even see the creek at the bottom of the hill in the light of the torches, though he knew it was there.

"Did you shoot a ball or one of the canisters?" Prue asked Hank, who was wiping his hands on his overalls.

"Hey, Mr. Prue. I didn't know you was back. We shot us off a couple of them balls. There's twenty men coming across the creek down there. Can't see 'em now for the smoke, but they's there. We're gonna bust out a canister this time. I think them vigilantes is close enough to make it a good idea. The balls don't do nothing. They go a ways then just fall to the ground. I guess they's for bustin' into a fort like or knockin' down a wall."

Short and Boarhog reached the top of the hill and joined Prue and the two men working the cannon. "Did you see McQueen?" Short asked.

"There's a tall feller down there," Dale said. "He's wearing a high-crowned black hat and he seems to be giving all the orders. He's riding a roan horse. Could be him, I guess. I don't remember what he looked like from when they attacked us. I thought that feller rode a yeller horse."

"Sounds like him," Prue said as he watched the two men load a canister shot. This kind of ammunition amounted to a big tin can filled with 148 mini balls packed in sawdust. Hank stuffed the canister into the cannon barrel and rammed it home.

"Get out the way," Dale yelled as he lit the fuse.

The five men raced for cover, giving the cannon its necessary thirty feet. The gun boomed and bounced backward, rocking on its wheels and dangerously close to tipping over. When the gun fired all 148 mini balls exploded from the canister and shot off in 148 different directions. The results were catastrophic.

Men and horses screamed all along the hillside and down in the creek. Thick smoke obscured Prue's line of sight. He had no idea how many men they hit or what had happened along the creek bed.

When the smoke cleared, Prue saw five men reduced to blood and rags laying up and down the hill. Wounded horses screamed and wounded men added their weaker voices. Prue was horrified. How had men been able to do this to each other in the name of war? He was defending innocent people and his home and he couldn't stand the destruction.

"Stop," Prue ordered the two gunners in a hoarse voice. "Don't fire that thing again."

Shots rang out of the trees as the snipers high on their platforms picked off the wounded and any man still on a horse.

Prue ran out into the open, risking his life. He didn't care. The killing had to stop. "Cease fire," he shouted, waving his arms over his head. "Stop shooting."

The men in the trees heard him. They quit taking shots and the men on the ground that weren't wounded began gathering up horses and heading back across the creek.

"Come on down," Prue yelled. A thrashing horse struggled next to him, shattered leg dragging uselessly behind. Prue pulled out his pistol and ended the animal's misery. All Prue could think was, *what a waste of good men and good horses.* He hoped never to see anything like this again. It was one thing to plan a battle like this but all together something else when it actually happened. He holstered his pistol and climbed the hill back to the cannon.

Men high in trees started climbing out of their roosts and making their way to solid ground. It was over from what Prue could see. The howitzer ended the battle before it got started. He'd thought of using the cannon more as a lark, a fun escapade that might stop some killing. He'd had no idea of the destructive potential contained in the weapon. He vowed never to fire those canister shots at anything again.

When Prue reached the top of the hill, Short shouted, "There he is!" Short pointed down the hill.

Prue turned around and stared down the hill. In the light of the dying torches, he saw Malachai McQueen standing beside his dead horse, a shocked expression on his pale face. His top hat was gone and his white shirt was stained red with blood, either his or the horse's.

"I'm going after him," Short shouted, leaping on his black horse.

McQueen looked up at them standing beside the howitzer on the top of the hill. He must have heard Short. He ran back across the creek, grabbed the reins of a loose horse as he went, and leaped into the saddle. Prue watched as McQueen turned the horse and galloped across the creek and into the dark. Short raced down the hill only seconds behind him.

"We got to clean up this mess and help the wounded," Prue said to Dale and Hank.

"This old gun is a terror," Hank said, his voice reflecting awe of what he'd just witnessed, a little pride tinged with horror and even some enjoyment. "The cannon balls didn't do nothing. I can't believe what just one of them canister shots did. It was fine the way only one of them shots ended the whole battle."

"I hope we never fire one of those rounds again," Prue said. "I almost feel sorry for the vigilantes. They had no idea what they were getting into."

"That'll teach them to mess with you, Boss," Boarhog said. "You done whupped them like they never been whupped. You done put the king of whuppings on them boys. They ain't never gonna forget this day not if they live to be a hundred. Yes sir, we done showed them. I tell you what."

"Yeah, we whupped them all right," Prue told his foreman. "Help take care of the all these hurt men and animals, Boarhog. Get the women out of the house to tend them. If you need to, hitch up a wagon and tote them into Arcadia. I'm going with Short. I want to be there when he catches McQueen."

Prue grabbed Satan's reins and leaped into the saddle without touching the stirrups. He pointed his stud's nose down the hill and let him have his head. He wanted to be there when Malachai McQueen went down.

28

Black thoughts filled Malachai McQueen's head, thoughts of revenge and killing and death. His entire life as he knew it was over, no more ranch, no more Sara Sota Vigilance Committee, no more being an important man in the county.

He had just watched all his men go down under a hail of destruction issued from the mouth of a mountain howitzer, a weapon with which he was well acquainted. He knew what one of those cannons could do. His unit had five of them. The guns were designed to be disassembled and carried on horseback. They were small but deadly. Canister shot had just shredded his vigilance committee.

He wasn't waiting around to find out how the men attacking on the east and north had done. He heard the stampede and saw the dust rising from a multitude of hooves. The Texan must have released an entire herd of cattle and deliberately stampeded them over his men. The Texan had won. Malachai McQueen was no more.

By this time Thelma McQueen had no doubt informed on him with the law. His imposture was over. With her knowledge, it would be foolish to continue the masquerade. The US Marshal was probably in town either in regard to his pretending to be McQueen or to investigate the vigilantes. Either way, his time here was at an end. His only option was to run, to get as far away from this place as he could before they caught him and put him in prison. He couldn't let that happen. Prison was worse than death.

The bone-shaker he rode clattered through the trees as he galloped down the trail along Horse Creek toward Arcadia and the road to Sarasota. He would ride to the coast and catch a boat out of town. Maybe he could start over in Tampa or further up north.

The thought of going back to the Rafter Q had occurred to him, but he quickly decided not to go. There was nothing there for him except the yellow stud. He sure would miss that horse. But Rooster was dead and Berryhill gone as well. All his friends were dead. It was better to cut and run. If he was going to have a chance to get out of the county, it would be now. And if the sheriff of Arcadia survived the massacre, he couldn't trust Daniels not to join up with the marshal and turn on him.

Edmund Daniels would take out his own mother for the right amount of cash. And to save his ass, Daniels would turn on McQueen in a minute. If that US Marshal was in town to bust up the vigilance committee or get him, Daniels would knife him in the back in a heartbeat.

As he rode, he kept hammering himself in the head with his failures. He'd become sloppy. He'd let the little things slide and now look where he was, running, that's where. He should have made sure Aunt Thelma was dead.

She sure looked dead when Gem was cradling the old hag's bloody head in her lap. It had been a terrible mistake to leave Thelma alive and now it was proving to be the mistake that finished his life here on the prairie as an important man. No doubt that kid Jeb McQueen would take over his ranch. The thought was enough to make him puke. There was another screwed up job. Berryhill should have made sure those two kids were dead and they never got out of that well.

Malachai rode on through the night. He was sure he was being followed. When he allowed the horse to walk, he could hear hoof-beats hot on his trail. When his poor horse began to fail, he drove him forward with whip and spurs. The sun was just coming up as the horse fell to his knees, completely finished.

Climbing off the exhausted animal, McQueen threw the reins to the ground. The horse fell onto his side breathing heavily. Cursing, Malachi kicked the down horse. The animal didn't even flinch when the toe of his boot connected solidly with its ribs.

"What a piece of useless buzzard bait," McQueen swore. It was almost dawn and he should be less than a mile from the Arcadia Road. There was no telling how much of a lead he had. By pushing his mount until it dropped, he'd probably gained a few miles. Without looking back at the suffering animal, Malachai took off walking at a steady pace, heading for the road.

When he climbed out of the creek bed and up on the road, the sun was creeping over the eastern horizon. That blister from the day Berryhill died was back. Walking in riding boots was not something he recommended. But what else could he do? He hadn't planned on his men being soundly trounced by a nobody from Texas. When he reached the road, he turned northwest and headed toward Sarasota. He had about seventy miles of walking to do to get there. But with luck, he'd soon locate some transportation.

Luck provided him with a mount before he walked even one mile. He heard the horse before he saw it. Spooked at the sound of hoof beats, he dove into the bushes on the side of the road as a cowhand came trotting into view around the last bend. Malachai sighed with relief. Pulling his sawed-off out of the holster, he climbed into the road right in the cowhand's path.

"Pull up there, partner," he ordered the man, signaling for him to stop with the shotgun.

The cowhand had the typical Florida cow hunter's gear strapped to the saddle, a slicker, a whip, a bedroll, and big bulging saddle pockets, all things Malachai needed.

Startled by Malachai and the shotgun, the man pulled his horse to a stop. The nag was old and skinny but Malachai did not care.

"Climb off that there *caballo*," Malachai said. "We're switching places. You be walking now and I be riding."

"Now wait a minute," the hand protested, trying to pull his rifle out of the scabbard.

"Get yer hand off that shooter," Malachai snarled. "I ain't got a minute. Climb down or I'll shoot you dead. Don't make no never mind to me."

The hand slid off the horse and quick as he could, Malachai leaped into the saddle and gathered the reins.

"At least leave me my rifle," the hand complained. "You can't leave me out here unarmed. I'll starve or be killed outright."

Malachai was already heading down the road. He called over his shoulder. "You're right. I'll drop it in the middle of the road half mile yonder."

The cowhand cursed and started plodding after Malachai. Mal took one last look behind to make sure no one else was coming down the road after him and set the boney old piece of crow bait into a rattling trot.

It seemed to Malachai that whoever was following him had either fallen way behind or quit the trail. He sure hoped it was the latter. But taking his recent experience, half-killing a good horse, into consideration, he paced the skinny nag he'd stolen, pushing him into an uncollected half-ass lope and then bringing him down into a bone-wrenching trot. But no matter how dreadful the horse's gaits were, it was way better than walking.

He'd been on the horse for an hour when curiosity along with a belly ache made him begin searching the saddle pockets. He found jerky and corn dodgers. Sucking on one of the cornbread cakes that was hard as a piece of sandstone and about as tasty, he began looking for the road that turned off this trail and headed to Sarasota. If he kept straight on this road, he would pass through Myakka and Ellentown and eventually end up in Tampa. Somewhere up ahead, he knew there was a more westerly trail.

The sun was high overhead and he still hadn't come across the turn. He began fretting. Maybe he'd missed it. When the sun started to drop behind the trees he looked toward it and realized, he had to have missed the turn. The sun was setting in front of him but slightly to the left. He hadn't been out this way in years. Maybe he had it wrong and the turnoff for Sarasota was further toward the west coast. And if that was the case, then if he wanted to go to Tampa, he'd have to turn to the right soon and head in a more northerly direction.

Since he'd acquired transportation, of a sort, he'd started thinking maybe Tampa was his best bet after all. Tampa was a bigger port with more opportunities. But he had one major problem. He was broke. His pockets were empty. He regretted not making an effort to stop in Arcadia and withdraw funds from the bank. He really regretted it. Being broke was not something he was used to and he didn't like it. But he'd been so scared of the Texan and worried about the US Marshal being in town, he'd run like a chased rabbit. And now here he was, flat busted and riding a horse that felt like it was fixin' to trip and fall down at any moment. The nag was a shuffler, dragging each hoof at every step.

The more he pondered his situation, the more he liked Tampa. In Tampa, he could find a bank that would accept a check from him drawn on funds he had in the First State Bank of Arcadia. He'd take out enough money to catch a ship to just about anywhere with enough cash left to start his life over again.

Satisfied he'd thought of a good plan, one that would work, he began thinking about what beginning a new life would mean and what he might do. He liked town life and he missed Texas. Maybe he would take a ship to Galveston and go inland from there. He'd heard Houston had grown and was turning into a regular city. Maybe he would settle there. He'd read they even had newfangled electric lights in Houston. Maybe he'd invest some of his money in electricity. He had a feeling it was the wave of the future.

When the sun finally set and the sounds of insects and tree frogs filled the air, Malachai started looking for a good place to camp for the night. He should be getting close to Myakka. He'd been through there a while ago and couldn't remember if there was a bank in Myakka or not. If there was, he could probably convince the banker to give him some money against his accounts in Arcadia and Brownville. The McQueen name and the Rafter Q were known everywhere, even this far from the ranch. That would solve his most immediate problem, no money.

Malachai's mind was busy rolling these thoughts around when he turned a corner and saw a traveling carriage parked under a tree on the east side of the trail. Four husky horses rested on a picket line strung between two trees along with a little mustang mare.

A creek crossed the trail in front of him. Malachai rode down the bank to cross at the ford. The sorry crow-bait he was riding wouldn't go into the water. Every time Mal tried to put the animal into the creek, it planted its front hooves and refused to budge.

Tired of fighting him and tired of riding him, Mal climbed down and stood staring up the trail at the carriage camped in the trees. Maybe he'd hail the camp and go sit for a spell with these travelers. They might offer him some hot food. He'd really enjoy a meal right about now. Corn dodgers and jerky was fare for lowlifes but not for him. Mal sniffed the air. He smelled wood smoke, coffee, and frying bacon.

Grabbing the nag's reins, Mal dragged the protesting horse across the creek. When he got to the other side, he grabbed the left stirrup in his right hand and prepared to stuff his left boot into it. He was almost in the saddle when he heard the first scream. It was a woman in terrible agony or really frightened. The sound cut into Mal's head like a lightning strike. He'd heard his mother scream like that many years before.

Jumping into the saddle, Mal yanked his shotgun out of the scabbard and spurred the nag into a fast trot up the bank, a trot so rough it just about knocked him out of the saddle. When they got to the top, Mal laid into the horse's sides with his spurs and it broke into a gallop, which turned out to be the nag's best gait and actually pretty fast. The horse put his rear under him and dug in as they tore into the campsite on the other side of the carriage and Mal pulled the horse into a sliding stop. Loose sand and dirt flew from under the horse's hooves as Mal flung himself off and looked around, shotgun ready.

Two black men sat by the fire. When he jumped off the horse and pointed his weapon at them, they slowly raised their hands in the air. Mal scanned his surroundings, taking in the fire with the food he'd smelled cooking, a child covered with a blanket on the ground next to the fire and the carriage. The door of the carriage was closed and more screams and sobbing could be heard coming from inside it along with curses and swearing from both a man and a woman.

Mal's teeth pulled back in a snarl and the hair on the back of his neck and his arms rose. There was nothing he hated more than a rapist. When he opened the door to that carriage, he knew he'd find some poor woman fighting off the advances of some brute of a man.

Holding his fingers to his lips, Mal signaled the two darkies to be quiet. One of them had a rifle laying on the ground next to his boots. Mal strode over to the fire, picked up the rifle and rapped both black men over the head with the butt, knocking them out. When he bent over to hit one of them a second time to make sure he was out cold, he glanced at the child. She seemed to be sleeping or unconscious. There was something terribly familiar about her, but Mal's attention was all on the carriage.

He looked back at the two black men one more time to make sure they were unconscious, then moved toward the carriage. He holstered the sawed-off and pulled out his pistol. The screaming had stopped. Now all he could hear was grunting and sobbing. It turned his stomach so bad, he feared he would vomit.

It was an effort to control his raging emotions as he snatched the carriage door open. The sight that greeted him was worse than he'd expected. A fat man with his trousers around his ankles was raping a very young woman with long red hair. Her face was bloody and there were bite marks all over her arms and her breasts.

The shock and rage on the man's face when Mal snatched open the door gave him back his composure. Once more he was fully in control of himself. Without hesitating he shot the man in the knee with his pistol. The man screamed and fell to the carriage floor. The girl pushed her skirts down and turned her back on Mal. He could see her adjusting her white blouse and looked away. There was something familiar about her as well but all she'd offered him was a quick glimpse of her face.

Mal grabbed the fat man by one of his wrists and hauled him out of the carriage. He dropped heavily to the sandy ground crying and blubbering as he clutched his ruined knee.

"Shut up," Mal growled. "You got worse things to worry about. You know what we do to rapists in these parts?"

The man didn't answer. Mal hadn't expected him to. He grabbed the man by the wrist and pulled him across the ground toward the trees. One of the darkies was sitting up. Mal called out to him. "Get yer ass over here and help me stretch out yer master. I'm gonna show you some real cracker justice."

Rope was found and it didn't take long for Malachai to tie each arm and leg to a different tree, stretching the fat man tight. When he had the rapist tied, Mal wiped sweat off his brow with his sleeve and stopped to breathe deeply. Fatigue had him now. The long night with no sleep followed by the day was catching up to him. His eyes were blurring and a wave of dizziness flowed over him. He'd been okay up until now. He was suddenly so tired.

Pulling himself together was an act of extreme willpower. But he had a job to do. He had to exact justice for the rape of the woman in the carriage. He remembered how much he hated a rapist and slid his knife out of the sheath, bending down to cut off the man's creamy white suit, now covered with mud and sand.

"Stop," the fat man cried. "I have money. Take it. Take anything you want."

"Oh I will," Malachai said. "But that ain't gonna stop me from what I'm bound and determined to do. This is going to be the final act of cracker justice dispensed by the Sara Sota Vigilance Committee. As the judge and leader of the committee, I hereby convict you of the act of rape and condemn you to live out the remainder of your life as a eunuch."

Malachai displayed the small knife for the bound man. "Now I always use me a sharp knife when I geld a horse or cut a calf." He ran his thumb over the blade. "Out of respect, you understand. This one seems to need a little sharpening."

He turned to the black man. "You got a strop or a wet stone?"

The black man nodded, eyes wide.

"Well get it for me," Mal said and grinned.

The black man disappeared for a minute and returned with a small wet stone. Mal spit on it and began stroking the small knife back and forth across the rough surface.

The bound man lifted his head to watch every stroke of the blade across the stone. When Mal tested the blade by shaving the hair on the back of his hand the fat man began screaming.

Malachai's smile widened. "Now you better hold still, mister. I'm real tired. I ain't had me a lot of sleep lately. One slip of this here knife and you could die. Or I could cut off something else. There's worse things than being gelded."

The procedure was over in a matter of seconds. Mal had done it twice before on men and many times on animals. It was one of the only ranching chores he enjoyed. "Cut him loose," Mal told the two black men watching.

Mal stood up, put the knife back in its sheath and dusted off the knees of his britches, job done, justice dispensed. Soon he would be able to lay his head down and close his eyes.

The screaming and commotion woke up the little girl sleeping by the fire. She slowly stood up. Mal saw the movement, glanced over at her and froze. His mouth opened but he could only croak out one word. "Jenny."

29

Out of the frying pan and into the fire was all Harriet could think as she adjusted her skirt and pulled her blouse up over her shoulders and buttoned it. Of all the men who could have ridden down the road right at this moment and come to her rescue, the one that showed up had to be Malachai McQueen.

She climbed out of the carriage just as Uncle Buford began screaming like a woman. As she surveyed the scene she realized how appropriate that analogy was. McQueen was fast. He had her uncle on the ground, stretched out and gelded like a horse in mere minutes. Harriet watched, her heart cold, her emotions flat. When it was over McQueen turned and saw Jenny.

Harriet looked at her uncle splayed out and cut like a bull calf. With her emotions suddenly released from their icy coating, she was screaming inside with exultation and joy at revenge, the ultimate revenge on a man that had mentally and physically abused her for so many years. He would never be able to hurt her or any young girl or woman again. For this one thing she would always be grateful to McQueen.

Even though she was glad her uncle would no longer be able to hurt women, she felt horrified by the blood and gore, though outwardly her face revealed nothing of her inner struggle. She stared at her uncle with her features composed and hard.

She knew she shouldn't be feeling happy or relieved Uncle Buford would forever be a eunuch. It wasn't Christian to be rejoicing as a man she knew, a relative, lay suffering. Her uncle had just been brutally castrated. But Uncle Buford deserved exactly what Malachai McQueen delivered to him, Christian feeling or not. And she felt no pity or remorse. Surely he had never felt any for his victims. And there was no doubt in her mind that she had not been his only victim. Men like him would torture those they controlled and would crave that experience over and over again. With all his power, no doubt he'd found other victims for his amusements, but no more.

Jenny saw McQueen and realized who he was at the same moment McQueen recognized Jenny. Harriet saw the girl's face change as realization hit her. Hardly knowing what she should do, she opened her arms and Jenny ran to her.

"It's him," Jenny whispered into Harriet's ear. "He's the one that stole me."

"I know," Harriet said. "He's dealt with Uncle Buford for us but now we have to deal with him. And I was just starting to believe in God again."

"Maybe God sent Mal to us and he won't hurt you like your uncle did," Jenny said staring at Uncle Buford with loathing.

"Don't count on that," Harriet answered her, then softened and hugged the girl. "I'm sorry, sugar, I shouldn't be scaring you. Maybe you're right, maybe God did send Malachai McQueen here to save us and maybe he won't hurt us either."

Across the clearing at the site of the recent gelding, Buford was trying to get to his feet with the aid of Henry. Tiberius sat beside the fire with one hand holding the back of his head.

Seeing Jenny seemed to freeze McQueen in a state of shock. Harriet stood tall and faced him, holding Jenny's hand.

"Is it really you?" McQueen asked and then scrubbed his eyes with the back of his fists. When he walked toward them, Harriet saw him weave. McQueen looked utterly whipped.

Harriet tried to hold her hand steady as she held it out to him and tried to smile. In her present state of mind, it was almost too much to manage. "Thank you for saving me."

McQueen gave her the briefest of glances. "My pleasure," he muttered as he knelt down on one knee in front of Jenny. "You're alive," he whispered then looked around. "Why are you here?"

Jenny stared her biggest fear, Malachai McQueen, right in the face. Harriet felt so proud of her. She was proving to be a strong young lady. Jenny pointed at Uncle Buford. "That man stole me and Miss Harriet. He's a horrible person and he hurt Miss Harriet bad. I could hear her screaming. The only thing I could do was cover my head."

McQueen tried to put his arms around Jenny but the little girl was on the watch and backed up quickly. McQueen stood up and shook his head, wiping his eyes once more. "No, of course, I'm so sorry. Of course you don't want to be hugged. You've been through a terrible ordeal."

McQueen turned his attention to Harriet. "You must be Harriet Painter. Pelo Berryhill told me so much about you. I apologize for stealing little Jenny away from you that day at the Arcadia House. It must have seemed the act of a madman. I knew her parents, you see. Such a tragedy. I just wanted to take Jenny where she could be safe and cared for."

Harriet tried not to sound as desperate as she felt. McQueen had just spouted the biggest load of horseshit she'd ever heard in her life. He must think she was a moron. Well, if pretending to be stupid kept her alive long enough to get Jenny out of here then a moron is what she would be. "Thank you for saving me," she said in sugary tones all the while gazing up at him vacuously and batting her eyelashes. "That man is my uncle. He came to Arcadia to take me back to Savannah." Harriet allowed her voice to grow harsh and stared McQueen straight in the eye. "He abused me as a little girl and I think he was interested in Jenny."

Her ploy seemed to work. Mentioning her uncle's possible future abuse of Jenny drew McQueen's eyebrows low and caused him to narrow his eyes and shoot a look of pure hatred at Uncle Buford still blubbering and once more sitting on the ground.

"You must be exhausted after such an unsettling experience," McQueen said bringing his attention from Buford back to Jenny. "Why don't you and Jenny come sit by the fire and I'll have your uncle's servants fix you a cup of tea or coffee. Come now, come and sit down."

He took Jenny's hand in his and led her to the fire. She snatched it away as soon as she'd sat down on the blankets she'd been under earlier. Crossing her legs and folding her arms over her chest, she stared at the flames.

"Fix these two ladies some refreshments," McQueen ordered Henry. "Make me some coffee."

Harriet sat down next to Jenny and watched McQueen's every move. If he was as tired as it seemed, maybe he would be careless or maybe he would have to sleep. That would be their chance to get away.

Tiberius propped her uncle up against one of the trees. Harriet thought Uncle Buford looked in pretty bad shape. His head lolled on his shoulders and his eyes kept rolling back in the sockets. Tiberius had covered him with his torn clothing.

Leaving Uncle Buford against the tree, Tiberius walked over to Mc-
Queen and with his head down, eyes averted, addressed him.

"Please sir, may I get Mr. Buford some clothes out of his trunk?" Tiberius
asked.

"Bring it over here and open it in front of me," McQueen said. "Let's see
what the old man has packed away."

Henry made two cups of hot tea, sprinkled in some coarse sugar, and
passed the cups to Jenny and Harriet. Then he handed McQueen a cup of
coffee out of an enormous pot boiling on the fire.

McQueen slurped coffee as he watched Tiberius open a large leather-
bound trunk. After moving some things around, Tiberius carefully removed
a small pile of folded clothes. McQueen watched, hand resting on the butt
of his ugly little weapon.

When Tiberius had taken the clothes to Uncle Buford, McQueen rifled
through the trunk. He pulled out a brightly colored waistcoat and threw it
on the ground with a disgusted expression on his face. When he found a
small leather-covered box, he pounced on it. Holding the box in one hand,
he opened it.

"Lookee what we got here," McQueen crowed, holding up a gold insignia
ring. He threw that back in the box and held up Buford's tiger-eye cufflinks.
"Got me a little treasure here," he said, winking at Jenny. "Hey you," Mc-
Queen yelled at Henry. "What else you all got hid in that carriage?"

Henry led McQueen to the carriage and began unloading boxes, leather
satchels, and several carpet bags. McQueen soon had a pile of money, jewelry and other valuable trinkets. Not satisfied with the pile of accumulated
booty, McQueen began searching inside the carriage, cutting open the seat
lining and pulling the fabric off the interior walls.

Harriet and Jenny sipped tea, as Harry's mind scrambled for a way to get
out of this mess. She thought of grabbing one of the carriage horses and
making a run for it when McQueen went to sleep. McQueen's sorry-looking
nag didn't look very quick. If he woke up and set out after them, maybe
they could outrun it. She put a protective arm around Jenny's shoulders.
The little girl rested her head against Harriet.

"What are we gonna do, Miss Harry?" Jenny whispered.

"I don't know, Jenny, but I'm thinking."

30

Prue caught up with Short in no time. They both agreed speed was not as important as consistency. The two men set a good pace, one that wouldn't kill their mounts, and kept it up until morning. The sun had been up for a couple of hours when they found McQueen's horse. He wasn't dead, but looked completely exhausted.

The animal was on its feet. Reins dragging, it cropped grass as though it barely had the energy to eat. From experience, Prue knew the horse would recover. He'd seen enough reach this point. As long as the horse could stand and eat, he'd survive.

"I can't believe the man left the saddle on this horse," Prue said to Short. "Couldn't even be bothered with helping out an animal in distress, especially when it was his fault the animal was half dead."

Prue climbed off Satan and picked up the tired horse's dragging reins. The animal looked at him with heavy eyes as he loosened the cinch strap and pulled the saddle and blankets off its back. Then he stripped off the bridle and let the horse go.

"We might as well take us a break," Short said.

Prue took a look around. They were about a mile from the main road into Arcadia. "Good idea. The Arcadia Road is up ahead. Looks like McQueen is afoot. We should be able to catch him quick enough."

The two men made a small fire and boiled some water for coffee. Prue needed some bad, he was about done in. He'd caught a few winks on the ride here, napping in the saddle like he used to when he was riding herd in Texas. But he was tired. His muscles ached and his brain yearned for sleep.

The two horses were tired and hungry. Prue let Satan's reins drop. The mustang could go for days on a mouthful of grass and a few sips of water. Prue knew this for a fact, having asked the horse to do exactly that many times. But Short's older, larger mount was weary. The big black horse slowly cropped grass next to Satan.

The coffee woke Prue up. Short had some hard tack and some jerky in his saddle pockets that he shared. "You sure that big hoss of yours is gonna make it?" Prue asked as they prepared to remount.

"He'll have to," Short answered tightly. Apparently the man was tired and cranky just like his animal.

Prue shrugged. The marshal's horse wasn't his problem. He knew Satan could keep up the pace. The two set off again, soon hitting the Arcadia Road. Four miles later they came upon a cowhand walking.

"Hello there," Prue called to the man trudging down the road.

The hand was wearing boots and spurs. It looked like he was used to riding, not hoofing it.

"You lose your horse?"

The cowhand stopped and looked up at them. "What's it to you?" The hand answered as he took his black, large-brim floppy hat off his head and mopped at the sweat gathered across his brow with a red handkerchief. "I was held up at gunpoint and relieved of my mount by a low down hoss thief."

Prue leaned down to hear the cowboy speak. "What'd he look like?"

"He looked like a low down hoss thief," the man snapped.

"We're tracking a man who left his horse back by the creek. I need to know if he's the man who stole yer horse."

Marshal Short rode up and flashed the badge pinned to his lapel. The cowhand straightened his back and adjusted his demeanor. "What did this man who stole your horse look like?" Short asked in a very official-sounding voice.

The hand was only too happy to answer Short. "I don't remember much. He was wearing black and he pointed a sawed-off shotgun at me. Would that be him?"

Prue nodded, gazing down the road. "Yeah, that's our man."

"How long you been walking?" Short asked.

"A little over two hours I guess. He stole my horse right after sunup."

"Let's ride," Short said. "We got some time to make up."

Prue spurred Satan. The horse bucked twice just to show Prue who was boss and that he wasn't that tired and then settled into a lope. Prue glanced

at the sun. The shadows were still long, the sun up for maybe two or three
hours. It looked like McQueen had a fresh horse and was probably six or
seven miles ahead of them. Things looked bad for catching him, but they
kept on.

When sundown came, they stopped for another break. They'd picked
up the trail of the horse stolen by McQueen. From his hoof prints, Prue
could tell he was a plodder with rough gaits and pigeon-toed to boot. It
looked like McQueen was tired and moving slow just like they were. His
fresh horse gave him an advantage, and they would have lost him by now if
the horse had been a good one. It was this fact that kept them pressing on.

Short's mount was whipped and kept falling behind. Even Satan was off
his usual pace. The two men barely spoke to each other, not out of malice,
just because they were too tired to talk. They built a fire and hobbled the
horses. After a couple of hard biscuits and a bite of jerky, Prue put a pot of
coffee on to boil and shut his eyes.

The horses grazed and the two men slept for about four hours. The full
moon was up when they woke. Prue poured himself some of the coffee, still
warm from the fire, and sat down. Short got up and lit himself a cheroot.
He sat smoking it and sucking on a tin cup of coffee.

"Think we should go on or stop?" Prue asked.

"I'm heading on," Short said. "McQueen's riding in the direction of
Tampa. I got to go that way anyway. I'll follow him. You coming with me?"

"Might as well," Prue said. "I feel pretty rested. You ready to hit the road?"

"Let's ride," Short said and dashed the rest of his coffee into the fire.

The moon was bright enough for Prue to see McQueen's tracks. They
rode for two hours and came to a creek. As they trotted up the bank, Prue
saw a carriage in the moonlight parked in a grove of oak and willow. He
held up his hand for Short to stop.

Six head of horses were tied to a picket line in the trees. One of them was
a tall piece of crow bait, boney and plainly old.

"He could be riding that horse," Prue said. "That there nag looks about
the right size to be leaving the tracks we been following. I'll be able to tell as
soon as we get close. The horse toes in bad on the front. I'll know if it's him."

Short nodded and slowly pulled his pistol out and rolled the cylinder to
make sure he had a full load. He put it back in the holster and pulled out
the rifle, laying it across his saddle.

Prue checked his pistol and loosened his lariat, swung it over his head a
few times, and hung it off the saddle horn. Never knew, he might need it.
"Got a plan?" he asked Short.

"You seem to be the plan man. What you got in mind?"

"I was thinking I might scout the position while you wait here out of sight. When I know what we're facing, we'll go in."

Short climbed off the horse, bringing his rifle with him. "Make it quick."

Prue nodded as he jumped off Satan and securely tied the stud to an overhead tree branch. He slipped off his boots with their noisy spurs and headed for the campsite in his stocking feet.

Running quietly, Prue made it to the carriage and leaned against it to catch his breath. He listened. The camp was quiet. Making his way cautiously around the carriage, he risked a look. The trees shadowed the moonlight and the fire was low, making it hard to see. He spotted what looked like five bundled figures sleeping beside the fire, one a very small bundle.

He stood there for five minutes trying to figure out if one of them was Malachai McQueen, and he still couldn't tell. He could go check the horses for the one with the toe-in, but they might put up a fuss which would wake the sleepers. Heck, he was just as well off going in to take a closer look. With his pistol in his hand, he crept toward the sleeping figures.

The first one he came to was a black man. So was the second one. Then he came to a large man barely covered by his blanket with blood on his face and clothes. He seemed more unconscious than asleep. Even in the dim light Prue could see this guy was in a bad way. But none of them was McQueen. The last two bundles slept close together. They looked familiar. Just as he was bending down to get a better look, he felt a tap on his shoulder and the unmistakable feel of a gun pressing into his back.

"Hold it right there, Texan," Malachai McQueen spoke in a cool voice with a familiar Texas drawl. "Stand up slow, turn around, and hand me that pistol."

Prue handed his gun to McQueen as he rose to his full height and turned to face his enemy.

McQueen wasn't wearing boots or spurs either. In fact, he was in his longhandles and his feet were bare. He tossed Prue's pistol to the ground and pointed his sawed-off at Prue's gut. "Ain't it wonderful? All my wishes have been granted today. Now lookee what providence just dropped into my lap."

The two figures laying side by side behind Prue stirred at the sound of McQueen's voice. Looking over his shoulder, Prue saw Harriet sit up, holding her tied hands in front of her. When the blanket fell away, Prue saw the figure beside her was Jenny. The two of them were individually bound and then linked by one rope that was tied around each of their waists.

Prue's heart jumped when he saw Harriet. As always, she looked beautiful, even though she'd just woken up, serene as a Madonna and vulnerable at the same time. What was she doing here? She was supposed to be in Arcadia working.

Prue took a step backward toward them and was stopped by the barrel of McQueen's sawed-off poking him in his stomach.

McQueen wanted to gloat.

"Hold it right there," he said. "You know, I thought I had lost everything in this world I cared about. And it was all taken away from me by you, Jesse Pruitt, some nobody cowhand from Texas. No more Rafter Q, no more vigilantes, no more yellow stud, no more friends, no more Jenny. And then I rode into this camp and got back the one thing I discovered was most important. When I was allowed to save Jenny from that evil, disgusting child raper over there, I was given back all I care about in this world. Ain't it strange when you start thinking about the things that mean the most to you? That little girl means more to me than all the ranches in the world put together. She means more to me than being some big high muckety-muck head of the committee. I got her back and I ain't letting her go, ever."

Jenny rose slowly to her feet and stood beside Harriet, clutching a fold of Harry's skirt in one bound hand. Her eyes were wide and staring, probably from shock and still being half asleep.

McQueen walked around the fire, moving behind Prue and the two women, all the time keeping his eyes on Prue and the shotgun aimed at his chest. Prue moved with him, turning to watch McQueen and the sawed-off. McQueen slipped behind Jenny and with one eye still on Prue put a hand on Jenny's shoulder and dropped a kiss on the top of the girl's head.

Prue guessed it must have been the kiss that pushed Jenny over the edge, or it could have been the proprietary hand on her shoulder. Whatever, apparently the little girl had reached her breaking point. She turned and shoved McQueen, taking Harriet with her and all the while screaming at the top of her lungs that awful high-pitched noise Prue remembered from the first time they had met. It was an unmistakable noise and shot into his eardrums like a piece of slick wire.

"Don't touch me," Jenny screeched as loud as she could. "Don't ever touch me again. You killed my ma and pa. I hate you. I hate you. I hate you."

When Jenny screamed, a bolt of black and gray fur came streaking out of the underbrush. Buzzard must have been laying there. When he heard the girl scream, he charged McQueen, hitting the tall man in the chest and knocking him flat on his back. Before McQueen could stop him, the dog had McQueen by the throat and was shaking the man's head, growling horribly. The shotgun fired, hitting nothing but a tree. Leaves rained down on everyone.

Prue leaped across the fire, grabbed the sawed-off out of McQueen's hand, pulled back the twin hammers and stood there watching as Buzzard tore into McQueen's throat. Why jump in and interfere when the dog was doing such a fine job? Blood seeped down McQueen's neck and puddled on the sand. It seemed fitting to Prue that McQueen should die at the hands of a dog. He was afraid of dogs and hated them.

"Call off the dog," Short's voice came out of the darkness. "Call him off, Pruitt. I'm taking McQueen to jail. He's gonna hang, not die like this out on the trail."

Short walked slowly into the campsite, pistol out and pointed at Buzzard. "If you don't call off the dog, I'm gonna have to kill him."

"Oh damn," Prue cursed. He wanted to watch McQueen die like an animal in the dirt. But he believed Short would kill Buzzard and besides being an outstanding cow dog worth his weight in gold, the dog was a hero.

"Buzzard!" Prue said sharply, grabbed the big dog by the collar, and pulled Buzzard away from McQueen.

Jenny, dragging poor Harriet with her, fell on the big dog's neck. "You came to save me, Buzzard. You came." Jenny looked up at Harriet, tears sparkling in her eyes. "He followed us, Miss Harry. He remembered about me and he followed us."

The dog panted softly and looked up at Jenny. His one blue eye and his brown one were shining with love and devotion for the girl. A thin string of bloody slobber rolled out of his mouth and fell on Jenny's white smock.

Jenny hugged the dog's neck with her one free arm and kissed Buzzard's big spotted head over and over again. "You saved me, Buzzard. You saved all of us."

"I guess he just got here and crawled into the bushes to rest," Harriet said, grabbing one of Buzzard's big ears and stroking it.

Taking his knife out of the belt scabbard, Prue cut Jenny and Harriet's bonds so they could be free and free of each other. Jenny wrapped both arms around the dog and hugged him tightly.

Prue pulled Harry into his arms and buried his face in her red hair. "When I saw you here, I got such a fright, Harry. Don't ever do that to me again."

Staring over Harriet's head at the scene unfolding around him, Prue thought this had to be one of the weirdest he'd ever encountered. The two black men were up and working. Both wore burgundy velvet livery with white shirts and gold waistcoats. One tended the hurt man. He'd propped the man's bandaged knee on a green velvet cushion, probably removed from the carriage, and was tenderly bathing his forehead with some liquid Prue thought smelled like lavender. The water's odor was so strong Prue could smell it over the wood smoke, horse manure, and the odors of creek water, willows and damp ground drifting in from the creek and the woods on the clear night air. The smell added a note of the bizarre to an already creepy and peculiar situation.

The injured man was very fat and wearing a pair of fawn-colored britches with one leg slit up the side to allow room for the swollen, bandage-covered knee. The crotch of the britches was unbuttoned, revealing another large bandage, this one stained with blood. He had on a fine linen shirt with ruffles at the neck and a multicolored satin smoking jacket. The man's face was pale, his flesh like bread dough, his cheeks twin circles of bright red. He looked like he'd been attacked by something or someone and he was dressed for a drawing room.

The other black man stirred the coals of the fire then peered intently into a large blue-speckled coffee pot. All were watching Short as he jerked McQueen to his feet, pulled his hands behind his back and slapped a pair of handcuffs on him.

"What are you doing here anyway?" Prue finally asked McQueen. "And who are all these people?"

"You were gonna let that animal kill me," McQueen croaked, his voice rough and raw sounding. McQueen's red long-john shirt was torn at the neck. He gingerly touched his throat, which was wet, probably with Buzzard's saliva. Several large puncture wounds around his Adam's apple oozed blood. "Ask your little girly friend why I'm here. I probably saved her life."

Harry hugged Prue as tight as she could. His arms felt wonderful wrapped around her. She reached up and touched his face while he looked around and spoke a few words to Malachai McQueen. His face was lined with fatigue and worry and covered with bristles. "You need a shave," she murmured.

Prue looked down at her and after smoothing her hair he caressed her cheek with one callused finger. "I've been chasing McQueen for a day and a half with little sleep and no time for such things as grooming," he said. "Tell me what's going on. And what in tarnation are you and Jenny doing here?"

Harriet didn't want to tell Prue about her uncle. It had been her personal pain for a very long time. Something she didn't wanted to share with anyone. What Uncle Buford had done to her was shameful and embarrassing. And now she had to tell this man she loved her awful secret.

Prue held her away from him by her shoulders and stared into her eyes. "Harry, tell me what's going on. Who are these people?"

Harriet took Prue's hand and led him to the fire. Henry had made coffee. She poured a tin mug of the hot liquid and handed it to Prue. "That man is my uncle. And the two black men are his personal servants. I had to live with Uncle Buford when I was very young, younger than Jenny. He has unnatural and twisted desires. He gave me the bedroom closest to his own and he would come to me in the night through the connecting door and force himself on me. He's a very sick man, Prue, very sick. And I was terrified of him. He's the reason I ran away from Savannah. He's the reason I became a prostitute. Because of him I'm a ruined woman."

Prue started to say something and Harriet held up her hand. "No, let me get this said. Let me finish. My uncle found me in Arcadia. I always worried he'd come after me. I tried to take Jenny and run but he caught up with us right after the bridge. He was going to take me and Jenny to Savannah. Yesterday, McQueen rode in late, after dark, and found my uncle forcing himself on me in the carriage. McQueen gelded him for his crimes against me because I believe he thought my uncle was going to hurt Jenny in the same way he hurt me. And I'm sure that was his plan and he would eventually have done just that."

Prue threw the cup of coffee into the fire. His face was distorted with pain and disgust. He stared at her uncle, then glanced at Jenny, and then looked at Harriet. His lips were drawn back in a snarl, his nostrils flared, and his eyes were flinty little slits. He looked like he hated her. His expression said everything. Harriet backed away.

It was just as she'd feared. It was happening just as her uncle had said it would if anyone found out. Prue was sickened, revolted by what she'd done, by what had been done to her. Now he would turn away from her forever. Prue knew she was soiled and ruined. She was guilty of the crime of incest. She'd knowingly had carnal knowledge of her own kin. No man would ever want her, just as Uncle Buford had told her every day of her life in Savannah. All hopes of having any kind of life with Prue had just gone up in smoke. The only thing she could do was leave. Leave before she had to listen to him repudiate her.

Harriet turned and ran, ran into the darkness, ran away from her pain and the look on Prue's face. She lifted her skirts high and ran across the creek and into the woods as fast as she could. She came across Prue's horse tied to a tree, grabbed the reins and jumped on him, galloping away into the darkness. She would find somewhere to hide, somewhere, a place where no one would ever know what had happened or know her burden, the burden of eternal shame she would carry to her grave.

31

Harriet's words burned into Prue's brain like a hot branding iron. He could clearly see the incredible pain she suffered. Her shame and embarrassment were written all over her face. As he listened, red-hot anger boiled in his chest. He wanted to kill Harry's uncle. What McQueen had done to the man did not seem harsh enough. Prue wished he could have been there to watch. He wished he could have done it to the man himself.

When Harriet finished telling her story, he looked down at her and he couldn't think of a thing to say. He guessed she must have taken his silence as shock and revulsion. When she took off running, he figured she'd come back after she cooled off or got over being embarrassed. But that's not what happened at all. Call him ten kinds of a fool.

"What'd you say to her to make her run off like that?" Short asked.

"I didn't say nothing," Prue said. "Maybe that's the problem. I should have comforted her or said something to make her know how I felt. She was telling me something very personal and I guess I did the wrong thing."

Short laughed. "Story of my life. It's the main reason I ain't married."

Prue was just about to say she'd be back when he heard hoof beats. A horse was galloping hard down the Arcadia Road and from the sound heading back toward Arcadia.

"I hope that ain't my horse," Short said.

Prue's eyebrows flew up. "Well if it ain't, it's Satan and he's no horse for a woman to handle. Damn! And I left my boots on the saddle."

Prue spent the rest of the night trying to sleep beside the campfire. His strange companions coupled with worrying over Harriet kept him tossing and turning. When morning came, he was not rested but determined to ride after Harriet and make her understand how he felt about her.

Finding her here out of the blue, in trouble and hurt, had made him realize he loved her. From now on, he wanted to protect her and keep her safe. He knew he had a lot to learn about handling a woman but he wanted to try with Harriet. She was the only woman he'd ever known as strong and as wonderful as his mother.

Jenny was up and ready to ride before he left his bedroll. "Mr. Prue, you got to go after Miss Harry. She's so upset. I'm afraid of what she might do." Jenny pointed her finger at Buford Simpson. "That man hurt her. He's a bad man."

Prue nodded. "She told me," he said to her, thinking for the hundredth time what an ass he'd made of himself. "At least McQueen took care of him."

Jenny looked up at Prue with eyes old and wise for a girl her age. She tilted her head toward Malachai McQueen sitting with his hands tied behind his back, a dejected look on his face. "Ain't it strange that he was the one that come and saved us?"

"This whole situation is nothing but weird and strange," Prue said. "About the craziest thing I've ever been involved in."

Harriet's mare was on the picket line. Prue found her tack and saddled her.

"Jenny, I got some business with Harry's uncle. Wait here for me."

Prue walked over to Buford Simpson still reclining beside the fire. The man was awake, his face very pale. One of his servants was trying to spoon broth into him. Brown liquid ran in a continuous stream out of the corner of his mouth, down his cheeks and onto his satin jacket. He looked up at Prue standing over him but said nothing.

"You better load up in that carriage and git," Prue said through his teeth. "If you ever show yer face in Arcadia or these parts again, I'll make what McQueen did to you look like a walk in the park."

Simpson blinked but said nothing. The two black servants looked at Prue and said nothing. Prue shook his head. What a group. Well they were on their own. They would either make it back to Savannah or they wouldn't. Simpson would either live or he would die. Thanks to McQueen, none of it mattered to Prue one way or the other.

Prue walked away from Harriet's uncle and didn't look back. Marshal Short was busy brushing his big horse.

"I ain't sorry the gal took your stud," Short said. "I've had this big guy for a lot of years. He's old but dependable. And I saw she threw your boots off the saddle. They're over there."

Prue stuck out his hand. "It's been a pleasure riding with you, Marshal."

"Well if you don't mind, I'll stick with you to the Pine Level cutoff. I'm taking McQueen back there to jail."

"I'll be glad of the company," Prue said to Short as he tossed Jenny into the saddle. "We're gonna have to ride double," he said to the girl. "Miss Harry done stole Satan."

Still in his socks, he gingerly walked back across the creek and up the bank into the trees where he'd left his stud. There under the tree where he'd tied Satan lay his boots, spurs still buckled over them.

Flopping onto the ground, he pulled the boots on over his wet socks. "If this don't give me a blister, nothing will," he told Buzzard, who sat next to him, the blue "watch eye" on him.

It was a quiet group that headed back toward Arcadia. Marshal Short leading McQueen on the boney nag rode beside them. Jenny slept most of the way sitting in front of Prue. No one seemed to want to say anything. Besides being worn to the bone, the events of the night before had about taken Prue's ability to talk away.

"I guess this is where we part company," Short said when they reached the trail heading west to Pine Level. "I'm gonna slap this man in jail and go round up what's left of them out at your place."

"Better check to make sure the sheriff is there," Prue said. "I'm pretty sure I saw Sheriff Drawdy riding in that bunch that got mowed down by the stampede out at my place."

"If he ain't, there should be a deputy and he better damn well pay attention to me," Short said as he shifted his weight in the saddle. "Dang my ass is killing me. I ain't used to this much riding. I've been pushing a pencil for a couple of years."

"Good luck to you," Prue said, holding his hand out to shake the marshal's gloved fist.

"And you," Short said as he tipped his hat and turned off the road, taking the trail south along Buzzard Roost Branch.

Prue watched Short ride away, watched Malachai McQueen hunched over, his hands tied in front of him resting on the front of the saddle.

"I guess that's the last we'll ever see of Malachai McQueen," Prue said to Jenny, who sat in front of him, head resting on his chest.

"I never want to see him again," Jenny said. "But he did save Miss Harry and for that I'll say a prayer for him tonight before I go to bed."

The two of them rode on. Prue couldn't figure out what he should do. Where could Harry have run off to? When he reached Horse Creek, he got off the horse to stretch and check to see if he saw Satan's hoof prints turning onto the trail that led to his ranch. He found Satan's familiar prints coming up onto the main road. He saw Short's horse's big old prints but he didn't see Satan's prints going back toward his ranch.

Prue stood holding the mare and looking down the road to Arcadia. Maybe she went back there. It wasn't much of a choice for him. He mounted up and turned the mare toward Arcadia.

"Let's go see if Miss Harriet went home," he said to Jenny.

"I sure hope we find her," Jenny said. "I was kind of hoping you two would be together and I could live with you."

Prue tightened his arms around her. "I was kind a hopin' that, too."

Malachai's brain was numb. He couldn't think. One minute he'd been on top of the world, the next a prisoner of this US Marshal and on his way to a hanging, his own. The only bright spot in a miserable situation was as of this moment, the only charges against him concerned the vigilantes.

Short hadn't discovered what had happened out at his place when he'd gone on a rampage and killed his cousin Clara, old Rooster, and wounded Aunt Thelma. Malachai chuckled, a hoarse rasping sound. Well, they couldn't hang him twice.

He lifted his hands and touched his injured throat. The dog bites were deep and the wounds swollen. He could barely talk or swallow. Damn, he hated dogs. Well, maybe they'd wait until he healed to string him up.

The ride seemed to end too quickly. Before he knew it they were in Pine Level. When they climbed the steps to the Pine Level courthouse, an unimpressive building constructed of small peeled logs, they found Sheriff Drawdy was not in. The deputy, a sanctimonious, tee-totaling, sawed-off runt named Bailey Harris was only too glad to lock him into a cell next to a drunk Indian charged with shooting off his pistol inside Pine Level Methodist Church. The cell was small, the floor covered with sawdust, and as soon as Malachai sat on the bunk a hoard of fleas attacked him.

"I'm going back out to the Pruitt place and round up the rest of the vigilantes," Malachai heard Short say to Harris after locking him inside the stinking cell. "Keep a close eye on McQueen. He's got friends all over this county. I don't want him escaping."

"Don't you worry," Harris replied, pulling a long-barreled forty-four out of a holster hanging across his crotch. "I'll guard him with my life."

"If you got a dog, put him to guarding," Short said, leering at Malachai. "McQueen don't much like dogs."

Malachai could hear Short laughing his ass off as he clanked down the steep steps. When Short was gone, all Mal had left to do was sit. Sit, scratch his numerous flea bites and think about what he'd done and what had gone wrong. It didn't make for much of an afternoon.

32

Prue and Jenny rode into Arcadia close to supper time. Prue was dirty, still tired from his recent travels, fighting, and the emotional butt-whipping delivered by Harriet when she took off. Jenny was sound asleep leaning against him. The quick trot Harriet's mare started the day with had turned into a foot-dragging plod. Prue found it hard to push her any faster. He knew exactly how she felt.

When he got to the livery stable, he found Satan stalled at the end of the barn by himself munching on hay from an overflowing bier. Instead of being overjoyed to see him, the stud pinned his ears and turned his butt to him, all the while stuffing his face.

"I'm sorry, old man," Prue said to the horse. "I couldn't help it. She stole you."

Satan finally relented. Turning in the stall, he came to Prue and nuzzled his hand. "Thanks for taking care of her," Prue whispered to his horse.

Satan nickered his answer and returned to the hay.

With Jenny's hand in his, the two walked to the Arcadia House. Prue checked in and took Jenny up to their rooms. The little girl dropped onto the bed without taking off her clothes and immediately fell asleep. Prue wished he could go into his room and climb into bed as well, but first he had to see Harry. He had to apologize for whatever it was she thought he had done and beg her to marry him. There was no way he was going back to his ranch without her.

Harriet put her pencil down and looked at the clock. It was four-thirty, almost supper time.

"I'm finished with this piece on the church supper," she said to Mr. Jeffers. "I'm tired out. Do you mind if I go home?"

Jeffers pushed his glasses up on his nose and looked thoughtful. "I was kind of hopin' to get you back out to the Pruitt ranch so you could find out what's been happening out there. I heard a bunch of rumors yesterday about a big to-do out there involving the vigilantes. Could you leave in the morning?"

Pain stabbed through Harriet's heart, and when she tried to speak her throat felt closed. The Pruitt ranch was the last place on earth she wanted to go. But this was her job. She loved what she was doing. "Sure, Mr. Jeffers, I'll go."

"Great," he said and handed her an envelope. "Here's a little something extra for all your hard work on those stories. We sold a bunch of advertising and we sold out every printing of the papers with those stories. You did a great job, Harriet, a great job."

Harriet took the envelope and held it close to her chest. If her heart wasn't in her shoes, she would have jumped with joy. She was a success. Men on the street tipped their hats to her and the ladies stopped her to say hello. Even though her byline read Harry Painter, most everyone in Arcadia knew that was her.

So why did Prue's reaction to her past hurt so much? Why did it have to ruin everything else?

"Thank you, Mr. Jeffers," she said forcing a smile. "You don't know how much this means to me."

Clapping her once on the back, Jeffers turned back to his work setting up the paper for printing. Harriet left the shop, closing the door softly behind her.

Her mind raced as she thought over this new assignment while she walked back to the Arcadia House. She knew she'd have to face Prue again. She just hadn't expected it to be so soon. Her mind was in the clouds as she climbed the steps to her room. When she ran into a man coming down them, she didn't even look up.

"Harry!" The man said grabbing her in a bear hug, pushing her bonnet off her head and crushing her velvet wrap.

"Stop," she said sternly. "You're knocking my hat right off my head." But when she looked up into warm brown eyes and realized it was Prue, her heart melted and she burst into tears.

"Oh no, don't cry, Harry, please." Prue's voice held an edge of desperation. "I'm sorry if I hurt your feelings. I love you, sugar. Whatever you done in the past don't matter to me at all. I just want you to marry me and be my wife. Please don't cry."

Prue's words were like music to her ears. It was tempting to melt into his arms, hold him tight as she could and never let him go. But first she needed to get a few things straight, straight in her mind and straight with him. "Then why did you look at me like I was . . . like I was diseased?" she demanded.

"I was upset," Prue said softly pulling her closer to his chest. "And I was mad. I couldn't stand to hear you'd been hurt like that. It made me want to kill your uncle."

"McQueen took care of him just fine," Harriet said with satisfaction. "Almost made me like him."

"Come on up to my room, darlin'," Prue said. "Jenny's sleeping and we can talk."

Harriet pushed him away and straightened her poke bonnet, retying the lavender ribbons under her chin. "I'm a respectable woman, Jesse Pruitt. I can't be seen hugging you on this walkway or going up to your room. But I am glad you brought Jenny with you. I missed her."

"Fine, if that's the way you want it, then I'll ask you right here," Prue said dropping to one knee. "Harriet Painter, will you marry me? I do love you so much. You're strong and sweet at the same time. I know you'll make a wonderful rancher's wife."

"But what about my job?" Harriet asked softly. "I was just getting comfortable in it."

"Sugar, I can understand you wanting to keep your job. You've come so far in such a short time and you're good at what you do. I would never take that away from you. But I sure would like it if you'd consent to become my wife. You can keep a room here in Arcadia to work from and come home when you can. I'll leave that up to you."

"Get off your knees, Jesse Pruitt," Harriet said feeling her cheeks flame. "Someone will see you."

"Answer me, Harry, or I'll stay here all night."

Harriet looked around. Sooner or later someone was going to see her with Prue on his knees in the middle of the walkway outside the rooms. "I'll marry you, Prue," she finally said. "I'll be happy to be your wife. Maybe I can work for Mr. Jeffers part time."

Prue climbed to his feet and pulled her into one last embrace. He kissed her deeply and she felt love for this handsome man filling her heart. "I love you," she whispered. "I'll always love you."

EPILOGUE

Marshal Short returned to the Pine Level courthouse after capturing only two more vigilantes. The three members of the vigilance committee were tried and convicted in one of the country's first media circuses. Reporters from all over sat in the small courtroom scratching flea bites and taking notes as the verdicts were handed down.

Malachai McQueen and two other vigilantes were convicted and sentenced to ten years each. But McQueen and Bud Dawkins escaped and were never seen in Desoto County again. Duron Grey served three years and was released. The reign of the Sara Sota Vigilance Committee was over.

In 1889 a man named Ben Jones moved to Houston, Texas, and invested in oil. He made millions but lived quietly, often traveling to El Paso where he started a home for orphans. Some folks said he moved there from Florida.

Moccasin Bob became close friends with Thelma McQueen, eventually marrying her and moving into the Rafter Q. It turned out Malachai McQueen's Aunty Thelma enjoyed a snort or two of corn liquor every evening and Moccasin Bob was happy to supply her. She never did develop a taste for snake venom.

Danny Painter was quickly hired away from Jesse Pruitt by Jeb McQueen. The two became lifelong friends. Danny worked on the Rafter Q his entire life, becoming a famous cowboy and helping to start the Arcadia Rodeo in

1927 when he was in his fifties. Danny never married, preferring the free life of a cow hunter.

Jeb McQueen married Jenny Buttons in 1893. They had seven children, six girls and one boy. Jeb died in 1910. Jenny never remarried. It was said she had a relationship with her foreman Danny Painter, but no one ever knew for sure.

Jesse Pruitt married Harriet Painter in 1889. Harriet stayed with her job as a reporter until she became pregnant with their first child in 1890, at which time she made a permanent move to the Pruitt ranch. Jesse and Harriet had five children. Jesse introduced the first Hereford bulls into the area in the early 1900s, breeding them to the local cattle and cows he had crossed with Brahma stock. His ranch became one of the first to breed Florida Cracker horses and attempt to keep the bloodline pure.

Buford Simpson's recovery from his tragic accident was slow. He finally made it home to Savannah where he became a recluse, hiding inside his big home with no one but servants to keep him company.

Sarah Painter made a trip to Arcadia to find her daughter in 1890. Harriet and her mother reunited. Sarah stayed in Arcadia, opening a bakery. She often traveled to the Pruitt ranch to spend time with her grandchildren.

ABOUT THE AUTHOR

Janet Post is an adventurer who has lived in 40 locations including Hawaii where she served as a polo groom for 15 years. Upon moving to Florida she lived the Cracker lifestyle. She is the author, along with her son Gabe, of several young adult novels including *Voodoo Science* and *My BFF is an Alien* as well as the book *Vagrant* that was a finalist in the International Book Awards. She now lives in Hastings, Florida, with her 15-year-old granddaughter and many dogs.

Made in the USA
Columbia, SC
18 August 2020